The Autobiography of Miss Huckleberry Finn

Gina Logan

DEDICATION

To the memory of my beloved grandparents, in whose library I first encountered Mr Mark Twain and his literary creations.

ACKNOWLEDGEMENTS

To Professor Xiaoping Song, for her help in devising appropriate Chinese names for three of my characters, and to my dear husband, for his loving help and encouragement.

Introduction

Newspaper headline:
Dowager Philanthropist's Remains Found in Earthquake Wreckage

(San Francisco, April 21, 1906) The body of Mrs Theophilus V. Osterhouse was recovered this morning from the smoldering ruins of her Nob Hill home by soldiers searching for survivors of the earthquake and subsequent fires that continue to devastate the city. Mrs Osterhouse's servants were, fortunately, able to effect their escape before the building collapsed.

The deceased, whose remains were the latest to be discovered among the victims of the disastrous seismic upheaval of April 18, was apparently stunned by a fallen roofbeam, which pinned her to the floor of her bedroom on the third story of the mansion; unable to free herself, she succumbed to her injuries, which an Army surgeon described as "numerous and serious—any of [her] wounds would shortly have proven fatal."

That Mrs Osterhouse survived long enough to inscribe a farewell message in the floorboard nearest her right hand (using, for that purpose, a hairpin, found in her clenched fist), was, according to her acquaintances, "a tribute to the remarkable constitution of a remarkable lady." The message, in a cramped but legible script, reads "And I Am Gone Yes I Am Gone Alas." Alas, indeed: her presence will be much missed.

Mrs Osterhouse, widow of the late Mr Theophilus VanDerWalk Osterhouse, was well known in the Bay area for her charitable activities, including several eponymous foundations begun after her husband's demise. Mr Osterhouse departed this life in 1901. Under the circumstances, there will be no memorial services. Burial will take place privately.

In accordance with Mrs Osterhouse's will, friends may offer a suitable contribution to any of the following charities: The Osterhouse Refuge for Indigent Females, The Osterhouse Foundation for the Relief of Orphaned or Abandoned Children, The Osterhouse Fund for The Education of Indian and Colored Youth, The San Francisco Home for Little Wayfarers, and the San Francisco Chinese Consolidated Benevolent Association.

Newspaper headline:
Philanthropist's Will Probated

(San Francisco, April 21, 1907) The Last Will and Testament of Mrs Theophilus V. Osterhouse, probated yesterday, contained, in addition to the expected disposition of her estate to various charitable organizations and foundations, a sealed envelope of several inches' thickness, apparently containing written documents, and marked "To Be Opened on the One Hundred and First Anniversary of My Death."

As Mrs Osterhouse met her final end, as far as can be scientifically established, not earlier than April 18, 1906, the date in question will arrive not sooner than April 18, 2007.

The writer of these words would give a great deal to be present on that day; however, no one now living can reasonably expect such a privilege. It will be our descendants who will learn what mystery is contained in a sealed manila envelope now in the possession of Mrs Osterhouse's attorney and executrix, Miss Philippa Carruthers, Esq.

Miss Carruthers, one of the few attorneys of her sex in this part of the country, and the only female attorney of color now practicing in our fair city, declined to answer this reporter's queries. She stated only that the envelope would be conveyed to a safe-deposit box at the San Francisco Bay Bank, and there lodged until the day appointed for its disclosure to the world.

Newspaper headline:
1906 Earthquake Victim's Century-Old Mystery Unveiled

(San Francisco, April 18, 2007) In accordance with instructions issued 101 years ago, a sealed envelope was removed from a safe-deposit vault today and opened in the presence of a notary public by a representative of the legal firm Carruthers, Lefkowitz, Muhammad, Hong and Estrada. A spokesperson confirmed that the envelope contained a handwritten manuscript of nearly four hundred pages, apparently the memoirs of the author, a celebrated resident of San Francisco in the glory days of the late nineteenth century.

Mrs Theophilus VanDerWalk Osterhouse, widow of a patent-medicine tycoon who made his fortune in the decades following the Civil War (and who, before his own death in 1901, had devoted a significant portion of his wealth to the benefit of San Franciscans), and a noted philanthropist in her own right, died in the 1906 earthquake. Among her effects was this manuscript, which has reposed in the vault until today; it has been turned over to experts at The San Francisco State University for authentication and evaluation.

Newspaper headline:
Osterhouse Manuscript Termed
"Literary Hoax of the Century" by Twain Scholars

(San Francisco, November 26, 2008) After exhaustive study, scholars at The San Francisco State University have declared that Mrs Theophilus V. Osterhouse's manuscript, uncovered last year after a century in a safe-deposit box, constitutes a hoax of "rare magnitude," as historian Dr J. Thomas Frelinghuysen characterized it. A colleague and specialist in Nineteenth Century American Literature, Dr Andrea Sapolinsky, confirmed Dr Frelinghuysen's assessment, saying, "The author of this document, whoever she or he may have been, was a person of rare imagination but unquestionably poor scholarship. There is absolutely no merit in the claims expressed in this manuscript."

When pressed, however, both professors admitted that the claims made by Mrs Osterhouse were, although preposterous, just barely possible. Since the document is, at this time, public property, the City Commission will make copies of it available to scholars of American literature, in the hope that whatever germs of truth it may contain can be uncovered, analyzed, and published.

As an historical document, the manuscript—though presumably a hoax—still has some worth. "When you consider that these papers call into question over a century of scholarly research into *Adventures of Huckleberry Finn* and *The Adventures of Tom Sawyer*, as well as casting doubt upon the veracity and the creative ability of Samuel Langhorne Clemens, well, then, you can see why we hesitate to declare their contents anything other than false, if not falsely malicious as well," declared Dr Sapolinsky.

Upon further questioning, Dr Freylinghuysen concurred with

3

his colleague's opinion, adding, "For Americans—for anyone in the world who reveres American literature—to believe that Huckleberry Finn was a girl—and, moreover, not a fictional character but a real person, a person whose story was stolen, for all intents and purposes, and then recast by Mark Twain himself to suit an antifeminist, racist political agenda of which Twain was an unconscious agent and unwitting dupe—casts into doubt the entire enterprise of literary historians, of the role Mark Twain himself played, and of the place he continues to occupy in American letters."

Newspaper Headline:
Huck Finn Was a Girl

(New York, February 12, 2010) A panel of scholars from more than thirty American, African, Asian, and European universities has spent the past fourteen months studying the *Osterhouse Manuscript,* as it has come to be known in academic circles.

Yesterday, the panel's chief expert in Twain Studies, Dr Gad Ali Hussein of Cairo University, revealed that several members now believe that the document, far from being a hoax, is in fact the true story of the events that Mark Twain changed, rearranged, and retold in the novel *Adventures of Huckleberry Finn.*

"Ladies and gentlemen of the press," Dr Ali Hussein said, "We cannot ignore the evidence any longer. Huckleberry Finn was *not*–at least, not wholly–the fictive invention of Twain's genius: Huck Finn was real; and moreover, Huck Finn was a girl."

The prestigious monthly journal *The Atlantic* immediately announced intentions to serialize a critical edition, in twelve installments. The first will appear on the 100th anniversary of the death of Samuel Langhorne Clemens (which occurred on April 21, 1910). Meanwhile, critical debate continues to swirl around the manuscript, its supporters, and those who would deny its validity, its provenance, and its significance.

The Memoirs of Mrs Theophilus VanDerWalk Osterhouse
AKA
Sarah Mary Williams,
BORN and RAISED
And
FIRST SEEN IN PRINT
As
(Miss) Huckleberry Finn

***

Chapter One: Boy or Girl?

If you have read Mr Mark Twain's books, the one about Tom Sawyer and the one about me, then you know enough to go on with. I intend to set a few things straight, but I won't waste time and paper going over the whole as *he* told it. This is the story of what happened to me *after* the incidents that Mr Twain related in *his* book.

Now, *Adventures of Huckleberry Finn* is true enough, mostly, though the parts that Mr Twain had to change to make me into a boy was stretched far and away more than the rest.

I asked him, of course, *why* I had to be changed into a boy, and he said, first of all nobody would believe a girl could have done such things, and second of all it would be offensive to the proprieties, and third of all t'wouldn't sell, as the reading public was too moral to put up with such a scandalous tale.

Worst of all, he said, his having wrote the story from a girl's point of view would destroy his literary reputation. Now, in *Tom Sawyer* I didn't matter much, as I was only a minor character. However, Mr Twain said he couldn't afford to take any more risks than he was already taking with the Huck Finn manuscript, since people was telling him already that it was trashy. He said *he* knew it wasn't; it was a "rattling good yarn." But if he let on I was really a girl, he'd be a ruined man and nobody would ever buy anything he wrote ever again. And then he offered me $5000 to shut up, so I did. And that $5000 come in mighty handy, as I was right short of cash at the time.

Lest the reader of these pages assume that my story is too far-fetched to believe, let me point out that I was not the first and certainly not the only girl to masquerade as a boy and also to fool all and sundry whilst doing so. Mr Henry Morton Stanley, the great explorer of Africa, mentions such a case in his own memoirs, of a fellow sailor with whom he bunked for some days before discovering, by happenstance, that "Dick" was actually "Alice." And there are tales told of girls who served in the War Between the States (dressed in both Blue and Gray) alongside their sweethearts and brothers, and no one the wiser until a wound made the sex of the wounded one plain to the surgeons on the battlefield and to "his"—that is, "her"—comrades in arms.

It helps, if a girl wishes to pass for a boy, that she be somewhat taller than average for a female, slim-shanked and flat-chested withal, and that she be accustomed to wearing breeches and to spitting and smoking and swearing, and also to avoidance of over-indulgence in soap and water and clean linen and all such effeminacies. She should be indifferent to cold, hunger, and rough sleeping conditions; having, as well, a head for strong waters and the ability to take promptly to her heels at the slightest hint of danger to person or property. Further, she should be able to lie quickly and convincingly.

All of these qualifications I possessed from my tenderest years.

What I do *not* possess is any likeness of myself at the time of my adventures as chronicled by Mr Twain. If I had, you would see a gangly youth, or so you would suppose, with a shock of dark hair that curled stubbornly—"cowlicks" is the term for such wayward tresses— and eyes that seemed black at first but on closer examination proved to be dark blue. The skin of this youth was tanned by wind and weather (and somewhat tinted also by dirt) but was under its coating of soil indisputably what is called "white"; the youth's limbs were long and ill-clad in men's clothing that was still a bit too large, but that "he" wore with a certain dash. I refer you to Mr Twain's own prose description In *The Adventures of Tom Sawyer*.[1]

Of the two of us, Tom Sawyer was (I thought) the more likely to be the subject of a story-book, for he ended up a famous lawyer and in time a federal judge and (if you will believe it) a Senator. Men like that may see their early lives turned into pages for the

---

[1] Eds. note: *The Adventures of Tom Sawyer*, Norton Critical Edition, 2007, 40.

edification of the young and the profit of the chronicler thereof. But something persuaded Mr Twain that my story might be altered to suit the tastes of the book-buying public—at least, such of them as warn't too particular.

The way Mr Twain and I ended up literary collaborators could be taken as pretty much a coincidence, if you believe in such things. I don't.

I was visiting Hannibal—this would have been in 1880—where I had come for Aunt Polly's funeral, she having gone to what Tom's cousin Mary called "her eternal reward"—and Mr Twain called to pay his respects whilst I was there.

Like everyone else in America and most of Europe, I was familiar with Mr Twain's work, but in addition, the man himself was far from a stranger to me. I had come to know him some years earlier in Virginia City, Nevada, when he worked on the staff of the *Territorial Enterprise,* under his real name of Samuel Clemens. I, too, was using a different name at that time.

I knowed Mr Twain had used my real name, Huckleberry Finn, in his book about Tom, which I had read when it was published, in '76. So, at the time he wrote *The Adventures of Tom Sawyer,* Mr Twain, like the rest of the folks around there, had plainly thought Huckleberry Finn was a boy. No reason for him to think otherwise—in those early years I did in fact pass myself off as male, and quite successfully, too, as has been related.

Well, that first book was about Tom anyway, though I come into it, mostly as Tom's accomplice, but Mr Twain did say more than once in it how my character—that is, the Huckleberry Finn of that book—was everything boys like Tom would have wished to be: free and independent, without any cares nor responsibilities.

What Mr Twain's book don't tell is how I eked out a meager existence on scraps and leavings, and how the only shelter I had was an old sugar hogshead. Tom Sawyer slept in a bed with sheets and a counterpane, but all I had to keep off the cold and wet was a couple of hemp sacks. And Tom ate regular, and hot food, too, whilst I was lucky to cobble together a single cold meal, most days. And then there was the way folks treated me, like I didn't have a right to live. The only people who was ever nice to me was colored folks— slaves. Truth to tell, I used to envy them, and not a little: they belonged to someone, and even the miserliest slave owners fed, clothed and housed their property better than I ever was.

And always I was afeared Pap would show up and take whatever pitiful small amount of food or clothing I'd managed to accumulate and then whip me within an inch of my life.

No—Mr Twain was not trying to be fair to my character, nor even accurate: in *Tom Sawyer*, Huckleberry (who is me and *not* me at the same time, if you catch my drift) is pretty much there as a contrast to Tom, who is a member of the better classes and can afford to make-pretend, since his real life is one of relative security.

Still, my character does have a few scenes of significance in that book, in particular when we run off to Jackson's Island and all of us was supposed to be drowned. My character is the comic relief in that chapter, especially when at the end Aunt Polly makes over me the way she done. And I am still the unredeemable son of the town drunkard in those scenes, a foil to Tom and to Joe Thatcher and Ben Harper, respectable boys with families and property, boys who was worth caring about, worth mourning when it seemed they had been lost.

So: back in Aunt Polly's parlor in 1880, when Mr Twain come in (that is, Mr Clemens, but I will continue to call him by his *nom de plume*), we spent quite a bit of time catching up on our old acquaintanceship. Mr Twain was eager to hear what all I'd been doing since he and I both left Virginia City, but he was more eager to learn how I knew Tom Sawyer. (He was puzzled about our acquaintance, you see, since he couldn't place me, as the saying goes, in Tom's past.)

Well, during the conversation that took place, it become clear to Mr Twain that "Huck Finn" was really me. So I had to explain everything, and I did, including how and why on earth I come to be sitting there in a very stylish walking costume,[2] (complete with bustle) and my best paisley shawl, and sporting a hat the size of a coal scuttle, trimmed in real egret feathers to boot.

Of course we couldn't go into the whole story right then, so Mr Twain, he come to visit me several times over the next week—I was stopping at the Sawyer home—and he was interested as could

---

[2] Eds. note: This consisted of a dress, rather more tailored and a trifle shorter than a dress for dinner or for a party, paired with a jacket or short coat of complementary fabric, color, etc.; this "costume" was intended for, as the name suggests, "walking" or going out in the daytime to visit, shop, etc.

be, wanting to know exactly what did happen after the gold was found, and if the Widow Douglas really did take me in and try to civilize me, and so the whole story come pouring out, all about Jim and the raft and what happened after.

And then he said he'd like to make another book, but this time mostly about me; only, he said, my character would have to stay a boy, as I'd been in the first book. And I was agreeable, for I was never averse to money—and that too was something I had in common with Mr Twain, who spent a great deal of his life trying to become rich. (And that is a story that would fill a book, too, though I can't imagine anyone wanting to read it.)

And that was how *Adventures of Huckleberry Finn* come about.

Mr Twain had great fun with some of the aspects of my being a girl, for example when he had me—the character, I mean—pretend to be a girl and try to fool Mrs Judith Loftus (and end up not fooling her in the least).

Of course, being Mark Twain, he left out some of what I told him *did* happen, and he made up some more stuff that *didn't*. That being the case, I will try as I go along to make clear what is true and what was made up, by either of us.

I guess I do need to go over some of what really happened, just to set the record straight.

First of all, about my sex. Tom Sawyer and Joe Harper and Jeff Thatcher knowed I was a girl and they didn't care. I made them swear to keep mum, because if people like Tom's Aunt Polly and the schoolmaster and minister and judge found out, I'd be put in a Home, or bound out to somebody, and I didn't want that.

Pap warn't around much, but decent folks didn't care for him, and while it was nobody's business how he dealt with his son, if it turned out his son warn't a son but a daughter, why, then everybody's nose would have been poking into my business, and I was the one would have had the worst of it. People had funny ideas about girls then—still do—and I had always been used to being free and easy and on my own. I warn't about to stop now.

I never wore girls' clothes in those days except when I was pretending I was a girl, which Mr Twain took pleasure in putting in the book in a couple of places, as I have said, since it was true and also made sense as far as the story went.

But as Mrs Loftus was quick to spy, when I did put on a dress, I acted like a boy in a dress would. I didn't know no other way. Point of fact, I never had worn girls' clothes in my life before Jim and I found those things on the wrecked steamboat.

At that time, Jim didn't know I was a girl—that is, when we first got acquainted with each other, back when I was living at the Widow's— but when I run into him on Jackson Island I had to tell him. He was awful scared.

Well, you can see why. If he'd been caught with a white girl it would have meant a rope party for sure. And some fancy knife work before the noose, too. I said I would swear on a whole entire stack of Bibles that he'd never done me any way but friendly and proper, but he just looked glum and said if we was caught he'd thank me to push him overboard and hit his head a good thwack with an oar. He said he'd just as lief drown as be lynched, gelded, and turned into a human torch.

Well, that never happened, thank goodness, but it was a close call now and again. Especially with the King and the Duke.

The King, he nearly give me a stroke of apoplexy one time— he got me inside our little wigwam when the others was out foraging and what not—and put his arms around my waist and tried to kiss me. I'd a'most fainted, thinking he'd found me out, but it warn't that. He liked boys, is what it was, and he still thought I was one, since his hands hadn't strayed below my belt buckle as yet. I kneed him hard where it hurts and told him to keep off.

"I don't care what your habits are," I said, "But I mean to tell you that they aren't mine. Leave off, and don't touch me no more, or you'll be sorry."

"What," he sneered, "Going to tell your big nigger?"

"Yes, I will," I answered, "And Jim knows ways to kill you that won't never be found out—African ways, with poison—herbs and suchlike. Jim, he c'n work roots, too, and he knows all about witches."

"I'll bet," he muttered.

He moved away from me, and never did touch me again—but he hated me, and Jim, worse than ever. That was just before we landed at the Wilks place. It is a good thing for the King that he wasn't found out—if those people had got any notion as to his tendencies, they'd have done more than just tar-and-feather him. (He *pretended* to lust after young girls, but I never saw him do more than slobber over those who come within his reach.) About the Duke's inclinations, I never was certain, though he and the King

10

didn't seem any thicker than thieves are customarily.

Don't get me wrong, I have no quarrel whatsoever with inverts or what-you-may-call-'em, including those females who belong to Sappho's league, as you will see. As for the males, those I've known personally (excepting of course old Looey the Seventeen) have been among the many kind friends I've had in my life, especially down on the Barbary Coast. It was the King in particular I objected to. His high-and-mighty ways notwithstanding, he warn't over-clean in his habits; his breath was enough to make your knees buckle, and his feet stank, when he took his boots off, so's you could smell 'em a mile upriver *and* down.

Well, finally we got shut of old Looey and Bilgewater, not without a lot of grief, and then there was all that foofaraw with Jim and the Phelpses, and Tom showing up and me having to pretend to be Sid, and Tom getting shot.

True, all true, except the part about Jim being a prisoner and Tom's schemes to "rescue" him—that was pure Twain, pure invention, put into the story just "to illustrate how Tom's character has been corrupted by his addiction to Romance," was how Mr Twain put it to me.

Mr Twain seemed to find it entertaining, to speculate how someone like Tom would put his signature on such a chain of events as freeing someone who was already free—just the sort of nonsense that Tom might have enjoyed, but I did not find it diverting, myself, and doubt that future readers of Mr Twain's attempt at retelling my adventures will, either.

Though of course they are not really my adventures, being re-told by a man who seldom told the truth when a lie would sound better.

Which is another thing Mr Twain and I have in common.

There are so many memories that did not make their way into Mr Twain's book, along with a few that did, but in significance if not in form almost wholly changed.

The chapter about the Grangerfords and the Shepherdsons is factual, as far as it goes, in the chronicling of events. But Mr Twain was so interested in using the situation for its satirical possibilities that he didn't even come close to depicting the truth about that family (and he used different names for them, thanks to goodness, because if the real families ever read the book and recognized theirselves, they'd take out after Mr Twain with guns a-blazing, you

11

can be sure). Buck Grangerford, now, was the only boy I was ever true friends with, aside from Tom. Mr Twain did not do Buck justice. He was a fine boy and would have made a noble good man.

Of course, Buck knowed about me being a girl—I made him swear not to tell, and he never. Buck was like Tom Sawyer, always reading about King Arthur and Sir Lancelot and Queen What-you-may-call-her and such folk, and he saw me and Jim as romantic, like people in one of his storybooks. He swore wild horses could not drag the truth from him, and at night when we went up to bed he always scooted far to one side "so's you don't think I'm trying to take liberties," he said. His death changed the way I looked at a lot of things—book learning, for one.

Now, Mr Twain done pretty well telling how I come to leave Hannibal— though he had to change the reasons around, some.

In Mr Twain's book, I aim to escape Pap and the Widow and society in general, and when I meet up with Jim, we decide to light out for freedom together. Well, that was more or less true. We *was* intending, Jim and me, to float the raft down to Cairo, then sell her and use the money to take a steamer up the Ohio to the free states; then I was a-going to head on to Tennessee, where I had an errand I wanted to attend to—but I will tell about that later. (In any case, we missed Cairo entirely, as Mr Twain's book tells.)

No. The reason I decided to leave Hannibal was pretty simple: I just couldn't deal with Pap one day longer than I had to.

During our conversations back in 1880, I asked Mr Twain did he know Pap, and he allowed that he had seen him, on occasion— mostly drunk, which was normal enough for Pap. Mr Twain said he'd never actually *spoken* with Pap, but he'd heard some of his talk, and Mr Twain didn't believe he'd missed much by "not holding conversation of any substance with the man," as he put it. He did say he had never seen a man as filthy in his clothes and his person who hadn't been dead for at least a month.

Well, I had been used to Pap, filth and all, but after going to live with the Widow, seems I noticed it more the second time; that is, after he come and took me again.

Mr Twain does not say how that was done, only saying that Pap watched for me and catched me and took me upriver. What happened was, he sprung right at me whilst I was walking home to the Widow's from school, larruped me a good one with a piece of stove-wood, and tied me up tight before I come to.

12

When I woke up I was bound hand and foot, and I stayed that way, with the rope tied up to a big iron ring he'd drove into the wall.

I'd seen slaves tied up, and I felt bad, to reflect how I'd never been bothered much in my mind about it. But when you have to spend hour after hour, day after day, without being able to move more than a few feet in any direction, you start to thinking. I suppose that some of my feeling about Jim come from the time I spent tethered in that cabin. I'd've run off myself, of course. Like a shot.

Pap knowed it, of course, and he watched me. When he left me off the ring to go outdoors to relieve myself, he went right along, holding the rope, and though he turned his back, he was never more than an arm's length away. And after a while I begun to feel like I would never be free.

I begged him to let me loose, and promised I'd stay put and be good. He only laughed that screechy laugh of his. But one day, just when I'd got to thinking I couldn't bear it no more, he untied me. He said if I run away, this time when he caught me he'd kill me. And I could see he meant it. So I promised, but I kept my wits about me and waited for my chance, which I knew would come, if only I could be patient.

That was hard, considering Pap's deportment. He was, as I said to Mr Twain, awful handy with his hickory. Sometimes he forgot I was a girl and beat me half to death, more than once so's I could scarcely walk. And then sometimes I could see he was remembering, and it was only a matter of time before he would get drunk enough to try something funny—and maybe not too drunk to accomplish it. I wasn't sure I'd be able to fight him off when the time came, and I was sure it *would* come.

These things happen, and happened then, too, though nobody likes to talk about them.

Then he had that awful episode of the DTs and thought I was the Angel of Death. It didn't happen that he actually killed me that time, but it was close. Between being killed and being raped, I didn't see much benefit in lingering.

No. The time to leave had most definitely arrived, before my being a girl become something I couldn't hope to hide.

I knowed I had only a year or so, two at best—I was fourteen or fifteen when I struck out for Jackson's Island, and I figured I had til maybe sixteen before it all caught up with me.

I had asked Tom when his cousin Mary started in to be a woman, and he said it was around the time she was sixteen when he found the washtub with bloody cloths soaking in it, in the woodshed.

I asked what the cloths were for, and he said girls bled every month; he'd read about it in the schoolmaster's book (the one he got whipped for tearing even though it was Becky Thatcher that done it) and it was called *ministration* or some such word. It meant you could have a baby.

Jeff Thatcher said he had overheard his mother talking to Becky once, and Mrs Thatcher said it was the curse. I asked him, what curse?

"'Eve's curse,' she said it was," Jeff remembered.

"Why," I said to Jeff, "I recall Miss Watson reading me about Eve and Adam and how God called down a curse on them on account of that persimmon or whatever it was they et."

"Yes," Jeff said. "She got cursed for eating the fruit—I remember from Sunday School. Don't you recall it, Tom?"

Tom said he didn't, but he would take Jeff's word for it.

"Where is Huck going to get cloths and a washtub?" Jeff wanted to know. "You can't keep them things in a sugar-hogshead."

I was pretty cast down at that. But Tom said, "By the time Huck needs 'em, Huck'll figure something out. Right, Hucky?"

I said I guessed so. "I'll have to," I said.

"Acourse you will. It's so hot—let's go a-swimming," Tom said.

So he and Jeff went off, leaving me to my thoughts. It was times like that I missed having a mother. Even an Aunt Polly would have done me some good, I suspected.

I felt a little low in my mind, especially since I couldn't go a-swimming with the others. But we only swum together out at Jackson's Island. So, whenever Tom and Jeff and Joe enjoyed a dip off the town dock, or down by the old abandoned tanyards, I stayed behind. People might've seen them go on without me and thought it was because I was—what was the word Mr Twain used?—oh, because I was the town pariah.

But I knowed the situation wouldn't last too much longer. I was *growing*.

I was most as tall as Tom now, and he was near a year older, as far as I could reckon. I could tell I was growing fast, too, by the way my trousers didn't need to be rolled up so much any more. The curse couldn't be far off. (I still warn't sure exactly where the blood come from, but I had a fair idea.) At any rate, it was clear I'd have to make plans, and make them quick, too, in preparation for what lay ahead.

Keeping my secret whilst living with Miss Watson and the Widow Douglas was the hardest. I was always in a sweat in case one of them might come in whilst I was taking a bath. However, they was both so prim and proper about bodily matters, bathing posed small risk of discovery, specially as it warn't more than a weekly occurrence.

Who else had caught on to the fact I was a girl? Well, before I went to live at the Widow's, that time when I was so sick after giving the warning about Injun Joe, the old Welshman, Mr Jones, learned my secret. But he said he wouldn't tell.

I remember I come out of the fever just as he was levering my arms into the sleeves of a clean nightshirt. I started up and begun to babble, but Mr Jones, he put his finger to my lips.

"There, now, rest easy; you needn't try to explain," he said, when I couldn't seem to put two words together to make sense. "You've had a hard life, and none of us should judge you. Why," he said, and his eyes kindled and seemed almost to throw off sparks, "Why, it's that father of yours that brought you to this pass, isn't it? I thought as much."

I didn't ask him to explain his thoughts. For one thing, I was still pretty sick. Later, I figured out what he meant. But he kept his promise not to tell, and the Widow and her sister Miss Watson took me in all unknowing—and I meant for the situation to stay that way. When Pap finally showed up I was all in a fever to know if he'd told. He hadn't, and I believed he wouldn't, for it they'd known, they'd have gotten me away from him for good and all, but still it was an uncomfortable time.

Well, as I have said, Pap did get me away from the Widow, and if you read Mr Twain's book you also know how I got away from him. I still think I done it nearly as well as Tom Sawyer ever would, though not with as much style. Mr Twain invented a lot about Tom's doings later on in the book, but Tom's ability to spread himself in such a situation was a fact.

But there's one important thing that Mr Twain didn't put in his book, for I never told him about it. I found out about my mother.

Chapter Two: I Learn Some Astonishing Information

It still seems curious to me that Mr Twain wrote almost nothing about my mother, or even about the fact that I didn't have one.[3] If you overlook a couple of brief mentions, it seems like it was always just me and Pap.

Now, even though I had never lived what you might call an ordinary life, I knowed every child had two parents to begin with, though it was pretty frequent in those days to lose a mother or father or both. Even amongst my own acquaintance: Tom Sawyer's parents was both dead, and his stepmother too, for him and Sid both had only Aunt Polly to bring them up, and she had lost her own husband years earlier.[4] Jeff Thatcher's mother died when he was small, and his sister Becky's mother was the Judge's second wife.

But I had no memories of my own mother at all.

Finally, after Pap come and took me from the Widow's, I got my courage up to ask.

That was a conversation that deserves to be put into print if ever there was one.

"How come I don't remember my mother?" I asked. "How old was I, about, when she died?"

"Died? She never," Pap said.

To say I was stunned is like saying water is wet, or fire burns.

It had been a fine evening. We'd just had ourselves a good dinner—fried catfish and cornbread—and we'd lit our pipes and was lolling around feeling comfortable. Pap had started in on his whiskey before supper, and was improving his digestion with a second round; consequently he was in a talking mood.

"How come you always told me she died?"

"I dono—she might's well have. I didn't figure you'd remember her. Why, you was just a babe when she left," he said, hoisting the jug. "Two, three year old or thereabouts—I disremember."

---

[3] Eds. note: *The Adventures of Tom Sawyer*, Norton Critical Edition, 2007, 121.

[4] Eds. note: Some of Clemens's readers have received the impression that Aunt Polly was a spinster, but she had been in fact married to a Mr Reese Penniman, the father of Tom's cousin Mary. Mr Penniman died of cholera in 1835.

"Well, where did she go? *Why* did she go?" I asked, though it took some effort to get the words out, and my voice sounded funny in my own ears. I hoped Pap was paying too close attention to the jug to notice.

"I dono *where*," he said, taking another long swig. "Back to her own people, I reckon. As to *why,* that's easy to answer. She hated my guts, the whore, and I come to hate hers just the same."

I shivered at the coldness in his voice, and the flat way he said "whore," but asked the next question, in a voice I tried to keep steady. "Where was she from? Her own people, you say? Who were they?"

"Well, I dono as I ever met them in person. But 'twas in Tennessee I met her."

"Is that where your folks come from?"

"Hell, no," he said. "My pap and my ma was both from Ohio."

"How'd you end up in Missouri?"

"We come here after the British war.[5]" He drank and belched. "My pap fit in the war, but never got nothing for it."

"So you growed up here, in Missouri."

"I did, but I didn't stay long. Hired me to a flatboat for a while. Got down as far as Natchez and decided to take to trappin'. That's how I got myself to Tennessee. Lord, what godforsaken country that is."

"How do you mean?"

"Wild an' misty an' dim. Woods full of hollers that never see the light of day.'

Pap tipped the jug back, swallowed, and belched. "Ghosty-like. And folks're queer, too. Shy as deer, an' just blame full of religion—queer kind of religion, too, snake-handlin' an' speakin' in tongues 'n' hymn-singin' in part-harmony[6]; they sing fit to wake the dead whilst twirlin' all around like spinning-tops. Tall an' lean. Part Indian, a lot on 'em, too. Cherokee and Choctaw and Chickasaw an' sich. Good with their guns." He shook his head. "They don't

---

[5] Author's note: He meant the 1812 war, not the Revolution.
[6] Eds. note: Probably shape-note singing, which evolved from 18th century English country parish hymn-singing and was developed in America largely through the work of composers like William Billings and a variety of singing schools (see *The Southern Harmony* and *Sacred Harp*).

cotton to outsiders much."

"But you met my ma. How'd that happen?"

Pap settled the jug so's it rested more comfortably in the crook of his arm, leaned back in his chair and pondered the question.

"Well, let's see. It was long about, oh, 1828; Old Hickory'd just been elected, so I guess that was the year. The Natchez Trace was still open. I'd been traveling, just bummin' along. Taken plenty pelts in the last few years, but beaver was gettin' scarce, and I guess I got tired of movin' and decided to settle down and stay put, find a wife and raise some crops and young'uns. That was some fine country, back then. Plenty of game, and the Injuns mostly gone, and the few still left was peaceable.

"I was making my way along the Trace, studying the land, how it lay, where the water was, and the high places and low, and I come to that ridge in the afternoon of a late summer day.

"The light was all goldish an' shinin' on the ground and the leaves an' all, and there was a little soft wind up high in the trees— no clouds to speak of, and I stopped to rest a minute. It was warm that day, and the bees was tumblin' over each other in the flowers and grasses . . .

"An' we met up, an' so, well, one thing led to another."

He stopped for a moment, staring down at the jug, then he raised it again, and drank deep before he went on.

"We come back here, an' she had you. My mam and pap had just died, and the old man left me this-yer cabin and what-all was in it."

"How'd they die?" My Ohio-born grandparents, which I had never seen.

"Sickness—a cough an' a fever an' flux. Fust he went, then she." He jerked a thumb. "They's buried out back a ways. No marker, but you kin see where the ground's been tromped an' it's sunk in, like."

"So you and she come back here."

"An' you come along. She started another young'un when she took you off the titty, but that 'un died. Too bad. Would of been a boy. She said t'was my fault." Pap took a long pull at the jug. "Well, it might could of been, I guess."

"What happened?"

"Well, she'd been sickly, 'n' she wanted me to go for a doctor,

19

but I give her a good dose o' salts instead. An' she drapped that baby, dead."

"And then what happened?"

"She tried to kill me. *Bitch*," he said, and the look on his face made me shiver. "She wouldn't give me my husbandly rights. Said I'd never touch her again. She near cut my liver 'n' lights out one night when I tried—kept a skinning knife around her neck on a strip of rawhide. I tried to get that knife away 'n' got *this* for my trouble," and he pulled his shirt open to show the long, silver scar that run acrost his black-furred chest.

I'd seen that scar before, a hundred times, but never knowed what caused it.

"What happened then?" I managed to ask.

"Well, I might of done for her myself, right then, but I'd been drinking, you see, an' she was too quick for me. She run off to the woods, and time she come back, I was sick's a dog. She taken you with her. I remember her coming back into the house with you tied up in a shawl, an' me out of my head with fever." He drank some more whiskey. "I laid there for a week or two, limp as a dead hare, 'n' then you took sick, yourself."

He drank some more, then resumed. "Well, she took on so, I said I'd fetch the doctor, this time, an' I did go, but he just laughed at me, the bastard, an' wouldn't come. So I rowed on back here 'n' when I come to the cabin an' tolt her the doctor warn't going to come, she said she was goin' to go herself, an' get him, but I said no. It was dark by then, an' a storm blowin' up. So," he went on, "She staid here, crouching over you an' weepin' and cryin' til I told her to shut her trap or I'd throw her, 'n' you too, into the river."

"And what happened then?"

"She went to sleep, finally, 'n' so did I. I woke up an hour or so later 'n' she was screeching like a stuck pig that you was dead. An' she throwed her shawl over her head, cryin' an' wailin' 'n' carryin' on 'til I went over to see. You looked dead, sure enough. So I tolt her I'd dig the grave come morning." He glanced at me. "But we was both wrong. You warn't dead at all—though I never see a living child look as bad as you did, and that's a fact. You was the color of clay, an' cold as stone. But time I found out you was still alive, it was too late."

"What happened?"

"Well, she run off."

"Run off?"

"Ain't I a-telling you? She started up 'n' rushed on out of here, grievin' at the top of her lungs, out into the wind and the wet. The trees was lashin' an' the rain coming down just in torrents, you know, an' I could hear the river runnin' fast n' deep, an' I called out, but she didn't answer—an' in a minute or two I couldn't see her no more, so I come back inside. An' in a little while you woke up 'n' called for her, but she never come back."

"Did you look for her the next day?"

"Happen I did, but she warn't nowhere to be found." He was silent for a moment, then shrugged and hoisted the jug again, taking a long swallow. "I figgered she must of fell in the river in the dark, and drownded."

I was so staggered, I didn't really take it in when he begun to grumble, but pretty soon his voice rose, and soon he was a-goin' like a house afire: "And so I had all of the trouble of raising you an' learnin' you to be anyways useful," he kept on, "An' then you go 'n' take up with that damned Douglas bitch, an' put me to all the trouble to have to go fetchin' you back. Folks ought not to interfere with how a man raises his child, an' I say—"

Well, he was off again on one of his favorite tirades—nothing I hadn't heard a hundred times before. And so I continued to pay him small mind, until he said something that brought me to attention.

"There warn't no body ever found, but that happens sometimes. The river don't always give back what it takes."

He didn't say anything more for a time.

I sat back and considered.

She had thought I was dead. Had she aimed to die, herself? Or had she made a bid for freedom, no matter the cost?

I wondered how any mother worth the title could have left a living child alone and unprotected, with this man.

Pap's voice broke through my reverie. "She's how you got your name," he said.

"What?"

"She named you," he said. "Huckleberry. For your eyes. She said they was like two huckleberries, so big and dark-blue an' shinin' up out o' your face."

So I got my name, odd as it was, from my mother, the mother who was gone from me before I had a chance to know her.

21

"I always did wonder how I come to have such a name," I said.

"It's heathen-sounding for sartin," Pap agreed, taking another pull at the jug.

"What was hers?" I asked.

"Mother" was not a word I could remember ever using, nor Mam, nor any sound like it. "Pap" was what I called him, this man whose real name, I knew, was Jimmy Finn. But I had never thought of him by name, only as Pap, the dark and fearsome man who was my only kin—or so I believed—and who owned me, body and soul, as much as if I'd been his slave.

Or his wife.

"Her name? Hagar," he said. "It's in the Bible."

"Hagar," I said, trying it out. "What was her surname?" I asked, then, but got no answer at first. Pap was too drunk to notice that I was talking to him. He was smiling and humming to himself. Every once in a while he shook the jug to hear how much was left. I calculated that he had enough for about an hour of steady drinking; then, if I was lucky, he'd fall off the chair and roll into the corner and sleep until noon next day. But he spoke up all of a sudden, and near startled me into falling off *my* chair.

"Cantrell, that was the name," he said. "I met her brother oncet—a snake, he was. Pure pizen. Rifle-totin' schemin' snaky son-of-a-bitch." He stopped and took a pull at the jug. "No," and he shook his head. "It's just as well she went. She warn't no good to me nohow, an' as for *you*," and he put his head down and leered at me from under his eyebrows, "You know what side your bread's buttered on, don't you?"

I didn't say anything for a minute. Then I couldn't help myself.

"What did she look like?" I asked.

He didn't speak for the longest time, and I was afraid to repeat my words, for fear he'd take out after me, but at last he answered.

"Like a panther, she was. Tall but slim. Quick an' slick-like in her movements, like as not to come up spittin' an' scratchin' as to curl up an' stretch out under your hand. Dark hair'd, an' dark-skinned too, like 'n' Injun almost, but her eyes was gray, gray like fog in the morning, down in the hollers."

He was quiet after that, and I got pretty quiet too, thinking, so that I jumped in fright when he slipped off the chair, just as easy and nice, and rearranged himself on the floor.

It warn't much later, a few days or thereabouts, when I made my escape.

And when I left that cabin for the last time, I took along all of the gear and food and blankets and truck, but I took something else, too: my mother's name, and what there was of her that remained in me.

I took the hurt of her leaving, the hurt raised by the questions I would never get to ask her, and I carried the burden of both these hurts for many years thereafter.

I suppose that that is why Mr Twain decided to tell my story in his own way, making me a boy, for a man does not think of his mother in the same way a girl does, and a man is not burdened by his sex the way a woman is. A man can tell a story and see it as a rattling good yarn, but if he is a man of genius—as Mr Twain most certainly was—he can tell the story and make the reader feel it as if it were his (or her) own. For *Adventures of Huckleberry Finn* is in a way my story and in another way Mr Twain's, and it is also the story of how we all come to know our own selves. Or don't.

Chapter Three: I Decide on My Next Step

Getting back to what actually happened: when I first struck Jackson's Island, I hadn't planned to hide out there, just get my bearings before I decided what to do next. Meeting Jim was Providential, as the Widow would have put it.

Then, after me and Jim decided to head down river,[7] Providence struck again, as you might say. It was pure Providence that led me to the Wilkses. And Providence again that saved those girls their money (and got rid of them two old frauds). And, after it was all put about how Jim was really free, and Tom and me helped him get situated, it was Providence put me in the way of taking the next step in my own life.

And it must'a been the Widow's Providence, because he seems to be the only one I've ever heard of that is willing to give a person any kind of a show.

I'd had to come clean about myself to Aunt Sally and Aunt Polly, and though both of them tried to explain it to Uncle Silas, I don't think he ever got it straight, but kept right on calling me "Tom" and Tom "Sid" until his dying day.

Aunt Polly, she took charge of everything, which was her strength in most difficulties that came to folks. She could roll up her sleeves and have everything just so whilst the rest of us would be twirling around like dust devils, going everywhere and nowhere at once.

I do believe Mr Twain done Aunt Polly an injustice, portraying her as a foolish old woman when in fact she was one of the sharpest folks, male or female, you could ever hope to see—and one of the kindest, too.

Well, the first thing was to take me in hand and put me in proper attire, for it was a sin and a scandal, she said, for a girl to wear men's clothing. She set to and cut down a dress of one of Aunt Sally's older girls to more or less my size and bundled me into it, then sent me to set at Uncle Silas's big desk and write a letter to the Widow Douglas. "She's entitled to know what has become of you," Aunt Polly said, and I could see that she was right. So I done it.

Here is what I remember of that letter:

---

[7] Eds. note: See *AOHF*.

Dear Widow Douglas,

I am sorry for leaving you and Miss Watson, rest her soul, in such circumstances. I hope that you will allow me to call on you and explain myself fully when I return to Hannibal. You was always very good to me and I want you to know that I have thought of you always with respect and gratitude.

Yours very truly,
Huckleberry Finn

When I read the letter to her, Aunt Polly snorted.

"Ain't you left something out?"

"What?"

"Huckleberry, you need to tell her that you are a girl." Aunt Polly looked even more than usually peeved. "Huckleberry! Huckleberry! That ain't no name for a Christian. Seems t'me we had ought to do something about that."

I felt some consternation at this. I had always been able to conjure up something to call myself—George Jackson, Sarah Mary Williams, George Alexander Peters—but I did not think that I was ready to be called out of my name by somebody else.

"What was your mother's name, honey?"

"Hagar."

Aunt Polly brooded over this for a few moments. "No," she decided. "It's a good strong name, and Scriptural, too, but I don't feature it for you."

I had an inspiration. "Aunt Polly, can I choose for myself? Since I can't be Huckleberry Finn, can I at least settle on a name I'd admire to have?"

She reached over and patted me on the hand. "Goodness' sake, child, acourse you can. What name be you a-thinking of?"

"Sarah Mary Williams." It had seemed to come into my head all of a sudden, but I knowed in my bones it was the right choice—it was the name I'd used when I'd pretended to be a girl, the name I'd give Mrs Judith Loftus (although she'd immediately seen through my use of it).

"Well," Aunt Polly said, slowly. "It sounds a decent name, for a fact. Where'd you come by it, child?"

I didn't answer her for a minute or so, because my mind had suddenly plunged me back to that little shack by the wharf in

Hannibal, just after I'd staged my own violent death and run off to Jackson's Island, only to meet up with Jim, who'd run off too.

Mrs Judith Loftus. I had spent all of two hours with the woman, and she a stranger to me then and since, and yet not a week has passed without her wandering across my mind. She was a plain, ordinary, ignorant cracker—like me—but sharp of judgment for all her stream of gossipy talk. (She was one of those women Pap had spoken of as having their tongues hung from the middle and a-going at both ends.) And yet she told me if I ever got into trouble just to send word to her and she'd do what she could to get me out of it.

If you recall Mr Twain's book, I met with Mrs Loftus just before Jim and me started off down the river.

I'd took the canoe over to the village to see if I couldn't find out some news. (Jim had hitched me into a girl's dress we'd found on the wreck.) I tied up below the town and crept along the bank, just as Mr Twain tells it in his book [8]:

There was a light burning in a little shanty that hadn't been lived in for some time, and I wondered who had took up quarters there. I slipped up and peeped in at the window. There was a woman about forty year old in there knitting by a candle that was on a pine table. I didn't know her face; she was a stranger, for you couldn't start a face in that town I didn't know. Now this was lucky, because I was weakening; I was getting afraid I had come; people might know my voice and find me out. But if this woman had been in such a little town two days she could tell me all I wanted to know, so I knocked at the door, and made up my mind I wouldn't forget I was a girl.

'Come in,' says the woman, and I did. She says, 'Take a cheer.'
I done it. She looked me all over with her little shiny eyes, and says,'
'What might your name be?"
'Sarah Williams.'
'Where'bouts do you live? In this neighborhood?'
'No'm. In Hookerville, seven mile below. I've walked all the way and I'm all tired out.'
'Hungry, too, I reckon. I'll find you something.'
'No'm, I ain't hungry. I was so hungry I had to stop two miles below here at a farm; so I ain't hungry no more. It's what makes me so late. My mother's down sick, and out of money and everything, and I come to tell my uncle Abner Moore. He lives at the upper end of the town, she says. Do you know

---

[8] Eds. note: From *AOHF*, 73-80.

him?'

'*No, but I don't know everybody yet. I haven't lived here quite two weeks. It's a considerable ways to the upper end of the town. You better stay here all night. Take off your bonnet.'*

'*No,' I says; 'I'll rest a while, I reckon, and go on. I ain't afeard of the dark.'*

She said she wouldn't let me go by myself, but her husband would be in by and by, maybe in an hour and a half, and she'd send him along with me. Then she got to talking about her husband, and about her relations up the river and her relations down the river, and about how much better off they used to was, and how they didn't know but they'd made a mistake coming to our town, instead of letting well alone—and so on and so on, till I was afeard I had made a mistake coming to her to find out what was going on in the town, but by and by she dropped on to pap and the murder, and then I was pretty willing to let her clatter along. She told about me and Tom Sawyer finding the twelve thousand dollars (only she got it twenty) and all about pap and what a hard lot he was, and what a hard lot I was, and at last she got down to where I was murdered. I says:

'*Who done it? We've heard considerable about these goings-on down in Hookerville, but we don't know who 'twas that killed Huck Finn.'*

'*Well, I reckon there's a right smart chance of people here that'd like to know who killed him. Some think old Finn done it himself.'*

'*No—is that so?'*

'*Most everybody thought it at first. He'll never know how nigh he come to getting lynched. But before night they changed around and judged it was done by a runaway nigger named Jim.'*

'*Why, he—'*

I stopped. I reckoned I better keep still. She run on, and never noticed I had put in at all:

'*The nigger run off the very night Huck Finn was killed. So there's a reward out for him—three hundred dollars. And there's a reward out for old Finn, too—two hundred dollars.[9] You see, he come to town the morning after the murder, and told about it, and was out with'em on the ferryboat hunt, and right away after that he up and left. Before night they wanted to lynch him, but he was gone, you see. Well, next day they found out the nigger was gone; they found out he hadn't been seen sence ten o'clock the night the murder was done.*

---

[9] Editor's note: Mrs Osterhouse had at some time penciled into the margin these words: "Reckon Pap would have been some put out, his reward being for less money than a black man's. Serve him right.'

So then they put it on him, you see; and while they were full of it, next day, back comes old Finn, and went boohooing to Judge Thatcher to get money to hunt for the nigger all over Illinois with. The judge gave him some, and that evening he got drunk, and was around till after midnight with a couple of mighty hard-looking strangers, and then went off with them. Well he hain't come back sence, and they ain't looking for him back till this thing blows over a little, for people now think he killed his boy and fixed things so folks would think robbers done it, and then he'd get Huck's money without having to bother a long time with a lawsuit. Oh, he's sly, I reckon. If he don't come back for a year he'll be all right. You can't prove anything on him, you know; everything will be quieted down then, and he'll walk in Huck's money as easy as nothing.'

'Yes, I reckon so, 'm. I don't see nothing in the way of it. Has everybody quit thinking the nigger done it?'

'Oh, no, not everybody. A good many thinks he done it. But they'll get the nigger pretty soon now, and maybe they can scare it out of him.'

'Why, are they after him yet?'

'Well, you're innocent, ain't you! Does three hundred dollars lay around every day for people to pick up? Some folks think the nigger ain't far from here. I'm one of them—but I hain't talked it around. A few days about I was talking with an old couple that lives next door in the log shanty and they happened to say hardly anybody ever goes to that island over yonder that they call Jackson's Island. Don't anybody live there? says I. No, nobody, says they. I didn't say any more, but I done some thinking. I was pretty near certain I'd seen smoke over there, about the head of the island, a day or two before that, so I says to myself, like as not that nigger's hiding over there; anyway, says I, it's worth the trouble to give the place a hunt. I ain't seen any smoke sence, so I reckon maybe he's gone, if it was him; but husband's going over to see—him and another man. He was gone up the river; but he got back today, and I told him as soon as he got here to hours ago.

Well, it was at that point, of course, where I got nervous and started in to fiddle around with that needle and thread, according to the way Mr Twain told it. And she asked me again,

'What did you say your name was, honey?'

'M—Mary Williams.'

Somehow it didn't seem to me that I said it was Mary before, so I didn't look up—seemed to me I said it was Sarah; so I felt sort of cornered, and was afeard maybe I was looking it, too I wished the woman would say something more; the longer she set the uneasier I was. But now she says,

'Honey, I thought you said it was Sarah when you first come in?'

'*Oh, yes'm, I did.   Sarah Mary Williams.   Sarah's my first name.
Some calls me Sarah, some calls me Mary.*'

And she started in to talk about herself and her husband
again. Just as I got to feeling easy, she up and tested me with that
knot of bar-iron, getting me to heave it at a rat, to see how I
throwed it, and then she plopped it into my lap and I shut my knees
on it, and that was that. She had me.

'*Come, now, what's your real name?   Is it Bill, or Tom, or Bob?—or
what is it?*'

Acourse, as Mr Twain's book goes on to explain, and this part
was true, I launched into a story about who I was and what I was
doing there in girls' clothes, only it was all a lie (despite my telling
her "I would just make a clean breast of it") and in point of fact,
nothing I told that dear good woman was the truth or anything near
to it. I was only interested in any news she could give me about
me—the real me, Huck Finn—or Pap, or Jim.

It was the most strangest experience, being a girl pretending
to be a boy pretending to be a girl, and I have always thought that
that was the reason she caught me out in the first place. I could
pretend to be most anybody—and done so—but this was a new
thing for me.

And I never saw her again, but I think of her often with
respect (for she was sharp as tacks) and affection (for she treated me
exactly like what she supposed I was—a runaway 'prentice—and
she'd said she'd help me and not tell on me, and I believed her then
and still do). So, perhaps my taking the name I'd tried to fool her
with was a way of trying to make up for the lies I had to tell her.

And maybe, thinks I, maybe the name "Sarah Mary Williams"
would help me remember that being a girl was something I had no
choice but to learn.

Aunt Polly broke in on my reverie, so that I looked up,
startled to be back in the present.

"It's a good-sounding name at that . . . Sarah Mary Williams,
Sarah Mary Williams." Aunt Polly tried it out. "Where'd it come
from? Any of your folks named Williams? Maybe your ma's
people?"

"No'm. I just like the name, that's all." There was no way I
could explain the episode with Mrs Loftus to Aunt Polly, so I didn't
try, but took another tack. "Sarah, she's in the Bible, ain't she?" I
knew how much store Aunt Polly set on Holy Writ.

"Yes. Mmmm. Well. Maybe you don't know it, but your Aunt Sally's christened name is Sarah."

"No'm, I didn't know that."

"And Mary . . . did you have in mind my own girl, my Mary?"

"Maybe . . . " I tried to look as if thoughts of Mary Penniman were pleasant. "She's always been kind to me."

(This was not strictly true, for Tom's cousin Mary often slapped me and ordered me out of the Aunt Polly's kitchen when she caught me there, but then again, she'd given me more than one slice of bread-and-butter-and-sugar, too, when in a good mood.)

Aunt Polly laughed. "Don't try so hard, child. What I meant to say is, my name's Mary, too. Polly's a common enough nickname for Mary, don't you see."

I decided to be honest, for a change. Well, at least partly. "Aunt Polly, ma'am, I'm glad to know that your name's Mary, and Aunt Sally's is Sarah, but—ma'am, Mary is the name of somebody else, too, somebody I admire—very much. Ain't that enough?"

Aunt Polly patted me on the shoulder. "Sure*ly*. Well, now. Sarah Mary Williams. If that's the name you want, that's the name we'll call you by, and let Huckleberry Finn go for good and all."

"Yes'm."

I thought for a brief second of a woman's voice I could not remember saying that my eyes looked like two huckleberries, dark blue and shining; I thought of Jim calling me "Huck, honey." I thought of Tom and Sid and Joe and Jeff and the Widow and Mr Jones and even poor old skinny Miss Watson calling me "Huckleberry," and I turned my back on all that was past and looked ahead to the new life of Sarah Mary Williams. Which I was about to embark upon.

But first I had some business to attend to.

***

Aunt Polly had made arrangements for us four—her, Tom, me, and Jim—to travel back upriver to Hannibal. Tom, he wrote Judge Thatcher explaining all of the circumstances, and telling him that we intended to buy Jim's wife and children and set them up on a farm of their own, as free negroes (which there was more than a few of in Missouri, mostly in the western part of the state). I signed under Tom's signature where the letter said I wanted money took from my share of the gold—the six thousand apiece that the Judge had invested for us.

Tom was pleased as he could be. "When we get back, I'll hire a land agent and we'll find the farm that suits you best, Jim," he said.

Jim was so happy he could hardly sit still. "In a few days I'll see my Eliza and my Johnny and Elizabeth Ann," he said. "Won't they be joyful! "

I was happy for him, but sad too. This meant that he would be going far from me, with his family—which I had never met, since they lived on a farm about six mile from Hannibal. Jim had a family that I was not a part of. Jim was a father and a husband, and his freedom meant that he would have a home for his family. "You will always be welcome where I am," he told me, when I ventured to say how much I would miss him.

We was standing together in front of the slave cabins, near the pump. Neither of us felt comfortable with each other inside the house, for he was not a prisoner nor a slave any longer, but still a colored man, and everyone knew now that I was a girl, a white girl. We could not sit down together like folks, like the way we had done back when we were together, back on the raft.

"I know it, but it ain't the same," I said, trying to say it lightly, like it was something pleasant to remember. But inside I felt a kind of sinking. "We had some good times, didn't we, Jim?"

He smiled and started to say something, but Tom called from the house, "Jim, I need to have your mark on this letter, too." So Jim went back inside, and I went for a long walk up the road, as far as the pasture where the cows grazed, where I sat on a fence rail and waited until I trusted myself to be around folks once again.

When I was ready, I found Tom and took him around behind the cow barn where we could talk private. "Tom, I got to slope," I said.

"Why, Huck, you can't! We're taking the steamboat tomorrow. Why, we'll be cabin passengers, Huck! Won't Jeff Thatcher and Joe Harper just be pea green with envy when they see us!"

I knowed what he meant. Cabin passage was the height of luxury on a steamboat. But, "I can't help it," I told him. " I'll slip off, Tom, quiet as quiet, a few miles upriver. Then I'll come along to Hannibal when I've done what I have to do."

"You can't just—well, you can't, Huck. Aunt Polly will skin me alive."

"I have to, Tom. You go on ahead. Tell her I'll do anything

she wants me to do, when I get back."

Tom started in to argue with me, then, but I wouldn't budge, so he quit. "All right, but Aunt Polly will take it out of both our hides when she sees you," he said.

"I won't be but three-four weeks behind you, Tom."

He warn't comfortable about it, I could see, but I knowed this was my only chance. I might never be in this part of Arkansas again. He made me explain everything to him, and once I'd done so, he saw things my way, though he still predicted dire consequences.

We had to make our farewells to the Phelpses, and I didn't want to raise Aunt Polly's suspicions, so me and Tom and Jim was up at sunrise next morning, all of us ready for our journey. I was wearing another one of those pesky cut-down calico dresses and a bonnet, and I know I looked as uncomfortable as I felt. The linen shift I wore under the dress (as my sole undergarment)[10] was bunching up around my waist, and the dress was too tight under the arms, making me sweat like the dickens. Also, the strings of my bonnet chafed me mightily underneath the chin, and the sides of it cut off my vision like a pair of horse-blinders, but Aunt Polly said that no respectable woman went about with her head bare, and unless I was under a roof I had to keep that bonnet on, or else. She, herself, like Aunt Sally, wore caps inside the house and around the property, and under her bonnets when she did go abroad, white starched caps snugged down tight so that only her front hair showed, and she trimmed them with ribbons on Sundays. But she said caps was only for married women and widows, not for young girls.

Well, so it was come time to take our leave, after one of Aunt Sally's noble good breakfasts of wheat cakes and molasses and fried salt pork and gravy and hot biscuits and coffee with thick yellow cream, and peach preserves and three kinds of pickles—she was, sure enough, one of the best cooks that ever lived—and she and

---

[10] Eds. note: In the early 19th century working-class and rural people (and slaves of both sexes) commonly wore a long (thigh- or knee-length) shirt or shift as a night-garment, putting the outer clothing on over it in the day. Undergarments were not commonly worn, except in wintertime. Slave children, as Huck notes in *AOHF*, often wore nothing but a coarse "tow-linen" shirt.

Uncle Silas and all the children and servants come out to see us off. Uncle Silas had one of his slaves get the wagon ready for us and he was to drive us to the boat landing , a tall dark-brown man named Cuffy. His wife was Aunt Sally's head woman in the house, Lize, and the two of them had become good friends to Jim ever since he had been brought onto the place. At the news that he was free, they both—and all the servants acted the same—just as joyful as if it had been they theirselves. So all of them was smiling and some of the women was weeping a little, too, whilst Jim stood there straight and tall and thanked Aunt Sally and Uncle Silas for taking such good care of him, and me, and Tom.

I hugged Aunt Sally, and she kissed me, and said, "Don't be a stranger, now, come back to see us sometime," and Uncle Silas took my hand in his and smiled his gentle smile, and Aunt Polly hugged and kissed her sister and Uncle Silas and Jim histed her box and bag into the wagon along with Tom's valise and the little cloth bag that held my gear.

"I will pray every day of my life for the Lord to bless all of you good, kind peoples," Jim said, smiling but a little teary, too, and Uncle Silas helped Aunt Polly up onto the wagon seat, and Jim, he helped Tom and me up over the tailboard, where we could sit behind the driver and Aunt Polly on bales of hay, then clumb in himself and settled down in the bottom of the wagon box with the baggage. And we drove off down that dusty track towards the town and the river, all of us waving and smiling, until the road bent and hid us from each other's sight.

***

That river voyage was the first time I had ever been a passenger on one of those great glittering floating palaces called "steamboats"—and what a plain-sounding name that is for something so rich and fine—all smart paint and fancy carving, and shining brass, and the people on board dressed up like swells, especially those fortunates booked into staterooms, with sleeping accommodations and meals provided.

(I should explain that "cabin passage" meant staterooms; the actual cabin, on the upper deck, was a big room, furnished handsome, that served as a lounging place and was where meals was served for the cabin passengers. Deck passengers got no meals and had to sleep on the bare decking, and do without other conveniences as well.)

Aunt Polly kept a watchful eye on me, so I did not get the chance to explore as I would have liked, but Tom, who was let to go where he wished, reported that there was not only a barbershop with red leather chairs and white china shaving mugs but a barroom with solid gold spittoons, though I think they must have been only brass, even on such a rich boat as the *Roxane*. Jim too was enjoying himself, for he was traveling with Tom as Tom's own personal servant, and shared his stateroom.

I figured on slipping over the side some time after Aunt Polly went to sleep—I knowed she was a sound sleeper, having shared a bed with her at the Phelpses'—and so I made sure to have Tom fish me out a pair of britches and a shirt beforehand from his luggage, for I would need to be a boy again for this part of the trip. He made me take along his Barlow knife, too, for which I was most grateful.

Aunt Polly took quite a time to get ready for bed, first making sure that the stateroom door was bolted shut. I took off my dress and hung it on a nail. Then I washed my face and hands and cleaned my teeth at the little washstand whilst Aunt Polly put on her own voluminous flannel nightgown[11] over her dress, undressing under its tent-like cover, and replaced her daytime cap with a nightcap. Beneath its ruffled edge her pointed nose stuck out like a hen's beak. She knelt down on the floor beside the bed and motioned to me to do the same, and when I was kneeling too she said prayers for both of us. I was praying too, that she would not discover the bundle of boy's clothes that I had stashed under the bed, and my prayers was granted, for a wonder; she finished with "Amen" and a deep sigh, then plopped into bed and scooted over, leaving a space for me to join her.

"Are you comfortable, Sarah, dear?" she asked, drowsily.

"I'm just fine, Aunt Polly." In fact, the bed was wonderful soft; the mattress was a real horsehair one, not straw or corn shucks, and the sheets smelt of lavender.

The engine sounds was kind of muffled, or else I had gotten used to them, for I heard only a faint rhythmic pulsing far below us,

---

[11] Eds. note: Aunt Polly shows her "respectability" or perhaps adopts the customs of a higher or more citified class by wearing a special, dedicated sleeping garment and not simply removing her outer clothes to sleep in her shift, as Huck does.

and the voices of people on deck, of passengers and crew, could scarcely be heard.

"Sleep well," she murmured, and was snoring in an instant.

I waited at least half an hour, until I judged she was as fast asleep as she would ever be this side of the grave, and then I slipped out of bed—slowly, slowly—and changed into Tom's clothes in the dark, for I dasen't light a candle.

I left my girls' clothing under the bed, and as silently as I could I slid the bolt of the stateroom's inner door and let myself into the cabin, from which doors opened off on either side to the staterooms. I had judged earlier that I would do better to leave our stateroom by the inside cabin door rather than the outer door that faced the boiler deck balcony—the latter would, I thought, be noisier, especially at night.

I was right; the cabin was deserted, and I slipped down the stairs at the far end without seeing or hearing anyone. The passengers seemed all to be sleeping, from the sounds of snores that followed me. The officers' day crew was all asleep in the texas; the black hands slept behind the officers' staterooms (in what was often called the coon pen).

I looked round for the mud-clerk,[12] but he too was asleep, sitting on a pile of rope and leaning against a bulkhead. Such other hands as were awake and not engaged in keeping the boilers going were up in the bows where they could keep an eye out for snags, and the pilot up above the texas in the pilot-house was keeping his eyes ahead as well.

The boat was plowing along steady but slow when I let myself over the starboard side and struck out for the Arkansas shore.

---

12 This was a low-level job for a boy or teenaged male, who might work his way up to a better-paying position by being industrious, running errands, fetching and carrying, and taking on the really dirty chores, hence the name.

Chapter Four: I Learn How to Be a Girl

It didn't take but an hour to make land, for the current warn't over-strong just there. After my swim, I was cold and tired, but I had to wait until it was light to make the rest of my journey. There was a plenty of underbrush, and I hacked a way through to a little copse, where I curled up at the base of a tree and slept for a while.

When I woke it was dawn, with the birds making an enormous racket over my head. I was hungry, but there warn't no prospects nearby—no orchards nor gardens—so I started on my way.

I knowed approximately where the town was, and also that the Wilks place was some distance south of it, a brick house, which was unusual in that place and time, so I reasoned I would not miss it as long as I kept to the main road. However, I looked less than respectable, and did not wish to attract attention, so it took me rather longer to get to my destination, as I kept having to dive into the woods or take to a ditch or field whenever I heard or spied someone coming along. I think I walked a half-mile extra for every one I actually traversed on that day. The weather was fine—it was early autumn, the middle of September—and before too long I did manage to find something to eat in the way of windfall apples and a hunk I cut off a ham that was hanging in a smokehouse with no one watching it.

Finally I come near to the house. It was mid-morning, but there was nobody outdoors, neither out front nor in back, which was lucky. I took a deep breath and knocked at the back door, which was one of those half-doors, you know, with the door in two pieces so you can shut the bottom half to keep out the chickens and dogs and whatnot.

"Anyone to home?" I called out, though I could see them, setting at the table. It looked like they was doing the household accounts, for there was a ledger, and pens and ink, and a stack of papers and a tin money-box. One of the slave women was standing at the fire, stirring something in a big pot.

"Why, it's–" cries Joanna (the one everybody called Harelip, because she had one, poor thing). She opened the door.

"Adolphus, only I ain't," I said, and stepped into the room.

Miss Mary Jane took charge. "Why, you *are* a sight," she said. "(I was pretty muddy and dusty and covered with bits of hay and chaff, you see, from hiding in ditches and ducking into barns.) "Joanna, take these things away,"—pointing to the papers and truck— and you"–this was to the servant–"run get this child a towel and some hot water—and some clean clothes."

Well, you can bet everyone scurried, then. Joanna picked up the papers and whatnot, and the servant scooted off straight, and Miss Mary Jane started in to come at me with her arms outstretched. I got behind a chair and said, as fast as I can, "Miss Mary Jane, listen! I ain't what you think."

"Oh, you poor boy," she said, "You know how grateful I am to you! You ain't a criminal like those other two characters. They forced you to go along with their evil schemes."

"Yes'm," I said, "But—"

"No one here holds any of their wrongdoings against you, Adolphus," Miss Mary Ann said, flushing a most becoming pink.

"I'm glad to hear that, ma'am," I said, "But—"

Just then the slave woman come back with a pair of men's britches and a tow shirt. "I taken these off the line out'n the drying yard, Miss Mary," she said. "And this-here's a clean towel." She brandished it in my direction. "An' they's hot water in the kettle." She eyed me with suspicion.

"You go on and wash up and get dressed," said Miss Mary Jane to me. "Then we'll talk some more. Now, Bella"–this was the servant's name–"Pour some hot water in the washtub, and then go on and bring something for this poor boy to eat. I vow, he must be just famished."

Well, I took the clothes from Bella, who I remembered from before—a tall, heavy light-brown woman in a calico gown and starched white petticoats and headscarf—and followed her and the kettle of hot water out to a lean-to in the yard, next to the cookhouse.[13] There was a wooden tub hanging on the wall. She set it on the ground, poured the water in and handed me a piggin of soft soap, then left me to it, with a last direful look in my direction.

I stripped off and cleaned myself up as best I could. The

---

13 Eds.note: In many middle and upper-class homes, it was usual, especially in the Deep South, to have a separate small building (often of brick, when brick was available) for cooking, partly due to concern about fires and partly to keep the house from becoming overheated, a major concern in the summer.

britches was too big (being a full-growed manservant's, I supposed, as there wasn't no other males on the place) and the shirt hung down a mile, but I put 'em on anyway. (I never see such a girl as Mary Jane Wilkes for bossiness, but it didn't seem to matter—everybody loved her, because she was still sweet as pie, most of the time, in spite of that red hair.) I left Tom's clothes on a peg.

When I got back to the house, Bella had a dish of cold peas and bacon on the table, with a big slab of corn-bread and a pitcher of buttermilk, and I set to.

I was most famished, and didn't stop until plate and pitcher was nearly empty.

Miss Mary Jane had left me alone to finish eating, but she come out as soon as I had done, and set down across the table from me.

"Now, Adolphus," she began, but I cut her off.

"Miss Mary Jane, excuse me," I said, "But I have to tell you right now. I ain't no Adolphus—in point of fact, I ain't a boy."

I looked around for Bella, but she had disappeared, which didn't mean nothing. All the servants would know, probably before I even finished telling Miss Mary Jane. Slaves know everything there is to know on a place, long before any white person even has a clue.

"What I mean," I said, trying to find the right words, "Is that I ain't who you think I am, but it's even more complicated than that. Why, Miss Mary Jane, them two frauds had me in such a fix, on account of a friend of mine, but I c'n swear on the Bible if you want me to, they'll never trouble any of us again, because they've been rode out of town on a rail, and my friend is all right, so I can tell what I couldn't tell before. I mean—" I stopped. Miss Mary Jane was looking at me, her hazel eyes steady and kind of seeking.

I knowed what they was looking for.

"I reckon you expect I'm just telling more lies, like I done before," I said.

Miss Mary Jane looked at me kind of quizzical but not flustered in any way. "Why don't you tell me the whole story, then?" she said. "It might save you telling lies, if that's what you're really afraid of."

"I don't know what-all I'm afraid of," I said, struck by this. "Except I can't go on being who I was—not Adolphus, I mean, but the real me, Huck Finn, only the real me ain't real neither." I stopped. "Miss Mary Jane, before, when I come here, it was under false pretences."

She nodded encouragingly.

I went on, "And now, the way you see me, it's false too, but I ain't out to swindle or hoodwink nobody. In fact I want to live a true life for the first time in my life, but I need help." She looked interested and not mad, which perked up my spirits no end, so I plowed on with it.

"So, Miss Mary Jane, here it is: I'm a girl, and I don't know how to be one, and I'm counting on you to teach me. If I have to be a girl, and I guess I do, I want to be one like you are, at least as best I can, in my own way. Will you show me, Miss Mary Jane?"

There. I had got it out.

I sat back and held my breath and waited.

She looked thunderstruck, but only for as long as it took her to rearrange her face—then she started in to laugh. It was a good laugh, a real laugh, not the kind that folks give out with when making fun or intending to shame you, and I let my breath out and joined in.

She reached out her hand to me then, and we shook on it, and she said, "All right, let's see what we can do with you!" She looked me over with interest. "I never would have thought it. You fooled everybody a right smart, didn't you?" She called the servant back in. "Bella, do you know where those old clothes of Joanna's are, the ones she wore before she put her hair up last year?"

Bella appeared to ponder for a long minute, then smiled broadly. "Yes'm. They's in the big trunk in the front room."

"The missionary box? That's fine, Bella," Miss Mary Jane said. "Would you light the lamps in the front room, and bring my workbox back here, when you have a moment?"

"Yes'm." Bella picked up the plate and mug and the pitcher of buttermilk (not that there was any much left in it) and swept off, the pointed ends of her headscarf standing up atop her head like rabbit's ears.

In the front room, Miss Mary Jane closed the door and locked it, and pulled the curtains over both windows so's nobody could see in. She took the ring of keys that hung at her waist and found the one for the trunk, a big brass number, and turned it in the lock. I looked over her shoulder as she raised the lid.

There was a lot of women's clothing in there, in neat rolls— blue, and pink, and lilac, and some variously sprigged. Miss Mary

Jane pulled out a garment and held it up. "These are under-drawers," she said. They was open from crotch to knee, and had a frill on each leg at the bottom.[14] Then she took up a cream-colored object and shook it out. "This is a chemise," she said.

"Miss Mary Jane, ma'am," I said, "I have never heard of such a thing."

"Goodness sakes, child, you don't have to call me 'Miss Mary Jane' all the time," she said. "We're friends, aren't we? Come to think of it, what ought I to call you? 'Huck Finn' don't sound very girlish to me."

"It's really 'Huckleberry,'" I said, "But I do see your point. I have decided to change my name to Sarah Mary Williams."

"That's a good strong-sounding name," she said.

"I chose it for myself," I said.

She looked interested, so I plunged on.

"And the 'Mary' is for you," I said, "if you'll let me, Miss Mary Jane, ma'am."

"For me?"

"Yes'm. I never knowed any girls before, Miss Mary Jane, and truth be told it was knowing you give me some hope for myself as a female."

"Is that a fact?"

"Yes'm." I was starting to feel uncomfortable, but when I looked into her eyes I saw she was only teasing me.

"I expect you know what I mean, Miss Mary Jane," I said.

"I believe I do. Well, Miss Sarah Mary Williams, I am pleased to make your acquaintance, indeed," she said, and bowed to me like you do to a grown person. "Now, back to the lesson: a chemise is a little short dress with short sleeves that you wear over your drawers," she went on. "Then you put on your corsets and petticoats, usually two of those—I generally wear one at home, or on an especially warm day; two if I'm going to town, and in the wintertime I often wear three, and woolen drawers and woolen hose beside—and then the dress goes on top of everything," she paused to laugh at me again. "You do look thunderstruck," she said.

---

[14] Eds. note: Such ladies' underdrawers as existed in those days were slit open from crotch to knee for ease in elimination of bodily wastes. Modern underdrawers for women (knickers or panties with closed crotch seams) did not come into wide use until later in the century.

"I guess I am. *Three* petticoats?"

"Well, only when it's *very* cold."

I shook my head. "I can't seem to see myself got up so."

"You will," she said. "Now, these are women's clothes. Little girls usually wear just a chemise and pantalettes underneath—those are like long, frilled drawers, with closed legs, for modesty, because little girls' skirts are much shorter than grown women's—until they get old enough for long skirts and corsets."

"When is that?"

"Mostly around fourteen or fifteen or thereabouts, but since you've never worn any, I think we'll start you off with the least little bit of lacing until you get used to being in skirts." She handed me the chemise. "All right, just strip right down to your skin and then put that on, and the drawers," she said.

I did so, and she watched me, critically. "You're awful thin and bony," she said. "Must be you don't get enough to eat."

"I do tolerable," I said, "At the Phelpses–where I been all this while–I ate like a drover. But it's been thin pickin's lately."

"We'll fatten you up some," she said.

Over the chemise, she helped me put on the corsets, or "stays," she said most folks called them, which laced up the back. She said she was not going to pull them tight, but even so I felt trussed like a chicken. Next she had me step into a petticoat, and showed me how to tie the tapes of it around my waist. I had to tie them around twice. The petticoat was made of cambric, and the chemise she said was muslin.

"And a lot of girls wear a corset cover too, which is like a little sleeveless shirt with buttons or ribbon ties up the front, and rows and rows of little bitty ruffles sewn inside it, to smooth you out and make you look nice and round up top," she said.

I must've made a face, for she laughed.

"All right, Miss Sarah Mary, we'll forget about the corset cover for now," she said, and then proceeded to explain matters further. "There's all kinds of underclothes for different seasons and uses," she said. "In cold weather most womenfolks do wear long woolen underdrawers, as I said. And your stockings, you keep them up with garters, of course. And then there's hoops—they're very fashionable right now but hard to manage. I have trouble with mine at times, for I don't wear them often, and you tend to lose the knack if you don't wear them regular. There's ways you have to handle your hoops when you sit down or go through doorways and such—and oh! They do fly up—seems like they have a mind of their own. Well, we'll try those later on. You'll pick all this up quick, I don't doubt."

I wished I had as much confidence. It seemed a powerful lot of information, and I warn't sure I understood it all. The chemise and the top petticoat didn't seem that different in feel, though the petticoat was whiter, and had a couple of frills around the bottom, unlike the chemise which was plain. I resolved that later on I would spend some time looking at the things more closely. It puzzled me why there had to be so many difference pieces of cloth just to cover one female body,[15] and I said so.

"That's the fashion," my teacher told me, laughing. "You can't argue with it."

I didn't see why not, but I decided not to say so, and she showed me how to fasten the parts of a dress together. It seemed that dresses made all of a piece, like Aunt Sally's calicos, was only for little girls, or else for country folks or servants. The skirt she handed me, and then the top part—the bodice—had to be hooked to each other, and all the hooks, which was extremely tiny, had to go into the proper tiny little fasteners, which was called "eyes." It was tiring work, and I was sweating by the time it was done, but I had the dress on, and I had it on properly.

My hair was the next difficulty. Mary Jane poked at it and fiddled with it and combed it this way and that and finally gave up. "We'll just wash it tomorrow morning," she said, "And I'll trim it up some and use the curling irons on it. That will have to do until it grows out." I could see that hair would be yet another trial of mine, for up til now I had simply hacked it off with my knife when it got to brushing past my eyebrows and down my neck.

I looked at Mary Jane's hair, which, despite being red, was

---

[15] Standards were, as mentioned earlier, different for different classes. Working-class and rural women wore fewer and less elaborate clothes than their sisters in the middle and upper classes or those who lived and worked in towns. (Slave women also tended to wear only under-shift, gown, apron, and head-scarf, with stockings and shawl in cold weather, if their masters were thoughtful enough to provide these extras.) Little girls' dresses were also usually made in one piece, with shorter skirts than those worn by women.

thick and glossy, worn in a neatly braided twist and coiled around her head. My hair was that coarse and bushy, I despaired of its ever being long enough to braid, but Mary Jane said that it would, as long as I left off chopping at it whenever it got in my way.

Next, Mary Jane looked down at my feet. "I declare, I don't know what-all we can do about shoes," she said. "Joanna's feet are a sight bigger than yours."

"It's still warm enough to go barefoot," I said hopefully.

"Ladies don't go barefoot," Mary Jane said positively. "Only children, sometimes, and country folks, and servants . . . and trash," she added.

I foresaw difficulties here, but once more held my tongue.

In the end, she decided that we would go into town next day and visit the cobbler, for I would need more than one pair of shoes— I didn't think I should ask why just now—and we could have my feet measured and order them all at once. Meanwhile I could wear a pair of Joanna's old slippers with some sheep's wool stuffed in the toes to make them snugger.

"You'll want stockings," Mary Jane said. "Joanna's are all ripped to rags anyway—that girl is awful hard on stockings. Meanwhile, you can borrow some of mine—I think they'll be long enough. Were your parents tall people?"

"I don't remember my mother," I confessed. "She went away when I was little. Pap said she was tall, and he ain't far from six feet, himself."

"You are nearly as tall as I am, " Mary Jane observed, "And I am uncommonly tall for a woman, or so I've been told."

"I've been growing lately," I said.

"Yes, I know," she said. "You were a deal shorter when you were here before, and that was only a few months since. How old are you?"

"I don't know for certain. Fifteen, I think."

"Have you—" she dropped her voice down low, and came closer to me—"have you had your flowers yet?"

"My what?"

"Your flowers. Your 'health' is what the old ladies call it. Your woman-times."

I still didn't know what she meant.

"Some folks call it Eve's curse," she said patiently.

"Oh, that. No, I haven't had it yet," I said. "I know what it

43

is—I mean, I think I do. When women bleed every month?"

She was blushing now, but she nodded.

"I have only just heard of it," I said. "Where does the blood come from?"

She blushed even harder. "It comes from—down below," she said, in a funny strangled sort of voice. I must have looked uncomprehending, for she tried again. "Down by where you— make water," she said finally.

"Oh!" Another mystery solved. "Why?"

It took some time for her to explain, and I was sure she had some of it wrong, but I didn't say so, not wishing to make any trouble.

Later on she showed me where the rags was kept, and the tub for soaking the used ones in salted water, and she promised to show me how to care for myself when the time came. "You mustn't ever mention it in front of men," she said.

"Why not?"

She blushed again. "It's one of those things that women just don't discuss with men. It's—it's just not ever spoken of. Decent women just don't mention such things."

I didn't see why not, but I recalled my conversation with Tom and Jeff, and figured that this must just be one of those strange aspects of civilized life that I would never understand.

Mary Jane went on, "And don't ever wear light colors when it comes, for if you bleed heavy it can show through, easy, even if you wear *three* petticoats. And then you'll have all that extra scrubbing to do. It stains something terrible, that blood. Worse even than regular blood."

I wondered why about this, too, but she didn't say, and I didn't like to ask, for it was clear that the subject troubled her to talk about.

I figured this must be true of women in general, for I'd never heard Aunt Polly or Aunt Sally say anything, nor Mary, or either of the older Phelps girls, though one was nearly seventeen and must surely be having her woman-times, but I had never seen any evidence, nor noticed any female in that household becoming faint, or having stomach pains or the sick-headache, which Miss Mary Jane said was common though not everyone suffered the same.

(I might as well say now that my acquaintance with my dear friend Doctor Thannheimer, who I met on my first trip West, cured me of these kinds of notions. He was a man of great knowledge of the body, having studied medicine not only in Europe but also back in New York State, where one of his classmates had been Dr Elizabeth Blackwell, who became the first female to practice medicine in this country. Dr Thannheimer told me where the blood actually came from—he even lent me a medical book that showed all the organs and what not—and he explained that women (at least some women) was wrongly encouraged to act weak and ill at such times even though there was no reason for them to feel any different unless there was something physically the matter with them—and usually there wasn't. It was the Doctor's opinion that modern women was being ruined by fashion and by fashionable magazines and fashionable doctors—even by their own clothing. He was against lacing, for example—not just tight lacing, but any kind of corsetry. He said it was bad for the proper development of the lungs and the abdominal organs, and he said it hindered breathing and made women prone to pleurisy and phthisis. He said the wearing of high-heeled shoes was near as bad as the Chinese custom of foot-binding—he was right, there—and he didn't think it was healthy nor sensible to wear long sleeves and long skirts and two or three or more petticoats when a woman had any heavy work to do, or when the weather was hot and steamy. For a long time I adopted my own version of female dress partly as a result of his prescriptions, and so my life as a woman was a sight more comfortable after I met Dr Thannheimer, I can tell you. But that was some years in the future, and I will tell more of these things, and of him, later.)

As it turned out, I would not have my first menstrual period until nearly a year later, but Mary Jane decided to show me how to fold the cloths that went between my legs into a pad, and also how to secure this pad in another, longer strip of cloth, fastening the ends of the strip around a kind of belt or sash, fore and aft, also made of a piece of fabric, the whole enterprise to be worn underneath all of those petticoats.

"And you should keep all your old linen to make your little cloths—old sheets and towels, everything," she said, "Because you can't have too many. No matter how you scrub, after a while the stains won't come out completely, and the cloths get stiff and hard, and you have to get rid of them—bury them or burn them. And you will need them for the next twenty years or more, all the times

45

when you are not pregnant or nursing a baby."

"It don't come then?"

"No. So make sure you keep a good supply."

I was not happy to hear that I'd have this to deal with until I got near as old as Aunt Polly, but there was no help for it. I must just get used to it, as Mary Jane said, and try not to mind too much.

(I may say here that this is one area of female experience where the younger generation has the advantage, for there are companies now that sell disposable towels for "women's hygiene,[16]" the advertisements say. I had quite a bit of trouble back in my traveling days, until I discovered how to use a plug of sheep's wool stuffed into a kind of cheesecloth pouch, or bag, which could be inserted into the vagina, and the used wool pulled out and washed or thrown away, and the bag rinsed out and re-stuffed with fresh wool. (I learned this from an Indian woman). I found that the wool plugs worked very well, especially if I also used a small piece of sheepskin, wool side in, as a barrier between my skin and my trousers. This stopped any leaks and could be washed or thrown away and replaced. But girls and women today have a much easier time of it.)

Well, I staid with Mary Jane and Joanna for close on two months, and we become fast friends in that time, almost like sisters, I guess, though having never had a sister nor a brother, I had no experience to go by.

(I have to say that Bella stopped aiming those baleful looks at me once Mary Jane explained that it was me who helped get the Wilks' girls fortunes back from them two frauds, and also that it was me sent the message that the slaves who got "sold"[17] would be returned once the King and the Duke's scheme was exposed— Bella's son had been one of those slaves and she had, she eventually told me, all but give him up for lost. Mary Jane told all the other servants, too, and I never had to lift a finger for myself in that house after that, which made me uncomfortable, but I had to stand it,

---

[16] Hartmann's; also Johnson and Johnson made a disposable sanitary pad for a while in the late 19th century. Several European companies made washable pads and disposable pads as well, including some bandage companies, such as Curad, but these were not widely available at the time.
[17] Eds. note: *AOHF*, Chapter XXVIII.

because it was the only way the servants had to show they was grateful.)

Mary Jane and I had many long comfortable talks, and she told me all about her life with her sisters and their father. There had been another sister between her and Joanna, named Sophronisba. (I privately thought that such a name was enough to send anyone to an early grave, but then, some folks might have felt the same about "Huckleberry.") This sister had died at the age of twelve of measles. Their mother had died when Joanna was born, so Mary Jane was like a mother to both her sisters, as well as taking care of the household for her father.

"He was always so kind," she told me, "And he often said he wished he were a wealthier man, so that I could go East to school, maybe, and not have to waste my youth as his unpaid housekeeper." She smiled a sad little smile. "But I wouldn't have left him, even if he'd been as rich as Croesus. It was my pleasure to help him with his burdens, truly it was—and I also meant to show him, and everybody else, that being a female didn't mean I couldn't turn my hand to any tasks that were needful!"

She looked so pretty and spunky when she said this, that it made me wish I had had such a father, not to mention a sister of my own. Mary Jane had asked me about my own family, and I had told her what I judged she might understand, leaving out some of the worst parts as not really fit for a girl like her to hear. I did tell her that I wanted someday to find out about my family, where we all had come from and so forth, though I let on that my mother as well as Pap had died.

I was most dreadful sorry to say goodbye to Mary Jane, and made her promise to come to Hannibal soon for a long visit, and to meet Aunt Polly and the rest, and she said she would.

Well, she did come to Hannibal, and I visited her again, and so on, and I was present at her wedding to a nice young lawyer, that same Lawyer Bell who'd featured in Mr Twain's story about me, the time those two old frauds tried to steal all the Wilks' girls inheritance. And she and her husband and their oldest son visited me here not too long ago, when they brought their youngest grandson out to California to go to college at Mr Leland Stanford's new school. And of course we have written many letters back and forth over the years.

She is probably my only female friend, come to think on it,

for Aunt Polly and Aunt Sally were more like mothers than friends, and Tom's cousin Mary and I never did get along real well, whilst Tom's wife Becky was much too ladylike for me to ever feel comfortable around her (the same can be said for Mr Twain's—that is, Mr Clemens's wife, Olivia, who I also never felt at ease with).

It is strange to think on, but Mary Jane is close on eighty years old now, and we have not seen each other for five years and a bit. When we last met, her red hair had turned nearly all white, but her eyes had the same old mischievous sparkle; they was still the eyes of the girl she had been when I first met her.

Chapter Five: Hannibal and I Are Not Congenial, and
It is Decided That I Should Go East and Become Educated

Well, Mary Jane tried her best to help me explain myself to the Sawyer household and to all the folks back in Hannibal, but the visit was not a success.

For one thing, Aunt Polly took an instant dislike to Mary Jane—maybe because of her red hair[18]—and was barely civil, so after a few weeks, Mary Jane went back down river and I had to take up my own cause again, so to speak.

Aunt Polly had good intentions, but the rest of the town had not been consulted, it seemed, for when she tried to include me in her activities, folks did not seem eager to welcome the Sawyer family's newest addition. Even in church there was whispering when I come in and more when I went out, though it stopped short when Aunt Polly's bonnet turned in the whisperers' direction.

And I have to say that my own conduct did nothing to mend the situation.

I had always been accustomed to going where I pleased and doing what I wanted. Now that was impossible.

It seemed there was a sight of rules for how a respectable girl had to behave, and I warn't following them nearly close enough.

Well, I was ready to wear girls' clothes, and did so, but that was not all that was required.

I was forbidden to go outdoors alone after dark, that not being proper for a girl.

I warn't supposed to swear—swearing not being proper, neither.

Now, I had tried to give up swearing once before, when I lived with the Widow, and it did seem that I was making some progress once again, but every so often something would slip out, and it usually did so when the minister was to tea or when I went a-visiting with Aunt Polly or Mary, who seemed to feel obliged to help me "learn how to behave in decent society," as she said.

---

[18] Red hair was not admired at this time. (Perhaps not altogether coincidentally, Sam Clemens was himself a redhead.) Huck apparently does not impute Aunt Polly's dislike of Mary Jane to any personal feelings of Aunt Polly's beyond sharing this prejudice--for instance, to jealousy.

Well, I knowed they had my own best interests at heart, but it was something hard on me, just the same.

And then I warn't to smoke, nor go into taverns, nor hang about the river-front, nor talk to strangers, nor be too familiar with servants—and that meant I warn't even supposed to visit with Uncle Jake, Mr Rogers's slave who was always so good to me in the old days.[19]

I did go to see Uncle Jake when I first come back to Hannibal, for I intended to give him five dollars for old time's sake, but he wouldn't thave anything to do with me.

"Please, Miss, go away and leave Uncle Jake be," he begged me. I was standing in front of the barn, looking up at the loft where he used to let me sleep, sometimes, when it rained.

"Uncle Jake, I brung you a present—do come out and see."

"I dasen't, Miss, please don't make me." I could just barely out the shape of him, the loft was so dark. His white hair and beard was about all I could see of him, in the gloom.

"Why, what's the matter, Uncle Jake? It's only me. Won't you come down?"

He would not say anything for the longest while, but finally, when I told him I would just sit down on the mounting block and not budge until he explained, he come out with it.

Well, it was just the most disgusting rubbish you can imagine.

His master had forbidden Uncle Jake—all of his slaves—to talk to me, because I had helped to free Jim.

"But Jim was *already* free," I said.

"No, indeedy," Uncle Jake said positively. "You stoled him. He warn't on'y free when old Miss, she sign freedom papers for him, and Master Jack [that was Mr Rogers], he say we none of us can talk with you count o' you might steal us away."

Turned out that Mr Rogers had threatened all of his slaves with whipping or worse if they spoke to me.

"I won't. And I won't say nothing about it, neither, Uncle Jake," I told him.

"Just go on away from here, please, Miss," he said.

"All right. But I want you to have this," I said, and stooped down to put a gold coin on the ground next to the mounting block.

---

[19] Eds. note: *The Adventures of Tom Sawyer*. Norton Critical Edition, 2007, 135.

"It's by way of thanking you for being so kind, when I was so poor and alone."

"Thank you, Miss," he said. "I don't want it."

"Don't want it? Why not?"

"I'm feared Master Jack will whup me, do I take it."

And no matter how I urged and pleaded, he would not budge, so I finally went off, sad and angry.

I left that five-dollar gold piece there on the ground, and I heard a few days later that Uncle Jake never did pick it up, but a peddler passing through found it and took it. So I never was able to show Uncle Jake how thankful I was.

And it turned out that there was not a single slave in the whole town who was allowed to speak to me, on pain of whipping.

Jim, of course, was living out at the Widow Douglas's, and it near broke my heart that he was uneasy around me, too.

"You ought not to come by here, Miss Sarah," he said, when I stopped by to pass the time of day after seeing the Widow.

"Why not?"

"It ain't proper," he said. "Now, if you come by with Mister Tom, we could have a visit, but you ain't to come alone—it could make trouble for me, too."

I had not thought of that. "All right, Jim," I said, but it irked me none the less. Tom was my friend—but Jim was something more.

And it appeared that that was precisely the problem.

"People talk," Tom pointed out when I complained to him. "They can't sell Jim back into slavery until he's been in the state six months,[20] and they ain't a-going to lynch him, not 's' long as he's under the Widow's protection, but there's a powerful lot of feeling against him. If you want to do him a good turn, we ought to see the Judge and get him and his family settled as soon as we can, for he's in danger here."

In danger—and largely because of me!

I was a danger to Jim, and also to his family, and to the negotiation to buy Jim's wife and children. Tom pointed out that their master did not have to sell them to anyone, let alone to someone who planned to free them.

"You know as well as I that there's a-plenty don't think black

---

[20] This was the law.

folks should be free," he said. "Sometimes those folks take the situation into their own hands. You don't want that."

"No," I agreed.

"So keep away from Jim," Tom said patiently.

"All right."

"And try to act respectable."

"I will."

And I did try, but it was awful hard.

I was a liability to the Sawyers, for folks who respected them did not respect me. Because of my history, I was not someone who could simply drop out of sight—not in a town the size of Hannibal—and I was not someone who could be forgotten, either, because my presence was the excuse for a passel of gossip, which folks in small towns depend upon, their lives being mostly without interest otherwise.

Even though Aunt Polly and Tom and even Sid and Mary did their best, it seemed that Hannibal was not ready to accept the former "juvenile pariah of the village" as a respectable female, and a wealthy one to boot (for I still had my share of Injun Joe's gold), even when the Widow Douglas and Judge Thatcher and Mr Jones all stood up for me and tried to show that I was truly a reformed character. Which goes to show just how far a body will go, all of them being respectable folks who ordinarily would not tell lies. There was even talk of taking Aunt Polly to court and having me bound out to service, but the Judge, he put a stop to that.

It might've been easier if the Widow had still been around, but she had gone to live in Lexington, Kentucky, where her older brother was. He was a widower, himself, and needed her to run his household for him—he was a Senator and lived pretty high on the hog, or so everyone said. I missed the Widow more than I had thought I would. Although she wrote to me from time to time and always encouraged me not to let small minds hinder my progress, I did not find life in Hannibal any featherbed of ease, I can tell you.

Finally, what everyone decided was that I ought to be sent away to school.

At first I was totally against the idea, having learned well enough, as I thought, to read and write and cipher while at the Widow's. But Tom, he argued otherwise.

"You don't aim to stay in this burg for the rest of your life," he said. "No more'n I do."

"True."

"And you'd like to be rich—just like I would," he said.

"We *are* rich," I pointed out. Six thousand apiece was more than most people saw in a lifetime.

"Well, *more* rich," Tom said.

I couldn't argue with that.

"So," Tom went on, "What's the best way to keep our fortunes—and add to them?"

"I give up."

"Education!" Tom said. "It takes an education, these days, to achieve wealth and position in society. Why, look at Judge Thatcher. He——."

"I c'n see the attraction of wealth," I said, "But I don't much feature the part about position."

"Acourse not," Tom said. "You ain't never been part of society *before*; you ain't going to see much good in it *now*."

"Getting back to the part about wealth," I said, "Tell me again about how education is involved."

Well, he tried, but I couldn't make head nor tail of his argument.

Seemed to me then—as it still does now—that becoming rich happened to a body more or less by accident, like Tom and me finding Injun Joe's gold. But according to Tom, such accidents was rare—what happened to folks as was trying to become rich who actually succeeded was that they had a system, which, Tom maintained, come from having an education, in these modern times.

"Look here, Huck—I mean, Sarah Mary," he said, "A man with an education is a man who's going to go far in this world."

"How far?" I said. "And you ain't said nothing about a *woman*."

But the Judge agreed, and also said that if his own daughter Becky had an ounce of intellect (which he allowed she hadn't) he'd send her to school back East, too.

Well, they both simply stuck to the same argument and said I was being pigheaded, which I was.

(Later I would find out that Tom's being bit by the education bug was all the fault of the Judge, who talked about his own university days (he'd been to Yale College, himself) in a way that was certain to make somebody like Tom—somebody with romantical inclinations—think of it as the only path toward true gentlemanliness—which is the estate Tom said he intended for himself, because it was time to put away childish things.)

"This is exactly like it was last time, when we was planning Tom Sawyer's Gang," Tom said, in disgust. "You didn't want to go back to the Widow and be respectable then."

"And I still don't want to be respectable," I said. "But I guess I ain't got a choice in the matter, do I?"

"No more you do," Tom said. "It's out of your hands—mine, too. Don't you see, Huck, we ain't children no more."

Now, I have to say that that is a reflection of Mr Twain's attitude as well as Tom's own. Nostalgia for those carefree boyhood years—that was Mr Twain's problem. I often heard him say he wished he could go back to being twelve or fourteen years old—and then drown. And Tom also looked back and grieved for those bygone days.

Which I myself was only too glad to see the end of.

But if Tom wanted to mourn the loss of his childhood, the least I could do was let him do so without being a hindrance. And he won me over, finally, by proposing that the two of us go East together, him to Yale College and me to a girls' school nearby.

And so Judge Thatcher, he made all of the arrangements.

But there was still one more thing to be done before we could leave, and that was to settle Jim and his family on their new farm.

***

We went by train, St Joe being the end of the line at that time. Although I dislike train travel, it was interesting—for a while at least—to see the country go by so quick and to hear the rails singing under us. If we had gone by wagon it would have taken close to two weeks, and been hard going, but the railroad trip lasted only a bit under two days, and we—the white folks anyway— was able to take rooms at the railroad hotel whilst we gathered ourselves and what would be needed for the family on their new land. Jim and Eliza and the younguns stayed with a black preacher just outside of town. He was a freedman himself, and he and his wife made them very comfortable, Jim said.

It took another two days to purchase the remainder of the goods we needed and the wagon to carry them in, plus a team of mules. Jim and Tom looked over all of the animals for sale and chose four that seemed sturdy, all warranted for haulage as well as trained to the plow. We also bought a milk cow and her calf from a farmer with extra stock to sell.

The farm wagon we'd already commissioned—Tom had gone ahead, when he met with the land agent and made over the deed— and it was ready, a good sturdy buckboard, with the driver's seat mounted on springs so as not to jolt one's teeth completely out of one's head on the bumpy, rutted tracks that were all that region could boast of for roads, back then.

We loaded the wagon with the household goods: a table and benches, a couple of stools and a rocking chair, Eliza's spinning wheel, a dresser and bedstead with bedding, and a couple of crates of crockery and cutlery and bread pans and such. The clothes-trunks and carpetbags and two pallets we put in the bed of the livery stable's wagon, which Tom and I would drive back afterwards. Eliza and the children would ride there on our way out to the farm, Jim driving, whilst Tom and I come along in the farm wagon.

The journey took all of one day and half the next. But it was a grand trip—the weather mostly sunny (it being the first week in May) and we jogged along quite comfortable, chatting with each other and enjoying the children's antics.

Johnny I remember at that time was about eight years old to his sister Elizabeth's five or six, a likely little chap, light-complected, sort of a biscuit-color—both of the children being much lighter than Jim, who was deep brown, and each one with crinkly black hair and perfect white teeth. Johnny's eyes I thought very beautiful, kind of a deep goldy-brown, the color of good whiskey, with long curling lashes like a girl's. He could sing, and whistle, too, and evenings he sometimes brought out a jew's-harp and played some—lively tunes that made a body want to dance.

Oh, yes, those was fine days and nights, and I treasured them, knowing that soon I would have to say goodbye to Jim and he to me, which I will not write about here, but in another place.

***

Well, after we settled the family, Tom and I headed East, Tom to Yale and myself to Miss Edwards's Female Seminary in Meriden, Connecticut.[21] I was going to be an educated woman if it killed me, which I thought it just might—especially after the two years I spent

---

[21] A number of Twain scholars suggest that this may have been Miss Porter's School for Girls, located in Farmington, Connecticut, founded in 1843 by Sarah Porter to provide a college-preparatory education for young ladies.

with Miss Edwards and my fellow female seminarians.

Indeed, I would not even take the time nor the ink to report on those same two years, but for what happened to me under her tutelage.

She, Miss Edwards, reminded me powerfully of the Widow Douglas's sister, old Miss Watson: another tolerable slim old maid with goggles on, but more in the way of brains—a deal more—and much less in the way of religion, though she was devout enough, always having prayers before meals, and recommending improving books to us "young ladies," and going to church every Sunday, rain, snow, or sleet. I had learned to sit through a church service and even to listen to a sermon without dying of boredom, though most of it still seemed pointless to me, especially the Old Testament, which seemed mostly about God smiting someone or other; now that I think of it my mental picture of God in those days was of someone more or less like Pap, only more powerful and a good bit cleaner in his habits.

But, back to Miss Edwards— she was as unbending a woman as Miss Watson had been, quick to point out errors big and little, and quicker to jump on a body for not making the necessary corrections with lightning speed. She was constantly after me to use better grammar and not to swear, and she refused to let me wear breeches even to ride, but had me learn to use a side-saddle, which is an instrument of torture if ever there was one.

It probably goes without saying, but I'll say it: I detested her before I'd been there a week, and it was mutual. Only the regular payments forwarded from my account via Judge Thatcher persuaded her to keep me, and only my determination to make something of myself allowed me to stay.

So I stood it for nearly two year—and that was as much as I *could* stand, no matter how Tom scolded at me.

"You ain't a quitter," he said one Sunday, visiting with me in the Seminary's front parlor. Miss Edwards was always pleased to allow him to call on me, he being a Yale student, and therefore most likely rich, and good-looking besides.

"No, I ain't—am not," I said. "But this is no life for me, Tom, and you know it as well's I do."

"You just ain't used to it."

"Maybe I don't want to be used to it. Maybe you ought to catch the train back to New Haven and leave me to hell alone."

"You oughtn't to swear," he said. "It ain't ladylike."

He sounded just like Miss Edwards, only with worse grammar. "Maybe I don't want to be a lady."

He leaned against the parlor door and looked down at me, a lazy look but full of mischief. I could see it in the curl of his lip and the lift of one eyebrow. "Well, that's good, because you sure ain't one."

That did it. I give him a glare that should have frosted his liver, then stalked away.

"Sarah Mary! I didn't mean it."

"Well, I don't want to be friends with someone who says what he don't mean."

The look on his face when I said that made me wish I hadn't. He stared at me for a moment, not speaking, then he whirled round and left, slamming the front door so hard a pane of glass fell out and shattered into a dozen pieces.

I ran over and tried to pick them up, but grazed one finger on a sharp edge. A thin trickle of blood dripped onto my skirt.

"Drat you, Tom Sawyer," I said, and went at the spots with my balled-up pocket handkerchief. "Men!" I snorted. "Think you're all lords of creation and we women exist only to do what you think we ought to. Whoever give *you* the right to decide what's best for *me*?"

I shook out my handkerchief and looked balefully at the bloodstains that streaked it, then down at the spots on my skirt, which I realized would probably never come out. "Damnation!" I rang for the maid and asked her to bring a dustpan and brush, then stomped upstairs.

I was in a foul mood indeed.

One thing more, I thought, *just one thing, and I will leave the dust of this infernal place behind me and never look back.*

That one thing came just a few days later, but it warn't my doing, at least not only mine.

***

I had gotten pretty far with my education, though Miss Edwards tried to make me give up bookkeeping and economics, and learn fancy embroidery and French, and she also disliked my spending so much time with her cook and butler (who was also her coachman), both of which I was heartily fond of—they was colored folks, not slaves but free colored people (like Jim and Eliza and their

57

children had become), though these folks worked as house servants and had never, they told me, even been on a farm. They was city-bred, Pompey and Clytie, and both their families had been free clear back to the Revolution. I learned a great deal from them, especially Clytie, about household management.

(It is interesting, but the maids in that place was Irish girls, not colored; I do not know why this was. Howsomever, there was two of them, one named Peggy and the other Patsy. I think they may have been twins, for they looked alike as two peas, both freckled as quails' eggs, with blue eyes and hair as red as Mary Jane Wilks's, but curly. They worked as hard as any slave, too, and I never did get to know them very well, for they was always busy. Too, they was hard to understand, speaking a heathenish-sounding English, very different from anything I'd ever heard, full of strange words like "bejasus!" and "begorrah!")

In spite of feeling odd and awkward, and lonesomer than I'd ever been, I made one friend at Miss Edwards's school. It makes me feel strange to recall how out of place I felt in those days. In addition to what Miss Edwards called "my doubtful origins," I was hell-bent on getting an education, which set me apart. Most of the other girls was too silly to care about learning anything but the words to the latest popular songs, and several was spiteful and mean; the remainder didn't interest me one way or another, being there mostly to acquire what Miss Edwards called "a smattering" of knowledge before being put on the marriage market. I can only dimly recall their faces, and none of their names, except hers.

She was vastly different, as different as a swan is from a crow.

(And why I should think of a swan in connection with her is no puzzle at all, for although they are beautiful birds, graceful and sleek with their long curving necks and spreading white wings, they are neither kindly nor noble. I have seen one try to drag a child under the surface of a pond, when the little one ran out of the bread he'd brought to feed "the pretty birds," and it took the boy's mother and a man who come a-running, both, to save the child from that white, raging fury.)

Her name was Antoinette d'Iberville, which, she told me, was a French name, and very old; her family was from New Orleans. She was just sixteen, and I was at least a year older, but she was well ahead of me on the road to young-lady-hood.

Indeed, I learned more from Antoinette about proper clothes

and the way to arrange one's hair and what colors became one (and suchlike) than I ever could have gotten from Miss Edwards, who was neat and businesslike but far from fashionable (in fact, she deplored fashion as being oppressive to women, one of the few matters in which we was in perfect agreement.)

And I also learned about love.

***

Antoinette was a kind of girl I'd never even seen before, from a high-placed family, but she was an orphan like me, so that was a bond between us. Her papa had left her well-fixed, and she had an aunt and uncle back in Louisiana who sent her to school when she told them she wanted an education—they had no children, and was getting along in years.

I met them once, when they come North for a visit, a comfortable, well-dressed couple in early middle-age, he plump and ruddy-faced, she slender and pale. It was the aunt who was sister to Antoinette's father, and I imagine it was from that side of the family she got her looks: slim and fair-complected, with black eyes and shining black hair that she wore parted in the center and brushed into clusters of curls over both ears.

Antoinette was going to be a writer, she said. She was going to write books when she grew up, [22] and she planned to be famous. She would work for women's rights, and she would never marry, she told me.

"Why not? You're pretty enough that some man will snatch you up as soon as you're old enough to wed," I said.

"Marriage is no life for a modern woman," Antoinette said. "When you are married, your husband owns you, like a slave. You have no rights of your own any longer."

That had never occurred to me. I had not much experience of married folks, to tell the truth, except for Jim and Eliza and the Phelpses; the former I hadn't observed enough to form a judgment, and in the latter case they seemed pretty equal in terms of rights, or maybe the weight was heavier on Aunt Sally's end. The other women I was acquainted with was all widowed or single: The

---

[22] Eds. note: The name used here is clearly a pseudonym. The true identity of Antoinette remains to be discovered. Possible candidates include Olympia Brown, Anna Elizabeth Dickinson, and Julia Sears (although the latter in fact never married).

Widow, Miss Watson, Aunt Polly, Tom's cousin Mary, Mary Jane Wilks (at the time) and her sisters, and of course Miss Edwards.

In any event, Antoinette read a great deal from the works of a writer named Margaret Fuller, who was plainly someone of deep thought—far too deep for me—and also various essays by Elizabeth Cady Stanton and Amelia Bloomer and other ladies whose names I disremember, all of them high up in the women's rights movement. She sometimes read from their works aloud, whilst I was sewing (I had learnt to, finally, for it was a useful skill, though I didn't esteem it as a recreation) in the evenings, in our room, for we shared a chamber. She took several papers, too, including an abolitionist journal, and she read me about the great convention for women's rights that had taken place in Seneca Falls just that past year.

"I wish that I could have gone there," she said wistfully. "I would give a great deal just to hear the speeches."

I privately thought I would give as much to be delivered from such an occasion, but refrained from saying so.

"I am going to Oberlin College[23] after I finish here," she said, "And I will study law and history, and someday, yes, I will be able to do my part for the struggle. Come with me, Sarah, do!"

"This is as much education as I care for," I said, laughing. "You study your old books, and I'll study how to make lots of money." For that had become my goal, to become exceedingly rich, so rich that I could do whatever I pleased and never have to answer to anyone ever again.

'Toinette flung herself across the bed and hugged me, fierce. "You think you are so practical, Sarah, but you are a romantic at heart," she said. "I know it."

"If you want to think so," I said, and silenced her with a kiss.

I heard many years later that 'Toinette had in fact married, and that she and her husband had moved to Greeley, Colorado with the Union Colony. I sometimes thought about what it might be like to see her again, being curious as you might say, especially about the man she married. But I never did.

As many as the years have been since then—more than sixty, now—I can still see her, slim and white as a young birch tree,

---

[23] If Antoinette is based on Olympia Brown, Brown actually attended Antioch.

breasts and flanks gleaming in the glow from the fire, her black hair rippling over the pillow, her dark eyes shining up at me, the candle-flames reflected in them, small but very bright.

Yes, we were lovers, and in spite of what transpired, I don't regret it for one moment.

And I was glad to hear, all those years later, that she had married—at least, I wasn't sorry.

Well.

It was Antoinette who made the first move.

I remember I was sitting at my desk, writing a letter to Aunt Polly. It was a rainy afternoon, and most of the Seminary's students was reading in their rooms, or napping. I could hear music very faintly; someone was playing the piano in the front parlor. Antoinette was half-reclining on the sofa in front of the fireplace, the novel she'd been reading in her lap. I remember the title. It was *Jane Eyre*—which had just come out that year, and had caused quite a sensation. She was gazing into the flames with a somber expression.

"Sarah," she said suddenly. "Do you miss your family?"

"I miss Aunt Polly, sure, and Jim, and Aunt Sally and Uncle Silas, if you call them family—I guess they and Tom and Jim are all the family I've got," I said. "Do you miss your folks?"

"No, not really," she said. "There is someone I miss, but no, not a relative."

"A friend?"

"You might say so," she said, and she got up from the sofa and began to roam around the room in a distracted sort of way.

I give up trying to write my letter and watched her instead. She crossed to the window, parted the drapes, and looked out, sighed a little, and leaned her head against the glass for a moment.

"What's the matter?"

"Nothing. I am sad, that is all." She returned to the sofa, falling back against the cushions with her eyes closed.

"Does your head hurt?" (She often suffered from headaches.)

"No—yes, it does a little."

"Would you like me to ring for a cup of tea?"

"No—sit here with me for a while, won't you?" She patted the sofa with one long, white hand.

I got up and went over and sat down beside her.

She reached over and took my left hand in her right one, and squeezed it a little bit.

"Do you want to know why I am sad?" Her dark eyes were shaded by long, curling lashes; I thought I saw tears brimming in them.

"If you want to tell me."

"Well, then, I am sad because I am remembering someone."

She seemed to want me to say something, so I did. "Someone you—cared about, maybe?" I thought it was some boy she'd known, back in New Orleans, and perhaps had a crush on, the way girls do, you know.

"Yes—someone I cared about very much." She was still holding my hand, and stroking it in a sort of absentminded way.

I tried to pull back my hand, but she held fast to it, and drew me closer to her, so close that I could feel her warm breath on my neck.

I had never been this close to another girl before, not even Mary Jane.

I could feel the heat from her body, and smell her scent— partly the French cologne she liked to wear, and partly the muskier fragrance that rose from her white skin and dark, dark hair.

I couldn't help myself. I drew closer to her, closer, breathing it in, that scent . . .

And she leaned over and kissed me on the cheek, quick and gentle.

It startled me, but I didn't move away.

Then she moved even closer, and brushed the corner of my mouth with her warm lips.

And somehow we were in each other's arms.

And there was all the wonder and the softness of her, the sweet-salty taste of her, the soft mounds of her breasts, the velvet skin and the perfumed secrets of her, for me to discover . . .

Even now I feel a catch at my throat, to remember how it was.

And when it was over, and we both lay there breathless, she kissed me again and said, "Now you are mine."

And so I was—until the end came.

***

We were—inevitably, I suppose—discovered.

Careful, always; but not careful enough.

I will never know whether our lovemaking was overheard, or

whether one of the other girls spied on us unseen, or whether Miss Edwards herself suspected, but one morning the door to our room opened without the opener's having given the customary knock, and we were discovered just as we had fallen asleep the night before, naked, twined in one another's arms.

Antoinette stirred a second before I did, and gave a little gasp, which brought me fully awake.

There in the doorway stood the Head of our school, and an expression on her face like someone who'd bit into an unripe persimmon.

I give Miss Edwards credit; she did not shriek nor fall down fainting, but simply stood there like the Wrath of God in a maroon dressing gown and said, "Put your clothes on at once, both of you. And come to my study as soon as you are decent." Then she stalked away, leaving her disapproval behind her like a bad smell.

Antoinette leapt from the bed like a young deer and began hurriedly to dress. I stood up slowly, stretched, and walked over to the washstand.

"Sarah, hurry up and dress. Maybe, if we explain—"

"'Toinette, there ain't—isn't—anything we can explain that won't get us in even more trouble," I said. "I guess we'll have to move to a hotel until we can sort this all out."

The look on Antoinette's face gave me a sinking feeling. "Sarah, I have no money," she said. "My aunt and uncle pay my fees, and there is a little spending money left over at the end of every month, but that is all."

"Well, shoot, I have plenty and to spare," I said, getting into my chemise and stays.

"I cannot take your money," she said, buttoning her basque.

"Why not?" I tied the tapes of my petticoat and reached for my corset cover.

"We are not related—we have no ties."

"No ties?" I stared at her. "I love you, 'Toinette. And you love me."

"That is true," she said. "But it doesn't matter any longer, does it?"

"Doesn't matter? How can you say that?"

"Because it is true. Listen, Sarah, listen to me: I love you, but you must have known before this that we could not go on this way, not forever."

"I don't understand." But I was beginning to. I watched as she finished dressing and began to unplait and then comb out her hair, that hair like dark rippling water that I had so often wound about her throat and breasts, hair that had fallen like a scented curtain about our faces; hair that smelt like musk-roses and felt like softest silk.

"Sarah." She reached out one slim arm, her long fingers curling.

I ignored the gesture. "You don't love me."

She did not contradict me.

"I need to stay here," she said. "You understand. I must finish my preparation, so that I can go on to college."

"Stay here? Do you think she'll let either of us stay here?"

"Oh, not you," she said. "But yes, I think she will let me stay."

I felt like I'd been sandbagged. "Why do you think so, Antoinette?"

"Because," she said, coming close to me, "You will tell her that it was all your fault, that you seduced me, and you will promise to go away and never see me again."

I backed away from her.

Even now, a lifetime later, I can feel it, the way my heart seemed to shatter and fall down inside my breast.

It was true. She did not love me. It was all a sham. She had only used me—

"Is this what happened before?" I asked, and wondered that my voice still worked. "To the other one? The one you pretended to love before?"

"It was not pretense. I did love her. And I did love you, Sarah. Truly."

"If that is love," I said, "Then I want no more of it, ever."

"Oh, Sarah." Antoinette walked to the door. "I am sorry."

"Are you?" I said. "I don't believe it. Just like I don't believe that you really think I'll take the fall for this."

"Ah, but you will," she said. "You will, because you cannot bear to see someone hurt that you care about. And you do still care."

As much as I wanted to tell her to go to Hell, I couldn't. She was right.

When I looked at her slim elegance, and thought of the times

I'd held that body to me, breast to breast, and when I looked at her red lips and knew they lied but still felt how sweet they had been, burning against my flesh, and when I heard her voice and remembered the times I'd made her cry out with pleasure—

I could only nod, and watch as she opened the door, went through it, and closed it, ever so gently, in my face.

My own interview with Miss Edwards was short.

"Miss d'Iberville has told me everything," Miss Edwards said. "She is—understandably—quite distressed, and I have put her under a doctor's care. You will not see her again, nor speak to her, and I forbid you to write to her. Do you understand?" Miss Edwards looked at me with loathing. "You betrayed the trust of an innocent young girl. I should have known better than to have taken a creature like you into my establishment in the first place."

I couldn't say a word, just stood and looked at her.

"Under the circumstances, you cannot remain here," she said. "I have arranged that your things be conveyed to the Meriden Hotel. A room has been reserved for you there. I will see that the remainder of this quarter's fees is returned to you before you leave this city."

"Keep it," I said.

"As you wish," she said. "I cannot convey to you how shocked I am at such a sordid state of affairs."

"I feel the same way," I managed to say.

"You will not be able to count on me for any future references," she said. "Goodbye, Miss Williams."

She did not rise, nor offer to shake hands, but directed her attention to the pile of papers in front of her on her desk.

The door opened.

Pompey, the coachman, was standing there. "I brung the carriage around like you said, Ma'am."

"Take Miss Williams to the hotel directly, please."

"Yes'm." He stepped back for me to precede him, and I walked out of the room, into the hallway, and up the stairs, feeling lightheaded, and as if my feet were not connected to the rest of me.

I went up to the room we'd shared—our room—and found that my bags and trunks were waiting on the stair-landing, and the door was locked.

That she was inside, I knew. And part of me wanted to hammer on the door, and scream, and part of me wanted to crush that slim stem of a throat between my hands, and part of me wanted to bury my mouth in her satiny flesh, and part of me wanted to fall down dead, but I didn't, and I couldn't, and that was that.

It was as if there were no one left in the house, all was so silent.

I could hear the clock on the landing ticking, its pendulum moving from side to side. I could hear the fire in the grate making its small rustling noise. And—so faint that I knew it was the last time my memory would ever summon the sound—I could hear 'Toinette's soft sigh and quickened breathing, joined with mine.

For Christmas, she had given me a pearl ring, which she said had belonged to her grandmother. I wore it on a chain around my neck, it being too small for even my littlest finger. I had thought to be buried with that ring. Now I reached up and lifted the chain over my head. I hung the chain with its circular burden over the doorknob of the room and turned, at last, to go.

That was my first experience with love.

The second would wait another fifteen years to find me.

Chapter Six: Knoxville:
I Meet Some Cantrells, and I Buy a Slave

I took my leave of Pompey and Clytie and Peggy and Patsy, and wired Aunt Polly that I was leaving school for good (though I did not, of course, say why). I told her to expect me in a few weeks, then left Hartford by train and continued on to Pittsburgh, where I boarded a run to Knoxville. From there I could go on to Nashville, and make a connection for St Louis. At that point, I'd head up to Hannibal and take my leave of the folks there, before going West.

I was about to light out for the Territory, as Mr Twain would later put it.

This excursion through Tennessee was a side trip, but one I'd been planning for years. Pap and my mother had met each other in Tennessee; Pap had said that her people were named Cantrell. It oughtn't to be too hard to find some trace of her, or them, if I put my mind to it. I had decided to make the attempt, as it might prove the only chance I'd have. Now I needed to equip myself for such a journey.

The usual difficulties attended my arrival in Knoxville. Most of my baggage I'd sent on ahead to Hannibal, knowing it would arrive eventually. I kept out a carpetbag with a shirt and trousers and jacket and clean linen, and wished I could change to men's clothes right away, they being much more comfortable and convenient, but that would not do for what I had in mind.

The livery stable near the station advertised reasonable prices, and I was able to bespeak a mount and gear for the next month at a price only a little above highway robbery. What I wanted next was a guide and escort, but that proved harder to acquire. There did not seem to be any men available. Finally, "I kin let you have one of my blacks," the livery stable owner said. His name was Betancourt, according to the sign hanging over the door. "I got a couple on 'em who know the country well enough, so far as I c'n judge, and trustworthy beside."

"How much?" I asked.

He named a sum I could have *bought* a slave for, easy, but I was not disposed to argue. "Let me see them."

He went inside and bawled out, "Cassius! Scipio! Get cleaned up and come on out here!"

"Them's pretty fancy names," I said. I had benefited enough

from my two years at Miss Edwards's to recognize the names as those of famous Latin statesmen and generals, like her coachman's, Pompey. It was a fashion amongst some slaveowners, to name their property so, as if they played at being ancient Romans. But it was rare to see it here in the back-woods, and in fact rarer to see slaves at all in this part of Tennessee. I said so.

"I got 'em of a gentleman from Virginia," Betancourt said. "An artist, he said he was. He traded them to me for a horse and a pack mule."

Cassius was about forty, a sturdy-built man, medium brown in color, hazel-eyed, with close-cropped coppery hair and a gap between his front teeth. Scipio was younger, a shade or two lighter and sparer in build, and his expression was one of unrelieved gloom.

I looked back at Cassius, who grinned at me and said, "How do, Miss."

Scipio, prompted by a glare from his owner, grunted a little and said, "Yes'm," letting his voice trail off while his eyes roamed the branches of the trees nearby.

Cassius stepped forward. "Don't mind him, Miss, he been having the toothache real bad, since last Sat'day."

Betancourt scowled at Scipio. "You didn't say nothing about no toothache."

"No, sir," said Scipio, still scanning the trees. "I ain't, sir."

"Well, take yourself off to the barber,[24] then, why don't you!"

"Yes, sir," and Scipio begun to shamble off.

"And don't take all day about it!"

"Yes, sir," his voice floated back.

I looked at Cassius. "Well, I guess I will take this man, then, Mr Betancourt."

"He's a good hand, very reliable," said the stable owner. "You, Cassius, I'm hiring you out to Miss Williams here. Now, you do whatever she needs doing, you hear me? You can keep half of what she's payin' me for you—I'll give it to you when y'all come back."

"Yes, sir. Thank you, sir."

"He'll come to your hotel tomorrow morning," Betancourt

---

[24] Eds.note: Barbers were, even at this late date, surgeons of a sort, lancing boils and drawing teeth as well as performing the tonsorial rituals of their trade.

said to me, and, to Cassius, "You get your gear together after work today, boy, and make sure these mounts're ready for you and the lady to use." He pointed to the horse I'd selected for myself and to one standing next to it.

"Yes, sir. I surely will, sir."

I shook hands with Mr Betancourt, paid over the sum he'd named, and nodded to Cassius, then returned to my hotel, hoping for a hot supper and a restful night. For all I knew, it might be the last sleep I took in a real bed for quite some time.

***

As it turned out, I was right—I didn't sleep in a real bed again for several months, with one exception, not counting staterooms during various river passages. That hotel bed in Knoxville, Tennessee was comfortable enough, or would have been had I not had to share it with a variety of insect life. I was pretty well chewed by next morning, but it turned out to be good training for the experience of being feasted on by mosquitoes and various biting flies as Cassius and I traversed some of the thickest-wooded trails in eastern Tennessee.

I had made inquiries over the past several months and had a good idea of where to start my search. There was Cantrells all over this part of the country, I'd been told; one of them run a post office and general store in a settlement on the Little Pigeon River. [25] This was where I aimed to go first.

It warn't much more than three days' travel, four at most, I was told, so I directed Cassius, when he arrived early next morning, to provision us for at least two weeks, figuring that delays were certain and also that our destination might not be the most hospitable. I told him to get a tent and blankets and some cooking gear; I give him twenty dollars and he come back midmorning with both horses saddled and a pack horse beside.

"Hope you ain't mad, Miss Sarah," said Cassius, "But I axed Mr Betancourt for another horse, beings you toting all this gear."

I warn't mad at all, but pleased he had taken the forethought, and I said so.

"I done some travelin' around in this country," Cassius said.

---

[25] Eds. note: This region was named for the enormous flocks of passenger pigeons (a once-numerous species, now extinct) that were native to the area.

"It don't do to go unprepared, no ma'am. Mr B., he say you can pay him the extra when we-all get back, and he won't charge but half again what you already paid out."

I said that was satisfactory and give him five dollars to keep for himself. Then I said we'd take to the trail as soon as I'd settled my bill, which I done, and we started off.

***

I had changed into male attire, and rode along feeling comfortable and easy.

It was a fine time we had. Journeying with Cassius was in some ways like being with my old Jim again, in that Cassius like Jim would always take the long watch at night, and he done all he could for my comfort, building smoky fires of green wood to keep off the mosquitoes (which was only partially successful), cutting pine branches to put under my blankets to keep me off of the cold ground, fetching water, and generally being agreeable. I thanked him for his trouble, and told him a little about me and Jim, and he said it was worth more than gold in the hand to have a friend you could trust.

"I would not be here except for Jim," I said.

"He taken good care of you," Cassius said. "Better than your own daddy done. And you say you set him up with a farm and all? And he a free man, too . . . living there on his own land now, with his own family, and all of them free?"

I nodded.

"It is a wonderful story," Cassius said. "I am glad to have heard it."

"Do you hanker after your freedom?" I asked him.

"Sometimes I wonder what it would be like," he said. "I hear tell of free blacks up North, in Philadelphia and New York and Boston."

"Yes. I have known some. Would you go North, if you were free?"

"I surely would. There is nothing to hold me in these parts, except I belong to Mr Betancourt and he would have me catched and brang back, did I try to get away."

"Have you ever known a slave who ran away?"

"One." He was silent, remembering. Then: "I was told that he was my father."

I'd heard the story before. Most people in the South had

70

heard it, or known of it, in different variations.

A slave who remembered Africa, who had been brought to these shores by men who tried to tame him with the lash, and who pretended to be gentled, but ran—at the first opportunity. And was hunted down, by men and dogs, and brought back—to be tethered to a stake and whipped until his back skin and muscle hung in bloody ribbons, and—if he recovered—to bear the scars for life.

"I never knowed for certain if he *was* my daddy in truth," Cassius said. "My mama, she say she thought he might be, for they jump the broom, you know, back before my mama and me was sold."

He looked at me. "We was sold. We never see the home place again. My mama, she sad, but she say: God have us in His hands. And then Old Master, he take her into his bed."

I knew jumping the broom was the slave marriage ceremony. I also knew that slave marriages were not legal, and if the master wanted a slave woman for his use, she had to do his bidding.

"What was his name, your daddy, the African?"

"I never did hear his real name. He ain't belong to our master, but to another man, a judge from the town. That judge give him the name Jehu because he good with horses.[26] And that how he and my mama come to meet—Jehu drive his master out to where we was, every week or so, on legal business. My mama say he, Jehu, use to talk to the people about freedom, because he remember being free, and she thought he the finest man in the world, tall and strong." Cassius shrugged. "But then, she tell me, master might be my daddy, too. No way to tell. I's lighter than that African man, but then, my mama, she very light herself."

He went on to tell me that his mother had been raised to be a house servant from the time she was a child. "She was *bright*," he said, meaning her color. "Tall and slim, skin soft and golden. Brown hair, long and crinkly, with golden lights in it. And green eyes, like mine but greener, like willow leaves."

"What was her name?"

---

[26] Eds. note: A reference to 2 Kings 9-10, about the King of Israel of that name, who drove his chariot "fast and furiously." The name was often used in both the States and England for coachmen and other drivers, both for slaves as personal names and as a general soubriquet for white wage-earning drivers.

"Leora."

And he told how she had become the Old Master's bedfellow.

"Old Master, his wife she die years back, and he don't marry again, just have him one slave woman after another. The one before my mama, she mighty upset when he turn her out and take my mama instead. But he keep my mama by him, long time. And he good to her—least, she hadn't to do much work but tend to him, and he give her lots of pretties."

Cassius reached into an inner pocket of his jacket and pulled out a piece of cloth. "Here, look." He held up a packet of some dark cloth, wadded up small, and unfolded it. Inside was a piece of linen, and within it a length of silk ribbon, perhaps twenty inches long, woven in a pattern of varying blues and greens. "I have always kept it by me," Cassius said. "As a 'membrance." He returned it, gently, to its linen shield, and then to its outer wrappings, and slipped it back into his pocket.

"Yes, I guess he good to her," Cassius went on. "In his way. But then—"

Then a baby girl was born—and died.

"I never see her, that child," he said. "My sister. My mama told me, she born dead."

I wondered—then, and still. Was it true? Or had the mother taken her own child's life, to spare her from slavery? Such things were known.

What must it be like, to be a slave, to go to the bed of the man who owned you, to receive his seed and bear his child? And was it better for such a child to be born dead or to live a slave, owned by the man who fathered her?

My old Jim, I knew, had lived for a long time in fear that his own wife might become her master's concubine—for he had told me, years before, of that ever-present worry. Eliza lived on her master's plantation, fully seven miles away from the Widow Douglas's, so that Jim could see her only when the Widow or Miss Watson went a-visiting there, and needed him to drive them.

Eliza was light-skinned and young and delicately made—like Leora.

Cassius's story made me want to weep—for him, for Leora, and for Jim. Not for the first time, I was passionately glad that Jim's daughter would never be owned by the father of her child.

Cassius and I sat in silence for a few minutes.

I asked, how had they come to Virginia?

He, Cassius, had been bought along with his mother—he thought he was perhaps seven or eight years of age at the time. "Well, like I told you, Miss Sarah Mary, first we was sold from the home place. And then we sold again, to pay some debts my mama said."

Cassius's new master, the owner of a vast plantation, decided he should continue being trained as a house-servant. "I remember, first time I see Old Master, he tip up my chin and look me in the eye, look close at my face and feel my arms and legs, make me stand up tall and walk back and forth across the room, and he look me over like you would a horse, you know, or a dog, and then say, 'This here a likely boy,' and he tell his butler to take me in hand and show me what-all I supposed to do."

This butler was in charge of the whole house, Cassius said, and had been with the family his whole life. "He train me real good," Cassius said. "Before I's half-growed I could wait table, polish silver, fold napkins, pour wine neat as neat, hand dishes from the sideboard, sharpen knives, make coffee the French way. . . all those things, and more beside. Old Master, he had a lot of company, and set a good table."

Cassius received a new name to go with his new duties. "Old Master, he give me the name Cassius," he said. "My mama call me Little J, you know, because my daddy name Jehu, like I say."

In any event, Cassius remained behind in the house after his half-sister was stillborn, but Old Master had apparently tired of Cassius's mother, who was sent to work in the plantation hospital, because she was skilled at tending the sick—she once told him, he related, that her own grandmother, Cassius's great-grandmother, had been a healing woman back in Africa—a herb doctor, a conjure-woman who could brew medicines and simples to cure many sicknesses. Leora too was good with illness and injuries.

"Not only that, but Old Master, he tired of her weeping and wailing, I guess," Cassius said. "She been a happy woman, 'til that baby girl died. Then she full of sadness and gloom, and cryin', so he sent her out an' buy himself a new wench, from over Williamsburg way, another light-skinned gal but younger'n my mama, fourteen or fifteen I guess."

And then, when Cassius himself was about fourteen, he and his mother were sold to a neighboring planter, who after a year or so sold Cassius to the Virginia man, a traveling artist.

"He painted folk who had money and wanted a picture of theyselves or they children," Cassius said. "Mr Parker, he buy Scipio first, you see, and then he decide one servant ain't enough. He need two of us to take care of him an' carry his canvases and brushes and paints and all. He had a right smart of baggage, and it was the kind need light handling, you see. He wanted me because I trained to care for nice things and I's warranted neat and careful."

And it was this man, a Mr C. R. Parker[27], who brought Cassius and also Scipio, whom he'd obtained elsewhere, this far into the wilderness and then sold them to Mr Betancourt.

"That Scipio, he from somewhere farther South, much farther than I ever been," said Cassius. "He say he been sold many times. I ain't been friends with him long, but he seem like he not all there, somehow."

I had gotten the impression, myself, that Scipio was somewhat chuckle-headed, but Cassio said he was not.

"No, just keepin' he head down, keep off trouble."

"Does that work?"

"Well, which one of us here with you? Him or me?" Cassius laughed. It was a good, rich sound, so I laughed, too.

"Maybe we see something good for the pot," Cassius said, looking around.

We was both carrying guns, for I give him one of my rifles to hold, my old muzzle-loading Hawken, whilst I kept my Sharps, which I was proud of, it being new and a breech-loader besides. But we did not run into any trouble on the route, and as it turned out, we didn't even fire the guns, not once. We didn't see anything that appealed to us, and we did not really need to kill anything for food (Cassius having packed more than enough). But it made Cassius proud and glad, I could see, to be riding along and carrying a gun.

The trail was fairly clear and straight, though the terrain was uneven, there being hills and low places more than any one level spot for the most part, and a lot of heavy undergrowth, especially

---

[27] Eds. note: C. R. Parker was indeed an itinerant artist who traveled widely about the Southeast during this period. There is no evidence that he worked in Tennessee or Virginia nor that he purchased slaves while in either state.

along the banks. The weather was fine, and so we dawdled, enjoying the sunshine and not pressing the horses nor ourselves, and sure enough in four days we come to the settlement.

***

It warn't much, being a grist mill and only a couple-three houses, not too large, and the store and post office, combined; there warn't no stables nor hotel in sight, so I judged we'd sleep out again that night, unless someone wanted to offer us house-room.

"Cassius, you stay with the horses," I said, and mounted the one rickety step of the general store. The door was on the latch, but the latch-string was out, so I let myself in and shouted into the gloom, "Hi! Is there anyone here?"

The single window was black with grime and would not have let in much light even so, being smallish, but I could see a counter, and boxes and barrels, and shelves. It was one large room, not too clean, and spiders had been ornamenting it for some time, or so it appeared, for the cobwebs themselves was hung with dust, and dust lay like fur on the table under the window, thick yellow-gray dust on a pack of papers tied with string, some of them seeming to be letters. I leaned over for a better look and blew some of the dust way. The top letter was addressed in faded brown ink to "John Cantril, Gen'l Store, by the Old Mill, Pigeon River, Tennessee."

"Well, Hallelujah," I said, and was leaning over, just about to pick it up, when I heard heavy footsteps and then a man's voice.

"Who's there?

I straightened up. "Sarah Mary Williams, from Hannibal, Missouri."

"What do you want?" the owner of the voice stepped into view.

He was an oldish man, tall and stooped, with a lot of white hair and whiskers, wearing an old blue coat with brass buttons, and nankeen britches. His footsteps raised more dust into the air as he shuffled along, and I sneezed.

"*Achoo!* I'm looking for information," I managed to say. "Who might you be, sir?"

"My name is Cantrell," he said, "John Cantrell."

Well, now. I looked closer at him. There didn't seem to be any resemblance between him and me, save for height. "Are you the postmaster?"

"Postmaster, postmaster," he droned the words.

75

"Postmaster—"

I tried again. "Is this your place of business, sir?"

He came closer and peered at me. "Do I know you?"

"I told you already, my name is Sarah Mary Williams."

"I don't know you," he said, and his voice took on a plaintive note. "Mariah! Mariah, where are you?" He pronounced it "Ma RYE uh," the way people in those parts often do.

"Is Mariah your wife, sir? Or your daughter? Mr Cantrell?"

"I'm a widow-man, and childless. Why do you want to know?"

I took a deep breath. "My mother's name was Cantrell, and she come from Tennessee, or so I was told."

"You was told? Don't you know?"

"I don't remember her. She—died—before I was three years old."

He came nearer to me. "What did you say your name was?"

"Sarah Mary Williams."

"I never knowed nobody name o' Williams from—you said Murfreesboro?" The old man sounded more angry than puzzled, and I hoped Cassius and the horses—and our guns—had not gotten very far away.

"Missouri. And my name warn't always Williams," I said, crossing my fingers behind my back for luck. "It used to be Finn."

His face never showed no sign of recognition. "Finn?"

"Did you ever hear of a Cantrell girl that married anybody name of Finn?" I asked.

"Not around here, no," he said, shaking his head. "My brother's girls, they all got husbands, far's I know, anyways, but none called Finn."

"Who is your brother?"

"His name's Samuel. He lives up north, upriver," and John Cantrell gestured toward the window. "He's a solitary man, now that his woman's died." He laughed a rusty laugh with no humor in it. "We neither of us can't seem to hold onto our wives, looks like. Mine died just a day afore his'n."

"What did they die of?" I had to ask.

"Cherokee," he said. "They was a lot of trouble with the Indians, oh, near forty year or more back, it was. They raided us, we raided back, and sometimes they took our hair, sometimes we took their'n. They's all gone now, or nearly—sent off to Indian Territory

76

by President Jackson, God bless 'im!" He blinked. "Who are you? Why you asking all these questions? What business is it of your'n?"

"I told you, Mr Cantrell," I said. "I have been led to believe my mother come from around these parts. Her name was Cantrell. She died when I was small. I'm trying to find out anything I can about her."

"John! John!" We both jumped a little at the sound of a woman's voice, just outside on the step. "John! There's a strange black man here! Where are you, John?"

I moved to the door and held it open. "That' s my servant, ma'am. Mr Cantrell is in here with me."

"Well, thank goodness," she said, and bustled in. "John Cantrell, what are you doing here? I had me the fright of my life—I thought you'd fallen in the millrace."

She was a sturdy woman of medium height, neither young nor old, blue-eyed, wearing a linsy-woolsy gown, buff-colored, and a muslin cap from which a few tendrils of black curly hair had escaped. Her feet was bare.

The old man looked guilty. "I was only looking around here, Mariah."

The woman reached out and brushed a cobweb from the old man's face, tenderly. "You don't need to go poking around in here no more, John. Just look at all this dust! Now come home."

"Ma'am." I broke in. "I am looking for information—about a woman named Hagar Cantrell. Do you know anything of her?"

"Hagar?" she looked at me for the first time, and her brows rose up in surprise, though whether she was more astonished at my question or my attire, I couldn't say. "No, no . . . there's no one in our family by that name, as far as I'm aware."

"Your family? Mr Cantrell here said that his wife and—and other female kin was gone, long gone."

"Oh, John," she said, and patted the old man's arm. "You forgot again."

"Did I, Mariah? I'm sorry," he said. "Let's go home. Can we go home?"

"Of course we can, dear," she said. "You come along, too, Miss Whatever-Your-Name-Is, and we'll see what's what."

I followed the two of them out and beckoned to Cassius, who was squatting on his haunches under a tree some twenty feet away, holding the horses. "Come on along, Cassius, we're going with

77

these folks."

He came up. "Miss Sarah, I told the woman you was in there, and who you was. She say that old man, he her husband."

I was startled. She looked closer to my own age than to his. I judged her to be thirtyish, whilst he was seventy if a day.

"Come on along, now," the woman was calling back to us. "It ain't far."

Cassius and I fell in behind the Cantrells, him leading both horses whilst I studied the backs of this strange couple.

We followed the river, past the grist mill, which I now saw had been abandoned. The trail wound up for a space, then down, and around a wide bend in the river. Some distance upriver I could see a new mill, bigger than the other one, and a large house built off the back of it.

"This is our place," Mariah said. "And the town is yonder."

I peered ahead and saw, farther down a short incline below the mill-race, a flat space containing a cluster of houses, some of them clapboarded, and a larger, brick-faced building in the middle of what seemed to be an open square. I could see a few more buildings on the other side of the square. Few people were about, it being the middle of the day.

"That's the court-house, and this is Setonville,[28]" Mariah said. "It's the county seat."

We had stopped at the top of the trail leading down, and I saw now that there were two rivers here, one flowing into the other in a broad, open curve. A wharf jutted out over the brown water.

"This is the Forks of the Pigeon River," Mariah said. "Back there, that was the Little Pigeon, where the first mill was built."

At her side, the old man began to mutter. "All right, John, let's get you inside," Mariah said. "Come on along."

We turned back to the mill and went around behind to the house door, which opened onto a broad verandah, shaded at one end by a thick leafy vine. There was a chair by the steps, and a loom set up close to the house-wall.

"I like to do my weaving out here when it's fine," Mariah said. "Now let me just get John settled." She and the old man

---

[28] Eds. note: Mrs Osterhouse appears to have changed the name of this settlement for some unknown reason. Most scholars now believe the town she describes here to have been Sieverville, Tennessee.

disappeared indoors.

I sat on the chair, and Cassius hunkered down again. He had the reins of the horses wrapped around his left arm, and with his right hand he reached down and traced a pattern in the dust, a circle inside a circle inside a circle. The trees stirred softly, though there was no wind, and the sun baked down. I was glad for the shade of the verandah.

When Mariah came out a short while later, she carried a kitchen chair and also brought out a dripping drinking gourd. We drank deep—I made Cassius drink first, for he'd been outside in the heat longer. The water was cold and tasted of limestone. We thanked her. She looked at me, and then at Cassius.

"Is he yourn?"

"No," I said. "He's been hired to help me."

"Oh," she said. "We don't see many slaves hereabouts, so I just wondered. You're from—Missouri, did I hear you say?"

"Yes'm," I said. "But I have been told that my mother came from these parts, and I have come to find out what I can about her."

"Tell me," Mariah said, and planted herself in the chair she'd brought out.

So I did.

It was getting on toward evening when I finished, and Cassius had long since unpacked and unsaddled the horses, fed and watered them and hobbled them in a small clearing , closer to the woods but near enough to the house for safety. He was sitting on the step, listening, and from time to time he nodded, though the story I was telling was as strange to him as to her.

I stopped talking at last.

Mariah shook her head. "It's a sad tale."

"If only I knew something more about her," I said. "If I could meet someone who knew her. But that does not seem likely."

"No," Mariah said. "It's too long ago, I reckon. And folks forget, with the passing of time. I know a little about that, as you have seen."

"Your husband—John. So his mind is gone?"

"Yes, mostly," she said. "I think sometimes he understands where he is and what is going on in the world, but those times get fewer and fewer. He lives in the past, now, which is why he was back in the old place when you found him."

"That was the original mill?"

"It was, but this site was a better one, so when enough folks came out to petition for the county seat, we moved the mill as well. Until he started to fail, John was a big man in these parts. A big man," she repeated, then sighed. "He was one of the first ones here, just a little boy when his daddy and his uncles and their wives come out from Pennsylvania, after the Revolution," she said. "He grew up on the Little Pigeon, and his daddy built the old mill."

She went on to tell me, while the evening light dimmed around us, of how the first settlers had fought the Indians, and the treaties that was made, and how just before the Cherokees was moved out to Indian Territory, a renegade band came whooping into the settlement and carried off three of them: John Cantrell's first wife and his daughter and his daughter's baby son.

"Where was her husband? The daughter's?"

"Killed earlier that year, in another Indian raid." She sighed. "That baby was never found."

"The Indians took it?"

"They did, or else kilt it and threw the body in the river or buried it deep, for the bodies of the two women were recovered—minus their scalps—but the child was gone."

"And you never heard of a girl in the family named Hagar?"

"No, I never," she said. "Are you" [I marked that she said "air ye" the way folks did in this country] "certain sure that was your ma's name?"

"Pap said so," I said. "No reason for him to lie about that."

"Some folks don't need a reason," she said.

"That's a fact," I said.

And Pap warn't necessarily wed to the truth under any circumstances, I thought. He'd just as soon lie as take another breath, in fact. It shook me, to think I'd maybe come all this way, following not only a ghost but a made-up one at that.

"Well, it's getting late," Mariah said, standing up and stretching. "We'd best light a lamp and have something to eat. I'd be pleased to have you stay the night," she said, looking doubtfully in Cassius's direction. He laughed.

"Missus, I'd be pleased to sleep on this-here nice verandah of your'n," he said. "I got my blanket roll, and I kin keep an eye on the horses. Miss Sarah, you have a good night, now."

"All right, Cassius; thanks," I said, and followed my hostess into the house.

The walls was all whitewashed inside, except for the gable-end where the fireplace was, which was plastered around the bricks. A pie-safe set close by a long wooden table with benches pushed underneath.

I saw a large bed in the far corner, a pencil-post bed Aunt Polly would have called it, in which John Cantrell lay sleeping, well covered with quilts that made a splash of color at that end of the room. The other furnishings was comfortable too: a press-back rocker with bright blue cushions, a chest or two, a tall armoire with a carved front, and a big dresser with blue-willow-pattern plates and a quantity of pewter ware—all of it shining. The floor was polished oak, with rag rugs spread here and there, and Mariah's spinning wheel—a walking wheel, fully as tall as she was—in one corner. The fireplace was well equipped with hooks and cranes, and the stack of spiders and kettles and such was blackened with years of use.

Mariah stoked up the fire and lit the lamp on the table with a spill, then stepped out to the woodshed, coming back with an armful of kindling. "I'll just stir us up some mush and milk," she said. "Then it'll be time for bed. I expect you're tired."

"I am," I said. I watched her make up the fire, then pour a handful of meal into a kettle of water. She added salt from a lidded wooden box and and begin to stir. There was a sudden cough from behind us, and a drowsy muttering from John.

"I can do that, if you want to see to your husband," I said.

"Thank you kindly—I will," she said, and give me the spoon, a long-handled one carved of some fine white wood, birch maybe. I kept the spoon moving in a dreamy rhythm through the thickening mush until Mariah returned.

"He's all right," she said.

"Won't he want his supper?"

"Oh, he don't eat much anymore, and I don't force him," she said. "He had a mug of milk, and I'll give him something hot in the morning—he wakes early. Now let's have our meal. Do you want to call your man in?"

I called Cassius, but he refused, politely, to share our table. "Thank you, Missus, but I'll take my share out here," he said, and would not budge.

Mariah give him a large bowlful of the mush, and a horn

spoon, and he retired to the porch. Mariah and I ate in silence. When we finished, she rinsed the bowls—wooden ones, ordinary enough but beautifully made, I suspected by the same hand that carved the big spoon.

"Those are handsome," I remarked.

"My daddy made them," she said. "He was the miller who come here to take over after John lost his daddy."

"How did John come to survive?"

"He wasn't to home. The Indians kilt everybody except John and his brother. They was out in the woods a good ways off, hunting, and when they saw the Indians go by, all painted up for war, they run and hid in a cave they knew about, and didn't come out til next day. And when they got back to the settlement, all of the folks was dead."

It was a sad story, sure enough, but one that was familiar enough in those times.

"So his brother stayed here, too?"

"He moved up north about six mile," Mariah said. "Married a German girl, and they have raised a good big family—five sons and five daughters, but none named Hagar."

"When did you marry John? Did you have any children?"

"Twenty years ago come April," she said. "I was fourteen. My daddy thought the world of John. John is book-learned," she said proudly. "He thought he might be a minister, after his family was killed. Folks got up a subscription to send him to preacher's college, and he went for a year, but he got lonesome and come back. That's when he built the store and took on the post-office."

"And you married him then."

"Yes, I was proud of him—still am—he's a good man. No, we never had children. It's been a sadness, but after a time, you stop grieving."

"When did he start to fail?"

She considered. "It started a time ago—in small ways. Forgetting to deliver a letter, or he'd think one had come for a body who was dead or moved away. And it just went on, until—" she waved toward the big bed. "You see how it is."

"I'm sorry," I said, and meant it.

"Well," she said, looking around, "At least we have this property, freehold."

"Will you sell it, when—"

"I ain't thought that far ahead," she said. "He's still strong in his body, and he's my husband, til death do us part. We'll manage."

I was sure of that. Mariah Cantrell was definitely the managing kind.

***

Mariah bedded me down on a pallet with a couple of quilts of her own making, so I spent the night comfortable and warm. Next morning Cassius and I breakfasted with Mariah and John, on biscuits and fried ham and clabber. Mariah insisted on giving us some cold biscuit and ham to take with us.

I planned to make one more stop before heading on to Nashville, and that was to visit John's brother.

Mariah said, "I don't hold out much hope that he knows anything, but you'd best talk to him anyway."

"Can I take anything for you? A message?"

"Just say we're as well as can be expected," Mariah said.

She walked out to the horses with me. "I hope you find out about your ma someday," she said. "Hope you find out the truth, what e'er it might be. Wisht I knew more to tell you."

I reached down and took her hand. "Thank you," I said. "You all take care, now."

And Cassius and I rode north.

***

The trail went mostly east-west, though, so Cassius and I had a hard time at first, often having to lead the horses whilst we hacked a way through the brush—it was a powerful lot of cane in those parts, which is painful to get through, believe me. Then the river bent north a mile or so beyond the settlement, and we left the woodlands and moved closer to the banks, where there was another trail of sorts, rutted in spots where wheels had sunk in deep. We stopped and ate our biscuit and ham and drank from a spring and filled our water-bottles before going on. The last few miles went fairly easy, and it appeared we would reach our destination by mid-afternoon.

We could hear the sound of axes before we come in sight of the house.

"Sound like two, maybe three," Cassius said, and I nodded.

He was right. When we come around the final bend, there was three men—no, two men and a boy about twelve—busy splitting rails for a fence.

83

I raised one hand and after a moment they did likewise. Cassius dropped back a length and I came up close to the men, slowing my horse to a walk.

"My name is Sarah Mary Williams," I said. "Is one of you men named Samuel Cantrell?"

"I'm Samuel," said the oldest man. I was prepared to see the usual surprised expression, at a woman in man's clothing, but he didn't seem at all astonished. "What can I do for you, ma'am?" He looked back toward Cassius, who lowered his eyes. The man spoke.

"He belong to you?"

"No, he's hired for wages," I said.

"We don't see too many blacks hereabouts," the man said, dragging his gaze from Cassius to me. "What do you want with us?"

"I would like to stop for a while and talk to you," I said.

"Go ahead," he said, and made a motion to the other two to stop what they were doing and draw closer.

I dismounted, as did Cassius, and I handed my reins to him. "Mr Cantrell, I spent last night with your brother and sister-in-law down by the Forks. Mariah Cantrell told me how to find you."

"They're well?" He spoke with a sudden swift concern, and I was quick to reassure him.

"Both well enough, though John Cantrell is wandering in his mind," I said.

"Been wandering a long time," said the other man—not the boy, but a youngish man, thirty or so, with the same dark hair and eyes.

"This is my wife's brother Henny," Samuel said. "The boy is his son Joss."

I nodded to them both, and they nodded back, solemn.

"Well, come in and set," Samuel said, and led the way to the house. Cassius tied up the horses and followed after.

It was a double [29] house, made of logs plastered together, and the roof was shingled—hand-split shakes, weathered to the color of old pewter. I could see two windows opposite the door, one glazed and one shuttered. The door was open, and we went in.

---

[29] Eds. note: Common in the Southwest, essentially two log or frame cabins with a roofed and often floored breezeway—a "dogtrot"—between them.

Inside was quiet and cool, and there was two chairs and a bench and a couple of backless stools on the puncheon floor. Samuel pushed a chair at me and I took it; he took the other. The boy sat on the bench with his father, and Cassius, hesitating a moment, picked up a stool and carried it to a position nearest the door, where he too sat down.

It took the better part of an hour to explain my errand to Samuel and his male relatives. I couldn't help wishing that the womenfolk were not away—they had gone a-visiting someone or another's female relation who was having a baby, Samuel said— women do seem to have more tolerance for such questions—but, finally, they seemed to grasp that I was trying to find out about my mother, and all I had to go on was a name.

Samuel shook his head. "I never heard tell of a Cantrell woman name of Hagar, far back's I c'n recall."

His brother-in-law said the same.

The boy said nothing at all, just looked at me and then at Cassius and back to me again as if he'd never seen a woman in britches nor a black man before. Well, maybe he hadn't.

We all sat silent for a while.

Finally, Henny ventured, "What about that woman of Tobias's?"

Samuel looked at his brother-in-law, and the two of them looked at me. "I forgot about her," he admitted.

"Who?" I wanted to know.

Samuel turned back to me. "It happened a long time since," he said. "My cousin Tobias—he had two wives—the first one died— and the second run off with a man she'd knowed before she wed Tobias—a fellow from back where she come from."

"What was her name?"

But neither man could recall, and the boy was too young and had never heard the story before. At least twenty years since, it was. And Tobias? Dead, too, these ten years or more.

I persisted, but to no avail. (I begun to wonder if John Cantrell's wandering mind was a family failing.)

"Do you recall where she come from?"

Somewhere back East . . . Ohio, maybe.

So there it was. I had come to a dead end in East Tennessee.

Now it was time to see whether the Natchez Trace held any evidence, or whether that search, too, would defeat me.

***

I thanked the brothers-in-law, who offered us hospitality, but I wanted to hurry back to Knoxville and make plans for the next leg of my journey. As we headed back up the trail, we could hear the sound of axes start up again. The afternoon was turning golden, and a small breeze hurried the leaves overhead.

"Well, Cassius," I said, "You'll have to put up with me for a while longer. How're we fixed for rations?"

"We all right, Miss Sarah," he said. "I think we c'n make it just fine, 'specially if we stops t' let me catch us some fish for dinner."

So that night before we bedded down Cassius cooked us some fine fat trout, and we drank our boiled coffee and finished the meal with a smoke.

And I fell asleep, to dream that I was a tiny child, calling out to a faceless woman who ran from me as I toddled after her: "Mammy, Mammy!"

***

Over the next several days we made good time, for the weather continued fair. Once or twice it rained a little at night, but our blankets shed most of the wet, and I was up and ready before Cassius, most of the time.

He shook his head and said he'd never met a woman like me, white or black.

"Well, I have had a different sort of life than most women, I suppose," I said.

He was silent for a while. Then, "I suppose you're bound to head out for the Natchez Trace, now."

"I am."

"It won't be easy. They ain't too much of it still open," he said. "It mostly has fallen back into wilderness."

"That is what I have heard," I said. "But there must be folks around, even so."

"Well, Miss Sarah, I do wish you luck," Cassius said. "I know you mighty disappointed, so far."

"So I am," I said. "But I intend to keep on—for a while, anyhow." I looked over at Cassius, who rode along beside me, serious and calm. I had found myself a good companion, and was resolved not to lose him. "Cassius," I said. "I would like you to go with me. Shall I buy you from Mr Betancourt?"

"Miss Sarah, I would be the most gratefullest Negro in this

86

world! Mr Betancourt, he ain't a bad man, but I *much* rather belong to you."

I did not say anything to Cassius about my decision—which I had already formed—to free him after I purchased him from Betancourt. There was one more matter to be resolved, though.

"What about Scipio? Is he kin to you, or a friend you'd hate to leave?"

"No, Miss, he ain't kin to me. And I likes him well enough, but I don't think you ought to buy all of Mr Betancourt's Negroes," he said.

"All two?"

"Well, Mr Betancourt, he ain't getting younger, and Scipio, he does tolerable well with the customers, picking up an extry dollar or two. I expect he could buy his own freedom in a few years, did he want it, if I warn't there."

I was pleased enough to be able to avoid purchasing Scipio, for he had failed to impress me. Cassius, on the other hand, was quite a different sort of a man. I was mightily glad to have him with me, and said so.

"Miss Sarah, you can trust old Cassius to the end of your days," was all he said, and I believed him. And would learn someday how much that trust was worth, in truth.

***

It didn't take much on my part to convince Mr Betancourt to sell Cassius to me. The price he asked was a deal more than he could have gotten at auction—seven hundred dollars plus fifty extra in gold, since he would have to wait for the full amount to come by bank draft.

Cassius took his leave of his former master and of Scipio.

"Was he sad to learn you was leaving?" I asked.

"No'm, he tolt me he dreamed I would be leaving soon," Cassius said. "That Scipio, he put a powerful stock in dreams. So I tolt him I had *me* a dream that he was going to die a wealthy man, and he said that meant he was a-going to live forever, since he didn't look to ever be rich."

I laughed, which was what he intended. I had learned already that Cassius preferred everyone to be cheerful, no matter how cheerless the circumstances.

***

I have little to say about the trip from Knoxville to

Chattanooga, and thence to Nashville. We went by rail, it being the fastest way, but rail travel has never been my choice of getting from one place to another. Given the chance, I'd go by water, every time.[30]

The first leg of the journey was just abominable.

The windows in the cars didn't ever quite shut, and the end doors likewise, so that cinders blowed in on us all the time, some of 'em live, and I ended up with burn-holes in all my outer clothes, just as if I'd been peppered with buckshot. Cassius fared some better, as he rode with the baggage in a closed car, but since there was chickens crated in there as well, he come out all over feathers and chaff. The two of us was quite a sight when we got to Chattanooga. Thankfully, there was few folks about, it being eleven o'clock at night (the trip having taken upwards of ten hours to go less than 150 miles).

We took rooms at a hotel close by the station—that is, I took a room, and paid for a bed for Cassius with the hotel's servants (all of them slaves). I found out next morning that Cassius had gotten very little sleep, however, as the others had kept pestering him to tell them about his mistress.

"They ain't seen many white women traveling alone," he said. "They wanted to know, was you really a woman, or was you a morphodite?"[31]

"What did you tell them?" I was amused, but not surprised. A woman of my size and shape—and wearing such unconventional clothes—was likely to perplex some folks. And still is.

"I told them you was a lady," he said.

That touched me. "Thank you, Cassius," I said.

This seemed like a good time to tell him my intention to free him. I wanted his help on the Natchez Trace, of course, but I wanted it to be his choice. For all I knew, he had other fish to fry, perhaps a wife or some other person he was close to—his mother, for instance.

---

[30] Eds. note: Mrs Osterhouse apparently overcame her distaste for rail travel, for she later went by rail to and from San Francisco several times, as well as trips to and from that city and Hannibal as well as back East.
[31] Eds. note: This term, a corruption of "hermaphrodite," was once common in the American South, as being applied to persons of indeterminate gender.

So I led up to the subject kind of sideways. "Did you ever see your mother again, after you left her in Virginia?"

He shook his head. "No, Miss Sarah; she was bought by a lady in Richmond, to be her maid, and she died a year or two after."

"She died? What happened? How old was she?"

He thought for a minute. "Around forty, forty-five maybe. She took the typhoy,[32] they told me. That was twenty year ago. I'm somewheres around forty myself, now, as far's I c'n tell from what my mama told me. She say I was born the year of the big quake."[33]

"Cassius," I said, "I have decided to give you your freedom. It is too late for your mama, but not too late for you."

Well, that man just about went to pieces. He cried and he cried, and he swore he'd never leave my side, no, not for a million zillion dollars, he wouldn't. He said nobody hadn't never treated him as well as I, and just the fact that I was willing to buy his freedom . . . well, he took on so, I had to to take him into a barroom and make him drink a glass of whiskey, for I was afraid he'd fall into a fit.

The barman give us the whiskey—not without some peculiar looks, but I stared him down. "My servant ain't—isn't feeling himself," I said. "He's just got some good news, and it's gone to his head." I ordered him a second whiskey, too—and one for myself, for I was feeling the need for some support as well, and tipped the man handsome. He went back behind his bar and started to polish glasses, but sent us a puzzled look now and then.

Finally, Cassius stopped weeping. He drank his second glass of whiskey without incident (the first had made him sputter and choke) and looked at me.

"Miss Sarah Mary, ma'am," he said. "I accept your kindness—and I'm grateful to have my freedom—but I do want to stay on with you, as your servant, if you'll have me."

I was no end touched. So we shook hands on it, and made our plans.

First thing we had to do, we had to get up to Nashville, and then start our way back down along what was left of the Natchez Trace.

---

[32] Typhoid fever, endemic in the South.
[33] Eds. note: The New Madrid earthquake, 1812. This would make Cassius 38.

Chapter Seven: I Receive a Sign, and Make My Decision

Cassius and I finally arrived in Nashville, after a train trip that doesn't bear description, it being just as uncomfortable and inconvenient as train travel could be (and was, back in those days, as I have mentioned). We rented horses and gear, as before, and set out along the Trace.

Well, it rained and it fogged and it drizzled, and the bugs was something dreadful—worse even than those in East Tennessee. Most nights we turned in hoping we'd wake up whole in our skins and not chewed to ribbons in the morning. I was still wearing men's gear, which was all that saved me, but even so those areas of skin that was uncovered stayed raw and sore for weeks. Cassius was much the same, but he bore it better than me, and was his usual cheerful self.

Which was all that saved me from despair, for we found— nothing.

At this time the Trace had mostly been abandoned as a route between Nashville and Natchez, Mississippi. It had started as an Indian trail, hundreds and hundreds of years before, and white men, trappers and hunters, had followed it for a long time, too, so that in places the trail itself was sunk deep in the ground, like a tunnel, with tree-roots and saplings growing up its sides.

In those places the light was always dim, and you felt the back of your neck kind of tickling all the time, as if you was being watched. I wondered if it might be panthers, and said so to Cassius, but he said the feeling was most likely just spiderwebs, and in point of fact there was an awful lot of them. (Some of the spiders bit, too, but lucky for us they warn't the poisonous kind.)

Snakes—now, that was a different story, but I was used to snakes—they didn't bother me—only I didn't feature either of us having to deal with being snakebit. But Cassius was careful, laying out our bedding, and we always searched around before getting up or lying down too sudden. I didn't want to repeat the experience Jim and I had had, years back,[34] and thankfully we didn't. But I was always wondering if a snake was a-going to slither acrost my instep or fall out of a tree onto my hat (or down my neck). It made

---

[34] Eds. note: *AOHF*, Chapter X, "What Comes of Handling Snakeskin."

traveling a jittery sort of progress.

And we stopped everywhere along the Trace that folks still lived, and talked to everyone we met—for some people still used the Trace, or anyway a part of it, in their journeying.

And nowhere did we hear tell of a woman called Hagar Cantrell who'd married a trapper from Missouri name of Jimmy Finn some twenty years before. If such a woman had ever existed, no one in these parts had ever heard of her.

You may think that surely some proof would exist. But back in those days, most folks couldn't write. A man's name might be found on a deed or a contract, but a woman's was rare. Even deaths were not always recorded, unless the departed happened to be a person of note or had an estate to leave.

And Cassius kept a-pointing out that I had no reason to believe that Pap had even told the truth. He might have been telling a tall tale for his own purposes, whatever those might be.

"Miss Sarah," Cassius said one night, just before we rolled up in our blankets to sleep. "Miss Sarah, you don't remember your mammy at all?"

I sighed. "Seems like sometimes I can just recall someone singing, real low, in the night, next to me. I can't tell the words or the tune."

"Would you know her, if you found her?"

I shook my head.

Cassius was right. It was time to give up—and go home. Only I had no home—Missouri could never be home to me, that I knew.

***

I have composed these next pages using the journal I tried to keep on the way out West, changing only what is necessary to make the sequence of events follow correctly.

We, that is, Cassius and I, spent a few months on the farm with Jim and his wife and children, now part of a sizable community of colored folk, some of which was freed slaves, and a good portion of mixed-race people, mulattoes and some part-Indian, despite the Fugitive Slave Law.[35]   Jim and his family was fairly safe, partly

---

[35] This law, passed as a gesture of goodwill to the Southern States, was variously enforced, but could result in freedmen's being returned to slavery if certain legal conditions were not met or if a judge so ruled.

because they had their manumission papers, but mostly because Jim was able (with Judge Thatcher's help, and on the Judge's posting a bond) to take out a license that allowed him to live as a free man, and later to obtain licenses for the rest of his family.[36]

Cassius and Jim got on together, thanks be, for if they'd taken a dislike to one another it would have grieved me. But it seemed they both agreed that I needed taking care of, and since Jim could not go with me, he and Cassius both were happy that Cassius would be the one to watch over Miss Sarah Mary.

Jim's farm was doing well, he having cleared and plowed for rye and oats and wheat, and his wife managing the milk cows—they had three by now, and three good heifer calves—and the chickens and pigs and geese. Jim had dug a pond and some irrigation ditches, and added a barn and lean-to to the house and shed that Tom and I had bought with the property.

The house too had been enlarged, with a wing added for a fine big bedroom for Jim and his wife, and a kitchen ell put on, and a root cellar dug, and the roof newly shingled.

"Store-bought," Jim said with pride. "I done traded a litter of pigs for the shingles, and Johnny and I, we nailed them on. Store nails, too. Johnny, he's my right-hand man."

Johnny smiled bashfully and went back to the barn, whistling. Jim and I watched him go.

"He is always a joy to me," Jim said. "An' Elizabeth, too; she doing better ever' day. Miss Sarah Mary, you saved this family."

I reached over and clasped his hand where it lay on the fence-railing next to mine. "Jim, your family is all I have for mine," I said.

"That makes me feel proud and glad," Jim said. "Amen! And now, let's go in and see what Eliza has fixed for supper. It surely smells fine."

The supper was fully as good as it smelt—fried chicken and gravy, green peas, hot biscuits, sour-cherry preserves, fresh-made

---

[36] Free blacks in Missouri were required to obtain licenses and post a bond with the county court, which bond could be sacrificed if the court decided that the black man or woman in question had become "a menace to society." In such cases, the person could be sold. Jim and his family would have had to post bonds of up to $500 per person, and might still be liable to being sold at any time. The Judge's protection was therefore of inestimable value.

cottage cheese with new green onions, and dried apple pie with thick cream.

Cassius passed his plate for another helping—his third—and grinned across the table at me. "Just getting ready for harder times and shorter commons," he said.

"Miss Sarah, are you-all fixing to go, soon?" Eliza asked, putting another hot biscuit on Cassius's plate and handing the rest to Jim to share around. "Here, take some more butter and some preserves."

"Thank you, ma'am," said Cassius, slathering butter and preserves on his biscuit. Elizabeth and Johnny stared at him with admiration.

"You children get along and do your chores, now," their mother said. She spoke in a clear voice, not loudly, and I marked how Elizabeth followed her mother's lips with her eyes, intently, and nodded when Eliza finished. The girl stood up and patted her brother on the shoulder, then pointed to the woodshed door.

"Excuse us, Miss Sarah, Daddy, Mr Cassius," Johnny said.

"Go on, son," Jim said. He watched them go. "I think Elizabeth's goin' to be as pretty as her mama," he said.

"You go along with your foolishness," Eliza said, clearing plates. "She's ten times prettier than I ever was."

"Not to me," Jim said, and half-rose up from his chair, leaned over, and kissed her. She feigned a slap. Jim smacked her on the behind, and she laughed out loud.

"You, Cassius," he said, laughing too. "Make sure when you wed, it's to a woman with some spice," he said.

Cassius finished his dinner, lovingly cleaning his plate of the last speck of preserves with a final scrap of buttered biscuit. "I hear you," he said. "When the time comes, I will remember."

I sat back in my chair, well content.

***

When I first decided to go West, I had consulted with Jim by letter. We had debated whether mules or oxen would be better for my purposes.

Mules was less apt to get sore feet, Jim noted, but oxen could pull more. Also, he pronounced oxen more docile and easier to handle. The major difference was that oxen meant having to walk alongside the team rather than sit on the wagon-seat and drive, but even mule teams rarely made more than a walking pace, Jim pointed out, when a wagon was fully loaded. And riding was no pic-nic, Jim said (and Cassius agreed), for the unsprung wagons bounced and jounced so, most folks preferred to walk. Another point Jim made was that mules need grain and hay, but oxen can live off the country. So oxen it was.

Having read quite a bit on the subject, and talked to a number of cattle breeders, I had ended up choosing Devons. They are not the largest breed but are very strong and do well on forage, and they are brisk movers. The two-year-olds I ordered had been delivered to St Joe a full six months earlier, and I had asked Jim to go ahead and use them on the farm, so that they would be accustomed to working by the time I was ready to learn to drive them. (I have to say that, although I started out unfamiliar with the habits of these beasts, I was to grow quite fond of them, and became well-skilled at their use.)

Jim also helped me with ordering my wagon and provisioning it for the trip. It might be of interest to someone reading this someday—if anyone ever does—to know what was considered necessary for a traveler on the overland journey back in 1851.

Per person: A hundred and fifty pounds of flour and twenty-five of corn meal. Bacon, fifty pounds. Sugar, forty pounds; coffee, ten. Tea, five pounds, and at least ten pounds of rice and five of salt. Fifteen pounds of dried beans, fifteen pounds of dried fruit, and two pounds of saleratus. These were the recommended amounts; I added another fifty pounds of meat in the form of two well-cured hams, and we also brought a jug of molasses and another of syrup, Cassius having a sweet tooth, and four gallons of good whiskey.

There might be opportunities to stock up on fresh meat en route, and being able to defend against Indian attack was a matter of course, so we took guns and powder and shot—my Sharps, my old Hawken, and four of Mr Colt's pistols—two apiece for Cassius and me. And I bought two new skinning knives and a set of scrapers for hides, and a hatchet. And an ax and a spade. I warn't going to farm, so we didn't need to pack a plow blade or handle nor harness nor nails nor hoes nor dibbles nor a shingle-knife nor an adze nor a plane. We didn't need to bring an anvil or a mattock nor a mallet nor a sledge. I did buy a kettle and a coffeepot and a spider with a lid and a set of tin plates and mugs. I bought two pair of forks and spoons, a ladle and some tongs, a bucket and some leather water bottles and a wooden piggin, a covered pail (for slops) and an enameled tin pitcher and basin, a pair of rubber sheets, two bed-quilts and two pallets, four pair of dark calico sheets, two pillows with pillow-cases of the same dark calico (so as not to show the dirt too much), and two or three changes of clothes, male and female, for myself; I give Cassius money to buy what clothes and gear he wanted.

I bought two pair of boots and six pair of woolen stockings, a canvas coat and a woolen one, a knitted hat and two pair of gloves, and a basket of old rags for my monthly need. I bought a wash tub and washboard and a small keg of soft soap. I bought a hair-comb, a mirror, some hairpins, a sewing kit, and a box of medical supplies: clove oil for toothache, a lancet, a roll of bandages, a pair of tweezers, a pair of scissors, some of Aunt Sally's goldenseal and beeswax ointment for skin rashes and irritations, and an assortment of medicines: laudanum, ipecac, rhubarb extract, blue vitriol, peppermint oil, clove oil, calomel, one case of Pain-Killer (Aunt Polly's old standby) and another of Dr Rush's pills—a powerful purge, known to users as "Rush's Thunderbolts." And I also stocked a quantity of Peruvian bark, which was unholy expensive, but the best remedy for fever at the time. [37] I hoped we would stay healthy enough to avoid taking any of these preparations, but it was as well to be prepared.

I also took some ready-made pens with steel nibs, a block of ink, a dozen or so pencils, a quantity of paper, including several blank ledger-books for accounting, and a money-box. This last was packed at the bottom of a chest under all of our goods, and the key I kept on a cord around my neck, but it contained only part of my treasury—I also wore six hundred dollars in paper money, well wrapped in oiled silk, in a belt around my waist, and had a hundred more in gold sewn into the lining of my heavy coat and another hundred in Cassius's brand-new fancy dark-blue military-style greatcoat, with caped collar and shining brass buttons. That coat hung nearly to his heels, and must have weighed ten pound even without the gold, but it was his first purchase as a freedman, and he wore it with as much pride as if he was George Washington or Napoleon Bonaparte himself.

---

[37] Eds. note: This bark was cinchona, from which quinine is derived.

So we had quite a bit to carry, of our personal items. And all that does not count the goods I took with me, to open my first store, as I wanted to begin right off, whilst I looked over the area and chose a permanent site. Therefore I had arranged with a St Louis firm via a Boston factor to fill my order in ten months' time and send it by ship.[38] Those goods would arrive some time after myself, taking into account the four months' voyage—if all went well.

To tide me over whilst I waited for the ship to arrive, I stocked up on items that were relatively light and easily packed, but reputed to be in high demand amongst the gold-seekers: pins, needles, hair combs, shirt buttons, shoe buttons, collar buttons. I had waxed thread, cotton thread, and silk thread. I had spices in tins, tea in tins, snuff in tins, candy in tins—peppermints and horehound drops, lemon drops and licorice. I had plug tobacco wrapped in paper and loose tobacco in leather pouches. I had woolen undershirts and woolen drawers and even some of the new-fangled one-piece underwear that was later called union suits. I had woolen gloves and canvas gloves and leather gloves and mittens. I had heavy socks in blue and gray worsted, and French silk socks with clocks on them—handkerchiefs and neckerchiefs and bandanas and woolen mufflers in red and white stripes. I had leather tobacco pouches and Lucifer matches and twenty boxes of fancy cigars. I even brought along some ladies' things: rouge and powder, silk sashes, seventy-five yards of lace trimmings and a box of assorted sachets, scented French soaps, hair-nets, fancy silk stockings and garters trimmed with satin rosebuds.

And I spent a good deal of money on having a cabinet-maker construct some ingenious little shelves and slatted holders and folding trays and bins and drawers to hold all of these things, for I planned to turn my wagon into a mobile shop—and live in it, too—until I got myself situated. So I had him build me a bunk bed on one side of the wagon (Cassius slept slung underneath the wagon, in a snug little hammock), with drawers underneath and above, and a pair of slatted doors, very cunning, that folded into little niches on either side at night, and folded out again to hide the bed from view

---

[38] Eds. note: Prior to the Panama Canal, going by sea from Boston to California meant a trip around South and Central America.

in the daytime. I could hang samples in front of these doors, there being hooks above for that purpose.

The whole larboard side was made to open up and fold back, being on hinges, with hooks to hold it open. This made a kind of overhang, protecting the counter-space that folded out below, with brackets that could be secured to keep it in place. It was just what I had pictured, and I paid the cabinet-maker a bonus when I saw how fine the work was, and how well everything fitted together.

The last job was to hire a sign-painter to make a signboard that I could hang up when open for business: this read "Williams' Emporium—Men's and Ladies' Furnishings—Notions and Necessities," in red and black, with gold edgings, on a blue background.

All of this meant that my wagon was somewhat bigger than most, so the team that Jim and I put together was also a bit bigger—three yoke of oxen instead of the more usual two. They was all healthy, beautiful animals. Cassius and I had spent several weeks with Jim learning both of us how to drive them, and Jim had trained them so well that you only to touch any of them ever so lightly with the goad—a kind of flexible stick, with a pointed brass tip—and that ox would do exactly what was wanted.

So we was ready to embark, and soon enough it was time to say farewell to Jim and his family.

I knew that this time it would not be easy. Those who started out on that journey in those days expected that years might go by without seeing the home folks, and who knew what changes time might bring? And whilst Jim was still a youngish man—being only around forty as near as he could tell—still accidents and sicknesses come to folks later in life, more frequent than not. So our goodbyes were made with deep emotion.

And Jim was still mightily worried that I was going with only Cassius to take care of me.

"Miss Sarah, you ought to take at least one woman or girl with you," he argued.

"I don't want no one else along," I said. "Cassius and I can handle everything needful."

"I knows you can," he said, "But does that mean you should? I would rest easier in my own mind if you took a woman with you. Somebody steady and dependable-like."

"Cassius and I will do just fine," I repeated.

Jim continued to fret and mourn until I had to tell him to stop. "The only other person I'd take with me is you," I said, meaning it really as kind of a joke, you know, but he seemed to be actually considering it.

"Don't be foolish, Jim," I said. "Your place is here, with your family and your farm."

"That's so," he said glumly. "Did I wish it, I could still go with you, though—I'm sure Eliza wouldn't mind—"

"Well, I know she *would*. But I'll be all right, Jim. You know I will."

So in the end he had to let it be, but he never was happy about it. You could tell. I never see such a man for worrying, and that's a fact.

At last it was time to go.

***

We set out just after breakfast on a Saturday morning in early March, with the birds making a dreadful racket in the trees. Johnny had the oxen all brushed and shining—beautiful dark red animals, they was, like polished mahogany—and he and Jim had put on their harness, all of it new. My wagon was bright and clean, and the wooden wheels with their forged-iron tires had been well rubbed and greased (and the grease buckets filled and hanging in place). The white canvas cover shone.

Cassius was wearing his blue coat, of course, and a low-crowned silver-gray beaver hat I'd bought him, with a jay's feather in the band. I had on breeches and leggings and a flannel shirt and woolen vest, with a canvas jacket and good sturdy boots, for along with Cassius and the rest of the train, I'd be walking most of the way,[39] and I had my hair braided up and pinned tight under my hat. I wore leather gauntlet-gloves and a neck-kerchief that Jim's wife Eliza had given me for good luck—blue, printed all over with little golden stars—and I carried my goad on a rawhide thong around one wrist.

"Bless you, honey," was all Jim could say. His eyes brimmed over with tears, as did mine.

---

[39] Editors' Note: being unsprung, as noted above, the pioneers' wagons were uncomfortable to ride in, jolting and bouncing unmercifully. Most people (including children), unless incapacitated by injury, illness, or advanced pregnancy or recent childbirth, preferred to walk.

"I'll miss you," I said. "Stay well, all of you."

And wiped away the tears, and turned, and shouted "Get up!" to my beasts, and we set out.

***

Looking over this journal now, I am struck by the recollection that our enterprise began with tears, for so it continued. Though there was sometimes laughter, more often there was mourning and weeping, on a trail marked more with tombstones than miles walked or ridden.

Independence, Missouri
March 6, 1851

We started for California this morning at about nine o'clock. I never see so many wagons and cattle and folks all ranged out across the landscape. And such noise and commotion, cattle lowing and mules braying and dogs barking and men and women shouting and children crying. I was most deaf when we finally had the call to move out.

Half the population of Missouri, seems like, has been waiting here for several weeks, for the grass to begin to grow out on the trail so that the teams can forage. It has taken nearly all that time for me to find a train willing to take on a single woman and her servant and gear—not an easy task. It appears that no single women ever make on this overland journey, or at least that is what I heard over and over again.

Finally, I was directed to Captain Sellers. "There's a fellow might let you come along with his outfit," a drover told me.

"What's different about him?" I asked in disgust. "Nobody will even hear me out. They just say 'we don't want no single women' and that's flat."

"Why, he's receptive to the crossing of his palm with silver," the drover said, snickering. He was a filthy specimen, wearing greasy, patched jeans and a ragged coat that looked like something he got out of the ark. "Captain Sellers, he loves that filthy lucre, Miss, so if you've got any laid by, you can make some good use of it there." He leered at me. "It's probably a better bargain than you might make with some others."

I glared down at the man (for I was at least a head taller). "That'll do," I said. "I can take care of my own business."

He clucked at his team and shook the reins over their backs.

"Hope you don't lose your shimmy in no bad deals," he called back over his shoulder as he drove away.

When I got to Captain Sellers, I strode up to him and spoke my piece.

"I have enough put by to see me to California and allow me to set up in business there," I said. "I owe nothing to no man. I can manage my own team, I have a servant who sees to my needs and his, I own all my own gear and to spare, I'm free, white, and over twenty-one, and I aim to make my own way."

Captain Sellers stroked his chin whiskers, which was brown and curly, like his hair, which he wore long, and pondered. "Let's head over to the train and introduce you to the folks," he said. "If they all agree on it, then you can come on in. Each household pays a share for the expenses," he went on. "Same amount for each."

"What's the tariff?" I asked.

"Four hundred dollars an outfit."

"Suits me," I said.

When we got to the encampment, Captain Sellers called a meeting. It did take a while for the folks to come in and draw close enough to hear him. "This here is Miss Sarah Mary Williams," he said. "She is a single woman with property who wants to join our endeavors. Are there any objections?"

Nobody said nothing, though one of the womenfolk–a sallow, spindly body with a brood of sallow, spindly young'uns–looked as if she'd swallowed a paper of pins. I thought of smiling at her but didn't. With that type of person, it don't do much good to act friendly or to *be* friendly for that matter.

Well, Captain Sellers called for a vote, and everyone said Aye, even the sallow woman, so I was in.

"Bring your rig on over," the Captain said. "And that four hundred dollars as soon as you can get it. And your servant—he'll have to work for the rest of the train when needful, not just for you. Agreed?"

I said it was, and we shook hands on the deal.

Next morning I went alone into town (in women's garb, so as not to attract undue attention), leaving Cassius with our belongings. I wanted to see if any letters had come for me. There was one from Aunt Polly, so I took it into the hotel dining room and ordered a cup of coffee.

The letter was a good long gossipy one, so I put it away to

savor later on, only taking time to note that all of the folks was well and Tom was home from Yale for the summer. I finished my coffee and was about to head back to camp, when I heard my name.

"Miss Williams?" It was the hotel clerk, a timid reed of a fellow with long stringy hair and a woebegone expression. "This—hem—this gentleman would like a word with you." He waved forward the tall figure standing at his side, and I looked up and laughed in pure pleasure. "Why, Captain Walker! I never expected to see you here at this time of year."

Joseph Reddeford Walker had been a mountain man, and twenty years earlier, he and his band of trappers, with their squaws, would in the ordinary way of things have been far away in the mountains, hunting beaver. But beaver hats had mostly given way to silk ones in fashionable circles, these days, and the trapper's trade had given way, in Captain Walker's case, to that of trail guide. He had led not a few folks out to Oregon, and in years to come would guide many more. I had met him earlier in the spring at Mary Jane Wilks's, for he was her uncle by marriage, and had come to her wedding, bringing as a present twelve pairs of beaded moccasins made for the bride and groom by his Shoshone wife, Otter Woman. (Mary Jane had given me a pair of those same moccasins as her going-away gift, and I had them packed away with my other gear as too good for ordinary wear.)

Now, as I shook hands with him, Captain Walker grinned down at me. He was a fine-looking man, hard-muscled, with long shining ringlets of black hair and curly beard and moustaches to match; he wore a beaver hat (twin to the one I had bought Cassius, I noted) with a cockade of grouse feathers, and his buckskins were splendid with fringes and colored quillwork. He sported a red flannel shirt on which reposed three heavy silver necklaces; from the longest hung a walrus tooth he'd traded for with a Eskimo, thirty years back, when he was faraway up North looking for seal pelts.

He pulled up a chair and sat astraddle of it. "What brings you to the jumping-off place? "

"I'm jumping off myself, that's what." I signalled the waiter to bring another cup and the coffee-pot.

His chair creaked ominously. "Going to Oregon, or Californy?"

"California."

"Thought so. Figured if you was for Oregon, you'd be

coming along with me. What for?"

I drank some coffee. It was hot and pleasantly bitter. "Thought I'd like to set up in the storekeeping business, out there in the gold camps."

He grunted. "You could make a fortune—if you was let to live."

"I aim to do both," I said.

"Got any experience keeping a store?"

"No."

"Got book-knowledge, is all?"

"That's so."

"It's a different kind of territory, where you're headed," he said.

"I guess I'll have to take what comes," I said.

He shook his head. "It's rough out there. You might end up rich, but you might end up robbed—even killed—or worse."

I looked at him. "Do you really think I'm such a fool as not to know all that? But I've made up my mind and I'm going to try anyway."

He got up from the table. "I know better than to get crossways of a female who's made up her mind," he said. "So, I wish you luck, and I can tell you, you'll need plenty. Would you take advice from an old man who's seen more'n his share of the trouble folks can get into? Don't lend nothing, don't borrow nothing, and keep your powder dry. " He smiled, drained his coffee in one last gulp, touched his hat, and left me staring into my own empty cup.

Captain Walker had asked the same question I kept on asking myself: why *was* I going West?

Was I running away from the life fate had chosen for me, the life of a well-to-do, educated woman? Just what did I think I was doing, anyway?

I had enough money put aside not to have to worry about where my next meal might be found. I had no living relations to keep me in any one place. My friends? All were occupied with their own lives—Tom Sawyer headed for a brilliant legal career, no doubt; Mary Jane Wilks-that-was newly wedded and settled in with her husband and the life of a lawyer's wife; Aunt Polly was busy with her good works and her churchgoing; the Phelpses' little plantation kept running no matter what Uncle Silas did or didn't do to help it along.

102

And Jim and his family were settled now, free and comfortable. I had no worries in my mind about them, nor indeed about anyone I cared for. Cassius was still with me, but when we got to California, I intended to make sure he followed after seeking his own fortune and left off guarding mine. And my questions about my mother? After scouring most of Tennessee with Cassius, I had come no closer to an answer, nor, likely, ever would. I knew that now.

All of these reasons might say, I had no reason *not* to go wherever I might choose; but what was my reason *for* going?

Well, maybe it was in my blood. Or maybe it was the pull of the new country—that was a powerful draw. After all, I had heard all my life of the West, listened to talk from men drunk and sober. Mountains as high as clouds; trees as high as mountains; herds of buffalo so vast a body couldn't see the other side of them; land free for the taking, free . . .

I'd been East and knew it was not my place; I'd lived in Missouri and never been comfortable there, and finally shaken myself aloose of it. Though there was people I would always love and cherish, it too was not for me.

Maybe the West would welcome me as I was, maybe provide me with room to become whoever I would become. A chance to, you might say, re-invent myself. Everyone in Hannibal knew me— and most didn't seem to care overmuch for what they knew. In the West I could be—why, anyone I wanted to be, anyone I wished to become.

If you have read that book of Mr Twain's you might recall how at the end I expressed myself of the aim to go westering. You might think that was Mr Twain speaking for himself, my own experience being, you might say, limited. After all, I was but fourteen at the time. And in pure fact I didn't much care where I went, long's as there wasn't no Kings nor Dukes about–but then Tom and me and Jim ended up at the Phelpses, and Providence, as Aunt Polly called it, stepped in.

Well, I think it *was* Providence sent me back to the Wilkses, and Miss Mary Jane done as good a job on me as one could expect, given the raw material she had to work with. I was a passable girl when she got through. And the schooling I had got back East, whilst it didn't put much of a polish on, had afforded me as much in the way of book-learning as I was ever to need.

I had thought I was ready to become a respectable member of society. But it was just the same as before, when I'd lived with the Widow all those years earlier, before I escaped from Pap, before Jim and me set out on the river. Being respectable, besides boring me to tears, just didn't seem possible. No matter what I did, I couldn't seem to carry it off. And —more even than that—it was like the life was being sucked out of me, day by day.

No. Civilization was not for me. (Maybe Mr Twain felt the same—indeed, I know that he did, for he said as much, and his books prove it.)

I smiled, recalling Captain Walker's remark that if I'd been headed to Oregon, I'd have gone along with him. That surely would have been the case. And in fact, first off, I *had* been interested in Oregon. Mary, Tom's cousin, had gone out there as a missionary, to the Willamette Valley. Her letters fired me up to see the sights that she described: how new it all was, how wild and wide, under a sky as high and broad as all eternity.

Of course, she also wrote how another missionary, a friend of hers, Mrs Whitman, was massacred by the Indians, along with her husband, a doctor. It seems measles come and struck the tribe, and a whole lot of Indians died, but no white folks, which made the Indians think that the whites—including Doctor Whitman— had brought the sickness on purpose,[40] to kill all the Indians and get their land without having to fight fair and square for it.

That kind of put me off Oregon, to tell the truth.

California seemed to promise more of what I was after.

Maybe it was the newspapers that done it–oh, the news was full of stories about the gold fields, remember. And the war with Mexico meant the United States got aholt of millions and millions of acres of Mexican and Indian lands (a theft of enormous proportions, as I was later to discover). You couldn't open a newspaper without having the riches of California, there for the taking, splashed all over the page. You couldn't hover 'round the edge of any group of people for more than five minutes but you'd

---

[40] Editors' Note: this was indeed the sadly mistaken rumor that led to the Cayuse Indians' slaughter of most of the population of the Whitman mission settlement, including Mrs Whitman, for whom the Cayuse felt a particular animus (she did not like Indians and in fact forbidden them to enter her house.)

hear about the West—great doings in the greatest land Americans had ever seen, or ever would. Why, even back in Hannibal, we heard how it was the plan of Almighty Providence for America (that is, for white men) to go West and take the land that lay there, waiting to be taken.[41]

What did I want? I know what I didn't:

I didn't want to go back to Hannibal and imprison myself like a fly in amber in Mrs Harper's boardinghouse, and I did not wish to marry—supposing anyone would want me, with my reputation—not featuring a future as a farmer's wife, or a grocer's, or a banker's, or anybody's wife for that matter.

Obviously, missionarying was not for me, neither, as anyone could tell who talked to me for half a moment, and I warn't qualified for much else.

No, it was the westward journey for me; the time was right, and I was young and strong and ready for whatever Fate might heave at me.

So I paid for the coffee, pulled my shawl around me, picked up my reticule, and headed back to camp. It was time for the next stage of my life story to begin.

---

[41] Eds. note: The author may be referring to the speech given in Hannibal in 1846 by Senator Thomas Hart Benton, a noted proponent of what would come to be called "Manifest Destiny."

Chapter Eight: Ghost Trails

24 March 1851

It has taken me a good while to sort out who is who amongst all the folks in our train. When we stop for the night, there's too much noise and commotion. By the time we all settle down, there's no chance to visit or say much more to your neighbor than "good night."

Days, we drive or walk, strung out along the trail when it is hilly or wooded, fanned out when the terrain is flatter or in the river bottoms, though Captain Sellers has warned us to stay out of the dry river beds. Flash floods come without warning, he says, and can sweep away a wagon and team quick as lightning.

This Captain Sellers, he appears to know pretty much all there is to know about this territory, or so he claims. He's been up and down the whole train ever since we started, telling us all about the trips he's made to Santa Fe, to California, to the Great Salt Lake, and to Oregon. "Whichever destination you might prefer," he says, "I can take you there by the most convenient of routes, without fear of hostile savages, and with no danger but what God in His wisdom sends to all men, namely wind and weather."

So far the wind ain't been much—it will pick up in the mountains, he says—and the weather has been damp. It is a good thing that I spent extra money on rubber sheeting to tuck in over my baggage and supplies, and on a double layer of canvas well coated with linseed oil for my wagon cover.

Captain Sellers has a wagon, but his servant, Ned, mostly drives it. The Captain spends his time on horseback, and I figure his horse has travelled twice again the distance we've come, what with all his to-ing and fro-ing. He is called Captain but it isn't a military rank, more of an honorary title, he says, because of his experience as a wagon leader and scout. I told Ned that I knew another man called Captain, Joseph Walker. Ned said he'd never heard of him, which surprised me some, as I thought most everyone out West knew the names of all the mountain men. I asked Ned if he had heard of Jim Meek and Jim Bridger and he said no.

This made me kind of curious, and I wanted to ask him what-all he did know, but just then he said, "Mizz Sarah, I has to go and look after the Captain's saddle horses now. Kin I go along, please?"

"All right, Ned, go along. But just one more question, please. What is the Captain's given name?"

"Hit's Beriah, ma'am."

"That's a strange name," I said.

"Hit's f'm the Bible," Ned told me. "The Captain, his family full of preachers and teachers. They know the Bible like the back of they hands."

I thought this over. Captain Sellers did have a preacherly way about him. His voice was rich and oily, going from loud to soft and back again like organ music. And he was full of knowledge, much of it out of books which he quoted often and with authority. It made sense that he come from a family of ministers and schoolmasters.

As it happened, nobody seemed to know anything about the Captain save that he was reputed to be an experienced trail guide and wagonmaster. I wondered at his choice of servant. Ned did seem more than a mite scattered in his wits at times, and wandered around muttering to himself when he warn't busy with the Captain's horses and gear. I asked Cassius to sort of nose around, but after a while he said it was only that Ned was, for some unknown reason, afraid of the Captain. So I put my curiosity to rest, for the time being.

We spent the next few days getting ourselves ready for the road. There was ten wagons in all counting mine—a small train, but Captain Sellers said the smaller outfits got through better. Some trains consisted of forty wagons or more, and he prophesized that half of these would founder along the way. "Not enough grass for their livestock," he said, "And they lose more time than they can make up." We had twelve hundred miles to go til the splitting-off point, where the Oregon-bound would take the northern route along the Snake River to the Columbia, and those of us headed for California would turn south for another twelve hundred and more.

The point of division was Fort Hall, Idaho; the goal, to reach it before the end of August. Then we'd turn southeast again to Fort Bridger, west and south to Salt Lake City, on to the Humboldt River, over the Sierra Nevadas and down past Carson City and on to the Sacramento Valley and beyond. (I had a map, which I studied over and over. Most folks had maps, and it was a matter of some interest to compare them.)

Of course, that first twelve hundred miles had to be gotten through, and only then would the hardest part of the journey commence. Everyone had wagons purpose-built to stand the strain, mostly not the "prairie schooners" folks think of, but heavy farm wagons made strong, engineered to take weight, to be maneuverable in rough terrain, and to pack enough gear and to spare.

The average load included over a ton of foodstuffs, tools, bedding, clothes and household goods. Captain Sellers scoffed at folks he saw bringing along furniture, and told us that we'd see most of it heaved out along the trail as we went by. He was right about that. I could've furnished three or four houses with the chests, wardrobes, bedsteads, and hall trees I saw lying alongside the wagon ruts between Independence and Courthouse Rock alone.

That, and I could have built the foundations of another twenty dwellings with the rocks that covered the graves we passed. Sometimes it seemed like more folks died on the trail that ever got to their destination.

If I'd been a one like Tom Sawyer, to believe in ghosts, or Jim with his "ha'nts", I might have slept less easily when we halted, as we often did, near to the graves of those who'd passed. But I still don't take no stock in dead people, even though Jim often told me that I would live to rue those words.

"Stands to reason, the spirits hear what you say, and it don't do to disturb them," he had said, way back when we were still on the raft, one night when we was talking about Heaven, and the other place, and what it must be like there. Jim, he maintained that some spirits hung around where they'd died, because they couldn't rest.

This was a common belief, and not only amongst Negroes, but I pshawed it. "Why, Jim, there's been thousands and thousands of folks lived most places; if their spirits hung around like you say, they'd be so thick they'd show up in plain daylight, seems like."

"Don't you make fun, Huck, honey," Jim said. "There is more things in this world and the next than you nor I can ever explain. The world of the spirits is hid from our sight, unless the spirits, they want to make theirselves known."

"So when a person sees a spirit, it's because the spirit wants him to see it?"

"Yes, child, that's a fact."

"I don't believe it. What would a spirit want with a person who's still alive?"

"They might could have a message for the one who's living, to warn him maybe or to set him on the right path. Spirits, they *knows* things."

Jim had a lot more to say on the subject, and we wrangled about it off and on for as long as we were together. He never could convince me, but he surely did try, and I had to admit that, as an African, he had more to say on the subject than I could ever muster. White folks, I told him, don't generally worry about spirits, unless they're in a graveyard at midnight doing something they oughtn't.

"That where you all just as wrong as you can be," Jim said. "You pay attention to the spirits, they work for you, not against you. But got to be proper attention."

"Like what?"

"Give 'em presents. Tobacco, whiskey, sugar best. But meat and other food work sometimes. Sometimes blood–kill a chicken or a goat, spill the blood for the spirits to drink. White chicken, white rooster if you can catch one. And you has to say the right words."

"What are they?"

Jim, he only sighed and said he didn't know but a few of them, and he warn't sure about those. This was African religion, he said, and since slavery times, most of the language, the prayers and chants, had been lost. But a lot of slaves still remembered to make the proper offerings, he said, and the Indians did, too. That was one place where Negroes and Indians had a lot in common, he said. They both paid attention to spirits, giving them presents to ward off any trouble or confusion that might come from mistreating or forgetting them. And of course Indians always took in slaves that run off, and adopted them into the tribe, so a lot of Indian spirit knowledge had become part of slave knowledge as well.

"I might've run off to the Indians," Jim said, "Ceptin' I wanted to get my freedom and then get freedom for my wife and children, and if I went to the Indians I knowed I'd never come back."

Thinking of Jim, I was glad that he'd got his wish at last.

I thought of our last goodbyes.

Jim had clasped me tight in his arms and prayed over me. "Oh Lord God," he said, in that rich dark voice of his, "Protect this child of yours from harm, and bring her safe through this worldly journey to your heavenly throne. Amen."

I didn't think prayers for me would do any much good, but I let him do it, because it meant something to him. And I figured it couldn't do no harm.

Now, whenever we went on past another file of graves, I wondered if I *would* get safe through this worldly journey—or if a rock-piled grave would be my end. Well, I told myself, no use in worrying over it. I meant to stay above ground if I could, and not let ghosts nor spirits nor the possibility of becoming one of them haunt my nights or days overmuch.

***

4 April 1851

Our train seems to be making good time, most days ten or more miles. Despite Captain Sellers's trying to keep us together, we tend to straggle out quite a ways over the prairie. Many of the folks are driving mules, which go just a trifle faster than oxen, which I and two other wagons employ, and then there are several milk cows coming along behind, herded by various children. These (cows and children) belong to the Swensons, who are foreigners and speak almost no English. They drive oxen, two yoke, red and white ones like their milk cows. There are about six little Swensons and the Mister and Mrs, all of them yellow-haired and fair-skinned and sturdy. They come at the end of the train, on account of the cows. In front of them are the Niedermeirs, German farmers from Missouri, also very fair and ruddy, a young couple with a baby coming, and three yoke of oxen, brown Swiss they tell me the breed is.

Up ahead of me are the Fieldings, a father about fifty and his son and the son's wife and their three boys, all in their teens—handsome lads. The Fieldings have mules, but also five beautiful saddle horses, bright bay with black manes and tails. They aim to raise horses in California and break them and sell them. The boys, all three curly-headed as young rams, and long of limb, are as much at home on horseback as on their own feet, and amuse themselves and the rest of us by doing trick riding, showing off what they and their horses can do.

There is a German doctor, Josef Thannheimer by name, who is traveling with the aim of setting up in practice out in California. He is a cordial man, about forty, with dark hair and beard, pale blue eyes, and a beautiful deep voice, and his wagon is an old-fashioned Conestoga, pulled by six mules, handsome gray animals, well cared

110

for by his nephew, who is also his assistant. This nephew, a dark, thin, bespectacled young man, is very quiet, spending most of his time reading thick medical books when he isn't driving the team or doing chores. His name is Ernst.

I feel a liking for the doctor on sight. There is something about him—a warmness and largeness of soul that kind of rays out of him, like sunbeams, which is the only way I can think to explain it. The doctor is tall, with an imposing, full, dark-brown beard, curling like his hair (which he wears cropped very short, so that it stands up all over his head). He dresses in a funny way, in a calico shirt cut like a boy's waist, and a wide, flat-brimmed straw hat and full-cut canvas britches, but over all this a long-tailed black coat like any doctor in town. He has a heavy accent, so's at first I found him hard to understand, but in time it got easier, and we have had many interesting talks, of which I will relate more at another time. (The doctor also enjoys talking with Cassius, which raises him in my estimation.)

Then there are two young couples, sisters lately wed to a pair of brothers named Hagen, and a Reverend and Mrs, named Aspinall; a carpenter named Orren with his wife and a widowed sister-in-law (the woman with the sour face who'd looked askance at me when I joined the train) and their two passels of children, six and five each, and Mrs Orren appears to have another one coming along, not too far off.[42] They have two wagons, for he has brought along all of his tools, and the sister-in-law and one of the older boys take turns driving the mules of the second rig. And there is a middle-aged Yankee bachelor from Connecticut, Hank Morgan by name, who has been in business all his life and has decided to try his luck at farming, he says, though a less likely-looking farmer I have seldom met. And Captain Sellers and Ned. And Cassius. And me.

I can look back in my mind and see the whole train, spread out for half a mile in a great fan, with the dust blowing and the long grass rippling and the clouds scudding pale across a sky without end. I hear the sound of the mules and oxen and the calling of voices as men shout and women cry out warnings to their children and the wagons rumble and squeak and the pans and pots tied to them clatter and jangle.

---

[42] Eds. note: It is a matter of record that many women who made the overland journey were or became pregnant en route.

At night the cookfires are shining and a lamp here and there sends out a glow, and I hear the sounds of families as they finish their dinners and make ready for sleep. Maybe somebody sings a lullaby or a hymn tune, low and soft.

Then evening, and the stars shining brighter than the dimming coals of the fires. Here and there a baby fusses or a small child calls out in a bad dream, and also here and there a wagon bed creaks as a man and woman take what ease they can from each other.

(Oh, yes, it made me feel lonely, yes, and still I wouldn't have traded my solitariness for anyone else's lot. I was solitary by choice as well as inclination, and I've never regretted that time I spent by myself. I often think that I would go back again to those days in an instant, even knowing what was to come.)

***

20 April 1851

Only six weeks out of Independence, and already half of us are sick with what some call camp fever and others trail fever. Fever, and chills, some, but mostly it is the bowels that are affected, with belly cramps and purging.

Dr Thannheimer says it is bad water that causes it. He advocates boiling any water used for cooking or drinking, and he has given laudanum to those worst taken, which binds up the bowels but renders the sufferer mostly unable to walk or stand, and lying down in these unsprung wagons would shake a body half to death if he warn't unconscious.

So far I have escaped, as has Cassius, also Hank Morgan, the Swensons, Dr Thannheimer himself, and the Niedermeiers. And Ned, and Captain Sellers, who is fretting, as we must halt so often for the sick to stop and relieve themselves.

The women seem to suffer more from embarrassment than from the flux. They try to go in groups of three or more, so that some can hold their skirts out and make a little tent to shield the one in the middle from the men's eyes. I myself don't think that any man, however woman-hungry, would look with any pleasure on a woman shitting and sweating in pain, but then, I warn't raised to such standards of modesty.

Also, since I am not wearing women's garb, when I do have to go out, I head for some bushes or a rock outcropping and do what I have to, which is harder, believe me, with breeches, for a woman, than with skirts and petticoats. The ability to relieve oneself quickly and conveniently is the only aspect of female dress that I would wish for, but at least I avoid the bother of having to wear the things at all other times.

The fact that I am wearing trousers has made the women even more suspicious of me, except for Mrs Swenson, whose English isn't much, and the younger Mrs Hagen—her name is Ida—who is something of a kindred spirit. She told me last Monday, when the train stopped to let the women do some washing, that she would have come west by herself if she hadn't been married. "Then you and I could have been partners," she said to me, and I hadn't the heart to say, "But I'd rather be by myself," because you could see how the idea had struck her as so pleasant. She laughed, showing pretty teeth, and I had to laugh too.

"Well, you have a partner anyway," I said.

"Oh, him," she said. But she smiled as she said it, and I could tell that she was pleased enough with her man. And he with her, for he came up just to help her with the wash basket and the look they exchanged said, plain as plain, *we two have a secret that is only ours to share.*

The other women don't have much to say to me. I spend most of my time walking or driving along alone with my thoughts, except for these occasional conversations with Mrs Hagen. One thing I have learned: nearly all of the women did not want to come on this journey, but came along because their husbands insisted on going.

"I told Mr Olmsted that I did not want to leave Ohio," Mrs Olmsted said. "But he said he was going, with me or without me."

It is hard to find time to converse with the other women, because they are so busy, making camp or breaking it, cooking meals and looking after their families. Even if prudence had not dictated keeping some distance, I shouldn't care to spend time with the men, who occupy their leisure mostly in bragging about their prospects or embroidering their past successes (the exceptions being Mr Niedermeir, who speaks mostly German and spends his time with the other men in nodding and smiling and saying "Yah, yah," over and over, and Mr Swenson, who likewise has little English, being Swedish, but keeps to himself, and Mr Aspinall, who is a Reverend and don't speak much to anyone, except when praying or conducting services, which Captain Sellers allows him to do on

Sundays or when we pass by a burial in progress).

Sometimes Dr Thannheimer and I pass the time of day, but especially in the evenings, I seem to have the most talk, besides of course with Cassius, with Ned, the Captain's servant.

Ned reminds me a bit of Nat, the Phelpses' slave who used to bring Jim his rations when Tom and me was rescuing him. Ned don't tie up his hair with thread like Nat, but he is about the same complexion—saddle color—and similar in size and shape. He knows the same old sayings about the weather, and he says he can work roots and make charms if need be.

Now, Mr Twain, he wrote about Nat as if he was feeble-minded, which was not the case—not by a long shot—and as if he was afraid of witches, which he warn't, at least not in the way Mr Twain wrote it.

I hate to say it, but there was an awful lot Mr Twain didn't understand about Negroes. Nat, now, he had a lot of respect for witches. The threads that he tied up his hair with wasn't done out of fear at all. He done it to show the spirits that he was willing to obey them if they called upon him. And sometimes they did. He could go into a trance and tell you what your dreams meant. The spirits told him, he said. I wanted to try it, but he said it only worked with colored folks.

Why, that whole rigmarole about the witch pie and Tom's having to convince Nat to take it to Jim was just more of Mr Twain's invention. And like most Negroes, Nat knowed perfectly well that white folks don't know shucks about spirits or witches. Even Indians know more than white folks do, as Jim had pointed out.

Captain Sellers's Ned talks about spirits sometimes—not like Jim or Nat, with respect and awe, but with fear in his voice, as if he'd seen something once that he never wanted to see again. He shivers a little when he mentions spirits, and clutches a little leather bag he wears on a thong around his neck.

I asked him what it was, and he said it was his *gris-gris*. His grandma was born in Santo Domingo, he told me, and she was a conjure woman from Africa. She made the *gris-gris* for him when he was a boy, and told him it would protect him always.

Ned wears a long, droopy mustache that is getting gray, like his crinkly hair, which he wears long, tied back with a thong. He keeps himself clean, and his clothes are much better than most slaves' are. He has a soft, gentle way with a horse or a mule: he hums a little tune when he curries the Captain's horses or gives them their feed. He runs his big hands over their flanks and backs and legs to feel for ticks or burrs, and he keeps their gear in trim and looks after their hooves and their teeth.

"You love horses," I said to him last evening, after supper. Which I shared with him and with Cassius, the Captain having ridden off to eat with both sets of Hagens. Ned is an awfully good cook, among his other talents.

"Yes'm, horses and mules, too, but I ain't care much for oxen," he said. He was doing some little chores. "Kin you pass me that bundle there, Mizz Sarah?"

I handed it over. He opened it and took out a skein of rawhide strips and begun to pick them apart and measure them into lengths.

"They ain't pretty like horses, but they pull like the dickens," I said.

Ned begun braiding his strips of rawhide into a hackamore. "I rather work with horses than go on this excursion," he said.

"Why, don't you want to go West?" Cassius said.

"No, indeed. Not me. I ain't never want to go nowhere but home."

"Where is home? Where are the Sellerses from?" I asked.

"Tennessee. *East* Tennessee," Ned said. "Sure do wish we was back there."

"East Tennessee? Whereabouts? We have been there, just recently, Cassius and me," I said. "Why, don't you like traveling?"

"Naw, Mizz Sarah, not me. I has all of the chores to do and the driving and cooking and looking after the horses, and the Captain, he mighty particular. I ain't had no rest yet on this trip, since we-all left Murfreesboro, and I don't expect to have none til we gets to Salt Lake City."

Cassius shot me a look.

"I thought we-all was headed for California," I said.

"I can't keep them places straight in my mind," Ned said. "They all just places to me. I don't care much where we be going, tell the truth, long's we don't see no Indians. I don't like Indians, no ma'am."

"Why, did you have trouble with them on your other trips out West?" I asked.

Ned seemed to hesitate. "No," he said, finally. "But I still don't like 'em. They's powerful strange folks, Indians is."

Here, Cassius looked as if he was about to say something, but I made a little motion, and he set back and kept quiet.

No matter how I cajoled him, Ned refused to talk about Indians in any greater detail, saying over and over that the Captain had told him not to discuss the subject. Later, I talked it over with Cassius. And we looked to the guns, to make sure they was all oiled and laid ready to use, and powder and shot to hand.

And again I thought to myself how smart I'd been to keep to men's clothing whilst we were on the trail. My clothes was still a thorn in some folks' side, but these mostly looked on me with disfavor for my ways in general, not just my attire.

It went against their notions of what was seemly for a single woman to drive her own team and live in her own wagon and shoot her own fresh meat and so on, though if I'd been forty instead of twenty-one they'd not have disapproved half as much.

These women mourned the loss of seemliness on the trail. They wanted their starched white aprons and shining-combed hair. They wanted their rocking chairs and bread dough rising under a clean cloth and the lamps trimmed and the door latched against the night. They rued the dark calico sheeting on their pallets and missed their crisp white bedlinen, ironed smooth and fine. Now they lived on the move and scarcely had time to braid up their hair, let alone wash and comb it; aprons were pieces of rough sacking, hands were grimed with pitch that wouldn't wash off, and bread dough rode in a crock tied to the wagon and got full of chaff and cinders by the time you set it out to bake.

And a wagon was no defense against the dark. I wondered how many of them lay awake at night, listening for wolves or bear or Indians, wondering if the husband sleeping an exhausted sleep beside them would hear in time to jump up and fire his gun—and hit what he was aiming at.

Most of the women in our train, like most who made the journey west, was in their late teens and early twenties, a few in their thirties, and married—and all except Mrs Hagen and Mrs Fielding had small young'uns underfoot. I noticed that several had their aprons high as well. Even the Reverend's wife was pregnant. I never see so many carrying women at one time as on that train. At least ten of them were showing by the time we got to Chimney

Rock. But I'll have more to say about that, and other women's matters, later.

***

6 May 1851

Finally, we are within a few days of Fort Laramie, after making our way through the Sand Hills in what Captain Sellers claimed was record time.

But first we had to stop for a day at Chimney Rock, which was exactly like it was named, a spire of rock in the middle of the prairie. A few of the younger men and boys wanted to climb up to it. Bill Hagen—he was the younger of the two brothers—even started out to do so, but his wife, Ida, raised a terrible ruckus. (She was one of those whose pregnancy was becoming evident by this time.) Captain Sellers added his voice to hers, saying that there was too much risk, and if a man fell and broke his leg or arm, he'd just have to be left, so Bill, he give up, though he said several times that a man ought to be able to judge for himself what risk he was willing to take.

The Doctor, he had kind of a stern look when he heard what Captain Sellers said about leaving anyone who injured himself. I myself thought that the Captain's words was mostly bluff, but held my peace.

This was a stranger country than most of us had seen before. The terrain in eastern Kansas was hillier. That had been a rolling kind of country, the grass spangled with wildflowers, more than I'd ever seen before. They seemed to spring up directly following the thunderstorms that came blowing in nearly every afternoon. The rain poured down in sheets and thunder roared like a hundred freight trains, whilst lightning flashes blinded man and beast alike, and then as quick as it came on, the storm rolled away and the sun shone again. As the train passed, the feet of oxen and mules and humans trampled the flowers and mixed their scent with the smells of dust and dung and heated metal and oiled canvas and the sweat of man and beast. Western Kansas and this part of Nebraska was far different—more sandy underfoot, and a great deal drier.

We followed the Platte, a shallower river than most, with islands in the middle—it was a broad, wide stream—where a few cottonwoods grew. The rest of the land was empty of trees, and we used buffalo chips for fuel. This was hard on the other women, who couldn't seem to forget that the so-called chips was in fact

117

dried buffalo shit. It took some of them quite a time to be able to pick up the chips without looking sick, but there was nothing else to burn for fuel, so they had to get used to it.

In fact these chips burn hot and give off little smoke, with almost no smell, and they are, or were, plentiful. The buffalo herds that made them were still around, and we saw them—and heard and smelt them, too, for we had to halt a good ways off to let them go past. Captain Sellers remarked that they were barely a tenth the size of the herds he'd seen just a few years since. He predicted that the Indians would suffer in consequence of losing their chief source of food and clothing (and so it would prove). We saw few Indians at this point, mostly small, wandering bands.

The weather also took a turn. It was hotter than blazes in the daytime and so chilly at night that we had to pull out our winter coats when we did the evening chores. Several times there was hailstorms, once a thunder-hailstorm with lightning that lit up the landscape for miles and miles in great white flashes, some of which struck a bit too close for my comfort. Cassius and I had to help Ned bring in the Captain's horses and hobble them near the wagons, so they wouldn't get far if they tried to bolt.

Ned was half out of his wits with fright.

"Hit ain't in nature," he said, "Lightnin' and hail at the same time! Something's wrong, Mizz Sarah. Judgment Day comin'!"

I didn't know what to say to that, except to point out that hundreds, maybe thousands, of people had traveled this way in past years and Judgment Day hadn't come yet.

"Maybe so," he said, "But too many of them folks dead, seems to me." And he dived into the Captain's wagon and pulled his quilt up over his head and refused to come out even when I carried him a bowl of hot stew. The hail had mostly died down, but the wind was whipping up, and I shivered.

"You go ahead and get yourself warm, Mizz Sarah," Ned said from the depths of the wagon. I left the bowl for him and went back to my own bed. I could hear Cassius snoring in his berth under the wagon—that man could sleep through anything, I do believe. Me, I could see the lightning flashes growing paler and paler as the wind died down. I thought of what Ned had said: "too many folks dead."

We passed so many graves I had lost count; on some days we passed five, six, or more at one place, then a little further on we'd see another half-dozen or so. No way to know if it was trail fever—which I now know was probably cholera, or typhoid—or a woman dead in childbirth, or a child crushed by a wagon wheel, or a stillborn baby, or a man pitched over a cliff in the dark, or brained by a falling tree, or killed by his gun misfiring, or any of the hundred other ways to die that there were out on the trail.

And we had also plodded by, on numerous occasions, wagons that had halted where people were burying their dead, or waiting for sick folks to die so's they could get on.

It must have been awful to lie there dying, *knowing* you was a-dying, whilst your folks dug your grave nearby, and to know that soon you'd be lying cold and still under a pile of earth and rocks whilst everything you'd cared for in life went on without you.

One woman we passed held her dead child in her lap as she sat by the side of the grave. She kept pleading with her menfolk: "Make it deeper! O, make it deeper!"

I knew—we all knew, by now—that a too-shallow grave meant that animals would dig up the body and feed on it.

Another likelihood was that some of those famished Indians we'd seen would dig it up, looking for clothes or trinkets to steal. (Which led to the sickness and death of a lot of Indians, who took contagion from the corpses they raided.)

I heard that mother's mournful words in my head for a long time. "Deeper! Oh, please, dig it deeper, for the Lord's sake!"

There was nothing to be done. So we passed on, leaving another small ghost to haunt the trail.

Dr Thannheimer grieved every death, I knew. He was gentle as a woman with anyone who was suffering, whether from sickness or grief. "It iss that ve so much of the knowledge lack," he said to me and to his nephew, one night when they came to share my campfire and supper. "Someday ve vill know, ja, vhat cause dis cholera morbus, what iss all dese t'ings dat make sickness and dying—dey have a cause, und ve vill findt it oudt."

(That is a sample of how he talked—I won't give out with no more of it, but stick to plain English from now on.)

The nephew said a few words in German to the doctor, who looked grim and said something back in the same language, then turned to me.

"Ernst says that it will be we Germans who do so," Dr Thannheimer said. "He has much feeling for his native country and its people, does my nephew."

I looked at Ernst, who nodded. "I love the fatherland," he said, and hummed a bit of melody in his sweet tenor voice.

"What is that tune?" I asked.

"It is a song by our great poet Heine," the Doctor said. "The words are these: *'ich hatte einst ein schönes Vaterland'*—'Once I had a beautiful Fatherland,' but the song goes on to say it was all a dream. So must we now dream, only dream, of the lovely land we have left."

"But I will go back," Ernst said passionately.

"If so, then so," the Doctor said. "But for this time, *ja*, we will do our best here in the new land." He spoke gently, but his glance at Ernst was sharp. "Here we must now live."

"I do not wish to forget," Ernst said.

"Then remember," the Doctor said. "But keep your mind and your heart to the present and the future. The past is all."

By this I guessed he meant that it was over and done. And I could see that Ernst took what his uncle said to heart, though he still hummed that tune now and again as we plodded on toward our destination.

Chapter Nine: Indians

10 June 1851

Past Chimney Rock we plodded on through the dry country. The Platte was more land than water at this point,[43] and the alkali dust began to take its toll.   Everyone's eyes became sore and inflamed, and Dr Thannheimer was kept busy concocting eyewashes from boiled water and boric acid, and measuring out doses of elderberry cough syrup for our raspy throats.

Finally we come in sight of Fort Laramie.

We spent a few days at the Fort, resting up, though most of the women took the opportunity to wash clothes. Some of us saw to our wagons, taking advantage of the Fort's blacksmith—there was much refitting of iron tires, as the wooden wheels shrank so much in the dry air. Generally, folks went over their gear and tended to their animals. Cassius and I looked to our oxen, who seemed to be doing pretty well, considering.

There was quite a number of Indians at the Fort, the first we'd seen in any great numbers.

From time to time we'd met with a few, mostly Pawnee and Kansas, who followed the wagon trains begging for bacon and coffee and sugar.

Captain Sellers liked to drive these folks off whenever they come too close, but they still managed to come into camp at times, and like to used up most of our sugar whenever they did, having a sweet tooth worse even than Cassius's. He, himself, used to measure out the sugar for our visitors whilst looking desperate grim, for the level in the piggin went down and down, and what was left in the barrel had to last us for some time more.

These Fort Indians was different. The young men who followed the trains was still wild and free, and looked it. They wore vermilion paint along their cheekbones and down the part in their braided hair, which they festooned with strings of beads and strips of fur and cloth, red and blue, and they sported fringed leggings and breechclouts below bare chests. Most of 'em had blankets, too, red ones or cream-colored ones striped in colors, that they pulled up

---

[43] Eds. note: A common saying of pioneers, referring to the Platte River, was that it was "too thick to drink and too thin to plow."

around their shoulders when they stopped to chat.

Once or twice a woman rode along with them, and I remember thinking how pretty they was, with long soft plaits of shining black hair, and deerskin tunics and leggings decorated in patterns with beads and quills. I wished I knowed their lingo, but had to content myself with smiles and nods, and they smiled back likewise. I could see that Cassius was mightily taken with them, and teased him, once, about taking an Indian wife.

"Well, if it came to that, I wouldn't be averse to such," he said.

"They do seem to be interested in *you*," I said, and laughed, for it was clear that the Indians—men and women alike—found Cassius fascinating. Several times he'd had to extricate himself from a group of them, all bent on feeling of his arms and face to see did his color come off on their hands—and some of them even pulling at his shirt and breeches to discover if he was dark all over. He was in fact not very much darker than they, but was clearly not a white man, though he wore white men's clothes. You could see them puzzling over it, and also over his kinky hair, which they tended to pat and pull at, so that eventually Cassius taken to tying a kerchief tight around his head and jamming his hat on over that, to keep them away.

So, from our few trailside experiences, I'd formed the idea that Indians were people I'd like to know more of, so the ones that were known as "Hang-Around-the-Forts" were an unpleasant surprise.

These Hang-Around-the-Fort Indians was a sickly, scrawny bunch. And dirty, too, unlike the wild ones out on the trail. These Fort Indians wore mostly white folks' castoffs, and in strange combinations, too, so that the first one I saw when we come up to the Fort had a calico waist on, but was wearing it like a pair of drawers, with his legs thrust through the sleeves, and the tails tied together around his waist, whilst his wife had on a petticoat over her leggings, but nothing up top, so that her breasts hung out all bare. This caused some of the women in our train to shriek and hide their eyes, which made the Indian woman gape at them.

It would have been a funny sight, except that both Indians were drunk, and so were nearly all of those we saw near the Fort. It got so every Indian we met was following after us, begging for liquor, which they did by pointing to their open mouths and grunting. It fair turned my stomach, but what was worse was some of the soldiers and traders giving the Indians whiskey and laughing at their antics. Once, too, I saw a trader take an Indian girl and push her to the ground and grope and claw at her—not gently—then climb on top of her, whilst she screamed and cried, but her man just sat on the ground in a drunken stupor.

All in all, I was glad to leave the Fort.

We spent some time, Cassius and I, going over the maps I'd brought and talking with some of the traders at the Fort, several of whom were on their way back East.

There was two possible routes from here on, they said.

After the Fort, most people elected to go on to South Pass and the Sweetwater River, and then on to Fort Bridger. Then it was a long pull up to the Bear River country and Soda Springs, where the trail divided, and those headed toward Oregon would take the northward leg, whilst those aiming for California would take the southern. This route carried travelers down to the Humboldt River and into Paiute country, and then followed the Truckee over the Donner Pass to Sonoma. But there was a shorter way, we learned: if we took Sublette's Cut-Off we could save near ninety miles.

"We'll miss Fort Bridger, do we go that way," Cassius said.

This was true, they said. But Fort Bridger warn't much.

Cassius and I talked it over. We could go on, a hundred and forty-odd miles after South Pass and the Continental Divide, heading almost due south and then turning northward again, or take the direct route.

"It's fifty mile, and no water," I said.

Yes, they said, but man and beast had done it before, would do so again.

I was tempted. But Cassius talked me out of it.

"We aiming to get there safe and sound, no matter the time," he said. "Maybe if the whole train was a-going that way, we could say we ought to go along. But 'pears to me that most of the folks plan on following the Captain."

That was so. Captain Sellers had already let on that he didn't think much of Sublette's Cut-Off. I was of the same mind as Cassius: we needed a short-cut less than we needed a safe road onward.

Well, with that question settled, we loaded up and rattled on out of Fort Laramie. Independence Rock was the next stop of any duration. We was late coming to it, also, that rock—which was less a rock than a mound of granite like a dome, maybe a hundred and thirty or forty feet high. It was covered with names and dates, mostly inscribed with axle grease but some carved into the stone. Bill Hagen put his and his wife's initials on, with the date, B H& I H July 1851; very pretty it looked, though Ida kept on calling out to him to finish up and come down. It was an easy climb, though, and no danger to speak of.

As I said, we was cutting it fine, coming up to the Rock. Most folks aimed to reach it by the Fourth of July, which would mean enough time left to get over the mountains before the snows got too deep. But Captain Sellers, he said he warn't worried.

"It's pretty clear going from here on," he said, and we all took heart at that.

***

We made Fort Bridger in good time, but now there was a serious decision to be made. Some amongst us wanted to take a detour to the Saints' new-built city by the Salt Lake. That meant going by the Hastings Cut-Off and rejoining the main route along the Humboldt, close to four hundred miles instead of three, and harder going, as it meant crossing the Wasatch Range.

The ground had been rising steadily, and some of us questioned whether the animals could make another long pull before the Sierra Nevadas. Going by Salt Lake City would be a longer route but maybe an easier one, and would avoid going through Shoshone country.

I had wanted to visit the Shoshone, myself, after having met Otter Woman, John Walker's wife, at Mary Jane's wedding. She had told me quite a bit about her people up there in Wyoming, and I had brought with me a supply of fine English embroidery scissors to trade with the women who did such beautiful beadwork.

So I put up my hand and observed as how I much preferred the northern route, and Cassius added his voice to mine.

Well, we couldn't seem to reach an agreement, so Captain Sellers called a meeting for that evening, to decide.

Cassius and I strolled over to the Captain's wagon after supper, where a small crowd of men and a few women had already gathered.

Ned had lit several torches and stuck them in the ground, and next he cleared off a space of level dirt where the Captain squatted, using a long stick to draw a map, which he explained as he drew:

"This here is where we are now, and we have two choices," he said. "We can head north by northwest, and make the main part of the California Trail right at Soda Springs," he said, drawing a long line, "And this here is the route to Salt Lake City. If we go that way, we can re-supply easily for the next stage. If we take the northward road, it's harder going, but a straighter route." He pointed with his stick to the last line he'd drawn. "It don't matter to me which way you choose."

"Which way's the one you knows best?" Cassius asked.

"Why, both of 'em's well known to me, one as much as t'other," the Captain said. "Like I told you—it's your own choice."

By now every man and most of the women had joined the group. Mr Fielding spoke up.

"I'd just as lief take the ordinary route," he said. "I had some run-ins with the Mormons back in Illinois, and I don't care if I never see another one."

Several men laughed, and most of them nodded. "They do have a reputation," said Mr Orren, the carpenter.

Mr Fielding leaned over and poked Orren in the ribs. "Why, so they do, Orren," he said. "If we stop with the Saints', you could marry your sister-in-law and have you two wives to keep you warm at night." Mr Orren was often cold, and just as often complained of it.

Mr Orren's wife let out a squeak at Fielding's words, and her sister scowled but kept her lips pressed tight together.

Mr Orren glared at him. "I don't think that's very funny," he said.

"Maybe you don't," said Mr Fielding, with a grin, "But I believe some of these folks do.'" It was true that there was guffaws all around, whilst Orren's wife and her sister stood balefully by, skinny arms folded over their flat chests.

I smiled myself at the picture of Mr Orren tucked into his bedroll, his sour-faced sister-in-law a-badgering him from one side whilst his wife—her sister—harangued him from the other. Orren was most dreadfully hen-pecked. His wife had not wanted to make the overland journey at all—nor had the sister—but while the wife belabored him mightily with her tongue, the sister, so far, had kept a discreet silence, as befitting her dependent status.

Orren darted a look of pure hate around him and stalked off, followed by the two women. As they left the circle of torchlight, I heard someone snicker, but Orren kept his back stiff and never let on that he noticed. Mr Fielding sighed.

"Well, now," he said. "What do you all think we should do? Should we put it to a vote?"

The final tally was clear: three men and one woman—me— voted to bypass the Saints and their new Jerusalem in the desert, and head instead for Soda Springs and the California Trail. (Cassius especially was concerned to avoid the Saints, as he had heard their attitude toward Negroes was less than cordial.)

The rest voted for Salt Lake City, so that was that.

(I must say here, in spite of what was to transpire, that years later I met and did business with a number of Mormons and found them pleasant enough to trade with, though drivers of a hard bargain, and somewhat patronizing of us who were "gentiles." As their colony, Deseret, grew, I followed its career with interest—as most Americans did. Brigham Young I saw only once but never forgot, a man built like a tree, with hands the size of hams and a fierce black beard big enough for two Prophets. I could well imagine him as the ruler of his own prosperous and orderly kingdom, and I was just as glad not to be his subject, though owning his many achievements.)

Well. As all of us was in agreement, we settled in to wait for the dawn and the next leg of our journey.

***

As I wrote earlier, I had long wanted to visit the Shoshones. A couple of the men in our train had ridden ahead the day before, and returned now with news that a band of Shoshone were camped just a few miles away. As this would probably be our only chance, I told Cassius that I intended to go and see them. I put on my Shoshone moccasins for the occasion.

"You ain't going by yourself," he objected.

"Somebody needs to stay with the oxen and with our wagon," I said.

"I'll ask Ned to watch over everything. He'll do it," Cassius said.

"I guess I can offer him a dollar. All right, see if he will." We arranged to borrow two of the Captain's horses (I paid Ned another dollar for the privilege) and were soon on our way. We had to tell Ned where we was going, of course, and he nearly had a fit over it, but I give him another dollar and he settled down, still grumbling.

When we found the camp, which was nothing to speak of—just a few wigwams and some fire-pits and piles of rubbish—I was startled to see that it was mostly women and children, with a few old men. No men between sixteen and sixty were in sight.

"Where have they gone? Hunting?" I wondered.

A Shoshone woman stepped up to my horse, took hold of my leg, and pulled on the fringe of my moccasin. I looked down and saw her looking up at me.

She was young and handsome, with a bright brown face, painted on the cheeks with circles of red, and her thick black braids were bound in red cloth. Her dress and leggings looked new—clean doeskin, almost white, ornamented with beads and quills in red and blue. I smiled at her. She smiled back and pointed at her mouth, then at mine.

"They want us to stop and eat with them," I said.

Cassius was doubtful, having heard that Indians eat dog (true) and human (not true), but I persuaded him. He give over the horses to a young boy, who took the reins and stared at both of us, but nodded when the young woman spoke to him, and led the horses away a short distance to a corral where a group of Indian ponies grazed.

It turned out that the young woman knew some words of English, and a woman who seemed to be her grandmother or an aunt knowed some as well, so we was able to hold a conversation, of sorts.

The young woman, whose name, I learned, was Little Rabbit, pointed to my moccasins and said, "Shoshone."

"They surely are," I said. "They was give to me by a friend. Do you know Captain Joseph Reddeford Walker?"

"Ah, Walker," Little Rabbit said, and smiled. Her teeth shone white against her copper skin. "Cap-tain Walker!"

"That's right," I said. I didn't know if she understood me, or was just repeating what I'd said, but I went on, "Captain Walker's married to Otter Woman. She made these," and I stuck my foot out so everyone could admire Otter Woman's work.

We was each given a bowl of stew—I didn't ask what the meat was, but whether it was dog or prairie chicken or rattlesnake, it was good, with a savory gravy flavored with sage, and some roots that might have been carrots or parsnips or something else I didn't recognize, but whatever they was, they was toothsome, and the whole enterprise set wonderful on the stomach.

Cassius belched. "Sorry," he said, but Little Rabbit laughed and pointed and clapped her hands.

"I think she taken a liking to you," I teased.

"Lord, I hope not," Cassius said. "I have had a time with these Indian wenches."

"You could do worse," I said.

"I ain't ready to marry anyone as yet," Cassius said. "Miss Sarah, I am going to make my excuses now. I'll get the horses ready and be waiting for you." He stood up and faced Little Rabbit. "Thank you for this good food, ma'am," he said, and bowed to her.

Little Rabbit rocked back and forth with laughter and said some words in her own language, then bowed back. "Good day," she said, as clear as anything.

"Good day to you," Cassius said, and headed for the corral.

Little Rabbit turned to me and said, "Hus-band?," pointing at Cassius' retreating back.

"No," I said. "Friend."

"Ah," she said. "Friend." And her eyes was thoughtful.

The camp, I noticed, was beginning to break up.

"Are you leaving?" I asked.

"We go—south," Little Rabbit said. "You, Big Water?"

"Yes," I said. "Big Water."

She reached out then and touched my cheek. "Friend?" she asked.

"Oh, yes," I said. "Friend." And I reached out and took her hand in mine, and held it to my cheek. "Friend."

She was silent a moment.

"Friend," she said, and eased upright, graceful as could be—only an Indian can rise up from that crosslegged sitting posture as if pulled by an invisible string—and walked away. I watched her go. Her back was slender and straight and her glossy braids shone blue-black against the pale doeskin.

"Friend," I said softly, under my breath, and joined Cassius and the horses. We rode back to the train, both of us thoughtful. I wondered what the Shoshone would find "south," and I wondered what we would find at the Big Water.

***

What happened to Little Rabbit and the others I did not learn, myself, until some years later.

The Shoshone went south, all right. It is a sad story, and too often repeated, for too many tribes.

They found no food. The game was all gone, and so they raided the white farms and settlements, and the whites demanded that the Indian thieves be caught or killed—killed being the preferred action.

The Shoshone moved on, those who survived—survived only to starve again in the southern lands, which was mostly held by the Saints, and so they marched north, to their old hunting grounds. And they was chased by the army, and finally hunted down at Bear River, and massacred, every one, down to the oldest old grandma and the littlest babe, the young maidens who would never be wives, and the boys who would never be warriors—and of course the soldiers killed what few remained of the last of the Shoshone warriors, too. Perhaps Little Rabbit was among the dead, perhaps not. I will never know.

I read it in the newspaper when it happened—in 1863 it was. I was living in Nevada then. I sent the clipping to Cassius, who wrote me, some months later, that he too had often thought of Little Rabbit. It was a shame, he wrote, a sin and a shame, that the Indians had to suffer so.

But most white folks did not think it a shame nor a sin. They was only too glad to see the Indians killed off. And as for the few whites who was less bloodthirsty, after the War Between the States most of those hailed the reservation system as the answer to the Indian "problem."

Somehow I could not picture Little Rabbit on a reservation, in cast-off white woman's clothing, dirty as only a Hang-Around-The-Fort Indian can be dirty, drinking the white man's liquor and lying under whatever white man gave her a taste of his bottle.

That was why, when I read about the massacre, I found myself hoping that she was one of those who perished. It would at least have been a clean death.

***

Well, we got to the Great Salt Lake all in one piece, for three days of repairs and replenishments. We dasen't take more than that, for we had a good ten weeks of traveling ahead of us, and it was already the end of July. None of us featured being on the trail when the winter snows began to fall in earnest. Which we was assured they would, starting in October.

Salt Lake City was a marvel even then, only a few years after the Saints had arrived. It was clear that they deserved their reputation as mighty builders, every man of them, and the women too was noble hard workers. The colony's emblem was the bee-hive, and in truth it reminded me of a colony of bees, every one buzzing along on his or her purposeful path, and never turning aside for any reason. The plot where the Temple was to be had been laid out, and the streets planned in a grid. It would be bigger than St Louis, I figured, by the time they was halfway done with the building.

Well, the colony prospered and grew, and one source of its prosperity was wagon trains, like ours, which stopped on the way West and required everything from new canvas to harness to livestock—all of which the Saints was only too willing to provide, at their price.

And I have to say here that the prices was fair, if steep; the argument advanced was the distance involved, and the hazards of doing business at such a remove from the centers of commerce. I doubt they made less than a hundred percent profit at any given time. And that was fair enough for me. I didn't begrudge the desire for any honest gain, and the Saints was honest to a man (or woman).

So we spent our time looking to our gear and our livestock and our supplies for the last long pull up to the Sacramento Valley. I would look back on that last leg of our journey with some satisfaction, if it hadn't been for what happened with Ned.

Ned had been having premonitions right along. Well, just as we was beginning to get ready to head out along the trail, we learned that Captain Sellers had sold him to one of the Saints, a big burly fellow who run a livery stable.

"You can't mean it," I said. "He's only lending you out, and he'll fetch you back on the return trip." After all, Ned had been with the Captain's family all his life.

"No'm, Miss Sarah, he has sold me outright," Ned said, and I could see he was near to weeping. "I can't stand it, Miss Sarah, I ain't never goin' to see the home folks again, and it's tearin' me up inside."

Cassius said, "Ned, are you certain? Maybe you misheard him."

"No, Mr Cassius, no. I hearn him plain as plain. He say to

this man, 'here is your new hand,' and the man give him a stack of money and Cap'n Sellers, he hand over a paper and tell me, get my things and go. 'You belongs to him now,' the Captain says to me."

Ned looked up at us through the tears that were falling now in earnest. "Oh, Miss Sarah! I ain't never thought to be sold away. I don't know none of these folks here."

Cassius cursed under his breath, then turned to me. "Miss Sarah, do you think you could talk to the Captain?" He looked at me with pleading, and I had to say, "All right, I'll try."

But I knew it wouldn't do no good. I''d met too many men like the Captain before. All they cared about was theirselves and what they could wring from every opportunity.

And so it proved. I said to the Captain, "Let me buy Ned— I'll give you half again what you was offered."

The Captain shook his head. "I have made a bargain and I aim to stick to it. This is business, ma'am, my business and my property, and you'd best leave mine to me."

"I'll give you *twice* what you been offered for him," I said.

"Ma'am, I wouldn't take your money if you was to offer me ten times over what I have sold him for. I said it before and I say it now for the last time: this is *my* business."

And that was that.

Captain Sellers was a hard man, and a sharp dealer, but now I was to learn that his sharpness was by no means confined to strangers. Next thing I knew, Captain Sellers had approached Cassius with a proposition: did Cassius want to earn some extra money by taking care of the Captain's horses?

"Should I do it, Miss Sarah?" Cassius asked me, troubled. "I ain't thinkin' he's wanting to do you a special good turn by taking over my labor—and I ain't goin' to have much time to take care of you and the oxen, and that's a fact."

"I can handle the team," I said.

Cassius sighed an enormous sigh that seemed to come right from his boots. "I come along on this trip to do for you, not for no Captain Sellers."

"But part of the agreement was that you were to work for the company, not just me," I reminded him. I pointed out that the Captain's horses and his gear were an essential part of the train, and without someone to care for them, the Captain would be unable to lead us.

"Maybe so," Cassius said.

"And he's going to pay you," I said. "You'll have a tidy bit put away when we get to San Francisco."

"I reckon I will," Cassius said.

"I'll take care of the oxen so you don't have to," I said.

"You ain't!" Cassius said. "That is not work for you."

Well, I argued and argued, and finally he saw reason. So I picked up the care of the oxen, and in doing so learned more and more to value those dependable beasts—and to look with new appreciation at Cassius himself, who had done this hard work all along, in addition to every other duty he performed. I perceived that I had been pampered, indeed.

Finally we was ready to depart that hive of busy, humming Saints. With a last look to our teams and our wagons, we headed out on the final leg of our long journey. It was five months since we'd left Independence, and if we wanted to reach our destination before the snows began to fall in the mountains, we'd have to pick up our pace in earnest.

But before we could leave, Cassius and I had to say goodbye to Ned.

We talked it over beforehand, and decided on what to give him for a farewell present. I counted out ten of my five-dollar gold pieces, and Cassius stitched them into one of the woolen vests I carried in my trading stock. I added some silk bandannas—red, blue, and yellow—which we wrapped the vest in, and I wrote out my name and Cassius's on a piece of paper, with the words *San Francisco* and *California* and *Williams' Emporium*.

"This is for you," I said to Ned, and Cassius handed over the little parcel. "And keep the paper, for someday you may come to California, and we'd be pleased if you'd look us up."

Ned cried and took on, saying—between sobs—how he knew he'd never see us again.

"Your new master might have some business out our way," Cassius said.

"It ain't no use," mourned Ned. "I goin' to die out here in the wilderness."

"This ain't no wilderness," I said. "It's a pretty big town, I'd say." I was trying to cheer Ned up some, but it didn't work. He just cried some more. He was still weeping when we shook his hand and took our leave.

I looked back down the street and saw him still standing there, his head bowed.

"I dunno why Captain Sellers wouldn't let me buy Ned," I said to Cassius. "He'd of made out by the deal."

"I expect he owed something to this man bought Ned," Cassius said. "You know how good Ned is with horses. Maybe he brung him all this way just to sell him."

"Ned said they usually didn't come this way," I said. "Could be you're right."

I warn't going to ask the Captain for verification, however, and we never did find out if Ned was part payment of a debt or if the Captain was simply being ornery when he refused to sell him to me.

Cassius pointed out that the Captain might have figured that I would simply free Ned, and the Captain, Cassius said, didn't hold with freeing Negroes.

"How do you know that?" I asked.

"He said so oncet when you wasn't around to hear," Cassius said. "I was getting water at one of our camping places and I passed by him whilst he was talking to that Mr Orren. The Captain, he said he wouldn't free any slave he owned and he was surprised that you did so. He said God intended the black man to serve the white man all his days."

I said I had heard that before.

"It's in the Bible," Cassius said.

"Is it?"

"Ain't you read the Bible?"

"No, I ain't. I don't hold with religion much, to tell the truth," I admitted.

"Is that a fact." Cassius shook his head. "I thought you was a Christian."

"Are *you?*"

"Surely."

"How can you follow a religion that says you are supposed to be a slave?"

Cassius allowed as no human could understand God's plan.

"I believe I don't think all that much of God," I said. "Seems to me I could have arranged a lot of things much better than He has." I gestured at my clothes. "This whole business of what's proper for women or for men, for instance. If I want to wear men's clothes, why is it wrong?" For I'd heard Mr Orren's sister-in-law say so, more than once. "Does God think He knows what's best for me? How can He? He ain't here! And why should He even care? It don't make no difference to Creation what-all I wear, or anybody else."

Cassius was shocked. "You oughtn't to talk that way, Miss Sarah. God is everywhere. Everybody knows that."

"Well, I don't."

It took a while to convince him, but finally Cassius give up attempting to save me, which was just the way I wanted it.

Later on I found out from Dr Thannheimer that the Bible was a whole lot of different books, all of them written by different folks, a long time ago and far far away, and there was plenty other religions in the world didn't even know about the Bible, they having their own books and stories. I figured that showed the Christian God warn't any big shucks. And since lightning never did strike me for saying so, Cassius allowed as how I might be right. But that was a long time after, and we'd found out what happened to Ned in the meanwhile.

The Saints, as I said earlier, was good at trade, and they sent out plenty of expeditions, one of which was run by the man who'd bought Ned. This particular Saint owned several teams and wagons he hired out for such trips, and he soon put Ned in charge.

Well, the wagon train that Ned was part of was ambushed by Indians, and everyone in the train was killed. That led to an expedition of soldiers to punish the Indians, and the Indians struck back, killing a party of settlers, which led to more soldiers coming and killing more Indians. Ned was scalped, by the way. I had some bad dreams back then—still do, at times—when I picture his long, gray, crinkly hair, still neatly tied, hanging at the end of some war lance.

So Ned was right—he did "die in the wilderness." I wonder if those gold pieces was buried with him, or if the soldiers who buried the bodies found them and took them.

I have given money in Ned's name and Little Rabbit's both, to a school for colored and Indian children. I make sure to send a good sum every year, and I have put it in my will for the money to continue after I'm gone.

I hope Ned's spirit rests easy out there in the desert. Or maybe, as Cassius used to say, maybe it flew home to Tennessee.

Chapter Ten: Gold Mountain

We eased on over the mountains with no more trouble than a busted axle or two; it was tedious going, from there on up to the Sacramento Valley, but we was trail-hardened, and soon enough it was done, and we made it in fact with time to spare. The first snows was blanketing the high Sierras when we jolted down into central California and made our last halt before the end.

I didn't find it hard to say farewell to Captain Sellers. He had turned mighty chilly on me since refusing to sell me Ned. As for most of the others in the train, we'd been cordial but not over-friendly, except for Ida Hagen and Doctor Thannheimer and Ernst, his nephew.

I give Ida a lace scarf and three pair of silk hose from my stores, as a farewell present, and she was mighty touched .

"I don't have anything to give you," she said, hugging me. "Wisht I knew where Husband and me was going to settle. I don't figure I'll ever see you again, Sarah, but I hope you do right well."

"And you the same," I said. "If you are ever in San Francisco—"

"I can't imagine we ever will be," she said. "But I will not forget you."

And we hugged each other again, and she was gone.

As for Doctor Thannheimer, he promised to write and let me know where he was, and he did so. I was to see him and Ernst again, many times, of which I will relate more later.

And so the train was disbanded, and we all went our separate ways. And come at last to the Bay and the settlement spread out below us, with ships so numerous down in the harbor that their masts sticking up looked like a forest. In fact, San Francisco at that time, 1851-52, was mostly harbor and very little town.

It had started out as a mission, like so many California towns running in a long string from south to north, missions named for saints by the friars who come to convert the Indians and turn them into peons—which was kind of like slaves, but not owned as such, to work the rich farmlands of the missions for the glory of God. These was Catholic friars, of course, but they aimed to do God's work just the same.

The mission had been named by the Spanish who first settled

there for San Francisco de Assis—but most folk called it Mission Dolores for the creek that ran by, Our Lady of Sorrow Creek. There was far more sorrows than joys, of course, for any human enterprise will likely come to grief more than glory.

As it was with me. The history of San Francisco has been written in tears and blood and fire. My own part of that history is scribed forever on my heart; the scars ache still.

***

The town itself, just a few short years before I arrived, was called Yerba Buena. It didn't become San Francisco 'til 1848, when the Americans taken it from Mexico. And until the gold-seekers come it was a small place, with no more vice than any other settlement. But within just a year of James Marshall's finding the first flakes of yellow metal at Sutter's Mill, the Barbary Coast was as notorious a den of thieves as you could find in the civilized parts of the world, or so folks said.

When I arrived, the miners' city was yet to rise on the slopes and hills above the bay. Most of the activity, as I have said, centered on the docks; in fact, a number of business enterprises were actually located on ships and other craft moored there and ranging in condition from seaworthy to nearly derelict.

Cassius and I settled the wagon in a likely spot, at a point where two thoroughfares intersected—actually they was mud trails, not even streets, but you could tell that someday soon they might be. I let down the awning and signboard over my stock and commenced at once to make money.

Lord, lord, but the money poured in, you might say, as dependable as the rain and fog that kept me in oilskins half the day. Cassius, too, had regretfully to abandon his greatcoat in favor of more weatherproof gear (the coat taking on water til it weighed more than he did), though he kept his beaver hat on, beaver fur being naturally water-repellent.

Before too long I had made a small fortune with my store on wheels in that tent city the Forty-niners begun to call Frisco. I moved my business to a storefront a short distance from the wharves as folks began to build more permanent structures. The old mission town and the lawless wharf district and the miners' tent city begun to shape themselves into something new. All this of course occurred following upon the War with Mexico, when more

136

and more Americans like me found their way clear to make their fortunes.

Now, you'll recall that I'd spent a good deal of time before and after leaving Miss Edwards's learning about business; over the years, I continued to read everything I could get my hands on that told on how to make money. I was lucky, of course, to have a stake—the money me and Tom found in the cave—and that gold, let out at interest, provided me with enough to equip myself.

Well, when I got to San Francisco, the goods I'd brought with me—and, eventually, those that arrived by sea—ended up being worth ten and twenty times more than any retailer back East could have asked, so that a pair of fifty-cent suspenders I could sell for five dollars, in gold!

The same was true for socks, or woolen drawers, or combs, or buttons and thread, or pins, or flannel shirts, or watches, or match-boxes, or tin lanterns, or peaches in brandy, or jam, or biscuits in tins, or calico shirts, or collar studs, or bars of German chocolate, or fancy belt-buckles, or leather billfolds, or peppermint candy, or patent medicines, or scented soaps from France, or a set of Sheffield steel razors with ivory handles—in a fine red morocco case—or chamber pots, or brass spittoons, or painted china pitchers and slop basins, or coffee grinders, or moustache wax, or hairpins, or curling papers, or stays, or petticoats, or garters, or French silk stockings with clocks[44] on them—for I carried a full assortment of ladies' goods, including rouge, Florida water, rice powder, tortoise-shell combs, pomade, attar of roses—

Well, you get the picture. I aimed to be the purveyor of the most variety of goods that were the hardest to come by in that place and time, and the entire wagon-load I'd brought was sold in just forty days, but I had already ordered seven times seven wagon-loads more, this time coming by ocean around the tip end of South America and back up to that great Bay where San Francisco still stands.

Yes, I made a powerful sight of money in San Francisco in the next ten years—over twenty thousand in profits, after expenses, and after I paid five thousand to Cassius for his time and trouble, I invested half back East with Judge Thatcher. The rest I invested in

---

[44] Eds. note: A fancy design on the side or ankle of a sock or stocking.

various ventures, which in time I would use to make my next stake—but of that I will tell later.

Cassius continued as my right-hand man, overseeing the store and supplies and making certain we kept up with the demand. When Levi Strauss begun to market his canvas pants, for example, we stocked as many pair as he could furnish. If miners took a notion to desire a particular item—be it silk socks or senna syrup or Hungary water—Cassius found a supplier. We made money without even trying; when we tried, we made even more.

I spent a great deal of time scouting out the land, so to speak; finally I found exactly what I'd been looking for: a corner lot, going cheap because it was an odd shape, sort of a chopped-off triangle just below Market, where two streets passed and intersected with a third. The lot, while irregular, was nicely situated. I was able to secure a 99-year lease and immediately set up my traveling shop whilst I located the wherewithal to build a more permanent version of Williams' Emporium.

I was able, in just a few months, to put up a store building with a covered shed behind where we cooked and ate. I took a room at the cleanest and least bug-infested of the hotels nearby, whilst Cassius bedded down inside the store with my Hawken loaded and ready to hand. He handled a good bit of the daily trade too, for I had to spend an unconscionable time keeping accounts as well as drumming up new business.

It warn't that trade was hard to come by—quite the reverse. But many of those who come to buy was possessed of other than legal tender, and I was of no mind to take less than what my goods were worth.

Folks forget that in those days "money" was of a staggering variety—francs, pesos, rubles, reals, dollars, shillings, pfennigs, yen, and whatnot. Not to mention gold, in dust and flakes and nuggets. Much dickering and haggling went on, and many times I accompanied a Forty-Niner and his little bags to the claims office, there to witness an assay and later to take a promissory note, in value redeemable in gold.

Gold. The gold-fever brought men from every corner of the world, and some of them survived it, but more of them succumbed.

Cassius swore that men came to him at every hour of the day or night, hoping to fulfill the promises that they made under the spell of gold. And when all of their gold was not sufficient to the task, it was never themselves they blamed.

Well. Be that as it may. I made a ton of money, and I made it fast.

There was never any lack of opportunity. However, I would soon discover a kind of opportunity that disturbed me greatly—the greater, perhaps, as there was nothing that I or anyone else could do about it.

I refer of course to what has been called "the oldest profession."

It has been said that there was no nation on earth that had not sent one of its number to San Francisco in those days, in the form of a prostitute. That may be true. They came by sea, mostly. People called them—the white ones, anyway—"soiled doves."

One of the realities of business life in the city was the need to cater to these soiled doves, these Jezebels, these Magdalens. The moral question aside, it become more and more difficult for me to trade with them, knowing that most of what they bought from me was used to attract their customers. And the better the prostitutes' business was, the more mine prospered. I ought to have been happy with this success, but I couldn't seem to manage it.

As I said, it warn't the morals of the thing, necessarily—I have always held that a woman ought to be able to share her personal favors with whoever she chooses. But these women was for the most part not free agents. Their pimps—*macquereaux* was the word that was used—took the bulk of their earnings, and those few girls who worked in houses was pretty much at the mercy of the madams, who used them nearly as hard. And the life was not one of ease, no matter what it might have looked like on the outside.

Many of the girls had diseases, more than a few had given birth to children they'd seen die at birth or shortly after at in various dreadful ways,[45] and most themselves died young, from sickness or violence or pure heartbreak. Quite a few smoked opium or drowned their sorrows in the bottle—both escapes being easy to come by. Often a woman who chooses whoredom, or falls into it as

---

[45] Eds. note: The practice of infanticide was common among prostitutes in San Francisco (and elsewhere). Babies were a liability, and there was no foster care available. Midwives in the employ of madams usually strangled infants at birth or threw them into the bay. A few were rescued, only to become child criminals or semi-slaves.

may be, is too soft for that profession. So many of them seemed fragile as butterflies, their bright colors fading too fast, their wings too frail for the storms of life.

Despite my misgivings, I was like most folks: I knew these women existed, and I knew why, but I tried to keep from paying too much attention to what I (and everyone else) knew, that these girls' lives was mostly miserable and short. Their money (or their pimps') was as good as anybody else's, and—or so I told myself—if I didn't trade with them, there was plenty of others who would.

So I silenced my conscience, which had a habit of rising up at most inconvenient times and saying, "That girl there, she could be your sister, and how do you know she ain't?" The result was, when one of these soiled doves come into my store, I was brusque with her, more so than was my habit with customers, and grimmer-faced than I wanted to be, for I felt that to let my pity show would be both patronizing and unhelpful. After all, what help could I offer? A girl who sold her favors, then and now, was a slave as surely as any black had ever been. Her macquereau saw to it that she never forgot it, neither. I made the best bargain with myself that I could, by undercharging such girls by whatever percentage I thought I could get away with, and cursing their pimps and their clientele in the richest language possible as soon as they were out the door.

Things might have gone on this way forever, until—

Well. This next will take some telling.

The way it happened was, I was taking advantage of a quiet afternoon, going over my accounts and trying to decide if I wanted to expand into household furnishings. There'd been a couple of inquiries, as more folks come in with an eye to permanent settlement, and the supply of bedsteads and armoires, bureaus and sofas and wing chairs and washstands, was something less than the demand. (Too many of these objects was left behind on the trail, of course, as I have mentioned, a state of affairs contributing to the aforesaid lack.) I was making notes to myself and thinking I'd have to add on to the store for display space when the doorbell tinkled.

I looked up to see a woman closing the door carefully behind her.

She was about my height, which is to say taller than most; her hair, what I could see of it, netted up and peeking out from under her bonnet, was likewise dark as mine. She had a purposeful look about her, and I made a mental wager that she'd already scouted the competition—what there was of it—and a sale, of whatever goods she'd come out to find, was a virtual certainty. However, I was prepared to dicker, if necessary.

"Can I help you, miss?" I asked, coming out from behind the counter.

I sized her up as a promising customer. She had on a green velvet bonnet trimmed in ostrich feathers, with a thick veil over her face, and she was fashionably dressed for walking, in a green broadcloth suit with black soutache trimmings, with her skirt looped up just enough to show her ankles in neat gaiters over serviceable but stylish black buttoned boots, and an umbrella hooked over one arm, together with a green velvet reticule.

"I need bedsheets," she said, putting up her veil and stripping off her green suede gloves. "Two dozen, if you have 'em."

"I do." I steered her over to the shelves where I kept what were called "domestics." "These is silk, from France, and these is Egyptian cotton, and these—"

She pointed. "Is that Irish linen?"

"New England manufacture," I said. "But yes, pure linen."

She reached out to feel of it. "Seems a bit thin," she said.

"Three hundred count," I said.

"Are those the only kinds you carry?"

I nodded.

"Well, then, I'll take two dozen of the linen."

"That'll be fifty dollars, miss."

She dug into her reticule and handed me five gold eagles. "Can you send them around today?"

"I'll have my assistant do it," I said, writing out her receipt. "What's the address?"

She told me, and I made a note. She begun to pull on her gloves, then stopped and stared at me closely. "Do I know you?" she asked. "You look familiar."

"I don't believe I've had the pleasure," I said. "I'm the proprietor of this establishment. My name is Sarah Mary Williams."

"I'm Olivia Quantrill," she said.

The way she said it, I sounded like "Cantrell."

My heart most stopped. "That was my mother's name," I blurted out.

"Was she from Ohio?" She continued putting on her gloves.

"No, Tennessee," I said. "But I come from Missouri."

"That's Q-U-A-N-T-R-I-L-L," she spelled. "Is it spelled the same?"

"Oh," I said, disappointed. "No, her name was Cantrell. C-A-N-T-R-E-L-L, I believe."

"Well, I did wonder," Olivia Quantrill said. "It's not a common name." She paused. "Missouri . . . you *did* say Missouri?"

"Hannibal," I said.

"Well, that *is* a coincidence," she said. "Because my sister did spend some time in Hannibal, when she was much younger."

"What's your sister's name?" I asked. My lips felt stiff, and it was hard to frame the words; seemed like I knew what she was going to say before ever she said it.

"Hagar," she said, and almost before she got it out, the room spun around and everything went black.

***

When I come to, with my head in this woman's green broadcloth lap, and her green suede hand waving a tiny amber glass phial of smelling salts under my nose, it took a moment before I was completely myself.

"What—what—" I stuttered.

"You fainted," she said. "It's all right. You slid right to the floor, easy as pie—I caught you on the way down—nothing broken nor bruised, is there?"

I sat up and felt of my arms and legs and passed my hands over my neck and head. "Seems like I'm all right," I said. "I'm sorry—" and I started to get up.

"Do it slow," she said, rising with me. "You don't want to keel over again right off."

I obeyed, for my head still swam. "Thanks." I reached my stool and hauled myself up onto it. I steadied myself with both hands on the counter, and shook my head.

"You said—" I took a deep breath. "You said you had a sister name of Hagar."

"That's when your eyes rolled back and you went down like a felled tree," she said. "So I'm guessing that was your mother's name, too."

"It was," I said.

Olivia Quantrill looked at me. Close up, I could see that her eyes, which had seemed brown or black, were dark, dark blue—like mine.

"I think you'd better come along home with me," she said. "Can you walk, do you think?"

I took a deep breath. "I surely can."

Well, I locked up the store and went with her. Cassius would be by soon, so I left a note for him, saying only that I had gone on an errand and expected to be back by evening.

And that was how I finally found Hagar Quantrill, who had once borne a child to Jimimy Finn.

Yes, she was indeed my mother—of that there proved to be no doubt.

***

The house—it warn't a house, really, to look at, on the outside that is, just a jumble of shacks and sheds— was built—or accumulated, partly on purpose and partly by accident, it looked like—close by the wharfs. It was typical. San Francisco in those days consisted of one rickety pile after another, with the wharfs sticking out into the bay, or falling into it, which happened more or less on a regular basis, along with the fires.

A lot of the city's business establishments was actually *on* wharfs, or on ships moored up to them, and fires was common. There was many times the city was ablaze—six or eight, I disremember, and each time things went back to just such a state as before, until finally the sea wall was built and the city took on a more solid kind of feel. But that was after I left it; when I come back, it was to a San Francisco I didn't hardly recognize, but for a few landmarks that remained, and most of them altered even so.

In those early gold-rush days, it was less a city of actual buildings than a collection of boards and battens, with roofs that tilted crazily and streets that meandered in the smoky light from torches and whale-oil lamps burning yellow in the fog. Ships and small craft piled helter-skelter around the wharfs and piers, some of them seaworthy and others having come to their last mooring.

Finally, we reached our destination. Olivia steered me around to the back, through a narrow alley, and we pushed through a stout wooden door into a long, dimly-lit hallway. I could hear music playing, faintly.

"In here," Olivia said, pushing me through a set of swinging doors directly into the kitchen, where a stout Mexican woman in a long white apron stirred a big pot on a handsome cooking range. "This is Rosita," Olivia said. "Our housekeeper."

"The madam is not well tonight," Rosita said to Olivia. "She has the headache."

"Is that so?" Olivia pointed with her chin at the stove. "Did she eat?"

"No," Rosita said. "She took a bottle of wine upstairs with her, that is all."

"So she's three sheets to the wind by now," Olivia said. "Well, might's well go on up."

We left the kitchen by a set of back stairs, at the top traversing one long hallway, richly carpeted and painted in soft, subdued colors. That was the pattern of many such places: outside, things looked about to collapse; inside, the furnishings was solid, even rich. Oriental rugs lay on the floor of nearly every room, for instance, with crystal chandeliers and velvet draperies throughout, but the windows facing the street was hung with plain green baize shades that let no light escape.

To someone who did not know otherwise, the place might have seemed uninhabited—but the knocks on the back door never let up, and the neat colored maid in her black dress and white apron and cap was kept busy letting in men and taking their hats and coats and canes.

I realized, of course, what the place was.

"Look here," I said, tugging at Olivia's hand. "I don't think…"

"Ah, here we are," Olivia said. "Just a few steps more. Follow me."

She kept my hand in hers, a strong grip. I swallowed, hard, and came along. We mounted to a square landing that held a console table on which stood an ornate brass lamp with a red glass shade.

(Now, I didn't see much on that first visit, but later I had the chance to look my fill.

It was always the same: the two big parlors was kept full of girls and their clients, the former in various examples of fashionable undress, the latter taking their ease in Madam's comfortable sofas and overstuffed chairs. Wine and whiskey could be had for only slightly less than ten times the going rate at any saloon. Every few minutes a man would heave himself to his feet, take a girl by the hand, and lumber out of the room. The sound of their boots going up (and later down) the stairs was a constant drumbeat.

There was a parlor piano in the right-hand parlor, and every evening a colored man named Professor Jerry came to play it. He was good, too. I heard a man say, once, that Professor Jerry had studied at a music college back East. That may have been true; at any rate, his playing was wonderful easy on the ears.

He was an older man, with long, curly white hair that he wore brushed straight back and falling to his shoulders, and he sported a neat white mustache and goatee as well that showed up well against his coppery skin. He had beautiful hands, with long, elegant fingers, and his nails was polished like pink shells, and he wore a white linen suit every evening, and a soft white shirt and a black string tie—the same outfit that Mr Mark Twain become famous for, later on, and I never see a picture of him in it that I don't remember Professor Jerry.

On this first visit, though, I could think only of what waited for me at the top of the stairs. It was a near certainty that the woman I was going to meet was the woman who had given birth to me, and left me, and for whom I had searched for months before coming West. I'd given up that search, but now it appeared to have taken on a life of its own and come to find *me*. Which sounds strange, I know, but that is what happened.

Olivia knocked at a half-open door. "It's me," she said.

A voice from inside the room said, "Who's that with you?'

"Somebody you ought to see," Olivia said. She winked at me.

I didn't think I could speak, but I managed it. "Miss Hagar?" I said.

She was there, standing just inside the door, a tall, dark figure. The room was dimly lit by a small dresser lamp, well on the other side of the heavy four-poster bed. "Who're you?"

"I used to be Huckleberry Finn," I said. The name sounded funny in my mouth, I was so used to being Sarah Mary Williams.

She made a sound—kind of a screechy moan—and her sister pushed me into the room and said, "For sweet Christ's sake, Hagar, pull yourself together!"

I edged into the pool of light.

Hagar Quantrill come close to me, so close I could smell her.

She smelt of cloves and wine and tobacco and cologne water and clean, ironed cambric. She was wearing a white nightdress, with a frill around the neck, and her hair was loose, hanging over her shoulders. I could see that it was still dark and curling, like mine.

"I thought you were dead," her voice came floating toward me, a deep voice with a throaty note to it, as if she'd had a catarrh lately, or been weeping.

"No'm, I ain't," I said.

"How come you here?" she asked.

Olivia snickered. "She runs a tidy little establishment up off the Square," she said. "I just spent last night's profits there, on new sheets. She carries quite an assortment. A good businesswoman, like her ma."

"It's no matter for laughter," Hagar said, still in that heavy voice. "You, Olivia. Bring her something to drink, will you?"

"Surely," Olivia said. "What about you, sister dear?"

"Bring something for all of us," Hagar said to her. "And tell Rosita to send up some supper."

Olivia left the room. Hagar Quantrill and I stared at each other.

"It's hard to believe. Are you sure you're not a ghost? *My* ghost, from a time and a time before. Why, you even look like me," she said, finally, and her eyes held mine.

I found it hard to breathe.

She came closer. "You aren't dead. I don't know. It feels—I don't know how it feels."

She turned away from me and sat down abruptly at her dressing table. I could see her face in the mirror, her eyes still staring into mine. She looked away and picked up her hairbrush.

"You. What do you call yourself? You're in business, my sister says." And she began to brush her hair. It was dark and coarse like mine, thick and unruly, and hung in a tangled mass down past her waist. It crackled as the brush passed through it.

"Sarah Mary Williams. I have a mercantile establishment," I said. "Selling goods and notions. Williams' Emporium."

"That your married name?" She still avoided my eyes.

"No'm, I ain't married. It's the name I took for myself."

Well, she wanted to know what I meant, so I explained about becoming Sarah Mary Williams. And that led to explaining about Tom Sawyer and about my going to school in Connecticut and my journey through Tennessee and on to the West.

Olivia came back after a while with the maid, carrying a tray of supper—buttered eggs on toast—so I stopped for a bit whilst we ate, then resumed.

"So I never did find any trace of you in Tennessee, and I decided to give up and come out here," I ended.

"That is not surprising," Hagar said, and laughed. "It was Ohio I come from. The only reason I was in Tennessee at all was to accompany my brother on some business he had."

"So you all have a brother?"

Olivia nodded. "Two. His name is Walter. There's another brother, Thomas, back in Ohio, but he doesn't approve of your mother and me. Or of Walter, for that matter."

"What was the business your brother had in Tennessee?"

Hagar answered. "It was about some wench he fancied—she'd pledged herself to him, but her father married her to some horse trader, and she'd gone off with her husband. Walter was away at the time, but when he came back, he took out after them."[46]

Olivia laughed. "I remember that! She didn't last long, poor thing."

I thought Olivia's tone was less than pitying, and I wondered what Olivia meant, but Hagar interrupted. "It's bad luck to speak ill of the dead," she said. "What I want to know is what your Pap told you about me."

"He said you left. He said he supposed you thought I was dead. He said he thought *you* was, for you run off in a storm and was never seen nor heard of again."

"Do you want to hear the whole story? The true story?"

Olivia stood up at this point and said, "I'll be going to bed, Sister—and niece. I've heard this tale before, and it ain't interesting enough for me to suffer through it again."

Hagar was silent while her sister left the room. Then she turned to the bottle of wine that stood on the dresser, poured herself a glass, and motioned to me to help myself. I shook my head. She sat back down, and began.

***

"I will tell you how it started," and she began:
I was fifteen years old. My brother Walter had asked for my help in

---

[46] Author's note: this might have been that second wife of the farmer Tobias whose kin I'd met back in East Tennessee; they told me that she had gone off with a man she'd known before being wed. If it is the same woman, then of course the man would have turned out to be my uncle Walter Quantrill.

hunting for the girl he wanted. He thought—and he was right, it turned out—that he'd have need of a woman's help in convincing her to go along with him.

Well, he'd gone off in search of a good place to camp for the night. And not more than an hour later, I saw a man with a gun up on a ridge, black against the sky.

I thought he was hunting Walter—for Walter has often been a hunted man, as you will find—and I crept up low and slow behind him and downwind, thinking to take him quiet-like, with my knife.

Here, she smiled a smile that chilled my blood. "I have some skill with the knife—I've been told I'm almost as good as a squaw."

I remembered the long, silver scar across Pap's breast, but held my counsel, and waited.

She went on,

I got close enough to him to feel the warmth of his flesh, and the knife was ready, but he turned around and caught me before I could plunge it in. And I was ready for him to turn my weapon on me, or fling me over the cliff onto the rocks and finish me with his gun, but instead he caught me by one arm and bent it 'til it nearly broke, then twisted my other wrist so that I dropped my knife.

He kicked the knife away, took a firmer grip on me, and started in to laugh.

"If this ain't the beat," he said, still laughing.

I tried to free myself, but he was too strong.

He was a tallish man, dark, with his hair in an old-fashioned queue tied with a thong; I judged him to be about thirty. I scowled at him. "How'd you do that?"

"I guess I felt you, or smelt you," he said, grinning. "Why'd you want to kill me? For sport, or do you have a better reason?"

"I thought you was after me," I said.

"I don't usually hunt womenfolk," he said. "But mebbe someone else does?"

"My pa is after me, and my brother," I said. "My pa is a preacher, and him and my brother aim to take me and stone me for committing adultery."

I had to think fast, you see, and come up with a tale he could easy believe.

"Is that a fact," he said.

"I was in love with a man," I said. "He betrayed me."

"Did he, now," he said.

"And so I decided to run away and hide my shame," I said.

"Ah. But they come after you."

"Yes," I said. "They are getting closer."

"Are they good shots?" he asked.

"Best in the county," I said.

"Preacher's usually a man of peace," he said.

"They believe in the sword of God," I said.

"What happened to your paramour?" he asked.

"They skint him alive and burnt what was left," I said.

"The sword of God, eh," he said. "Well, now."

He rearranged his grip, pulled the thong out of his queue, and tied my wrists with it, behind my back. With his dark curly hair loose and blowing, he looked younger.

"Let's you and me get better aquainted," he said. "Up there." He pointed to an outcropping of rocks high above the trail. "We'll wait there for your pap and his sword. And your brother too, you say?"

I nodded, and he helped me up the steep slope to where the rocks lay tumbled. I sat down, and he did too, but out of reach of my feet should I aim a kick. I saw that he marked me noticing this, and I realized he wasn't nearly as stupid as I'd taken him to be.

"My brother's got his woman with him," I said.

"And your ma? She come along, too?"

"She's been dead ten year," I said.

"So your pap's a widow-man."

"He is."

"And you keep house for him, do you?"

I nodded.

"Well, now," he said. "It's an old, old story, ain't it? A fine-looking young girl. Strict family—no pretties, no dancing, no play-parties. And this man you fell for—was he a merry one, full of smiles and winsome ways?"

"He was," I said.

"A youngish man?"

"About your age," I said.

"I can see how it was," he said. "I see it in your eyes. Pretty girl like you." And his hand reached out and gently laid hold of my right ankle.

I remember I looked at that hand for a long time.

Finally he took his hand away and spoke.

"I believe that must be your brother, yonder," he said. "Looks too young to be your pa."

I rose up a few inches, shaded my eyes, and looked where he was pointing.

It was Walter, sure enough, about a quarter mile below us, moving in a straight line in our direction.

My captor shifted his gun across his lap, and his grip tightened on the stock.

I had to keep this man from killing Walter, and there was only one way that I could see to do that. I turned toward him and said, breathless, "Let's leave, before he sees us."

"I c'n kill him for you," he said.

"Don't," I said. "I have no quarrel with him." I made my face appear indifferent, while all the while inside I screamed, don't kill him, don't kill my brother!

"What about the old man?"

"I don't care about him either," I said. "Let's leave. Let's go away from here, you and me, together."

"You and me, eh?" he said. "What about the child you're bearing?"

"Could be anybody's child," I said.

"Could be," he said. "All right. Let's get moving, then."

And so I came with him back to Missouri, and left my brother there in Tennessee."

She stopped and took a deep swallow of wine. "That's how it was."

***

We sat there in silence for many minutes. Then I asked, "Was any of that story true, that you told him? Had you loved some other man, and he got you with child?"

"You mean, are you some other man's get, and not Jimmy Finn's?"

"Yes."

"You understand," she said, "I had no wish to be caught in a lie. Your pap had a special way of punishing untruths."

I knew that to be a fact—I'd taken my share of stripes from Pap's belt, for fibbing. He had a convenient moral sense about most things, did Pap, but when it come to truthfulness, he was a stickler.

Which made me wonder anew: whose story was the true one, hers or his?

"Do you think he knew?" I asked.

"I can't say," she said. "Does it matter?"

I shook my head. "I guess not."

"So, let there be an end to questions, now," she said.

"One more," I said. "Did you ever—care for him?"

She shrugged. "I used him—and he used me harder." She

drank some more wine, and went on, "From the minute you was born, all I could think of was how to get away."

"Well," I said, "You managed that."

"Not before I got caught again." She drank more wine. "That is hard to explain, but I was a warm-natured woman in them days, and, well, one thing always led to another. Your pap had a way with him, sometimes. But I lost the baby."

"I know," I said.

"Ah, but do you know how I lost it?" She finished the wine in her glass, and poured another. Her hand was still steady, I noted.

"Pap said you thought it was his doing."

"I did, and I do," she said. "But it don't matter any longer. The baby was gone, and then you fell sick, and I thought I'd lost you. I think I lost my mind, too, for a while. If it hadn't been for Walter, I might have died."

"Walter found you?"

"He'd been looking for me for three full years, asking everywhere he went, and he travelled far up and down the river in those days. He learned where I was. He was coming across the river from the town, in a skiff, and he found me on the riverbank," her face was rapt, remembering, "And he kept me from throwing myself in—he took and hit me along the top of my head and knocked me senseless, then bundled me into the skiff and rowed away to a landing downstream, hailed a steamboat, and took me back up to the Ohio."

"So you never did know for certain if I was dead or alive?"

She was silent, holding her wineglass between her thumb and two long white fingers. "I didn't know, but I believed you were dead. I did not stay to find out, or come back to see. Perhaps I ought to have, but I didn't." She raised her head. "You hold that against me."

"I do," I said. "But I am willing to forgive it, if you are willing to be forgiven."

"I don't know," she said. "It is all so strange. You, here—"

"It has been a long road that led us both here," I said.

"Somehow I can't feel that you are my daughter," she said. "Although I know you must be. You look so much like me, for one thing. And yet there is a look of him, too."

"Of Pap?"

"A trick of the light, maybe," she said. "But no. It is there.

151

You have his mouth," and she traced her own lips, which was broad but thin, the upper one precisely bowed. My own was fuller, the lower slightly protruding, and the upper not as sharply cut.

I laughed. "I don't believe I ever saw Pap's lips under all his whiskers!"

She smiled, a sad little smile I thought it was. "You spoke of forgiving," she said. "I will forgive you your hatred, if you forgive me for my lack."

"I don't hate you," I said.

"I am glad to know it," she said.

We shook hands, then, like two men.

"Come see me tomorrow," she said.

"I will." I left her, then.

When I looked back, as I stepped out of her room and into the hall, she was still sitting by her dressing table, her hair hanging around her in a dark cloud, an empty wine glass in her hand.

Chapter Eleven: Walter—and William

After that first meeting, I returned to Hagar and Olivia's brothel many times.

I was not exactly a part of the household, but Rosita and the Professor and Carlos and the other servants accepted my presence at any hour of the day or night, as did the girls, though I saw less of them, they mostly being occupied when I visited.

I was troubled by this trade of my mother's and aunt's, for —as I have wrote earlier—I knew what the girls' lives were, and had no reason to suppose that my mother and aunt were less harsh in their rule than any other bawdy-house proprietresses.

I fretted over it, and went over in my mind many times how I ought to say to Hagar and Olivia: *this trade of yours is wrong, wrong, and it is wrong of me to visit you, to drink your drink and eat your food and sit in your chairs that are all bought with the flesh of other women, women like we are.*

I knowed I ought to. But I never did. And why was that?

The question still bothers me, all these years since.

Cassius certainly had something to say about it—and what he said made me squirm. He said it was worse than slavery.

"Those Quantrill women. You know what they do," he said, and his voice dripped contempt, "How they get these girls to work for them?"

"I don't know," I said.

"You might ask," he said. "I can tell you they's a standing order on the docks, send any likely girls to Miss Hagar, Miss Olivia." He scowled at me. "Miss Sarah, you ain't use the sense God give you. What kind of woman takes up a life like your mammy an' your aunt? They worse than slave-traders, in my book."

"I hadn't thought of it that way," I said, unwilling.

"Well, you best think of it," he said. 'Woman ain't got no way to feed herself 'cept on her back is not a free woman even if she a white woman."

"What do you mean?"

"I mean she *bought*. Just as much as a slave be bought," Cassius said. "Where she gone go? Who she gone tell? What she gone *do*?"

I offered Olivia's argument, that she and my mother cared for the girls and treated them well, but Cassius would have none of it.

"What happen to these women if'n they can't work?"

"I don't know," I said.

"Suppose they sick? Suppose they in the family way? What then?"

"I don't know!" I was beginning to feel put upon. "Why don't you ask my mother or my aunt, if you're so concerned?"

"Not my place to be concern," said Cassius. "Your place, though. These women, they ain't got no other chance, no other choice for how to live, how to eat, what to do."

"It's my mother's business, not mine."

"Seem to me the Good Book say something about brother's keeper," Cassius said. "Sister, too."

But my mother and aunt seemed to find all such objections easy to dismiss.

"For heaven's sake, Sarah," Olivia said. "These girls come here in droves, looking for a life on Easy Street. We don't seek them out; *they* find *us*. We keep them safe, we dress them in lovely clothes and feed them and pamper them, and we pay them a share of their earnings. Why, there's no reason on earth any one of them couldn't save up and go into competition with us, isn't that so, Sister dear?"

"That's so," Hagar said.

"But they don't have the gumption. They're happy to let someone else take care of them. They're happy with us," Olivia said. "Most of them don't have the brains of a calf. They'd be lost without our guidance. Isn't that true, Sister?

Hagar obliged with several tales she had ready, about girls who'd tried to freelance, so to speak, and been raped or robbed, or who'd gone off, against orders, with clients who hadn't been properly vetted and suffered damage thereby.

And when I tried asking some of the girls directly how they felt about it, they all said the same.

"Oh, yes, Miss. We love working for Madamoiselle Hagar and Madamoiselle Olivia," they all said, nodding their heads like puppets and talking very fast and all at once.

Olivia popped up then, like a jack-in-the-box, and they all scurried back to their rooms, still chattering about how much they enjoyed their work.

Olivia looked at me and smiled. "You see?"

I did, but I also see that the girls was afraid of her, and that was not reassuring.

154

But then Hagar and Olivia was always pointing out that their girls was well fed and housed and clothed and had every opportunity of improving themselves. "Only," said Hagar, "They are too lazy. The kind of women who become whores, Sarah Mary, tend to be lazy by nature, you see. It's a shame, but it's so."

"That's right," said Olivia. "They enjoy the life, Sarah dear. And if they don't, why, they're free to go."

"Of course," said Hagar.

So I left it, still feeling mighty uncomfortable, like you are with a tooth that stops hurting but always threatens to start up again.

I couldn't figure out how to deal with the situation except to make a break with Hagar, and—this is hard to tell, harder still to explain to myself, even—I just couldn't. Not yet.

I didn't know Hagar at all, seemed to know her less and less as time went on, but I thought there might be something there, some feeling for me, something she hadn't told me, yet, about who I was and how I came to be, and I didn't want to leave off until I was sure there wasn't any more to tell.

For of course I did not believe the story she'd laid out for me, on our first meeting. She had lied, but how much? And what, exactly, did her lies hide from me? I told myself that I did not want to go away and give up my last chance of finding out.

Thankfully, I had my own business to run, and turned to it with new resolve. I dared not take too much time away, though Cassius was, as always, reliable and honest. He shook his head whenever I went off to the house, though, and predicted over and over that no good would come of my new acquaintances. Olivia in particular he seemed to dislike, and when she visited the store he always found a reason to be absent.

Slowly I grew to understand the relationship of the two sisters: Olivia handled the personnel side of the business, recruiting and training (and disciplining) the girls, whilst Hagar was responsible for record-keeping and what Olivia called "community relations." These consisted partly of Hagar's monthly dinners (with plenty of cigars and brandy and the pick of the girls, no charge) for San Francisco's most important leaders.

Oh, yes: Hagar presided at these feasts, with her hair piled high and pinned with rubies and black ostrich plumes, wearing a low-cut black velvet gown embroidered with tiny jet beads, in red

155

stockings and red-heeled black satin slippers, smoking her favorite small black cigars in a long, red-lacquered holder. I was present at several of these functions, and watched her tap this man on the shoulder, teasingly, with her fan; saw her look up through her lashes at another, and hold out her hand to be kissed by still a third.

She was a handsome woman, and more than that: she gave off a smoldery kind of effect that was like a scent in the air, drawing men to her. I thought of a black widow spider; I thought of an evil sorceress like the ones in the tales Tom Sawyer used to tell. She used her femaleness like a weapon, and the men fell without even knowing they'd been hit a deadly blow.

For she got everything she wanted from them: the Police Commissioner looked the other way when complaints come in about the girls and their trade. The Commander of the Fort kissed her fingers, one by one, and swore gallantly that he and his men were her devoted servants. The leaders of the business community vied with one another over who would be the first to offer her investment advice, and the bankers elbowed each other aside for the privilege of issuing her credit.

It has taken me years and years to acknowledge, and it is still not without pain, that whatever ability I have to clinch a sale is likely something she passed on to me.

Likewise my talent for lying—to give it its plain name. I have always been able to make up a story to serve any purpose at hand.

And that gift, if it is a gift and not a curse, came from Hagar, too.

For a long time I suffered with this knowledge, because everything she touched, she poisoned or dirtied. I was afraid, and I suffered with that fear for many years, that I had inherited that talent as well.

For what that was good had I gotten from those two who begot and bore me? That was the question. I was low-down and ornery from birth, and Pap had never showed me how to be different. But despite my rearing, I couldn't claim *not* to know right from wrong, for the Widow and later Aunt Polly and Aunt Sally had showed me and taught me. And Mary Jane, too. I had every example of proper, Christian womanhood before me. I could clearly see and choose the moral path. And here I was, consorting freely with a woman of ill fame—the madam of a bawdy-house— my own mother.

It didn't help that her sister, Olivia, obviously found me a threat, and though she never spoke any way but sweetly to my face, her expression gave the lie to her words. She complained to Hagar that I took up the girls' time when I visited, keeping them from their duties—which was a lie—and she also took every opportunity to criticize me, always doing so in a way that seemed as if she might be offering helpful advice.

This galled me, but I didn't know how to put a stop to it, so I tried my best to avoid her. Hagar seemed not to notice, mostly, though she did speak somewhat sharpish to Olivia once when she— Olivia—was going on about my clothes. I didn't dress stylishly nor follow the fashions. "I don't see how you expect to sell to folks who want the latest styles, the way you look," Olivia said.

"She looks fine as she is," Hagar said, and Olivia shut up.

I did like to look at pretty things, and I enjoyed seeing pretty women wear them, too, but somehow I never found the urge in myself to preen and primp. I looked best, to my own eyes, in clothes that were plain and simple, and with my hair braided and coiled neatly out of my way.

And then Walter arrived.

***

Hagar sent me an invitation to a private supper.

Dear Sarah Mary, please come to supper on the 15th of November, at 9 in the evening. Your Uncle Walter has come to town and wishes to make your acquaintance. Sister Olivia and I await your response by return message.

The note was delivered by Rosita's eldest son, Carlos, a tall, lean, sloe-eyed seventeen-year-old. Olivia and Hagar employed him around the place, doing various chores and errands—and, in Olivia's case, as I later discovered, performing some private duties as well.

"Tell them I will be there," I said, giving him a dollar.

He raised his cap a fraction and slouched out. I looked at the black letters on the white paper and wondered about my Uncle Walter. After all, he was, in a sense, the cause of my mother and father's meeting in the first place, or so Hagar had said, so I figured he might be considered as part of the reason I had come to exist.

Hagar often spoke of him with pride, Olivia never. This difference in their reactions interested me, as did the picture of Walter that Hagar kept on her night-stand, of a tall man, about forty,

I judged, slender and handsome, who seemed, somehow, very familiar.

I supposed that was because he looked a great deal like Hagar, which is to say, like me—he had dark, almost black curling hair, worn longer than common, and high cheekbones, with eyes a shade lighter than one might expect in one so dark-complected. (I knew from Hagar's description that they were deep blue, like hers and Olivia's and mine.) He wore a thin pencil-line of a mustache, and he held, in one hand (curiously, I thought, for a man) a fan, in fact the very one that lay atop Hagar's bureau, a carved ebony-wood fan with a black velvet cord. He seemed in the picture to be smiling faintly, though if so it was a smile that never reached his eyes.

***

I dressed with care for that supper, in a gown Olivia had ordered for me, having finally worn me down with her urging. Hagar had added her support, they both saying that my uncle was a man of fashion, and deserved to meet his niece when she was looking at her best.

I remember every detail of that costume: the gown itself was of deep golden-brown velvet, trimmed with tiers of gold lace and garlanded with velvet swags, and I wore gold-lace mitts and a Chinese shawl of heavy silk, cream-colored, figured with a design of dragons and phoenixes in gold and brown, with a ten-inch fringe. I twisted my hair into a knot high on my head and held it in place with gold combs, and in my ears (for at Hagar's urging I had had them pierced) I hung topaz ear-bobs. Round my throat I wore a golden chain hung with a single topaz the size of a hazel-nut. My slippers was cream-colored velvet embroidered in gold, with gold heels, and my stockings ivory silk. When I finished dressing, I looked at myself in the tall cheval mirror in my bedroom, and I saw not a trace of Huckleberry Finn anywhere—and very little of Sarah Mary Williams. I looked like a golden idol, my eyes shadowed and mysterious, my figure slim but with enticingly rounded breasts showing half-moons above the low-cut bodice. I touched my wrists, my temples, and the valley between my breasts with a perfume I'd ordered from France, a scent that smelt of jasmine and orange-blossoms.

Hagar's carriage came for me promptly at eight-thirty. When I arrived at the house, I was immediately ushered upstairs to Hagar and Olivia's private sitting-room. The square table of ebony inlaid with mother-of-pearl was laid for four, with candles already lit in their branching silver candlesticks, as well as three lamps, so there was plenty of light. And so I saw my Uncle Walter Quantrill for the first time, and I saw him very clear.

He was as handsome as his picture—more. Though he was old enough to be my father, he moved like a young man. He was slender and tall, beautifully dressed and groomed. Again I felt that strange sense of familiarity.

He bowed debonairly over my hand, then drew me to him and kissed my cheek. Although his lips were soft and his breath scented, I found myself repelled, and resisted an urge to scrub the spot with my mitted hand.

"Ah, shy as a fawn," he said, and chuckled, then drew my hand through his arm and turned me toward his sisters. "Thank you, my darlings, for this lovely surprise."

Hagar raised her wineglass. "To my dear daughter—your niece."

"*Our* niece," Walter said, nodding to Olivia, who said nothing, but looked (as usual) half-amused, half-scornful. William ignored her and turned back to me.

"Hagar has been telling me about your tribulations, my dear," he said. "I am sorry not to have known of your circumstances earlier. Perhaps I might have been able to assist you."

"I don't see how you could of known," I said. I didn't care much for his tone, patronizing as it was. "I ain't—haven't—had as many *tribulations* as some. And as for assisting me, I have done pretty well on my own, I think."

"Of course you have," he said, and poured himself some wine, then poured a glass for me and handed it to me with a little bow. "Of course you have. You can do still better, however, if you wish it."

"How is that?"

"Investing . . . in the right properties, of course."

Hagar rose and went to the bell-pull. "I think we'd best have our dinner before going on with this conversation."

"Certainly, sister," he said. "Come, let us enjoy the pleasures of the table. I have not had the pleasure of dining with three lovely ladies for some time."

Hagar preened herself at this compliment. Olivia curled her lips in a sneer, though he had spoken truly: both sisters were looking beautiful, Hagar in her usual black velvet and Olivia in a rich, rustling satin the color of the sapphires she wore at her neck and wrists and ears.

Walter himself sported a beautifully cut frock coat in deep forest-green, with black trousers, gleaming black boots, and a dazzlingly white, ruffled shirt. His waistcoat was cream-colored satin, embroidered all over with green leaves and vines, his cravat was wine-colored watered silk, and he wore an opal stick-pin that shot darts of fire in all directions. His hair was brushed very smooth and rippled close to his well-shaped skull, and his mouth, I noticed, was very red, the lips full. His teeth gleamed.

"Shall we be seated?" He pulled out our chairs and sat down himself, and Rosita bustled in with our meal.

I can't recall the details of what we ate—some kind of Frenchified dish, chicken and mushrooms in a creamy sauce, with rice—but I do remember that I drank several glasses of the pale-yellow, fizzy wine Hagar had ordered, and after the dinner was over I accepted a Cognac with my coffee, and puffed away on one of Walter's elegant cigarettes. "A new vice," he said airily. "They're all the rage in Europe."

"Have you been to Europe?" I asked, feeling a trifle muzzy.

"Not recently," he said.

"Not ever," Olivia said under her breath, but everyone heard her.

"Dear Olivia," Walter said in his silky voice. "It may or may not interest you to know that you are wrong." He reached over to refill my glass. "I was in a French prison for a full year, while you were stuffing yourself with pastries and growing fat."

Olivia made a sound, but Hagar shot her a warning look.

"What were you in prison for?" I asked. The Cognac, on top of the wine, made me feel muddled, but it was not an unpleasant sensation.

"Murder," he said.

Both sisters continued to sip their Cognac without expression.

"Who'd you kill?" I asked.

"A sensible question," Walter said. "Nobody—that is, the man was no one worth considering. A common thief—who tried to rob *me*." He laughed. "He ended up with my knife between his ribs, instead of the treasure he sought."

"What treasure was that?" I asked, thinking that Walter and

Hagar both were way too handy with their cutlery for my taste.

Walter finished his Cognac and lit another cigarette. "Jewels—from an Egyptian tomb."

This was beginning to sound, I thought, like one of Tom Sawyer's stories about caravans of Spanish merchants and rich A-rabs and a thousand sumter mules, all loaded down with diamonds, and whatnot.

"Go on," I said.

"Egypt," he said. "Ah, the pyramids of the Pharoahs! I stole the jewels in Cairo and fled the country with all the forces of Ali Pasha in pursuit, but I arrived in France with my booty intact. Unfortunately, on the voyage this low criminal, this Frenchman, had discovered my secret, and he attempted to steal the jewels from me. I killed him, but I was seized by the police and thrown into prison."

"How'd you get out?" I was fascinated in spite of myself. He gave out with lie after lie with a perfectly straight face. Olivia and Hagar likewise didn't crack a smile. I figured they was in on the joke. "And what happened to the jewels?"

"I smuggled them out of the country in your mother's lovely bosom," he said.

Hagar leaned back in her chair, smiling, her hands caressing her bodice lightly. "This very bosom," she said. "Ah, yes. What more natural than that a man's sister should rush to his aid? I took ship for Marseilles directly I heard of Walter's trouble, and I gained permission from the Sultan to visit my poor brother in his cell. And there he gave the jewels to me, and I brought them back—here." She gestured around her. "All of this was bought with those jewels."

"And so," Walter said, with a bow in my direction, "I own the largest percentage of stock in this establishment."

"Unfortunately," Olivia said.

"For you, maybe, dear sister," Walter said. "But I pay you a handsome salary, do I not?"

Olivia looked pointedly at Hagar. "And I earn every penny of it."

"Well, that is true enough," Walter said.

Hagar began to laugh. "You're a caution, Walter, you really are." She turned to me. "Of course you understand that your uncle here is the greatest liar this side of the Mississippi."

"I flatter myself that that is true on the eastern side as well,"

Walter said, sounding a trifle wounded.

"All right," Hagar said. "In any case, you understand, Sarah dear, that there were no jewels and there was no Egyptian tomb, no Ali Pasha, no French dungeon—"

"Prison," Walter said.

"Dungeon, prison, no matter," Hagar said. "It's all your uncle's imagination, don't you see? We three came to this place and acquired this property not with jewels but cold, hard cash."

"Mostly acquired through my skill at cards," Walter said.

"Some of it," Olivia broke in. "Some of that same cold, hard cash came from me."

"Of course, dear sister," Walter said, bowing. "Your professional skill has also been of inestimable value."

Olivia only looked at him with loathing. "You'd be the best judge of that, no doubt."

Walter bowed again. "You, dear sister, should know. And now, sisters and niece, I must take leave of you. I have some affairs to which I must attend. Au revoir."

And he left the room, calling for Carlos as he went. In his wake a thin curl of smoke wavered and dissolved.

I stared after him. What was it that nagged at me about this man? What? There was something I needed to remember—

Hagar and Olivia sat close together, talking in low voices, too low for me to hear.

What *was* it about him that pulled so insistently at a place in the back of my mind, a place I'd almost forgotten—and, I knew, had been eager to forget.

Where had I seen him before—and seen him as someone to fear?

And then it come to me.

I was back on the raft, with Jim. I could smell the brown water flowing under us, feel the damp air stirring faintly as we followed the current along.

Sixteen years fell away as if they had never been.

The Duke had had just such finicky ways, and just such a soft but poisonous air about him.

The Duke. Bridgewater himself—water?—Bridgewater? Oh, God—*Walter*—

My uncle Walter.

My old enemy—the thief and liar who'd sold Jim away from

me, who'd kept us prisoner on the raft, who'd almost succeeded in stealing Mary Jane's inheritance from her and her sisters—

I had recognized him. And he knowed me, too.

That being the case, I realized, my life warn't worth much.

But more than the danger I was in, the disgust and loathing I was feeling had me in a state. I wanted to vomit, but sat rigid in my chair, not daring to move nor even hardly to breathe.

Olivia rose from her chair, walked to the window, and stood for a moment, looking out.

"He's hatching something," she said to Hagar.

Hagar shrugged. "He is," she said. "As usual. I've no interest in his future schemes, not any longer."

"No. You have what you want," Olivia said.

"I have."

"But I don't." Olivia sat down again and picked up her glass. She swished the wine back and forth idly and said, "What about the boy?"

"Ah." Hagar said. "What about him?"

I managed to croak out, "I don't understand what's going on. Will someone please tell me? What boy?"

They both turned and looked at me. Hagar nodded.

"Your uncle Walter has a young protégé," Olivia said. "His nephew, and mine. Your cousin, William Quantrill. Only fifteen, but a promising specimen."

"You would be one to know," Hagar said.

"And what of it?" Olivia laughed, deep in her throat. "He's a sweet boy, your cousin. Wouldn't you like to meet him?"

"No," I said.

Hagar shot me a look. I realized, with a surge of nausea, that she knew I had recognized her brother. And didn't care.

I shrugged.

"Oh, come," Olivia said. "You'll like him."

There was a faint knock at the door. "Why, here he is. William, come in and meet your cousin, Miss Sarah Mary Williams," and she crossed to the door and opened it with a flourish.

In the doorway stood a tall boy, dark-haired and slender. He entered the room with a kind of swagger, holding his head high.

"Aunt Hagar, Aunt Olivia, good evening," he said. "Is this lady my cousin? How delightful." He smiled at me. "Pleased to make your acquaintance."

It was a sweet smile, and a handsome face. Why, then, did I sense danger? My blood shrieked in my veins: keep him away from me! Evil, evil. My stomach heaved.

"I don't feel well. I want to go home," I managed to say.

"Soon," Hagar said. "Soon."

"Yes," Olivia said. "We've much to talk about, we four."

"I don't want to talk to you," I said. "I want to go home."

William strolled over to my chair and stood there, looking down at me, close enough to touch. I shrank away.

"You know, she looks just like my oldest sister," he said.

"Does she?" Hagar asked. "How interesting . . . these family resemblances."

"Yes . . . " He paused. "My sister was a whore, too."

That made me angry.

"Well, I ain't," I said. I might fear him, but I was damned if I'd let him see it again.

"You are," William said, and his tone made me quiet right down.

I'd heard that note before, in my nightmares. It rang in the voices of madmen who rode down Indian children and killed them from horseback like vermin, who gloried in the killing and in the torture that led up to it, who boasted of slicing women's breasts from their bodies while their victims bled and prayed to die.

"You're a whore," he repeated, "And I'm going to kill you, same as I killed her."

"Don't tease your cousin. The poor dear," Hagar said to me, "He was very attached to his sister. Why, it broke his heart when she—died."

I wondered just what it was that the sister had done, to merit losing her life at the hands of this insane child, who looked at me and smiled so warmly whilst he spoke of killing.

Olivia yawned, stretched, then said to William, "That's enough for now. Ring for Carlos, dear. We must get your cousin to bed." She stood up and turned toward the door.

"I feel sick," I said.

William reached for the bell pull.

"Here, darling, drink this," Hagar poured something into a glass and handed it to me. "It will help."

I drank it down—it was sweet and strong—

And then I knew no more.

***

When I awoke, I was in Hagar's bedroom, lying full length on a chaise. It was daylight—I could see the light shining in at the windows. My gown had been removed, as had my stays, and I was in my chemise and petticoats, with a light blanket thrown across my lower body.

Hagar was sitting at her dressing table in her night-gown, brushing out her hair. It was lively, that hair, rustling and crackling under each stroke of the brush. I watched for a long time, transfixed by the sight of her: my mother, beautiful and deadly, as she brushed her hair and gazed into her mirror, her face calm as a lake and hiding secrets as deep.

I spoke. "What time is it?"

Hagar turned, still holding her brush. "Oh, you're awake," she said. "It's nearly ten o'clock in the morning, actually. I've sent for some tea. I am so sorry I had to drug you, dear, but it was best, really it was."

"The truth," I said. I was still feeling weak, and my face hurt, and my head.

"Truth," Hagar said. "Those who seek it seldom want it when they've gotten it."

"Tell me," I said.

"When you're feeling better," she said, and she rose and came over to the chaise, still holding her hairbrush. "Don't you think you'd like to sleep a bit longer?"

"No," I said.

"Of course you would," she said.

The door opened, and Olivia, in a dark-green velvet dressing gown, came in with a tray. On it were a teapot, a sugar bowl and cream pitcher, and three bone-china cups and saucers. She put the tray down on the dressing table and smiled at me.

"We were very worried about you, Sarah," she said. "Let me pour you some of this nice hot tea." She poured some into one of the cups and added sugar and cream, then took something from her pocket. It was a small glass vial with a cork stopper. She pulled out the stopper and let a few grains of some kind of grainy, glittering powder fall into the tea. She stirred it with a silver teaspoon and brought it over to me.

"Hold her," she said to Hagar, who wrapped her arms around me and held my hands tightly in hers. I struggled to pull free, but

165

she was stronger than I was.

"Drink this," Olivia said, and held up the cup.

"I won't," I said, but Olivia took me by the hair with her free hand and held the cup to my mouth, forcing it between my lips.

I tried to keep them closed, but the cup's edge cut me cruelly, and against my will some of the liquid got into my mouth. I tried to spit it out, but Olivia's hand now covered my mouth and nose so that I could not breathe, and I swallowed, while tears of rage came to my eyes.

"That's a good girl," Olivia said, taking her hand away and letting go of my hair. Hagar, too, released me and patted me on the shoulder.

"You'll feel better soon," they both said, but I heard their voices only dimly, and their faces receded from me. My last conscious thought was that a storm had come, for the light faded like their voices, and as the darkness took me I heard only the thudding of my own heart.

Chapter Twelve: Desperate Straits

This time I was unconscious for a long time, and when I come to I was in a small room, lying in a narrow bed and covered with a flowered quilt. I did not recognize the room, but it was equipped with a chamber pot, which I rose and used, feeling stiff and achy.

There were no windows. I tried the door, which was locked.

I waited. I was starving, and also thirsty. There was a half-cup of tepid water in the pitcher. I drank it and waited some more.

Finally, someone came.

It was one of the girls—the small redhaired Irish girl, the one with the orange freckles and pale green eyes like unripe gooseberries. I had talked with her a few times—I remembered her name.

"Annie," I said. "Annie, did you bring food?"

"No'm," she said. "Miss Hagar, she said not to give you none."

"This is your room, isn't it?" I said.

"Yes."

"How long have I been here?"

"Only a night. I stayed with you," she said.

Dimly I recalled someone beside me in the night, someone's helping me to squat over the chamber pot, someone's holding a cup of water to my bruised lips.

"You've been taking care of me. Thank you."

"The Madam—"

"She told you to."

"Yes'm. She—"

I decided to take a risk. "Annie—would you like some money? A lot of money?"

She looked at me, her face guarded. "What for?"

"For yourself," I said.

"Where you gonna get money?"

"I have a lot of money in the bank, Annie. I can get it for you, if you'll help me."

"You want me to help you get out of here," she said.

"Yes."

"I dursen't."

"We can slip out when everyone's asleep," I said.

167

"She'll find out."

"No, she won't. We'll be gone before she ever knows."

"She's got Carlos guarding the door. He has a pistol."

This was a bit of a poser.

Cassius. If I sent Annie to Cassius, he could get the sheriff to come, or some soldiers, maybe, from the Fort.

"Will you take a message for me, Annie, if I pay you?"

"Message to where?"

"Do you know my store? Williams' Emporium?"

"Miss Olivia buys us our stockings and notions from there," Annie said.

"Do you know where it is?"

"Yes'm."

"Well, my clerk, Cassius, is there. He's a black man—a free Negro. Have you seen him?"

Annie allowed that she had seen Cassius once or twice.

"Go to him and tell him where I am, Annie."

"I dursen't. We ain't none of us supposed to leave the house without telling Miss Olivia or Miss Hagar."

"But I need you to do this for me, Annie," I said, as persuasive as I could manage.

"How much you pay me?"

"I will give you my topaz earrings," I said. They still hung in my ears, though the necklace and ring had been taken from me.

"They real gold?" Annie said.

"Yes, real gold."

"I want money, too," Annie said.

"Cassius will give you money," I said. "If you get me a piece of paper and a pencil I will tell him to give you a hundred dollars—in gold."

"A hundred dollars!" Annie's eyebrows shot up her forehead. "I only make fifteen a month here."

"Just think what you can do with a hundred dollars in gold, Annie," I said.

"It is a powerful lot of money," she said.

"Will you help me, Annie?"

"I—I don't know," she said, backing away from me.

"Please, Annie," I said. "Please—haven't I always been nice to you?"

She wavered.

"Annie," I said, wheedling, "I'll tell Cassius to set aside a silk wrapper for you, and a fan like Miss Hagar's."

"A Chinese wrapper? And a fan?"

"A silk wrapper . . . in sea-green silk, to match your eyes. And an ivory fan, with ostrich plumes."

Annie refused to say yes or no, but she did tell me that she'd be back when she'd done her afternoon duties.

"Where will you be? This is your room," I said.

"Oh, Miss Olivia let me use Mr Walter's room for working," she said. "Whilst he is away on business."

"He's gone away?"

"Yes; he and Master William. They will be coming back next Tuesday, so I hear."

"What day is today?"

"Thursday."

"How long have they been gone?"

"Oh, they went right before you was brought here, Miss."

Gone to Hannibal, no doubt.

After Annie left, I spent the time wondering just what my aunt's and mother's next steps would be. Probably I would be made to sign legal documents. No doubt they'd keep me alive at least long enough for that.

I shied away from contemplating Walter—or William. The thought of seeing either one again made my blood run cold.

Unfortunately, Annie did not return that night. Hagar came instead, accompanied by Carlos, who stood guard with his pistol. I eyed him and decided that he probably knew how to use it.

"Well, what do you want with me?" I said to my mother. "What story do you have to tell me now, and how much will the hearing of it cost me? Or will you tell the truth this time?"

"The truth may cost more than you'd care to pay. A story? How about this: once upon a time two children found a treasure."

"That's true enough."

"And one of them is grown up now, and right here in this room."

"And the treasure?"

"The treasure? Ah. Soon it will belong to us."

"To you? How?" I struggled to get up from the bed, but Carlos pushed me back until I lay flat. Hagar covered me tenderly with the quilt, and smiled down at me.

169

"It should be fairly simple for Walter to make inquiries in Hannibal, as your lawyer."

"My lawyer? Hannibal? Is that where he's headed?"

"He has a letter from you, giving him authority to negotiate on your behalf, with Judge Thatcher."

I could imagine how he'd managed to contrive that letter.

"Forgery is a crime," I said. "What kind of negotiations?"

I had a pretty clear idea, but I wanted to hear her say it.

"Accusations without proof are worthless. Ah—the negotiations. Well, we intend to arrange for your income to be deposited to a new account here in San Francisco, with your lawyer as signatory."

"A new account? Where?"

She named a bank. I recognized it as one whose president was a member of Hagar's "community relations" committee. "Oh, and we intend to take over your store, of course."

"Cassius won't let you, without my say-so."

"Your Cassius was unwilling at first to give over your records, but Walter persuaded him."

I only hoped Cassius had not been persuaded permanently. "Where is Cassius now?"

"How should I know?" Hagar shrugged. "Gone."

"Gone," I repeated.

"Are you hungry, dear? Thirsty?"

I didn't bother to answer. She motioned to Carlos, who left the room briefly and returned with a pitcher in his free hand.

"Make it last, for there'll be no more until tomorrow. As for food—you'll be fed, in time," she said. "Just cooperate with us, like a good girl."

"And if I don't?"

"There are worse punishments than slow starvation," she said.

Carlos put the pitcher down on the washstand, holding his gun on me all the while.

"Oh, and Annie?" Hagar said. "You will not see her again. She is being punished. She tried to carry a tale out of school, you see."

"Punished, how?"

"She is working down on the wharfs for the next few months. She will learn her lesson."

I was silent.

"Ah, yes," Hagar said. "You must admire our scheme. It is a beautiful scheme. Walter and I conceived it."

"What about Olivia?"

"Olivia? I intend to dispense with her—ah, her services. Shortly."

There was no mistaking her meaning. "But she's your own sister!"

"She is no longer as useful as she was, formerly. And I want no one coming between me and Walter."

"You and Walter? What do you mean?" Though I thought I knew, before she answered.

"Well," she said. "Of course we are lovers."

"But—"

"Oh, no one outside the family—" she tittered—"knows of our relationship. And you see, Olivia has been his lover, too, and for longer than I have. Oh yes," she said, nodding at my expression of disbelief, "She thinks to hold him with her charms. But mine are far more appealing. And my business acumen is far greater. He will realize, as I do, that we no longer need her."

She rose, setting down her brush, and came over to the chaise. She sat down at the end of it, and leaning forward, she took my hands in hers.

"You know," she said, "It is still so hard for me to imagine that you are really my daughter, except at times like this, when you are feeling hurt and unhappy. Then I seem to see my little one again, my baby, my Huckleberry." She raised my hands in hers to her lips, and kissed them.

I wrenched my hands away. "Don't! I hate you!"

"Ah." She rose and walked to the door. "I suppose you do." She closed the door behind her; I heard the key turn in the lock.

And so I was alone once more.

I lay awake in the dark for hours, thinking of the four of them: two sisters and a brother and a nephew, and all of them like the snake in that story the Widow used to read me, the one that talked the woman Eve into eating the forbidden fruit.

That story had always bothered me. There was nothing in it for the snake as far as I could tell. Unless it was simply the power to do harm.

Suddenly, I did not believe that my money was all that they wanted—nor that gaining control of it would lead them to release me. Not enough harm would be done thereby.

***

I might have thought that Hagar retained some motherly feeling, for she refused to allow Olivia to get rid of me, or so she claimed. But on reflection, I think it was that neither wanted to kill the goose that laid the golden eggs, for alive I was worth far more than I would have been dead.

Nonetheless, I spent over a month in that house, a prisoner—kept alive (barely) on bread and cheese and water, locked up in the room that had been Annie's, stripped to my undergarments, never knowing at what hour of the day or night I might receive a visit from one of the members of my family.

Olivia came seldom, Walter almost never, but William showed up every day, sometimes twice a day. He rarely spoke, only looked me up and down and smiled.

How I dreaded that smile.

One night, Hagar came, bearing a tray with a bottle and two glasses. As always, Carlos accompanied her. Carlos, and his gun.

"I thought we might have a drink together, and a nice little talk," she said, pouring the wine and handing me a glass. She motioned Carlos to stand across the room, keeping his gun trained on me.

"A talk? What about?"

"Your future," she said.

"Do I have one?"

"Of course . . . " She drained her glass and poured herself another. "Drink up." She smiled. "Ruby port. My favorite. Oh, it isn't drugged. This time."

I sipped. The wine was sweet and strong. "What do you want?"

"Cooperation," she said.

"I want something, too," I said.

"You aren't in any position to bargain," she said.

"Maybe not," I said. "But I think you owe me, just the same."

"What do I owe you?"

"The truth."

"You want too much," she said, and drank more wine.

"Tell me anyway."

"What do you want to know?"

"That story, about Pap, and you and your brother, hunting

that girl. Was any of that true?"

"Most of it. Some of it. Perhaps—none of it. He might have thought it was. Why do you care?"

"Did you ever love him—Pap?"

"No."

"Did you ever love—the child? Me?"

"I hated both of you and wished you dead, both of you, a thousand times," she said. "If I could have figured out a way to kill you both and get clean away, I would have done it."

"What about the baby that died?"

"What about it?"

"Pap said—you said—it was his fault. Pap's."

"It was. I told him I wasn't going to have another brat of his. I knew what to do—"

"And he stopped you from doing it."

"He tried, but he was too late." She took another sip; the glass was nearly empty. "I'd already taken care of it."

"He beat you, when he found out."

"He beat me nearly to death."

"And Walter—Walter come for you?"

"Walter would have killed him, but your Pap wasn't there," she said. "He had run off and gotten drunk, as usual."

"And left me there alone."

"We both thought you were dead."

"But I lived," I said. "When did you find out I warn't dead after all?"

"It was a dozen or so years after," she said. "Walter learned—it was in the St. Louis papers—that Huckleberry Finn and Tom Sawyer found twelve thousand dollars in gold in a cave near Hannibal." She paused. "Some of that gold was Walter's."

"Walter's? How?"

"He and Injun Joe were partners," she said. "It was supposed to be share and share alike, but Injun Joe double-crossed him and went back to the cave for the gold—and got trapped there. And died."

"So Walter was the ragged man—the man in the tavern," I said. "Injun Joe's comrade—but the ragged man was drowned! They found his body in the river, by the town landing."[47]

---

[47] Eds. note: See *The Adventures of Tom Sawyer*, Ch. 32.

"A body was found," she said. "But it wasn't Walter's."

"Whose was it?"

"Some drunken fool," she said indifferently. "Walter strangled him and changed clothes with him and dumped his body in the river."

I believed her. After a body's been in water a few days, it could be anyone's—and Walter, I was sure, knew that as well as I did.

"What happened then?" I asked.

"Well, of course he ran—but not too far. When you and the Sawyer boy found the gold, Walter knew what he had to do," she said. "He kept an eye on you. Yes, he did."

"So, him and the King finding us—Jim and me—that warn't no accident?"

"Of course it wasn't! He was following you. He took up with that fat idiot—the one you call the King—along the way. "

I remembered how uneasy the Duke had always made me— far more than the King, who was an unwholesome old rapscallion, lewd and ignorant as they come, but who never made the hairs rise on the nape of my neck like the Duke done.

"What did he—your brother—think he was going to do, to get the gold away from me?

"Oh, he hadn't thought it out that far. He figured, if he had *you*, he'd find a way. You know, he told me, once, that if you-all hadn't had that trouble over the Royal Nonesuch, he was planning to give the King a push, along with that big black buck of yours, and take you under his wing. He thought," she hesitated, "He thought you had *potential*."

"That was why he sold Jim to the Phelpses," I said. "Potential as what? A thief and a murderer?"

She ignored that. "If only he'd managed to get rid of that old fraud sooner—"

But he and the King had gotten caught, and ridden out of town on a rail—

"The old fellow didn't make it,"[48] she said. "And by the time Walter was able to travel again, you'd been taken in by those dirt

---

[48] Eds. note: Riding someone on a rail usually meant serious injury, even death; the rail in question was a newly-split one, and the victim literally "rode" the sharp edge.

farmers, those Phelpses, and he couldn't figure out how to get at you."

"Did he follow us back upriver?"

"He did. He was on that steamboat, hoping to pluck you off along the way."

But I'd slipped off instead, myself, and gotten clear—gone to Mary Jane Wilks—made a new life for myself, and tried to do the best I could—

Only to end up captured at last, a thousand miles away.

And the worst of it, what made me sick to think of, was the time I'd spent looking for some trace of this woman, hoping to find the mother I'd never known—

Finding, instead, that half of my parentage was evil to the core.

Worse, far worse than Pap, who was dirty and crude and low-down and mean, and a drunken sot to boot, but who'd never, so far as I'd known, made a deliberate choice, when in his right mind, to do me (or any human being) the way this woman intended.

"It's wonderful, isn't it?" said my mother, setting her empty wine glass down carefully, and reaching out to take mine. "You don't want any more? All right." She finished what was left in my glass, and sighed. "All these years, and all that time. We lost you, you know, after you left Hannibal. We couldn't find out where you'd gone."

"So you didn't have me followed out West, on the trail."

"Oh, no," she said. "We'd given up, actually. No, finding you here was just a coincidence. Funny, isn't it? You'd slipped through our fingers, and then—"

"And fell right into your lap," I said.

"More or less." She smiled. "Olivia was in the right place at the right time, you might say. And had her wits about her. And so." She stood up. "We have you right where we want you, Huckleberry dear."

"You can have my money," I said. "Just let me go. I'll sign it over. You can take me to a notary tomorrow."

"A tempting offer," she said, turning toward the door.

"I could sign it all over to you—just to you," I said.

Her eyes gleamed. "What about Olivia and Walter? And William?"

"Do you really care about them?"

"No. No, I suppose not," she said.

"I can sign the money over to you—and the store, too," I said. "I'll leave town. I'll never trouble you again."

She shook her head. "I don't believe that's the best course of action."

"Will you think it over?" I asked. I despise myself for the wheedling tone I'd put into my voice, but I wanted her to think I was desperate. (As, in fact, I was.)

"Perhaps," she said, and left, once more locking me in.

That night I truly came closer to despair than I'd ever been in my life. I doubted that Hagar would take my offer. I was worth far more as a captive. I finally fell asleep, my eyes still wet with the few hot, bitter tears I'd been able to squeeze out.

Some time before morning, I awoke. Something had awakened me—what? The dark was close around me, no light showing under the door. I listened, but all was quiet.

And then—

"Miss Sarah," a voice whispered, a voice I knew. "It's me, Cassius."

I hardly dared to breathe. Cassius!

I heard someone fumbling with a key, and then the door swung slowly open; I felt rather than saw it, for the room was still pitch-dark.

"This way," and I felt a warm hand brush against my arm, then fingers circled my wrist. The hand tugged at me, and I followed, trying to move silently.

We glided along the passage and descended the stairs.

We reached the kitchen, where a night-light burned. I blinked. There was Cassius, and there—seated at the table, his head in his arms—was Carlos. He was snoring. An empty wine bottle and a smeary glass stood on the table before him.

And beyond him—the door to freedom.

"Quick," breathed Cassius, and reached out for the latch.

I stepped through the door, and almost collided with someone waiting in the porch. It was a woman. I could not see her face—the light was too dim—but I knew her.

"Annie !"

"Come on," Cassius said. "Run!"

And he grabbed my hand, and we ran—the two of us. I looked back once and saw Annie still standing in the shadows, but had no time to wonder then why she stayed behind.

We did not stop until we had reached the waterfront. At a splintery pier, Cassius bent down and spoke.

"Still there?"

A voice answered in melodic singsong syllables. I could not understand the words, but I'd spent enough time in San Francisco to recognize the sounds as Chinese. A small man peered up at us, his yellow face lined and anxious.

"Here she is," Cassius said, helping me down into a tiny, frail boat, following after. The Chinese man picked up an oar and pushed us off the wharf. For a while we slid between moored ships and small boats, their lamps shining yellow through the fog.

At last we were out in open water. The Chinese stopped rowing long enough to fix a dark lantern in the prow, then resumed his slow stroke.

"Where are we headed?" I asked.

"Angel Island," Cassius said. "I been camping there."

Angel Island (which become Camp Reynolds during the Civil War,[49]) had been mostly deserted since the Miwok Indians all died off. It was a refuge for criminals and fugitive slaves and such-like.

Cassius continued, "Time we head back, it be close on daylight. Annie, she fetch some clothes for you, a few days since. We get you dressed and fed, then we head for the bank, soon's they open for business."

"Right."

"I ain't been to the store in some time," Cassius said. "Don't know what they done there, what condition the place be in."

"How long have I been—gone?" I asked.

"Four weeks and a bit," he said.

"Where've you been, Cassius?"

I couldn't see him clear in the dim, but I caught the flash of his white teeth and knew he was smiling. "Working to set you free."

The humor of the situation struck us both at the same time, and we laughed until the tears ran down our faces. The Chinese man shipped his oars and watched us without any show of emotion.

"Oh, Lord, Cassius," I said, wiping my face with the hem of

---

[49] Eds. note: Later Fort McDowell, which eventually took over all of Angel Island, although from 1910 to 1940 the island also served as the main inprocessing facility for Asian immigrants to the mainland United States.

my petticoat. The night fog swirled around us. Dim rings of yellow light from the shoreline bobbed up and down and sideways in the gloom. I commenced to shiver.

"Got to get you some warm clothes," Cassius said. He stripped off his jacket and hung it over my shoulders. "Pull that around you."

"Thanks," I said.

The Chinese man resumed rowing, looking back over his shoulder from time to time. Our little boat was making headway, though slowly.

"Where is Annie?" I asked. "Where did she go?"

Cassius looked grim. "She say she have some business to tend to."

***

Before long, I felt our boat's bottom grating on the shell and gravel of a bank, and Cassius helped me out, while he and the Chinese man pulled the boat up on shore. Cassius led me to a small canvas tent, where I found a bundle of clothing and a hairbrush and other necessities.

Whilst I made myself as tidy as I could, Cassius and the Chinese built a fire and brewed coffee. The Chinese disappeared, but Cassius stayed close.

I drank several mugs of the hot, strong coffee while munching on the thick meat sandwiches that Cassius had fetched along.

"Don't eat too fast," Cassius said. "You don't want it-all to come back up again."

"I won't," I said, cramming the last crust into my mouth and washing it down with a final swig of coffee. "Lord, but that was good. Thank you, Cassius."

"When you be ready to go?"

"I'm ready now."

Cassius nodded and began to red up the campsite, putting the fire out with sand and scattering the ashes. He left the tent up, but retrieved a leather satchel from inside. Then he whistled, and the figure of the Chinese man appeared from around the side of a pile of rocks.

"Time to go," Cassius called. The man nodded, moved back out of sight, then reappeared, pushing the boat back toward the water.

Cassius helped me back into the boat, then climbed in

178

himself, with the satchel.

"What's in there?" I asked.

"Your papers," Cassius said. "From the store, and from your other property."

"I thought—they—had them," I said, unwilling to use the names of my captors.

"Sho!" Cassius grinned. "They never. I taken these right away, soon's you don't come back from your visit."

"Hagar said you give them what they wanted," I said.

"You ought to know better than that," Cassius said. He shot a look at me. "I give them a few papers—nothin' worth much. Then I run an' hide out. You know I don't trust your relations."

"You always did have more sense than I had," I told him.

"Time you knew it," he said. "We almost there."

We returned to the wharfs a few hundred yards from where we'd first pushed off into the bay. The day was near to breaking, and the color of the fog had lightened to pearl, whilst a few stray beams of pale sunshine picked out a coil of rope on a dock, or a triangular shape of sail, or the shifting bulk of a vessel as it swayed at mooring.

"Here we go," and Cassius handed me up and followed me nimbly, tossing a few coins to the Chinese boatman, who bowed and pushed his craft back the way we'd come.

From the wharf where we stood, I could see the masts and spits of a hundred craft, and above us the dark shapes of what I knew were buildings. And one of them was a house I hoped never to see again.

***

As it turned out, I never did run the risk of seeing that house any more, because it burned up that very same night. But, as fires was so common in the city in those years, it was a day or so before I learned what had happened.

The newspaper gave very little information. It seemed that the fire was set, by "a person or persons unknown."

Also unknown were the identities of several bodies found in the rubble, two women and a man, all in evening dress, another woman and man who appeared to be Mexican or Indian, and four women who were "in deshabille," the paper said, meaning that they was largely unclothed.

I went over the list of victims again and again, but it seemed incontestably true.

Hagar, Olivia, and Walter were dead, along with at least some of the women who worked for them—not all, which made me glad, to think that a few had escaped. But no boy's body had been found. It was equally clear, then, that William Quantrill had escaped the fire.

I shivered, wondering where he might be—into what unspeakable den he'd crawled.

The newspaper reported only one survivor, who'd lived a few hours after the fire, though terribly burned. She was able to give her name: Annie Casey, but she died before she was able to reveal (if she knew) the names of the other victims. The property had been owned by a business concern—I didn't recognize the name; nothing else was known, and what remained of the structure would be pulled down as soon as the embers had cooled.

***

Later that same week, I spent a trying morning and afternoon with a contingent of bank officers, trying to unravel the machinations that my relations had attempted regarding my property. In the end, I had to part with a substantial sum in "fines" and "fees," but at last I was satisfied that my money and other concerns had been safely restored to me.

"And," I told the bank president, "If a Mr William Quantrill should attempt to lay hands on anything of mine in future, you should know that he does not have my consent to act for me in any way, and in fact I'd be pleased if you'd call the police, did he show up. For despite his youth he is a criminal of the worst order."

The bank president (who, if he remembered me from any of Hagar's soirees, was canny enough not to reveal the fact) swore up and down that he held my account absolutely sacred and inviolate.

"I'm glad to hear it," I told him. "Good day to you."

And Cassius and I went home.

I spent a few days resting up, letting Cassius take care of the store. But as soon as I felt well again, I dressed myself in my best, for I had a special call to make.

St Patrick's Catholic Church lay on Mission Street, between 3rd and 4th. I chose it as the most likely for a woman named Annie Casey to have attended.

I'd never been inside a Catholic church before.

It was dark, with windows patterned in colored glass. A small red lantern burned beside a curious structure, like a little house made of shining brass, atop a white stone table. A few shawled women occupied the pews, and the place smelled of candle wax, smoke, and something pungently sweet, like the joss sticks the Chinese bought from me and burned in front of the images of their mysterious gods.

A tall man in long black robes came out to meet me and escorted me to his office. On the white plaster wall opposite the door hung a life-sized wooden cross on which hung the image, in some lighter wood, of a naked man with a crown of thorns and nails piercing his hands and feet. The light from the tall windows shone on this image. I looked away.

The man in black robes seated me in an upholstered chair before a large wooden desk. Its surface was shining bare. He sat down himself, folding his hands on the desk top, and raised his eyebrows inquiringly at me.

"I am not a Catholic," I said to him. "I don't know how to address you."

"You may call me Father Desmond," he said. "How may I help you, Miss——?"

"My name is Williams," I said. "I wish to give some money in remembrance of someone, someone I think may have been a Catholic. At least, she was Irish."

Father Desmond smiled. He was clean-shaven, with dark hair and eyes; his hands was long and fine. Around his waist he wore a black rope hung with another cross and image, this one in silver.

"Most Irish folk are of our Faith," he said. "Not all. What was her name?"

"Annie—Annie Casey."

"Ah." He was silent. Then he spoke again. "Yes, she was of my flock. I have not seen her for some weeks. You said 'in remembrance.' She is dead, then?"

"She is dead," I said.

"I am sorry to hear it. How did she die?"

"She was in a fire." I hesitated. "Down by the wharfs. A house——"

Father Desmond nodded. "I recall the incident, now that you mention it."

"Then you know—what she was?"

"I know what she did to survive," he said.

181

"Yet you speak of her without contempt," I said.

"All of God's children are precious to him," the priest said. "She was weak; she was a sinner. So are we all."

"Well." I took a deep breath. "How much money will you need?"

"Tell me what you wish," he said.

"Her body was taken to Potter's Field. I want her re-buried, according to your—and her—beliefs," I said. "Whatever services you usually have, I want you to hold them. And I want a stone to mark her grave."

"All of that can be done."

And so we agreed, and I give him the money he asked for—it was a good deal less than I had intended to spend, so I put the rest in a wooden box at the back of the church, marked "For the Poor."

Annie's final disposition was now assured. Hagar and Olivia and Walter would never bother me more. I only wished I could be rid as easily of the lurking menace of my cousin.

***

The figure of William continued to oppress my nights, though in the daytime I could pretend that I had few cares to concern me. Still, Cassius knew what was going on, and he watched me, distress showing all over him like it was painted on. Finally, he spoke up.

"Miss Sarah Mary, you ain't well. What I mean to say is, you don't *look* well, and that's a fact."

"Is it? I feel all right."

"No, you ain't."

Cassius and I were busy restocking the Emporium's shelves in preparation for opening on Monday morning. He went on,

"Look how thin you's become, and jittery too," he said. "Jump at the lightest sound, and always lookin' every which way, like something coming at you."

I tried to smile at him, to reassure him. He was leaning toward me, his gentle eyes puzzled and concerned.

I gave up. "Oh, Cassius," I said. "I just can't stand it here any more."

"You intends to go away."

"I—yes, I do."

"Well, where you thinkin' of goin'?"

"I ain't thought of where, yet."

"Best have a plan," he said. And of course, he was right.

So we made one.

It was Cassius who first proposed I should head east to the Sierra Nevadas, where the town of Virginia City was taking shape.

Silver had been discovered just a year ago in Nevada, a major strike just across the California line. Virginia City grew up overnight--a real boom town. Cassius and I decided I should go out there and open a branch of the Emporium, leaving Cassius as my partner and supply contact here in San Francisco.

I begun to feel some excitement at the prospect. On our journey west with Captain Sellers's train, we'd turned south at Fort Bridger, as I have written earlier, and so I had not seen any of the country north of the fort, though like everyone else I had read of its rugged beauty, and of the riches to be found thereabouts.

And so I said farewell to Cassius.

It was a hard parting. Both of us wept a little, but I could see how pleased he was at his new estate. And I was relieved to be putting some distance between myself and my nemesis. Surely Nevada was far enough away!

But just to be on the safe side, I made sure to take my Sharps with me, and also a pair of the new-fangled "volcanic" repeating pistols as well, which I wore in holsters hung from a gun-belt that Cassius had made for me, of red Spanish leather, tooled in a pattern of crescent moons and stars. I practiced with those pistols until I could be reasonably sure I'd hit whatever I was aiming at, and I vowed never to take them off during the daylight hours, and to sleep with them close to hand every night.

Chapter Thirteen: Silver Mountain

Well, for a marvel, everything turned out fine.

I'd more than a sufficiency of goods and cash to set myself up in Virginia City. There was already quite a bit of commerce, and the local officials were willing to do all in their power to help desirable businesses to locate. From the first, I liked what I saw.

As it turned out, I was to spend a number of years there.

I should add here that my move to Nevada led to increased prosperity not only for me but for Cassius. He ended up quite a wealthy man, partly due to his own enterprise—partly due to his wife's.

(As it turned out, Cassius *did* marry an Indian. She belonged to the Rogue River tribe, and she spoke five languages: French, Russian, English, her own native Shasta and a curious tongue called Chinook. This last was a jargon blended of tongues partly Indian, partly European, some Chinese and Japanese, and some Polynesian, used by traders up and down the Northwest. I learnt some over the years, but was never what you might call fluent in it.)

Tiring of store-keeping, a year or so after I left for Nevada, Cassius hired a pair of clerks (greenhorns, brothers from New York State who'd lost their shirts looking for gold) to oversee the Emporium, whilst he and his wife set up in the saloon business, Cassius tending bar and his wife, whose name was Snow-on-the-Mountains, acting as hostess.

She was quite a sight, near six feet tall and strongly built, with blue-black hair down to her knees, and deerskin dresses that could'a stood alone, they was so covered with beadwork and silver bullion. Cassius loved her dearly, and she give him five beautiful children, three boys and two girls, all of them tall and sturdy, rich dark copper in color, with masses of curly black hair and eyes like coffee beans.

Virginia City was a brand-new town in a brand-new part of the country. For a long time few whites had come through that part of the world, the high Sierras on the border between Nevada and California. Then the Comstock Lode was struck and silver—and gold, too—begun pouring out, and the streams of miners begun pouring in.

So I started my new life.

***

Dealing with folks was a mite difficult at first, as always.

People are always trying to find out about you, where you are from and who your relations are and suchlike. I never said nothing directly about myself, but once I set to work, of course, folks found out that I was a woman of property. So, eventually, despite my odd appearance, I was deemed acceptable.

Oh, yes, I had long since given up dressing as a conventional female. I made the concession, since I lived and worked in town, of wearing skirts (except, of course, for riding). But my skirts—made of corduroy or canvas or thick wool, depending on the season—I kept short, no longer than my boot-tops—that is, just past the knees—and the rest of me I dressed to suit myself, in woolen shirts and leather vests and jackets, though I kept my hair long (it being easier to handle that way, braided neatly and pinned), and out-of-doors I wore a hat with turquoise beads sewn on the band and a feather cockade at the back.

I liked to wear a red or blue or green silk bandanna at my throat, and leather gloves with silver-embroidered cuffs. My boots, too, was softest Spanish leather, crimson like the gunbelt I wore to hold my two pistols, and there was silver conchas on my boots, too, and silver earbobs with many tiny dangles in both my ears. I wore silver and turquoise rings, too, on every finger, like the Indian women, because I liked the way they looked on my strong, tanned hands. I felt that I cut a rather dashing figure, in fact, for I was tall and long-legged, and my skin while somewhat weathered was clear of blemish.

Once the people of the town knew who I was, and got used to seeing me, they acted cordial enough. It is always interesting to see how other people treat you when you are destitute, and then again when you have some means at your disposal. Of course, in those days women could pick and choose, there being so few of us amongst so many hungry males. Had I only the clothes I stood up in, back in San Francisco, I'd'a' been married forty times over the first week I was there, had I wished.

But money makes a difference, there's no denying it. I had no dearth of offers of matrimony when I was a single woman driving my own wagon and team; when it became known that I also had an income (from an inheritance, it was whispered) I found suitors littering my path like buffalo chips out on the prairie. There did not seem to be any who could not overlook the fact that I had no background to speak of—or at least none that could be uncovered by the most dedicated snoop amongst them. It took me a quite some time to get folks to understand that I was not looking for a husband, but was a businesswoman, and in business solely for myself.

Now, I had found storekeeping congenial from the first, for many reasons, not least that I enjoyed having a lot of goods in my possession. Perhaps it is because I seldom had more than the gaudy rags I wore as a child, little food, and nothing extra, I liked being able to survey, in my immediate surroundings, a plethora of items large and small, for which men, women, and children would eagerly pay whatever price I set. .

A woman who has her wits about her can keep a store pretty much by herself in a place like Virginia City, while a livery stable or saloon or hotel is less easy to handle and requires more help. True, in San Francisco I'd had Cassius as my right-hand man, but this establishment was a great deal smaller and with far fewer customers, or potential customers, I should say. I'd ascertained that the price for the business was a fair one, including not only the inventory on site but contracts with suppliers. I had no intention of paying for a going concern, only to have the erstwhile proprietor set up immediately as my competition, and keep the customer base and the sources of goods for himself.

That erstwhile proprietor was selling out because his wife had died shortly after they arrived in Nevada, and he—a man in his forties—wanted to go back East and live with their grown daughter. The price of the store would be his wedding present to her, apparently, and he was glad to receive it, promising me that "the business would run itself."

I thought that in his hands it apparently had, since much of his stock was furred with dust as if it had lain in one place a century or so, and some of the more perishable items appeared to have in fact perished. But all of that was easily remedied. The store was also the location of the only post office in the area, so I would be postmistress, too—a formal title to the post came with the purchase.

Well, so, the money was transferred without incident, and the papers signed and notarized, and I found myself the owner of a small self-contained expanse of retail space on South C Street and a warehouse out on the edge of town, near the railroad depot. There was living quarters upstairs of the store itself, two biggish rooms, and built on to the back of the first floor was a kitchen shed with a cast-iron range and plenty of shelves, hooks, cupboards, and bins. A privy and small barn completed the property (out behind the store building).

I had my wagon run into the barn, the axles and wheels greased thoroughly, the harness wrapped up against damp-rot and the teeth of varmints, and saw the canvas cover roped down securely and the whole swaddled in oilcloth; someday I might need to take to the road again, and I meant to keep all in readiness against such a chance. My mules (for I'd used a mule team to make this journey) I boarded at the livery stable, where I allowed them to be rented out and used to pay part of the boarding fee. So, all in all, everything seemed well arranged.

Meanwhile, I spent a good amount of time surveying my new home and its surroundings.

Virginia City was a mining town, its very existence due to the Comstock Lode. The population at first was mostly male—with the usual infusion of prostitutes and gamblers, gunslingers and dope fiends—however, by late 1861, when I arrived, more and more ordinary Americans—and Chinese, and Irish— was coming, some just passing through but others planning to stay.

It was a time when there was a great deal of money to be made—and the greatest immediate returns were, as always, to be made from the riskiest ventures. Mine was not one such. It was definitely not romantic to make one's profits from sundries and supplies of various kinds, from flour and molasses, kegs of nails and bolts of calico, sacks of beans and papers of pins. It took longer than the riskier kinds of endeavor. But it was a sure thing.

After I'd been settled for a few weeks, I begun to get invitations from local folks to come to supper or tea. I come to understand that it was good business to accept most of these. I had the excuse of minding the store, so I did not take up every offer that come my way, but I did begin to make a few acquaintances amongst my fellow townspeople.

Chief of these was Mr and Mrs Jacob Stroethers, who had come West from a small town in Pennsylvania more than ten years before, and numbered among the first settlers of Virginia City. They owned the livery stable, which furnished me with a horse or a rig when I wanted one. Their oldest son Coleridge was learning the business. He was a likely boy, about eighteen, and with his two younger brothers kept the stock and equipment in fine fettle. The brothers was fourteen-year-old twins, Byron and Percy.

I asked Mrs Stroethers where she had got the boys' names, being curious, and found out that all three was in fact named for famous English poets, she being a great one for reading poetry and even writing some of her own.   The newspaper, *The Territorial Enterprise*, had even published a few of her verses, which I found a bit melancholy for my taste, but many people enjoy such sentiments, as I have discovered.   (Her verses put me in mind of Evangeline Grangerford's, but I thought them much less artfully composed, to tell the truth.)

The Stroethers also had a niece who lived with them in their big house on F Street, her parents having died when she was small. Her name was Rowena Lothrop, and her mother had been Mrs Stroethers's sister, also a great admirer of literature, a taste that run in that family, at least as far as the women was concerned.   Mrs Stroethers hosted literary evenings in the wintertime at which she read aloud from the works of Sir Walter Scott and Charles Dickens, which is how I come to hear about Rob Roy and Oliver Twist and Mr Pickwick.

(And Sir Wilfred Ivanhoe and Rowena, a romance I had difficulty figuring out.   To my mind, Rebecca was far more of a catch than that addlepated wench Rowena.)

The literary goings-on at the Stroethers' was about all Virginia City could boast of in terms of social gatherings, and as such they appeared from time to time in the newspaper, especially when one or t'other of the guests was a newcomer, such as myself. So I found my name listed amongst the other "patrons of literature" in the Society Column of the Virginia City *Territorial Enterprise,* whose editor was a youngish man, also new to the region, Mr Dan DeQuille. He was the man who, some years later, hired a reporter named Samuel Clemens.

Yes, in 1862 I would have my very first face-to-face encounter with Mr Mark Twain himself (about which I will write at a later time).   He was just starting out as a journalist and editor, after having been a miner (and before that, a printer, and other things beside) and his books about Tom Sawyer and me was far and away in the future.

***

There was one other particular man with whom I also become acquainted, and it is of this I mean to write here.

I had never considered men much, other than as potential customers or competitors. I kept to myself, but let it be known that I was a good shot. (I practiced with my pistols, regularly, out behind my store.) Once in a while men would come round and try to make theirselves agreeable to me, but I was not interested and soon enough they would go away again.

I was past thirty now, as near as I could judge, and I had asked myself over the years whether my early experience with Antoinette had spoiled me, so to speak, for men, but I hadn't found myself attracted to any women in that time, either, at least none I could've imagined bedding, though I'd seen some I found appealing. Men, on the other hand, generally left me cold.

I was about to find out that one man at least could affect me differently.

He come to town in the early autumn, and took a room at the hotel. I saw him from time to time as I went about my business, and I noticed him—oh, yes; he was good-looking enough to notice! But we had no mutual acquaintances, I didn't go to church (and thus had no idea if he did), and so we never managed to introduce ourselves. Still, I nodded politely when I passed him, and he raised his hat to me and smiled gravely back.

He didn't venture to speak to me when I went out walking or riding. So as I said, I noticed him only at such times as he come into my field of vision—a handsome young fellow, with a pleasant smile that showed good teeth (unusual enough in those days).

And then, sometime in the winter, the situation changed.

He begun to come into the store. At first it was once or twice a week. He never pretended to buy anything, either, but just walked in and set on a keg, or propped himself against a shelf of merchandise and waited for me to speak.

"Can I help you, cowboy?" I had asked, the first time. It wasn't hard to figure out his occupation, as cowboys was a common enough sight, easy to recognize, and usually first distinguishable by odor—this one smelt relatively clean, which was a novelty.

"No ma'am," he said. "I'm just lookin'."

So he stood there and leaned on the counter and looked. He looked at everything in the store, and he looked out the window, and he looked at the door, and he looked at me.

I had never been looked at before, not in that way. He didn't stare, but I could feel his eyes boring into me, so to speak, and no matter where I went in the store, I felt those eyes; the sensation brought about a tingling in my midsection and a fluttery feeling in my chest, very odd sensations that I'd never felt before.

I decided to let him know I could look, too. So I stopped the figuring I was doing (could I afford to carry more harness? Should I order more variety in dry goods and groceries?) and rested my elbows on the other end of the counter and settled my eyes on him.

He was good to look at, too: tall, with wide shoulders and a narrow waist flowing into lean hips and long legs in tight buckskins. He had on a thick red woolen blanket-coat with blue and white stars embroidered on the facings. Silver conchas glittered on his belt and on the hat he held at his side. He wore a necklace of wolf teeth strung on braided horse-hair. His eyes, lighter than his coloring seemed to warrant, were fringed with thick curling lashes a girl might envy. His neck above his kerchief was smooth and his cheeks had a healthy flush like on the skin of a ripe peach.

I realized suddenly that he was not a white man. Nor was he Mex. His skin was the color of molasses candy, and those thick-lashed eyes was deep golden-brown; his hair was dark and rippled back from his temples like shining black water, and his straight, sharply-marked brows were black, like the little curly black mustache that made his teeth seem even whiter. I judged that he was a quadroon or maybe octoroon.

Something about the way he walked and stood seemed familiar to me, but I could not remember ever seeing him before. Indeed, I didn't see how I could have, for he was at least a decade younger than I. In fact, I judged that he might not be twenty yet, for his skin was unweathered and his lips full and red.

"Well, goodnight, ma'am," he said, startling me. I flushed, realizing that I'd been staring at him.

"Goodnight to you, cowboy."

"My name's Johnny," he said, as he went out the door.

Weeks went by, and he come into the store with more and more frequency, until at last I found that I could look up from my counter or desk at just about any given time and see him looking back at me, not smiling nor frowning, just looking.

And whilst this sort of conduct would have been a cause of some discomfort from any other man, I didn't take these visits from Johnny amiss. I found myself, oddly enough, looking forward to them—so much that I was disappointed if I did look up and he warn't there.

I asked around, and learned from the saloon keeper, Mr Liam Donahy, that Johnny—Donahy didn't know his last name— had been a Pony Express rider. When the Express closed down operations, he'd been in Sacramento, and followed a job offer to Nevada. He worked for a ranch nearby, Donahy said. He was quiet and didn't drink much, nor visit the girls upstairs (Donahy said this with a wink, which I ignored), and seemed altogether like a nice young fellow.

"What's your interest, Miss Williams?" Donahy asked. "Going to offer him a job, maybe?"

"Maybe," I said, not wanting to admit being curious.

Then one evening, I found Johnny at my elbow when I was closing up.

"It's closing time," I said.

"Well, shoot, so it is. Y'all let me help you with them shutters," he said, and shut them tight, latching each one. There was six of them across the front of the store, and with them all closed and locked, a thief would need a good axe and a lot of muscle to get in. Which in any event would do that thief no good whatsoever, for I slept upstairs, and would be down in a trice, loaded for bear, at the first sound of splintering wood.

"All right," I said, and wondered that my voice sounded so ordinary in my own ears. For I was feeling mighty peculiar all of a sudden.

Whilst Johnny put up the shutters, I took the money out of the till, secured it in the leather pouch I wore tied to my petticoat tapes, and put out the lanterns, except for the one I would carry upstairs.

I checked the padlock on the back door, turned, and saw Johnny grinning at me.

"Well, going to invite me upstairs, or not?"

"I suppose I might as well," I heard myself saying, to my own wonderment.

Now, what in the world made me do that?

For I'd never been with a man before, believe it or not. Nor really wanted to, until that moment. But when he flashed those white teeth at me and lifted one eyebrow, I felt as weak as a newborn kitten, and all I could think of was what it would feel like to taste those red, full lips, and lay my own hungry mouth against that smooth molasses-candy-colored throat

***

Well, as it turned out, I *had* seen him before, although in circumstances that warn't likely to have reminded me of that meeting in the present situation.

But that next morning, when I woke up and turned my head to see his on the same pillow, then it hit me, just who he must be.

I sat upright and leaned over, peering down at him.

Oh, lord. It was true—it had to be—even these ten years later, I could see it plain.

But I had to make sure.

"Johnny. Johnny! Hey! What's your last name?"

He opened his eyes, smiled up at me, reached, and gathered me to his chest.

"Why? Do you want it for your own?"

"I ain't the marrying kind," I said.

"Maybe not, but you need a loving man," he said, and pushed me over onto my back, where I lay whilst he traced the curve of my breasts with one finger. His touch made me yearn for more, and I shifted away from him.

"I managed until you come along," I said, feeling a little bit cross. "Now, answer me—what's your last name?"

"Finn." He shifted himself and sat up in the bed, grinning at me.

I'd expected it, more or less, but it was still a shock.

The cowboy in my bed was none other than the son of my old Jim!

(To explain, which I should a' done before: Jim had took my old name for his and his family's, when they got their freedom; he did not want to take Miss Watson's, even though she had freed him, and he said, as long as I was going to call myself by a new name, he would keep my old one to remember me by.)

"Johnny Finn, do you come from Missouri? Do you have a step-ma called Julie, and a sister Elizabeth Ann, and is your daddy Jim?"

He fell back against the pillows and stared up at me, wide-eyed.

"Johnny Finn, meet Huckleberry Finn," I said, and held out my hand for him to shake. Mechanically, he took it, and shook it, and then the sheer lunacy of the whole situation broke over us, and we dissolved into helpless laughter, and then once more to love.

Even all these years later, I can recall the feel of him in my arms. Through all the years of waiting I had come at last to know what it meant to hold a man, all muscle and bone and smooth honey-colored skin, in my arms—and love him.

For I did love him, with all my heart and body.

There hadn't been much love in my life, and my own experience hadn't been much like what storybooks said love was supposed to be.

I'd never read any book that talked plain about physical love. I'd seen what some folks substituted for love, in my mother's and aunt's bawdy house. That was fucking, to use the coarse term that the whores did, and whilst it could be pleasurable (some said) the pleasure didn't seem worth the trouble nor the risk. (I had seen, twice, pregnant whores sent away with their burdens. One returned with her belly flat again. I'd never asked what happened to the baby; I knew the answer would be a grim one.)

And so I had not thought of the love of a man as something that would ever come to me, or as anything I would welcome if it did.

Now I knew.

If a body has had that kind of love in this life, you do not forget it, but once it is gone there is a strangeness in the recollection, like waking after a monumental spree. For I was besotted with him, drunk on the sight and the scent and the taste of him. He had only to look at me and I felt my bones turn to butter.

And that is how it was. Every night after closing, we climbed the stairs to my room and my bed and all I have ever known of that particular kind of bliss.

And, old woman as I am, after all these many years, I remember, and love him still.

***

"Now tell me, what's been a-doing with Jim and the rest of the family?" I asked Johnny, some weeks later, as we lay in my bed and listened to the lonely wind in the Ponderosa pines. The breeze rustled through the curtains that hung at my window, red curtains made of fine wool.

"Why, Sarah Mary, didn't you know? He died."

I felt myself quiver. Jim dead!

Last time I'd seen him, seven years since, on my way back

East for Tom Sawyer's wedding, Jim's hair had turned gray, but his eyes were as clear as ever, and his voice as rich and deep. He was still tall and broad-chested, with shoulders wide enough to carry a barrel on each one and arms tight with muscle.

He'd not known me until I spoke to him, and then he'd wept and laughed and wept again, and held me to his broad chest with those great arms and patted me and called me honey over and over again, just like no time had ever gone by.

"I has prayed to the Lord over you," he said to me, his eyes shining through their tears, "The Lord knows I has asked to see you one more time before I die. And the Lord has done it–yes, He's done it!—He has vouchsafed you to me once more in this world! Oh, happy day!"

"Jim, you sound like a preacher," I said, and I reached up and wiped his eyes, and then my own, with my handkerchief.

"But I am a preacher, sometimes," he said. "I takes the congregation between visits from the circuit rider. You should stay over 'til Sunday and hear me preach on how to be thankful!" and he beamed all over his broad, brown face.

So I did. I stayed with him and his second wife, Julie, whom he'd married just a few months before. His first wife Eliza, the children's mother, had died of fever-and-ague, and Jim had mourned for several years until he found Julie. She was a plump, dark-brown woman with a comical high-pitched voice—the complete opposite of Eliza, who had been slender and light-skinned.

Jim put an arm around Julie and said, "Julie here saved me from a life of sorrow. She makes me laugh every day whether I want to or not."

Julie nodded and smiled. "He was grieving so hard, he scarcely saw these children."

"You remember my children, Sarah Mary?" Jim asked.

"Yes, I do remember them," I said.

Of course, they'd changed and grown.

"Johnny is my foreman on the farm," Jim said. "I couldn't run this establishment without him and that's the truth."

Johnny was twelve or so by the look of him, and he obviously took his job as foreman very seriously, for he swelled up at this praise and tightened his lips so as not to bust out grinning.

"And my Elizabeth Ann," Jim said, and beckoned the tall girl who stood behind her brother, her eyes alert and shining, glowing with interest.

I remembered that Eliza had had the same deep-tawny eyes, and passed them on to her children along with her light skin and slender height.

Jim put his hand out and drew her near to me, and tapped my shoulder and then his own chest, and nodded and smiled.

Elizabeth nodded too, eagerly, and taking my right hand in both of hers, she raised it to her lips and kissed it, then leaned forward and kissed my cheek. Her lips were soft and warm.

"She's smart as can be," Jim said. "Can't hear nor speak, of course—you remember?—but she knows what we tell her, and a lot besides."

Yes, I remembered all right. I would never forget, as long as I lived, that night when Jim told me about how he discovered that his daughter was deaf and dumb. She'd been four then, after the scarlet fever, and now she was fourteen or thereabouts, just the age I'd been when Jim and I set off down the river . . .

Johnny's voice put an end to my rememberings. "Yes, Daddy passed away out there in Missouri, on the farm, last year," Johnny said. "Mama Julie and Elizabeth are still there, I reckon. It's a small enough place. Elizabeth has probably got married by now, and her man will do what's needful."

Memory stirred again. *"Poor little 'Lizbeth! Poor little Johnny!"*

Poor Jim, to bear such pain and sorrow. I was glad he'd found his children again and made a good life for them. It made up in a way for all that he'd been through, although nothing could make up for the years of slavery, not completely.

My mind returned to Elizabeth. "How can she be married, if she can't hear or speak?"

Johnny laughed and tightened his arm around my shoulders. "A lot of men would be happy with a quiet wife," he said. "She makes signs, remember. You can understand her pretty good. And she's nice to look at, and a good, strong worker. There was three or four men used to ride out and talk with Mama Julie about her, even before I headed West. And Elizabeth no more than fifteen then. I'm sure she's wed by this time."

"Haven't you heard from your family?"

"Mama Julie wrote me a time back to say that the Secesh had the town, and not to come home for a while," he said. "Last I heard."

195

"The war's been going on for near two years, now," I said. "Shouldn't you go back and see them? See to the farm? Suppose somebody's took ill, or dead!"

"Nothing I could do if they was," he answered, reasonably enough. "The farm belongs to Mama Julie, and she's got Elizabeth to care for, and Elizabeth's man and her children, when they come. They're just as glad I'm gone. I didn't belong there."

No, I thought. He surely did not. He was no farmer. Nor was he a soldier or a merchant or a townsman of any sort. He belonged to a breed apart, and no woman could hold him, and only a fool would even try.

I loved him, but I was no fool. Nor did I intend to start being one.

And that was good, because of course, it could not last.

Within a month, the boss of his outfit sent word for him to join them for the next drive to Abilene.

"I got to go, Sarah. You know I'll miss you, but I reckon I'll be back before too long," he said, that last morning, as he dressed. I sat up in the bed and watched him knot a bright yellow silk kerchief about his throat.

"What makes you think I'll be here waiting?" I said.

"Where else is my girl going to be?" He crossed the room to me, smiling, and bent down for my kiss. "You keep that bed warm for me, you hear? And nobody else."

And he was gone.

He left me with the memory of his warm lips and hands, with the scent of his crisp-curled hair still on the pillows of the bed we'd shared, and with a sense of desolation I'd never felt in my whole life before, except perhaps when I said goodbye to Jim.

Was this what it was like for every woman who loved a man? It was poison-sweet, like too much whiskey drunk too fast, and too bitter a taste afterward.

I never saw him again.

I am glad that I did not know it, at the time. I waited and watched and hoped, until it was clear that he was never coming back.

But he left me with one thing more: his daughter, in my belly.

***

When I first suspected I might be pregnant, I considered my choices. That there were ways to keep from having a baby I was well aware—some of them close to hand on my own store shelves, though I eyed them with mistrust. Such things did not always work.

A baby. What would I do with a baby? I'd never imagined having a child of my own.

There was, of course, no way to get word to Johnny, and I doubted he'd be much help even if I were to ask him for any. If he returned, we would see what we would see. Marriage, I guessed, was not in his future—nor did I especially see it in mine.

No; if I went ahead with this pregnancy, I'd be doing it alone. And at thirty-four or -five, which was old for a woman to bear a first child.

I took the problem to the only person I could think of who might be of practical help, leaving my store in the capable hands of my assistant, Cheung Ka Yat—better known to Virginia City, Nevada, simply as Chung.

Yes, I had a Chinese as my right-hand man, and a better worker you'd go far to find. He'd come to me several years back, when I was advertising for an assistant. The store had grown so, along with the local population, that I was having trouble keeping up.

I'd made up my mind to haul out my old traveling shop-on-wheels again, this time to some of the remoter ranches and settlements in the area—at least in the good weather. I reckoned that the women especially would welcome a chance to look over my stock, and maybe, once the worth of my wares was recognized, the farm wives might send their husbands into town with an order that I could fill.

So I'd strolled over to the office of the *Territorial Enterprise*, to take out an advertisement for someone who could look after the shop if I warn't there, who could keep records in a tidy way, and who might want to drive the store-wagon out on a regular route once I'd determined what that route ought to be. (I didn't figure to go myself after the first few times.)

Of course, all this was in my mind long before I discovered that I was in a family way.

When I got to the newspaper office, I spoke with the young man who clerked for the editor, Mr DeQuille, who happened to be out of town just at that time, but the young man—I believe his name was Holbrook—assured me that he was capable of setting up an advertisement for me, and so I told him what I wanted. He said he'd write it out and set it up, and I could come back in an hour and see if I liked it. So I headed up the street to Miss Rowena Lothrop's tea shop.

Rowena Lothrop, as I believe I've mentioned, was the Stroethers' niece, and lived with them, but she'd gone into business just the previous spring, opening the tea shop in a tiny alcove that she leased from the hotel. (It was in fact connected to that establishment by a pair of French doors that she often kept open to attract hotel traffic.) She paid the hotel owner—that was Mr John Mackay—a portion of her earnings, and also supplied his guests with refreshments at four o'clock every day, in the lobby. Some of those guests drifted in to her place between times, and then there was plenty of custom from folks going by on the board-walk that lay before all of the city's commercial enterprises in those days. Farmers' wives come in to pass the time of day with each other whilst their menfolks dickered for harness and feed, or stopped in to the hotel barbershop for a shave or a trim-up. Ladies out shopping took tea or cocoa or coffee, with one of Rowena's excellent small pastries or a dainty sandwich.

I often strolled in for a quick cup of something hot and a chat with Rowena, who was only a dozen or so years my junior, and possessed of a lively wit. Much of her success was due to this, as well as those delectable treats that she turned out daily, her mother's servant bringing them over under snowy white linen covers, and arranging them in a glass-fronted case.

As it happened, Rowena was busy cutting a handsome cake (topped with glazed cherries) into precise eighths, so I helped myself to a cup of tea from the vast silver urn and sat down for a few minutes at one of the miniscule tables—all prettily painted in green and pink and white, the colors of the sugar frosting Rowena used to ice her little cakes, with chairs to match, and each adorned with a milk-glass bud vase boasting a sprig of greenery and one of Rowena's aunt's hothouse posies—Mrs Stroethers had a famous green thumb.

I stirred sugar into my tea and stared out the window at the passersby, noting idly that ladies' hats was piled higher than ever with feathers—I made a mental note to order more, in as many colors as were available, when I made out my next list of millinery trimmings.

Rowena finished with her cake and arranged the slices on

paper doilies atop cake plates painted with flowers and vines. She set them inside the case, added a small sign with the price per slice, then dusted off her hands on her spotless white apron and joined me.

"How's business?" she asked, handing me a plate with five sugar cookies on it, cut in shapes of stars and flowers, and sprinkled with pink sugar crystals that glittered in the bright sunshine streaming through the shop window.

"Just dandy," I said, taking a cookie. "You?"

"All right," she said. "I thought I'd look in on your place a little later. I need some more extracts." She got up and poured herself a cup of tea. It was the mid-morning lull; the place was empty except for ourselves.

"Just had a new shipment come in," I said. "Got some bigger bottles for you."

"That's wonderful," she said, patting her lips with a napkin. "I need lemon and vanilla and almond and—and some rum extract," she added. "I know there are folks who won't approve, but I have some new receipts I want to try, and they call for rum flavoring."

"I got some in," I said. "Go on and do what you like—I bet the same folks who object to demon rum will be lining up for your goodies once they see 'em and smell 'em."

"You're sweet, Sarah Mary," she said. "Here, take this last cookie—here's the houseboy coming with the next batch."

I watched as the houseboy, a Chinese, came carefully through the door with his tray. He seemed typical of the thousand or so Celestials we had in Virginia City in those days: medium-sized, flat-faced, with an ivory-yellow complexion, his hair in a queue halfway down his back, tied with a black silk cord, but with a clean-shaven crown under his small round cap with a button on it. His face was clean-shaven, too, with black eyebrows like ink strokes, and thin lips and square chin.

He was wearing the usual black sateen gown with long sleeves and frogged closures up the front, and black trousers and black cloth shoes peeping from underneath. A long white apron covered him from chest to knees. It was dazzlingly clean. I remembered that this houseboy also did the Stroethers' washing as well as their housecleaning, and he helped out in the kitchen, though Mrs Stroethers drew the line at letting him cook.

"I'd just as lief not have stewed puppy dogs or some such heathen concoction on my table," she told the assembled guests at one of her monthly Literary Dinners. The Chinese houseboy— what was his name?—had been bringing in the courses and handing them round, and I saw his face when she said this. There was the faintest twitch of the lips, and he lowered his eyes, but not before I saw the glance of amusement he shot at his mistress.

Chung, that was his name.

Now I watched as Chung finished transferring cookies and fancy pastries from his tray to the glass case, under Rowena's direction.

"That's fine," she told him. "Come back around two with the next batch, please."

"Yes, Missy Rowena," he said, and bowed his little bow, then went out with the tray, this time bearing a load of used cake plates, cups, saucers, and cutlery which he would take back to the house and wash, dry, and return.

"He's a treasure," Rowena said, watching him go. "I couldn't do this without his help. Mama lets him take the time, so I pay him something in addition to what she gives him. He wants to earn more, anyway, so he can send more money home." Almost all of the Chinese sent money home from Yin Shan, the Silver Mountain.

I said goodbye to Rowena and headed back to the *Enterprise* office.

Young Holbrook was waiting with the advertisement he'd written. I took the sheet of paper and read the following words:

"Clerk wanted for thriving mercantile establishment. Must be clean, sober and able to write a clear hand. Duties include keeping accounts, stocking supplies and merchandise, handling deliveries, managing store in proprietor's absence, and driving wagon and team. Excellent salary. Inquiries may be made care of this newspaper, to Box _____."

"Why'nt they come right to me, so's I can see 'em?" I objected. "And how do you know the salary's 'excellent'?"

"You always say it is—that makes folks want to apply. This way you can look over their applications, see what kind of hand they write, what sort of qualifications they say they have, before actually *seein'* 'em," young Mr Holbrook said. "You don't want to be bothered during business hours with a lot of applicants takin' up your time, hangin' around the place. Why," he went on, "Some on 'em might be all sort of rapscallions—con men and thieving rascals and what not."

Brother, I thought, *I have seen enough of those in my day to be able to recognize any more of the type*. Aloud, I said, "I suppose you're right. Well, then, sign me up for a box number, and I'll be in next week to see if there's been anyone inquiring."

"Yes, ma'am, Miss Williams," Mr Holbrook said. "Long's you're here already, ma'am, would you care to look over your advertisement for this week? Make any changes?"

He laid a proof sheet down across the table behind the big desk and motioned me to come inside the railing that set off the business end of the paper from the production end. The big presses was silent, for the paper wasn't due to come out for another four days, it being a weekly. But the big desks and drafting tables was full of paper and pens and such, and a boy in overalls sweeping up paper clippings in a lazy rhythm: swish-swish-drag-stop; swish-swish-drag-stop.

I cast my eyes down the columns of print. My ad was boxed neatly at the bottom of the page, with a border of fancy curliques and the name of the store very big and dark: WILLIAMS' EMPORIUM, followed by MENS' & LADIES' FURNISHINGS * HOUSEWARES * NOTIONS & NECESSITIES and the street address, plus the notation, at the bottom: open every day but Sunday, 9 am to 6 pm.

"It looks all right," I said. "Maybe you could say something about 'new shipments arriving fortnightly,' so's folks'll want to come and see what 'new' looks like."

"That's fine," he said, writing busily. "I'll just add that in above the street address; will that be all right?"

I told him yes, paid for the next month's advertising in advance, as usual, and walked thoughtfully back to the store. I'd hung the "CLOSED" sign on the doorknob. Now I turned it to the "OPEN" side and unlocked the door.

Inside it was cool and dim. I went behind the counter and sat on my high stool, resting my elbows on the counter.

Thinking.

I warn't going to lie to myself. Whilst I could lie easy as falling off a log to other folks, truth had an uncomfortable way of settling into my vitals, so to speak, and gnawing away there like the fox in the story about the Spartan boy.

For certain, a part of me thought that having a baby was the worst possible idea—I'd never been around babies, didn't know the first thing about them, wasn't even sure I liked them, had a business to run and all that—not to mention the scandal, though I didn't much care about what other people thought . . .

But a larger part of me kept right on thinking: a baby.

My baby. Who'll she look like, Johnny or me?

You notice I thought of the baby, right from the start, as *she.*

And as *mine.*

And one thing I knew, even then: soon as a woman starts thinking along those lines, she's going to go through with it, if she can.

The question was: how would I manage?

A question that was answered almost immediately, although from a strange quarter.

Chapter Fourteen: Many Changes

As I sat there, pondering, the string of harness bells attached to the door gave a cheerful jangle and Chung, the Stroethers' houseboy, entered the store.

"Good day, Missy Williams," he said. "Missy Rowena sent me to pick up those extracts, if you please."

"Surely," I said, levering myself off the high stool and reaching for my black silk apron, which I tied around my waist whilst I headed back to the store-room. I found the carton and carefully counted out one vanilla, one almond, one lemon, one orange, and one rum flavoring. Five bottles, six ounces each, best extracts. I added a flask of rose water, a bottle of aniseed extract, and another of mint essence, gathered them all into my apron, and carried them carefully back into the store, where I set them on the counter next to the till.

"Here you are," I said. "I'll just tot it up and she can pay me at the end of the month. Let me wrap these up, now—" and I turned around to tear some brown paper off the big roll I kept for wrapping purposes.

"I have brought wrappings," said Chung. "No need to bother." He held up a market basket in which were several sheets of newspaper. "These work nicely." He took the newspaper out of the basket and began to roll each bottle of extract neatly in the sheets, folding them in at the ends and tucking the bottles into the basket.

"You're very neat-handed," I remarked.

"Thank you," he said.

"I'm so sorry, but I don't know what to call you," I said. "Is Chung really your name?"

"Yes. More accurately, Cheung, in Cantonese. Cheung Ka Yun. Chung is close enough, in your alphabet."

"What does your name mean?""

"Ah. Missy Williams, I am honored. You are, if you can believe it, the first American to ask me that question. It appears that not many Americans know, or care, that Chinese names do in fact have meaning." He bowed.

"Go on," I said.

"Thank you. It means—ah, let me see? 'The master of bows,' as in archery? In its constituent radicals, that is; one family legend says that our first ancestor invented the bow. 'To open forth' is the meaning in literal translation. My second name is the name for my generation—Ka. And my given name, Yun, means 'profit.' So, my name is Chung-the-one-of-his-generation-of-the-clan-who-profits." He smiled. "Thus far I have not profited very much in America, but I am still young enough to have hope for the future."

"How long have you worked for the Stroetherses?"

"Since I came to Nevada, about three years ago," he said.

"Your English is very good."

"Thank you. I have studied it for many years, even before coming to America."

"Did you come here alone?"

"No; my elder brother came with me. He is here in town, also."

"Does he work as a houseboy, too?"

"No, he is a nursemaid."

(I should explain that this answer was not as odd as it sounds today, when I suppose most nursemaids are women—as indeed was the case in the East even then. But this was the West, and women were few, and the Chinese, being known as excellent house servants, had quickly established this as work for which they seemed well-suited.

I have often speculated, then and since, that one reason Chinese men became so easily accepted as cooks and nannies and such was that most white men didn't quite see Chinese men as male—part of it being the pigtail, I suppose, and the long gowns, and the fact that the Chinese was mostly clean-shaven—and mostly *clean*, for that matter, cleaner than white men anyhow, on the average. At any rate they seemed more feminine, I guess, and so for Chung to mention that his brother was a nursemaid didn't raise my eyebrows one whit.)

"However, Missy Williams, if you know of anyone who needs a servant like my brother, his post will soon have expired," Chung went on.

"Why's that?"

"The little boy and girl for whom he has cared all these years—since they were born, in fact—are going East to school. The boy is eight and the little girl is six, and they do not need my brother's services as nursemaid any longer."

"How sad he must be, to say goodbye after so long," I said.

Chung smiled slightly. "Yes, he is sad. And his employers are sorry, too, but they say he must go now. And so he is anxious to find work, that he may continue to live and also to send money home to our family in China."

"Ain't they given him any parting gifts?" It was customary, even in our rough part of the country, to give a departing servant some sort of bonus.

"They have told him he may use them as a reference, and I believe they have also given him fifty dollars in gold, for expenses," Chung said.

"Huh! Fifty dollars for eight years," I said.

"Yes," said Chung. "It is not a great deal of money, is it? Well, good-bye, Missy Williams. I will tell Missy Rowena that you are well, yes?" He paused.

"Why, don't I look well?" I had in fact been feeling uncomfortable all day, tired and nervy at the same time, and queasy in my stomach to boot.

"You look—weary, yes?" Chung said. "Shall I hang up the sign that says 'CLOSED' for you, and shall you lie down for a while? Maybe you have a place for reposement in the back of the store. Yes? Shall I make tea?"

It was true that I didn't feel well. "Thank you, Chung," I said.

I watched as he quickly changed the sign on the door, then darted to the rear of the store where I kept a spirit-kettle on a small table next to a low settee. Sometimes after a long day on my feet it was good to rest there for a while.

In a moment Chung had returned and was offering me his arm.

"I don't know what's come over me," I said. "I'm never sick."

"Lie down here, Missy," he said, lowering me to the settee and covering my feet with the quilt I kept folded over the back.

I must have dozed for a few minutes, but I roused when he tapped me on the shoulder and handed me a mug of steaming tea.

"Drink this, please. I will be right back."

I heard the faint ringing of the harness bells as he left. I lay back against the settee's arm and sipped at the tea. Damnation. It must be the baby, I thought. That's why I feel so queer—it's the baby. I reached under the quilt and felt my stomach. It didn't feel any different—yet. But, as I'd told Chung, I was never sick. Well, almost never.

This was a puzzler. How was I going to work if I kept on feeling dizzy and queasy?

I sipped my tea until it was gone, then set the cup on the floor and composed myself for another nap. This time, when I woke, I thought I was seeing double.

It was Chung and another Chinaman—same robe, same queue and little round hat, same shining yellow face, black garments, flat black shoes, and narrow black eyes—but this one wore spectacles, round ones with gold rims, and he was, I now saw, a few years older than Chung.

"Good afternoon, Missy Williams," he said. "My name is Cheung Ka Yat."

I blinked up at him.

"Please, I am the elder brother of this one—Cheung Ka Yun—you know him as Chung. I also am Chung."

"Of course. Sorry. Can I help you, Mr Chung?" I tried to get up, but he forestalled me.

"It is I who shall help you," he said, and pushed me back gently onto the cushions. "Rest, now, and I will take care of the store, yes?"

The younger Chung smiled down at me, bowed, and left us.

I sat back as bidden, and watched his elder brother.

The sign was reversed, and the door began to open and shut with regularity, whilst the bells jingled and I sipped the cups of tea that appeared at intervals. In between tea-brewing and the serving of some sort of hot, spicy soup, which I found immensely restorative, Chung the Elder moved quick and noiseless in those black cloth shoes, going to and fro, waiting on all and sundry, with a bow and a smile for everyone, until at last it was six o'clock and I woke from a light doze to find him smiling down at me.

"We have taken in forty-seven dollars and sixty-two cents," he said, "*And* we are now completely out of curling papers, hair pomade, and rouge. It appears that there is a social event of some significance this evening."

"There's a case in the back," I said. "Of rouge. Pomade's been ordered. And curling papers . . . I think I ordered some of those, too. You can check the book. What sort of social event?"

"Ah. Mr Dan DeQuille's reporter, Mr Samuel Clemens, is

206

reading from his humorous writings penned under the name 'Mark Twain,' for Mrs Stroethers's Literary Evening tonight."

"Guess I'll have to miss it," I said.

"I guess you will," he said, his narrow black eyes dancing.

"Mr Chung!"

"Yes, Missy Sarah?"

"Please step around to the newpaper office and tell that fellow Holbrook to withdraw my advertisement, the one I placed yesterday, for an assistant. If you'd like the job, you're hired."

"Thank you, Missy Sarah. I would like that very much. I will tell Mr Holbrook."

(I want to say here that I had gone to an earlier Literary Evening when Mr Twain had read from his work, a funny story about a jumping frog, which he read extremely well, changing his voice to suit the different characters; all in all it was a livelier Evening than most.)

And so I hired myself an assistant. How well and how fully he was to assist me would become clearer as time went on.

***

Cheung Ka Yat was an educated man. His name, he told me, meant "the one of his generation who excels."

"Although," he added, "So far I have not lived up to that name—at least, not in such wise as I was led to believe I would do, here in Silver Mountain. But perhaps, in time, I shall."

In addition to what he termed "a thorough grounding" in the classics—the Chinese variety—he could read and write English and French, and he was also skilled at mathematics.

I asked him why he hadn't gone to some big city and looked for a job more suited to his talents and education.

"It is not easy for Chinese to find jobs like that," he said. "The Yellow Man has his place, and like the Black Man and the Red, it is somewhat lower than that occupied by the White Man."

I understood that.

"Also," he said, "It is necessary to send money home to China. A scholar's wages—in such positions as I could hope to achieve—would not pay as much as I earned as a nursemaid, or as much as you pay me."

This *did* surprise me, but he assured me it was the truth.

In point of fact he sent money back to China regularly, even though he heard no more from any of his relations than a single letter at the New Year—the Chinese one, that is.

"They ought at least to thank you," I said.

"That is not the point," he said. "It is my obligation to send; it is theirs only to receive. Thanks would be a superfluity."

"I don't understand it," I said.

"Chinese familial relationships and Confucian values regarding the same are perhaps too complex for an American to understand," he said. "That is not a criticism; it is simply that your culture is too new, too unrefined."

"Better not let Leila Stroethers hear you say things like that," I said. "She'd likely have you run out of town for a heathen."

"And so I am," he said.

"Thank God," I said.

And that was how Mr Cheung Ka Yat, Chung-the-one-of-his-generation-of-the clan-who-excels, came to work for me.

***

Of course, his side of things was somewhat different.

He told me, much later, that his brother had come running to him, crying out, "Elder brother! Elder brother! I have found a job for you!"

"What sort of job?"

"Taking care of a pregnant lady—and the baby she will have."

"How did he know I was pregnant?" I interrupted.

"You were pale and your stomach was uneasy, and you had just recently said goodbye to your lover—and before him there had not been another," Chung said.

"Damnation . . . and I thought I'd been so slick, nobody'd noticed . . . does everyone in town know about Johnny and me?"

"No, Missy, not everyone, by no means," Chung reassured me. "Servants always know these things, their masters seldom. It is by such information that we who serve are able to maintain what small power we have over our own lives."

I knew what he meant. It was what Jim had always said about his white folks: study 'em, learn what they wanted and what they didn't want, then make sure they got the one and avoided the other. That way a slave could live out his days in some kind of comfort, if not security.

"So what made you decide you wanted to work for me?" I asked Chung, now.

"I made inquiries," he said, smiling.

208

"Of who?" I said. "Nobody here knows my business . . . I mean, I ain't close to nobody in these parts, except maybe Rowena."

"No, not Missy Rowena," he said. "I asked questions of the ones who serve you and who also serve those others who are big names here, Missy Sarah. You may not see them, or take note of what they do, but they see you, and they have long memories."

He would, in time, tell me more of these "shadow people," he called them, free white folk for the most part, a few free blacks, some Mexicans, and those Indians who came to town once in a while.

All whose lives were lived apart from mine, or Rowena's, or even Dan DeQuille's.

There was the women who drank with the miners and ranchers, and danced with them, and, yes, went upstairs with them, to rooms where the bed took up most of the space, and the dollars earned depended on a girl's being quick enough to turn her tricks without letting them feel unsatisfied.

And then there was the men who cared for my mules and for the horses I used for riding, sweeping up the livery stable, cleaning away the manure, keeping the harness bright and the leather supple and in good repair, feeding and watering the beasts and seeing to their coats and their hooves, their teeth and their wind.

The boys who ran errands and carried messages, who chased each other down the main street and tore off each other's caps and shrieked with laughter, darting in and out of sight.

The girls who shopped for their mothers and sometimes fathers, coming into the store for a paper of pins, a skein of yarn, a length of cloth, a longing look at the displays of hair combs and lace collars, kid gloves and fancy garters.

Those few free black men who made a living as freight haulers and mule skinners, living outside of town in a group of falling-down shanties, some of them with Indian wives and platoons of copper-colored children, all of them silent, respectful, watchful.

Those Indians who come into town for blankets and mirrors and knives, for red cloth and glass beads for their women to use in decorating their shirts and belts and moccasins, tall men with long noses and proud faces, wrapped in their blankets, saying little . . . and those few of their women who came with them, pretty as young deer, with fawn-eyes and smooth brown cheeks, some of them in fringed leggings and tunics, others in blankets like their men, all of them wistful-looking as if they would speak but had no words.

The miners who rolled like a noisy flood into town on Saturday night, only to creep feebly back to the mines come early Monday morning. If I rose before dawn I could see them, reeling into the street from the alleys and stables and back rooms where they'd slept off the most part of their drunkenness and lust, scrubbing their faces with water from the horse-troughs, beating the dust from their jeans and scraping the mud or horse-droppings from their boots, combing their hair back with their fingers before settling their hats down upon their eyebrows and lurching off into the breaking day.

Beside all of these, those of us who counted as the "respectable" members of Virginia City society were few in number, indeed. Even if you counted the ranchers and farmers, we were still only a few. The shadow people thronged below us, waiting, watchful.

I pondered. Who was I, among these? By birth I was one of the shadow folk. By my own doings I belonged, perhaps, to those who'd come to seek a new life here: ranchers and farmers who saw in this new land a new life—as I had, once.

I knew them, these farmers and ranchers who came into town to trade and to spend a little time entertaining themselves and being entertained—even if all the amusement that the town could boast was a stroll up and down Main Street and a pot of tea for the women at Miss Rowena's, a shave and a trim at the hotel barbershop for their men, and a peppermint stick or sack of horehound or lemon drops for the children who trailed after them.

I had come West with them, and indeed some of them I could still count as friends, although I saw them seldom: the Niedermeiers, the Swensons, the Olmsteads, and of course Dr Thannheimer and his nephew Ernst. The Niedermeiers had settled not too far from Virginia City, in the valley of the Truckee River, as had the Olmsteads and the Swensons. Dr Thannheimer and Ernst were still in California—in Oakland, where Ernst was pursuing his medical studies. Far away from where I was, but not so far as to be completely out of reach.

And so, after Chung had bowed himself out of the store, I opened the drawer of my big desk, took out a sheet of writing paper, and started in to write. *Dear Doctor Thannheimer*, my letter began, *I need your advice . . .*

And within a week I had his reply.

My dear Friend, he wrote in his funny German-flavored English,

Come Thou shalt immediately here, but have a care for thy health and the health of the child,

Thy loving Friend,
Josef Thannheimer

***

I will pass over my trip to Oakland, except to say that it was just exactly as uncomfortable as I imagined it would be.

I was jounced about unmercifully in the stagecoaches, and most froze myself as well, or else was prostrated with heat, but no harm appeared to have been done when I finally stepped out of a hired hack in front of Dr Thannheimer's surgery. I wondered if Ernst would be there, as it was near end of term at the new College of California[50]—Dr Thannheimer had told me so in his last letter. I shook out my skirts (in the interest of avoiding stares and the stains of travel I had dressed in female attire, a dark wool costume, with a deep scoop bonnet that made me feel like a gopher peering up from the bottom of his hole, and a grey shawl the size of a coverlet (necessary for cold nights in an unheated, drafty stagecoach).

I stepped up to the door and knocked

"Coming, coming!" called a female voice. The voice's owner opened the door and stared out at me.

"Surgery entrance to the side," the woman said. I judged she must be the doctor's housekeeper: a white woman, in her fifties perhaps, neat and tidy, and she spoke up crisp, in an accent I couldn't place—later I was to learn that she was from Vermont. "Surgery hours aren't until 2 pm. Doctor's still at his luncheon."

"That's all right," I said. "He's expecting me."

"Oh, my goodness. You must be Miss Williams!" she said. "My dear, of course. Come in, do." She ushered me in and began helping me off with my shawl and bonnet and coat.

"Is it Thou, Sarah Mary?"

I swallowed hard at the sound of the familiar voice, the sound of which threatened to bring tears to my eyes. "Yes, it's me."

---

[50] Eds. note: This College was the genesis of the University of California system. The College was located near the present University of California at Berkeley campus, north of Oakland.

He was there, beaming, his hand outstretched. "How good it is to see Thee, my friend! Come in—Margaret, another place, please."

"Right away, Doctor," and she bustled off. I sat down across from the Doctor and accepted a cup of tea.

"Thy wire said that Thou wished to consult me professionally," he said.

"Right," I said, as Margaret swept back in, bearing a platter of cold ham and potato salad.

"You'll want something to eat," she said.

I looked at the platter and swallowed. "No'm, I ain't—I'm not hungry, thank you."

Dr Thannheimer peered at me, no doubt recollecting that on our trip West I was as likely to turn down food as to take wing and fly through the air.

"How's Ernst?" I said, changing the subject.

"He is well," the Doctor said. "But Thou?"

"I'm all right—except—" I couldn't finish, for the tears started in to come.

The Doctor throwed down his napkin. "Margaret, clear the table, please. We will to the surgery go." He rose, stalked grimly to a door on the other side of the room, and opened it. "Through here, please."

I followed, without a word.

***

I did not speak, either, through the examination that followed. When he was through, Doctor Thannheimer helped me to sit up, went across the room to wash his hands in the basin that stood there, and with his back politely turned (whilst I dressed myself) asked the question I had been dreading.

"And so, where is he, the father of this baby Thou wilt have?"

"He's gone," I said.

"Gone." Doctor Thannheimer swiveled round and glared at me. "How is this happening?"

I tried to explain. Finally, the Doctor threw up his hands.

"How wilt Thou be having this baby with no husband?"

"Same as any other woman would, I reckon," I said.

"It is not a matter for humor," he said.

"I ain't living in Timbuktu," I said. "Virginia City is bidding fair to become a civilized place—leastways, some of the inhabitants think so."

"Thou wilt need much care," he said. "Thou art not young a first child to be having. Thou mayest deliver easily, or perhaps not, but Thou wilt need someone with Thee, and someone to help with the child when it comes."

"I have somebody," I said.

"Who?"

So I told him about Chung, whom I'd left in charge of the Emporium, not without some trepidation. I expected the Doctor to rear up in protest, but I had forgot he'd been in the West as long as I had, and was just as familiar with Chinese nursemaids.

"This man, he has experience with infants? Good." The Doctor tapped a pad of notepaper that lay on his desk. "I will write out all directions, ja? For infant formula, in case Thou cannot nurse the child, and for medicines, and tonics—"

I was touched. "Thank you," I said.

"And since to stay you will not, I will myself to Nevada come to see this child born," the Doctor said.

"It's too far," I objected. "You can't leave your practice that long."

"The child is due, I perceive from my examination, in mid-June," he said. "Ernst will have finished his examinations by then. He can take charge here, as my locum. I will come at the end of May, to be certain."

And there was nothing I could say to change his mind.

Well, I spent about three weeks with the Doctor. My stomach settled itself enough that I was able to partake of Margaret's cooking, which pleased her as well as the Doctor.

"Thou must eat well, but not too much," he said. "No sweets. And no coffee." He went on to warn me about other things I must avoid, such as very hot baths, horseback riding except at a slow walk, reaching up for objects on high shelves, and tight lacing.

"I never lace at all," I said.

"Thou wilt wish to wear a loose corset, laced very lightly, in a few months," he said. "It will give extra support to the stomach as it enlarges. It will also be well to wear comfortable clothing, and make sure to keep warm, but not so warm as to make much sweat."

I promised to follow all of this advice.

"And I will write all of this down for Thou and that Chung of thine," he said.

"All right."

And in fact, when I was dressed and ready to be taken to the stagecoach depot, the Doctor came downstairs with a sheaf of papers in his hand.

"I have written, so," he said, "For each week, a set of directions, ja? And Thou wilt these follow, or I will know it when I come." And he made a terrible face.

"I will," I said, trying not to laugh.

"It is not in jest I have these things written," he said.

"I know it. Thank you," I said, and without intending it, I threw my arms around him and kissed him on his bearded cheek. "Thank you, my dear friend. I will do everything you say."

"That is good," he said, patting me on the back. "I will see Thee in six months, ja? And a fine baby we will bring, together, Thou and I and this Chung."

And so I trundled home to wait out the next several months.

***

Well, of course, eventually I got about as big around as an elephant, and the day I found myself unable to see my own feet I let out a screech that brought Chung running, only to retreat in embarrassment at finding me in my nightdress.

But at first all that was noticeable was a thickening through my middle, easily dealt with by letting my waistbands out a few inches. My queasiness subsided almost as soon as I got back to Virginia City, and I ate heartily of everything Chung produced, especially the soups he brewed, which he said were Chinese medicine for a healthy mother and baby. Some of them surely tasted like medicine—bitter and sour and salty—but I relished them all the same, oddly enough. Everything went well, with one exception.

I was going over the books with Chung one evening toward the middle of January.

"Seems like a drop in revenues," I noted. "And last month was the same, wasn't it?" I flipped a few pages backwards, scanning the "net" columns. Sure enough, we'd been seeing a decline for quite some time. It warn't much—but up to then we'd been seeing a steady increase.

"Indeed, we have been losing custom," Chung said. "Christmas made up for it somewhat, but now that the season is over, we are seeing a small loss, yes."

"Whyever? Has somebody set up in competition without me knowing?"

"No, there is no competition."

"Then what?"

Chung did not answer, but looked down at my front and coughed discreetly.

"Oh. The baby. Oh, Lord," I said. "Folks have realized that I'm expecting."

Chung nodded. I got up and began to roam restlessly around the room. "Damnation," I said. "What business is it of anyone's? What harm am I doing to anybody?"

Chung shook his head. "People are very conventional creatures," he said. "In any society, there are mores. One violates them at one's peril."

"I don't know what you mean by morays," I said, "But this ain't Connecticut! Or even Missouri," I ended, somewhat lamely. "People come out West for freedom. Don't they?"

"Some do," Chung said. "But I fear more bring their prisons with them—prisons of mind and habit."

"So some folks are showing their displeasure by keeping their pocketbooks far away from me, is that it?"

"It would appear so."

"Give me that ledger again," I ordered. I scanned the last few pages and sighed. "Guess we'll just have to figure out how to tighten our belts for the duration."

I could see in his eyes that Chung was much amused by this figure of speech.

"And tomorrow," I added, "I'm going to find out for myself what the situation is."

"You should not open yourself to humiliation from those who are not your equals," Chung said. "Nonetheless, I perceive that you will not rest until you hear their perfidy from their own lips."

"Damn right," I said. "Pass me that box of chocolate creams."

"Doctor Thannheimer said 'no sweets,'" Chung said.

"I'm only taking one. Two," I said, grabbing before he could pull the box away.

"I will make tea," he said.

"You do that," I mumbled, through a chocolate cream.

"Thank you, Chung."

***

Next morning I dressed with care in a new skirt and jacket I'd had made for the winter, of slate-blue wool trimmed with rows of matching braid. It was a struggle to button the jacket, but I managed it. To my own eyes I looked very little different, until I turned sideways and viewed my outline in the glass. Yes, there was definitely a bump protruding from my front, and even the fullness of the wool skirt did not conceal it completely. I shrugged and wrapped myself in the fur cape I'd bought to set off my new costume—it was Russian sable, and cost a pretty penny, along with the matching hat and mittens I drew on next—stepped into the fur-lined tall kamiks[51] I used in winter instead of American-style laced boots—the kamiks being warmer and easier on my swollen feet, these days—and set off for Rowena's house.

When I got there, Chung the Younger opened the door with a smile and a finger to his lips.

"Missy Sarah, Missy Rowena will see you in the morning room," he whispered. "I will bring her, right away."

I let him hang up my wraps whilst I stepped out of my kamiks. In my heavy gray wool stockings I tiptoed with him down the hallway and into the "morning room," which was really a converted sun-porch that Rowena had taken over for her domain. She had painted the walls a soft gray. Pink and gray curtains matched the slipcovers on a white wicker settee, and white wicker armchairs and tables sat here and there on the rose-colored carpet.

I sank into a wicker rocker and Young Chung slid a footstool under my feet, covered them with a rosy wool throw, and then, with another placing of finger to lips, departed.

To pass the time, I counted the rosebuds in the printed-cotton covers of the round cushions at each end of the settee. Just as I got to one hundred, the door opened and Rowena slipped in.

"Oh, my dear," she whispered, "I am so glad to see you! But you shouldn't have come."

"Why not?" I whispered back. "And why are we whispering

---

[51] Eds. note: Kamik (the word is Inuit, as is mukluk, a similar type of footgear) are boots made of reindeer hide or sealskin, often with fur linings (as here). Properly, kamik is the plural form (singular kamak).

like this?"

"Aunt Leila doesn't know you are here," she whispered.

"Well, so what?" I said in my normal voice.

"Sarah Mary!"

"I don't care," I said. "If there is gossip about me, I want to hear it to my face!"

"Well, then," said a second voice, "You shall have your wish!"

Rowena shrank back as Mrs Stroethers hove into the room.

I had never disliked Leila Stroethers, though finding her versifications somewhat tough to digest, as I have written, but I had never been on the receiving end of her displeasure before. Now I found myself trapped and the recipient of quite an earful.

I was a hussy and a disgrace. I was not to be received by decent people. No one with any claim to morality would darken the door of my establishment again—she and the other custodians of public morality would see to that.

"You can't really expect to cut into my business," I said.

"It is a matter of principle," she said. She was in quite a state and resembled, at that moment, nothing so much as a hen with all her feathers in a kerfuffle.

"What gives you the right to sit in judgment?" I asked.

"I believe in upholding decency. You have harmed us all. You are a disgrace to public morality," she said.

"Because I'm having a baby," I said, "Without a husband."

She made a little shriek and pretended to swoon. "Rowena! Leave the room!"

"Aunt Leila," Rowena said. "Don't you think—"

"I said, leave the room!" Mrs Stroethers shrieked again, louder.

Rowena, with a glance of apology towards me, edged herself out the door.

Mrs Stroethers advanced. "Leave my house, you Jezebel!"

"Touch me, and you'll regret it," I said, and though I was at a considerable disadvantage (being wedged in the chair, so to speak), she subsided.

"You must leave these premises, and never return!" she said in a melodramatic voice.

Just at that moment, Chung the Younger arrived, holding my wraps in his arms, his narrow black eyes dancing at me from over the furry bundle.

"Missy Stroethers!" he said. "You go, Missy—I take care of this!" and he glared at me quite realistically and shook my kamiks at me before dropping them melodramatically to the floor. It was right funny—but I managed not to laugh.

Mrs Stroethers leaned toward me and stuck her fat finger in my face. "And I forbid you to see or communicate with my niece!"

"All right, all right," I said, finally managing to lever myself out of the chair. I stooped, puffing a little, and managed to yank my kamiks on, then stood up and faced Mrs Stroethers. I was taller than she already by some inches, and when I had jammed my hat onto my head and wrapped my cape around me, the advantage in height and bulk was well on my side.

"*You* listen to *me*," I said. "I had thought you was a friend of mine. I always treated you decent. You have got no call to act this way."

"You don't know what the word *decent* means. Trollop!"

"I know this," I said. "Your conduct, lady, ain't decent, not by anyone's definition." And I stepped around her (which took some doing, as she had considerable heft of her own) and made my way to the front door.

Rowena was waiting in the doorway.

"Here," she said, thrusting a folded paper into my hand. Behind us, a door slammed.

"Rowena!"

"Right away, Aunt Leila!"

And with a last apologetic smile, my friend was gone.

Chapter Fifteen: Sally-John

The paper that Rowena shoved into my hand, when unfolded, read thus:

Dear Sarah Mary,

You must know how deeply concerned I am for you, and how sad I am to learn of the difficulty in which you find yourself. My Aunt Leila has vowed that she will canvass all of our friends and institute a formal boycott of your Emporium; as I heard her tell the minister's wife only yesterday, "We cannot reward immorality but must cast it from our midst." I cannot at present do anything much to assist you (for Aunt Leila watches me like a hawk, and insists that Chung go with me every step I take outside the house, even to my tea shop), but please know that I am still your friend, whatever betide, and my fervent prayers are with you in your sad situation—

Your loving friend always,

Rowena

This communication made up, a little, for the tongue-lashing I'd got from Leila Stroethers. Nonetheless, I spent the rest of the afternoon in bed, feeling sorry for myself, and also feeling a very strange sensation, as if I'd been through the whole thing before.

Which in a way I had, back when Miss Edwards threw me out of her school for seducing an innocent young virgin.

I couldn't help feeling that life was just a bit unfair.

The only two times I had ever been in love had both ended the same: with me being branded before all the world as a villainess of rare aspect.

I decided that there would not be a third time.

After a while, I got up and splashed some water on my face and went downstairs to deal with the situation. Self-pity would not help.

I pondered what to do. "I don't believe most folks around these parts care whether I'm having a baby or not," I said to Chung.

"That is most probably correct. The influence of Missy Stroethers and her ilk is likely much less than she herself imagines. But the months ahead will not be pleasant."

"What do *you* think I ought to do?"

"You could perhaps retire to Oakland for a time, with the good Doctor, and bring your former partner, Mr Cassius, here to take over for you," Chung suggested.

I had in fact thought of Cassius in that role, but dismissed the idea. "He's happy with his own place and his wife and children," I said.

"But he would come if you asked him."

"Of course he would. That's why I can't," I said.

"I understand," Chung said, and I felt that he did.

I determined to find out the extent of the hostility that was felt toward me. If it was only from the Stroetherses and their ilk, maybe I could manage to hang on.

Well, a trip around town next day did not encourage me. Not one of my "respectable" acquaintances met my eyes, none returned my cheerful greetings with any but the merest frosty nod, and in the end I slunk home, chilled more by the reception I'd got than by the winter temperatures.

Even Sam Clemens refused to stop and say hello, when I passed him outside the offices of the *Enterprise*. A shake of the head and a "Hem!" was all that I got from him, though I stopped dead in my tracks, stuck out my hand, and called out his name as plain as plain.[52]

I didn't dare stop in at the saloon. Lord only knew what might come out of Liam Donahy's mouth—though you could guarantee it would be indelicate, if not profane.

So that was that. I could manage to turn a blind eye to the opinion of Leila Stroethers and her coterie. But I didn't relish being shunned by folks I'd thought of as friends.

This time, I sent Chung to the telegraph office, along with several other errands. And when he returned a few hours later, it was with the reply I'd expected.

So, making the best of it, I leased my store to the oldest son of the Niedermeiers, who was more than willing to leave cattle raising for a while. I wanted Chung to handle the lease arrangements for me, but he pointed out that most folks wouldn't take the word of a Chinese in any legal matters, so I engaged the services of Mr Trumbull, an attorney I'd had some business with from time to time. The details I left for him to finish, whilst Chung and I made ready to leave for Oakland.

---

[52] Author's note: I reminded him of this incident when I met him again, years later. He claimed to have forgotten the circumstances.

It was snowing when we set out, I well bundled up and seated next to Chung, who was driving my traveling emporium, the wagon I'd come West with just twelve years ago. I'd had it refitted for a ten-mule hitch.

We'd loaded it with a selection that I wanted to take of my inventory—I'd kept some items back from the lease, which I intended as presents for the Doctor and his household—and with my and Chung's personal belongings. I'd packed my trunk with everything I thought I'd need for the months ahead. And whilst I made piles of towels and underclothing, petticoats and stockings, shirts and trousers, I looked long at the place I was leaving.

Especially the bedroom, where I'd slept alone for so long, and then—for just a few short weeks—where I'd lain with Johnny.

The memory was—and still is— bittersweet.

"Why do you love me? I ain't pretty," I'd said once, my head on his shoulder, the two of us lying drowsy and content.

"You ain't pretty, for a fact," he said. "But that don't seem to make a difference. I can't explain it, but you make me feel all—*full,* somehow, in here," and he'd laid his fingers on his smooth caramel-colored chest, at the center, where his heart beat. I could count the pulses as I lay looking up at him. "Just plum-full of love," he concluded.

That particular plum must've been too hard to digest, I thought.

But, really, that warn't fair of me to think so, and I knew it. Nothing had been said between us of permanence. Nothing held him us to each other but a few weeks in my bed. I had burned like tinder in his arms, and just as quick as tinder caught alight and went up in flames, it was over.

He'd come into my life just like the Pony Express rider he had once been—quick to arrive and quicker to go. Then that short-lived enterprise ceased, and he took out for the life of a range-rover, a cowboy. The saddle was his home, and not any woman's world.

A woman's world might hold a child within it, but not Johnny's.

If it was left up to me, he would never know that a child had been born of those few weeks he'd spent upstairs of my store, in my bed, loving me.

He would never know, not because I did not believe he would welcome a child, but because I would not use that particular weapon to hold him to ransom. The child was part of him, a part that I could keep.

I *had* loved him. But now Johnny had gone for good, and taken with him all I would ever know of that kind of love.

The life that remained to me would have to take a different turn.

So I said farewell to Virginia City.

***

The trip was easier than I'd thought it would be, because Chung went slow and insisted we stop often. When there was a town with a hotel, we stayed (or at least I did, whilst Chung bunked with the wagon in whatever stable was available). Otherwise, we camped by the side of the road, in passable comfort. It took three weeks, but we finally rolled into Oakland at the end of March, and Doctor Thannheimer's Margaret put me to bed in the spare room, and sent Chung to lodge in the attic Ernst had taken over as bedroom and study. Ernst was still living at the College, so Chung was quite comfortable, he said.

"What are you going to do with yourself?" I asked him.

"Study medicine with your Doctor Thannheimer, until we are ready to leave here," was the unexpected reply.

"Go on! Do you mean it?"

"I do indeed," he said. "I know a great deal about Chinese medicine" (I recalled the soups and teas he'd made for me, and acknowledged that this was so) "but I know very little about the ways in which this discipline is practiced in the West."

"Well, as long as you're content," I said.

"I shall be happy to be of service," he said.

And it was true that he was very useful to Doctor Thannheimer, learning quickly how to make the various potions and pills and ointments the Doctor used, and helping him in his surgery.

"Ain't—aren't—folks funny about you having a Chinese assistant?" I asked the Doctor, one day when he was examining me.

"Yes, some of them are," he said. "But it makes no difference to Chung or to me. And it is also true that the same people believe that the Chinese have special knowledge of healing."

"That they do," I said.

"I also believe it," he said, with a smile. "Your Chung has taken excellent care of you. I believe I have seldom seen a woman in your condition who looked so well as you."

It was true that I looked well—better than I ever had, save for my huge belly. This the Doctor directed Margaret to massage me with, gently, every evening with a special oil he had concocted, scented with juniper and sage, which he said would help me in giving birth, and I laughed every time she did so, for it seemed that my baby was ticklish, as she jumped about when Margaret's hands passed over her.

And so the winter passed, and the Spring came on, and on a day in early May, when the morning fog was just lifting and the sun came through the curtains in shafts of soft gold, I gave birth to my daughter.

I named her Sally-John: Sally for Sarah—me—at least, the me I'd chosen to become on that day when I had faced the inevitable truth of my femaleness—now fulfilled at last in motherhood.

And John, for her daddy.

The birth was easier than I had expected, maybe due to the Doctor's herbal oil. Margaret come in and out with hot drinks and fresh sheets and clean towels, and Chung and Ernst were both there, to help Dr Thannheimer.

It hurt, all right—don't let nobody tell you childbirth is any picnic—Lord, it hurt like hell, and I yelled like the dickens, I can tell you!

At the end, just before the last push, I didn't think I could manage it. I was half-kneeling, half-squatting on the bed, held up on one side by Margaret's capable arms and by Ernst's on the other.

Chung and the Doctor waited by with clean towels to catch the baby, and I looked up between spasms of pain into Chung's clear black eyes. He smiled and said something. I didn't catch it.

"What was that?" I gasped.

"I said, you are brave. You are like the phoenix," he said, and smiled again.

I smiled back. Then—

"Push hard," the Doctor said, "Now!"

And obediently I pushed.

It felt as though my pelvic bones was being wrenched apart by giant hands—

And then—

She was born.

She slid out of me with a wriggle like a tadpole, and I lay back against the pillows, unable even to ask, "Is it all right?"

I heard a faint squalling noise and closed my eyes.

Then I felt a small, moving weight upon me, a warm, soft solidness. Chung had laid the baby on my breast. I put my hands over her warm little body and I felt no more pain, only joy.

I was peaceful, peaceful and happy, maybe for the first time in my life.

"She is beautiful," Chung said. Doctor Thannheimer and Ernst and Margaret all nodded. All four of them looked as pleased as I felt.

"Your uncles and your auntie say you are beautiful," I told her, and she opened her eyes and looked into mine, and at that moment I fell in love.

I know I'd sworn never to do so again, but it was so.

When you fall in love with your child, it is passionate and sweet and catches your breath in your chest like an ache and a rapture all at once.

I fell in love—and at last it was with someone who it was all right, finally, for me to love that way.

She was a beautiful child. And that is not just the mother in me talking. When she was born she was very pale-skinned (as are all babies with Negro blood; born light, their complexions darken later). And she had a lot of thick dark straight hair like an Indian baby, but that all wore off in a few weeks, and when her hair grew back, it was curlier than mine, and glossy black.

Her eyes was the same muddy bluish color all new babies' eyes are, but they changed eventually to a clear deep-golden color like good sherry. And by the time she was half a year old, her complexion had turned the warm shade of maple sugar—a little darker than mine, a little lighter than her daddy's. All in all she deserved to be called beautiful.

She was also smart.

I know every mother says the same, but Sally-John was sharp as a tack. She said her first words when she was only eight months old. "Opa," she said, addressing the Doctor, and thereby moving him to tears.

***

We stayed with Doctor Thannheimer and Ernst and Margaret for six months. It got somewhat crowded in that little house, with Sally-John and me in the spare room and Ernst and Chung crowded together in Ernst's attic room. But it was summertime. We spent much of it outdoors in the Doctor's spacious back yard, shaded by trees and filled with flowers and herbs, for he was a notable gardener and grew the plants he used for many of his herbal remedies.

The Doctor had built an arbor; flowered vines covered it with shade and scent, and I sat in it and rocked the baby and fed her and sang to her in a haze of light, for it seemed that the sun shone every day. Margaret was happy, having so many to coddle and cook for. It was a time out of time for me, as if life lay waiting just outside the door, taking its ease whilst I took mine.

Money was not a problem; I had the investments Judge Thatcher had made for me all those years ago, and income from the Niedermeiers' receipts as well, for the store continued profitable despite its owner's reputation as a brazen hussy. I was able to pay Chung his regular salary, and I made sure to pay over a sum to Margaret for our room and board (she and I kept this a secret between us, for the Doctor would have refused to take any money from me).

But I begun to think more and more about the future. Sally-John deserved the finest things life could offer, and therefore her mother had better get herself back to work.

With that in mind, I sent Chung off to San Francisco to talk to Cassius about some plans I had begun to formulate. Cassius, you may recall, had set up as the proprietor of a saloon with his wife, Snow-on-the-Mountain. I had no intention of taking him away from his chosen work, but I wanted to consult him about some ideas I had, including making a move to Tahoe City, California. The prospects there was improving all the time, and while it warn't so very far from Virginia City, I felt it was far enough.

When Chung came back, he brought news of some alarming happenings in Lawrence, Kansas, just two weeks since.

Doctor Thannheimer took the newspaper, regular, and I give it a glance or two most days, just to keep up with the war news. So I'd seen the headlines about "Massacre in Kansas" but hadn't read the articles.

Now Chung plunked a copy of the San Francisco *Examiner* down in front of me and pointed.

When I saw what he was pointing at, I just about jumped out of my seat.

This was a full chronicle of the Kansas massacre. It was now well known, the reporter wrote, that it was that famous Rebel,

William Quantrill, who'd led a force of bushwhackers to Lawrence and executed close to two hundred men, some of them elderly and some not much more than boys. He had done it to punish the town for its pro-Unionist sympathies, the article said.

Sickened, I read on.

Quantrill and his mob had robbed the Lawrence bank, set fire to most of the town's buildings, and rode off. That had happened on August 21, 1863. On August 25, just eight weeks ago, the Union general in the area had ordered the population of three Missouri counties to leave their homes, in retaliation for the raid. The paper said that Quantrill and his men had headed south, perhaps to Texas. A bounty was offered for Quantrill, dead or alive.

"So that's what become of him," I said, slowly.

The Doctor returned from his surgery and resumed his seat at the table. "Look at this, Doctor," I said, pointing at the headline.

He read the article quickly, then turned to me. "Is this the same man of whom Thou hast told me?"

"That's him."

"So." The Doctor frowned. "This War. He fights on the side of slavery, ja?"

"Ja," I said. I felt sick. I looked toward the cradle where my daughter slept.

What would William Quantrill do, if he knew I—his blood relative—had lain with a colored man, given birth to a colored baby? The newspaper article described the condition of the men and boys he'd massacred. I shuddered as I remembered his eyes, cold as a snake's, but deadlier. A snake, after all, kills only to eat or to defend himself. Unlike my cousin, who did others to death, it seemed, for the sheer love of killing.

I said a prayer that night, and for many nights thereafter, to the God I didn't quite believe in, that somebody might claim the bounty on William Quantrill, and soon.

***

Chung and I agreed that there was no need for me to head up to the Sierras until next spring. The snows in the mountains made the roads largely impassable until then. Ernst volunteered in late March[53] to go to Tahoe City for me, as my representative, and I gave him full authority in writing, as well as a draft on my Virginia City

---

[53] Eds. note: 1864.

bank account. Chung and the Doctor both had impressed on me the need to send a white man. Though the necessity made me angry, I was forced to agree.

So we saw Ernst off at the stage depot in Oakland, well wrapped in a fur-lined overcoat, for early spring in the mountains was still cold, with a thick woolen blanket for the chilly nights, and a large black leather satchel: my gift.

This satchel, which would in time hold his doctor's equipment, contained not only a change of underclothes and socks, but plenty of food, wrapped well in brown paper and tied in a clean tea towel: sausages and bread and honey cakes and a number of the little fried pastries stuffed with fruit that Margaret called "hand-pies," plus a bottle of the Doctor's best schnapps to ward off the chill.

Ernst, pink-cheeked and smiling, with the satchel tucked securely under his feet, waved at us as the coach jounced off, and I waved back until the coach was a tiny speck.

"The little one will have need of her mother," the Doctor said, taking my arm and turning me around. "So come, let us not linger here."

And so, for the next two weeks, we heard nothing from Ernst. Then, finally, there was a letter.

It came just before I went in to breakfast, having settled Sally-John in her cradle after nursing her and changing her diaper. Having washed my hands and face and put on a clean wrapper, I stooped by the door and picked up the day's mail from the mat. I sat down in my usual place and drank the buttermilk that Margaret had, as usual, set out for me. The Doctor approved of buttermilk for nursing mothers.

I sorted through the envelopes, seizing one and slitting it open with my table knife. I scanned it quickly.

"Good news?" asked the Doctor, buttering his toast.

"Very good," I said. "Ernst has done well and will be home in—" I looked back at the letter's date; one week ago—"in about ten days."

"God be praised," said the Doctor, handing me a platter of fried eggs.

Chung came in from the surgery and sat down in his place. "I finished that batch of cough syrup you wanted," he said to the Doctor.

"Thank you," the Doctor said. "Sarah has had a letter."

I passed the letter to Chung, who read it and handed it back to me.

"Very good," Chung said.

"I shall be sorry to lose you," the Doctor said to him. "You have been an excellent apprentice. You would make a fine doctor, yourself."

"But you are the master, not I. Perhaps you will come to Tahoe City with us."

The Doctor smiled, but shook his head. "I do not wish for more travel. To have come to the Pacific, this is enough."

"And you have patients you would not wish to leave," Chung said. "Of course."

"And Margaret!" I spoke up. "What would she do, if you were gone?"

"Ach," the Doctor said, but I could tell he was pleased with this kind of foolery, though he pretended to be far above it.

So I wrote to the lawyers named in Ernst's letter, and we made ready, Chung and I, and the baby, for the next part of our journey.

Just before we left, Chung asked me a question I'd not foreseen.

"Missy Sarah, are you intending to keep me on in your employ?"

"Of course—that is, if you want it," I said, slowly. It come to me that Chung might choose to follow his own path now, and not mine. I heard his next words through a sudden pang.

"May I make a request?" he asked.

"Sure thing."

"I wish to continue in your service," he said. "But—"

"Whatever it is, if it is in my power, you've got it," I said, suddenly giddy with relief. He did not want to go!

"Well, then. I have decided that an American name would be desirable for my new situation," he said thoughtfully. "Perhaps you will find it agreeable to call me David. That seems to me to be a name of good import."

"What do you mean?"

"It is a name from your Bible," he said. "You will recall that for some years I took the children of my employers to Sabbath School, and of course I remained for the lesson. And so I heard this story of David, many times, David who killed the giant and went on to greatness." He smiled. "Not that I aspire to a kingdom, you understand, but the metaphor pleases me."

"Well, there ain't too many giants nor kingdoms in America, far's I know, but I've no objection," I said, and extended my hand. "Pleased to meet you, then, Mr David Chung."

And we shook hands.

We set out in April. Now, at that time the summer is fast approaching the California coast, but the high plains are still bare of flowers and the snows still lie thick upon the Sierras. And so it was. We rode over the pass and a golden eagle soared up into the sky. Beside me David said something in Chinese.

"What was that you said?"

"It is a good omen," he said, smiling. "The symbol of wisdom. It says that the choice to come here is a wise one, Sarah Mary."

"I trust you're right," I said.

The golden bird soared out of sight. The air burned clear and dark blue, cold as well water.

And then we saw the lake.

So deep a blue, a color no human could invent, like a jewel set down amongst the rocks and the trees, ringed by granite mountains covered with Ponderosa pines. Sometimes I dream of those trees still, with their weird twisted black branches and their giant cones, the biggest I have ever seen, and the air sharp and cool, scented with resin and the dry, clean smell of stone and snow.

Well, none of us could have known it, but the war was over. In a few days President Lincoln would be shot by a Southern assassin. Soon John Wilkes Booth would be run to ground and killed in his turn.

The old folks say death comes in threes, and news of a third death came my way in August of that same year. Not two months before, on a day late in June, Union troops had shot and killed William Clarke Quantrill, in a skirmish with the few who remained of Quantrill's Raiders.

So the blood shed in Lawrence, Kansas was repaid in blood , and I could leave off the wearing of guns as a daily habit—though I kept a rifle, loaded, at the ready for such other ill-doers as might come my way.

And, with the end of the war, a new era in the history of the

West would also begin. Of that, too, we had no knowledge—although we also took part in those beginnings.

Chapter Sixteen: I Go A-Visiting

I took advantage of the time spent building the new store to go back East and visit my daughter's only relations—as well as those folks in Hannibal who I counted as close as I had to family. It had come to me belatedly that it was wrong for me to keep the news of Jim's granddaughter from his other relations.

I left David in charge. He wanted to come with me, of course, thinking that I would have a hard time with Sally-John, without his help, but I persuaded him that he could use some time to himself, without being always at a baby's beck and call, and also that I wanted and needed some time with my child.

"You manage all of her care—why, she don't know me from Adam's off ox, most of the time," I said.

"Sarah Mary, that is not true," David said. "She knows her mama."

"All right! Now David, listen. This is important. I need to take her to see her step-grandma and her aunt, for they're all she has of blood relations besides me and Johnny. And I want to show her to Aunt Polly and Aunt Sally Phelps. They need to know about her, too."

For I had not written, when she was born, to tell Julie nor the others about Johnny's daughter. I did so, now, not wishing to spring such news on them in person, and Julie wrote back, telling me how pleased and excited they both was, and that we was expected.

So we went.

***

The first leg was by stagecoach, to Sacramento, then by train—two different railroads, in fact—to Omaha. From Omaha we went by coach, then a short trip by rail, then coach again, to Kansas City, where we took another train to St Joe.[54] It took seven days, which may seem a great deal today, but when I recalled the months I'd spent on the westward journey just a scant fifteen years before, I could only marvel at how things had changed.

---

[54] Eds. note: The Transcontinental Railroad connected railways to both coasts in 1869, but in 1866 rail travel between the far West and the middle of the country was still a matter of patching together different lines, many of which were still unfinished, and by bridging the gaps with other means of transport.

231

Sally-John was a good traveler, indeed better than her mother, for she slept most of the time, nursed eagerly (under the shawl with which I covered us both), and appeared to take a serious interest in everything around her when she was awake, whilst I found (as before) that as far as I was concerned, despite improvements in speed and accommodations, rail travel was (and still is) the least enjoyable way to take oneself from someplace to someplace else.

However, even the worst trip has got to end, and ours did, as we got down from the cars in St Joseph. I looked from one end of the platform to the other.

"You, there—" I called to the porter, who was wheeling various pieces of luggage on a large, flat cart. I pointed. "You can drop that one." I tipped him two bits, and he pulled off our trunk from somewhere in the middle of the pyramid.

The stationmaster was a-sitting on a bench, enjoying the noonday sun; I asked him to keep an eye on my trunk whilst I hired some transportation.

"Of course, ma'am," he said, touching his cap.

The livery stable was right across the street. It took only a few minutes to bespeak a horse and buggy. The stableboy promised to load our trunk and bring the buggy round to the hotel in an hour. I trotted back to the platform and told the stationmaster that the stableboy would be stopping for the trunk. Then I carried Sally-John over to the station hotel, where I ordered a light luncheon.

After I ate, I took the baby into the ladies' retiring room and fed and changed her. I asked a woman who had just finished washing her own hands and face to hold her whilst I washed my own.

"Sure is a pretty little thing," the woman said, smiling.

"Thank you kindly," I said, as she handed my daughter back to me. "Yes, she is."

The stableboy was waiting, with the trunk in the back of a trim dog-cart. I tucked the traveling-basket containing my well-wrapped daughter at my feet, secure behind the dashboard, then swung myself up next to her, tucking in my skirts.

"Off we go," I said, clucking to the horse, a bay gelding, and giving the reins a light slap. He pricked his ears at me, then obediently moved off in the direction of the Finn farm, with my daughter, herself a Finn twice over, gurgling softly in her basket.

The farm was still there: house, barn, outbuildings. The

house was painted white, with blue shutters. It all looked much the same as the last time I'd visited, on my way to Tom Sawyer's wedding, nearly eight years before.

But Jim would not be there, I reminded myself.

Since Johnny had told me of Jim's death, I'd hardly had time to take charge of my feelings. Part of me still had a hard time believing it—

But then, I thought, looking down into my baby's face, part of him is still here.

I pulled up into the dooryard. The kitchen door slammed, and Julie and Elizabeth came running out to meet us.

I scooped up Sally-John and held her out to her step-grandmamma and her aunt.

"Lord, lord, come on down from there," Julie cried, handing the baby to Elizabeth and holding out both hands to me. "Let me get my eyes full of you!"

Elizabeth's eyes shone as she held her niece.

I hugged them both. In Elizabeth's arms, Sally-John screwed up her tiny face and began to whimper.

"Give me that child," ordered Julie. "She been bounce around too much. Let me put her down someplace quiet." And she bustled us all into the house.

Elizabeth took my bonnet and pelisse and hung them up on a peg behind the door, then motioned me to sit at the table. She poured me a drink of water from an earthenware jug and sat down across from me. Upstairs I could hear Julie's feet going to and fro, and the faint murmur of her voice as she talked to her granddaughter.

"You be hush now an' go to sleep . . . that's right, darlin', that's right. Shhhh, now; shhhh." I heard bedsprings creak, then the sound of Julie's shoes on the stairs.

"I put her in the middle of the big bed," she said. "With pillas all around. She ain't goin' to roll off."

"Thank you, Mama Julie," I said.

"Oh, lord," and her eyes started to well up. "That's what Johnny always called me."

"He told me how good you have always been, to him and to Elizabeth and to Jim," I said. "Good as gold, he said."

"I do thank you for saying that," Julie said, and fetched out a handkerchief from her apron pocket and wiped her eyes. "I wisht I had him in front of me right this minute—I'd wallop him good for the worry he's give me, and then kiss him twice as hard."

"I just bet you would," I said.

"You ain't seen him—since?"

"No'm."

"Does he know?"

I shook my head.

"Well, as soon as we know where-at he taken himself, we will tell him," she said. "A man ought to know when he's a daddy."

"Mama Julie," I said. "Let me be the one to tell him."

Across from us, Elizabeth, who'd been watching us both intently, began making sounds. Julie looked at her step-daughter, then nodded. "All right. Elizabeth, she think so too."

"It's my responsibility," I said.

"Well," she said.

But I could tell she warn't happy about it.

She reached over, all of a sudden, and stroked my cheek. "You—and our Johnny! I never would have thought it, not in a hundred years."

"It was a surprise to me, too," I reminded her.

"I guess it must have been," she said. "Now tell me: last you saw him—was he in work? Was he looking all right?"

"He was," I said. Elizabeth left the table then, and come back with a plate of molasses cookies. I took one and described Johnny as I'd seen him last.

"Sound just like him," she said, and shook her head. "Vain as a bantam rooster, and larky as can be. No thought for the morrow, long's today going well."

"Oh, he's a grasshopper, all right, not an ant," I agreed.

"Ah, so you know that old story," she said.

"Jim told it to me," I said. "When we was on the raft. Oh, he told me just a jillion stories, Mama Julie!"

"He did have a lot of them to tell," she said. "I never got tired of hearing them."

Elizabeth made a soft sound and put her face into her two hands, then took them away and pointed to Julie.

"Yes, child, I do miss him," Julie said. "Every sunrise and sunset, and all the time between."

"I can't get used to the idea that he is gone," I confessed.

"He didn't suffer none," Julie said. "He was hale as can be, and on'y sick a little time, maybe a couple days and nights."

"What was it?"

"Doctor say his heart."

"I never heard he had heart trouble."

"It come on real slow. He had him some pains, now and again. But he couldn't work as hard—look like he'd be losin' his breath, chokin', like—and his face get all gray. But then, after a rest, he say he feel all right."

"How did it happen?"

"He was hayin'—him and Johnny—an' it was awful hot. He come in for dinner but he didn't eat none, just drank a lot o' cold well water. After that he say his stomach don't feel so good. I try to make him lay down an' take a little rest, but he wanted to finish. It was a good day for bringing in the hay—not a cloud anywhere, and the hay'd surely been curing long enough." She sighed. "He went back out and started in on stackin'—and then he didn't come in for supper, when I called him. I went out, just as it was turnin' dark, an' found him layin' there."

Elizabeth made another of her soft noises.

"Yes, child. You and Johnny helped me get your Daddy into the house," Julie said. "And then Johnny run and got Mr Drewery to go for the doctor. Mr Drewery, down the road, next farm to ours," she said to me. "An' Mr Drewery brought Dr Miller. Doctor, he say make Jim comfortable. Elizabeth and Johnny an' I, we took turns settin' up with him, and next day too. An' then, a little after midnight of the second day, he be gone." She dabbed at her eyes again. "Never said goodbye. Slip' away in his sleep."

Elizabeth was weeping, too. I felt my own eyes fill.

"I'm glad he had you to love him," I said.

"Bless you, honey," Julie said. "How could I help it?"

She was right, of course. Jim had been of all men the most lovable.

We sat for a moment, remembering. Then Julie stood up.

"After you take you a little nap, we'll go along and show you where he's been laid. Mr Drewery, he helped me get the stone for the grave."

Mr Drewery, I learned, was Elizabeth's betrothed.

"He'll be along tomorrow," Julie said. Tomorrow was Sunday; Mr Drewery was expected for dinner, as had become usual. "He wants to meet you," Julie said.

"I'll be pleased to meet him," I told her. And Elizabeth smiled.

***

Next morning I helped Julie and Elizabeth with the chores, and whilst Julie set up her bread dough I fed the baby, rocking away in the cane-seat rocker that had been, Julie said, Jim's favorite chair.

"He like to set there in the evenings and tell stories," she said.

"Did he ever tell you about him and me on the raft?"

"He did indeed," Julie said. "How you help him to freedom." She finished kneading the dough and lalloped the mass of it into a wooden trough, covering it with a clean floursack. "There," she said. "That's done."

"If we hadn't missed Cairo in the night," I said, shifting the baby to my shoulder, and starting in to pat her on the back, "He'd have been free a heap sooner."

"Well," Julie said, beginning to mix up piecrust, "He done *got* free at last—thanks to you and that scamp Tom Sawyer."

"Have you-all heard from Tom lately?"

"We got a letter last Christmas," she said. "Said they all was well enough."

"That's what he wrote to me, too," I said. Sally-John let out a satisfactory burp, and I laid her back across my lap and fastened up my dress-front.

"I had Elizabeth bring the cradle down from the attic," Julie said. "It's in the front room, if you want to put her to sleep."

I put the baby down and covered her with the shawl that Julie had put handy, then went back into the kitchen. Julie handed me a mug of cold tea.

"Drink that right down," she said. "It's got ginger and 'lasses in it. Helps, in this heat."

"It *is* hot," I said. "Where's Elizabeth?"

"I sent her out to kill a couple chickens, for supper," she said. "Likely she plucking them right now. We goin' to have chicken pie, and buttermilk, and string beans."

"Sounds wonderful," I said, and drank my cold tea. "What can I do to help?"

"You just set," she said.

"Tell me about this Mr Drewery," I said.

"Robert. Well, he ask me for Elizabeth some time back," Julie said. She got out a big skillet and began to try out some salt pork.

"Do you think he'll be good to her?"

"I do, or I wouldn't have told him he could ask her," Julie said. "He say, 'how do I ask a girl to marry me that can't hear?' and I say, 'if you can't figure it out, you ain't the one she ought to be marrying.'" Julie laughed. "He give me *such* a look—and then it was like the day breaking. His whole face lit up, an' he say, 'thank you, ma'am!' and rush out, and next thing I see was him and Elizabeth comin' up the walk, arms aroun' each other and stars in both they eyes."

I said, "So she loves him."

Julie nodded. "The wedding set for October—Elizabeth's birthday, the 14th."

"How old is Robert?"

"Twenty-nine."

"And she's twenty-five. Oh, I wisht I could be here for the wedding," I said. "But it's likely I won't be able to come."

"That's all right," Julie said.

"I want to give them a present," I said. "What would you say they might need?"

"Well, now," and Julie paused. The salt pork in the skillet was making little hissing noises. "They could use a set of chinaware. Old Mrs Drewery—Robert's ma—she didn't have but the one set, an' I don't imagine all the pieces still with it, these many years a-gone."

"His parents are both dead?"

"Long since. His pa died in the war, and his ma—she went soon after."

"No other children but Robert?"

"No, he been alone. Good for him to have a wife, raise up some children around the place."

"I'll send a set of dishes for a wedding-gift," I promised.

"Well, that will be just fine," Julie said.

(And I did, too: a complete set of Wedgewood creamware,[55]

---

[55] Eds. note: This is an interesting choice. Josiah Wedgewood, who developed the pottery business that bears his name, was a noted British abolitionist.

dishes and serving-pieces and all, enough to serve forty people in style. I still have the note of thanks that the young couple sent me, signed by both, with a row of kisses at the bottom, 'to our dearest sister Sarah.')

Mr Drewery came, and we had a very pleasant Sunday dinner. I decided that I liked Robert Drewery; he didn't put on, just shook hands and said, hearty as could be, "I am pleased to know you, Miss Sarah."

Julie said, "Ain't no need to be so formal, Robert. Sarah one of the family."

So he kissed me on both cheeks, and when the baby woke up he took her and held her all through supper, and said he thought she favored her Aunt Elizabeth (which was true, but it made us all feel extra good to hear it said). All through the dinner his eyes kept coming back to Elizabeth's. She didn't blush or falter, though, but kept on filling his plate and smiling at him. So my mind was easy, and when it came time for Robert to leave, I said, "I am glad you are marrying Elizabeth. I have thought of her for a long while as the sister I never had."

"I will be your brother," he said, and took his leave. Elizabeth walked him out to his rig, and whilst she was gone, Julie said, "I think Jim would be glad."

"I think so, too," I said.

Next morning, before I set out for town, Julie and I walked up a slight rise behind the house, as far as a grove of cottonwood trees. The trees, still young and slight, made a little shade by a tall stone at the head of a solitary grave. I read the inscription aloud:

JIM FINN
BELOVED HUSBAND AND FATHER
BORN INTO SLAVERY
DIED A FREE MAN
1861
"MINE EYES HAVE SEEN THE GLORY"

Julie and I stood together for a long time.

"He was the closest to a father I ever had," I said. "My own Pap was a hateful, hating man, but Jim—"

"Jim never knowed what it was to hate. 'Twasn't in his nature," Julie said. "Don't cry, Sarah, honey."

"I wish he could have seen Sally-John."

"Where he is, he *can* see her," Julie said. "Leastways, I believe that's so."

"I'm glad if you can," I said. "If only I could."

"Someday maybe you will," Julie said. "Do you know, he planted these trees? I like to think of him resting here with them all around, watching over him."

And we walked back to the house, as the trees whispered above Jim's grave.

Next morning I made ready to travel. Julie packed me a luncheon, and Elizabeth dressed the baby and carried her out to the buggy. I hugged both of them and said, "Send me news of the wedding."

"We will," Julie promised.

I drove off, and as I turned onto the main road, I looked back and waved.

In her basket, Sally-John gurgled. I looked down at my daughter. "I wisht you could have knowed your grandpa," I said.

Behind me the road dust blew away in white clouds. I tightened my grip on the reins and drove on.

***

It was not to be thought of, that I'd come this far East without seeing the home folks in Hannibal. I'd written to Aunt Polly and told her to expect me in August—with the baby.

I hated lying to Aunt Polly, and had debated whether to go ahead and tell her the truth, but when it come right down to writing it out on paper, I couldn't seem to manage it.

So I told her, in my letter, that Sally-John's father had been killed in the war.

She'd answered that we was both welcome, and mentioned that, along with Aunt Sally Phelps, Tom and his wife Becky would also be there. Tom was working in Washington, I knew, as an aide to Justice James Moore Wayne[56] of the Supreme Court. That Justice

---

[56] James Moore Wayne of Georgia was an Associate Justice from 1835 until his death in 1867. He was a graduate of Princeton, not Yale (Judge Thatcher's alma mater), so he and Thatcher must have been classmates elsewhere, perhaps at an academy or preparatory school.

was an old classmate of Judge Thatcher's, Tom's father-in-law. So far as I knowed, they had no children as yet.

Well, Sally-John and I arrived in Hannibal early in the morning. It was the last week of August, and hot as hot. I'd forgotten how sticky it could be down along the Mississippi. Sweat was streaming down from under my arms and along my spine and the backs of my legs. Sally-John was fretful, and I tried to soothe her.

"Hannibal! Hannn-ibal!" The conductor called.

The porter handed me down from the train, and passed the baby to me. I held her and looked around.

Aunt Polly wasn't at the station, but Sid was—Sid Sawyer, Tom's half-brother. He'd brought along a wheelbarrow, into which he loaded my trunk, and he trundled it along whilst I walked beside him, carrying the baby.

"Aunt Polly said you-all would be staying for a few days," he said. "Tom's a-coming too."

"I know," I said. "Becky's coming with him, too, isn't she?"

"She is," Sid said. "It's her daddy's seventieth birthday, next week."

"Well, then, I hope to congratulate the Judge in person," I said. "He's been mighty good to me."

"They're planning quite a shindy," Sid said. "But Aunt Polly will want to tell you all about it."

"Is Aunt Sally here yet?"

"She ain't coming this time," Sid said. "Uncle Silas is poorly, and she don't want to leave him."

I was sorry to hear it, and said so.

We had reached the Sawyer home, and Sid opened the gate for me. "I'll bring in your trunk terrectly," he promised. "Go on. She's waitin' for you."

I hoisted the baby to my shoulder and advanced up the walk. The curtain in the front window twitched. Why wasn't Aunt Polly out on the porch to greet me?

Just as I got to the door, it opened, and there she was. "Bring that child in out of the heat," she ordered.

Inside, with the shade drawn, it was in fact cooler, and I allowed Aunt Polly to take my bonnet and traveling cape. The baby set up a wail.

"Is she hungry? Go on and feed her," Aunt Polly said.

I sat down in the chair she pointed to, and undid my basque. Sally John began to suckle. Aunt Polly sat down across from me. "She looks healthy enough. How old did you say?"

"She's seven months old," I said.

"Sad, not knowin' her pa."

I didn't dare look up. Aunt Polly reached out and touched Sally-John's cheek. "She looks a mite flushed."

"It's hotter'n we're used to," I said.

"He died in the war, you said?"

"Yes'm."

"Well, the Lord giveth and the Lord taketh away," Aunt Polly said. "Had you been married long?"

"No'm."

"Ummph. Did he leave you any property?"

"No'm. But I have enough for us."

"You aim to keep on in your business, then?"

"Yes'm."

"Who's running things whilst you're away?"

"I hired an assistant."

"Well, let's pray he's honest."

"Oh, he is."

"Did Sid tell you that Tom and Becky will be here in a day or so?"

"Yes'm."

"Judge Thatcher's seventieth birthday is Saturday."

"Yes'm."

"But my sister can't make it. Silas ain't feeling well."

"Yes'm. I heard."

"Sarah Mary Williams, is that all you have to say? Used to be you'd talk the arms and legs off a body, and now it's all I can do to get two words out of you."

"I suppose I must be tired, ma'am."

"You might be," she said. "But I have a feeling there's something you ain't told me."

I didn't answer. The baby had stopped nursing, so I buttoned myself up again.

"Let me hold her," Aunt Polly said, and I passed Sally-John over.

"Sssh, ssssh," Aunt Polly said, rocking back and forth, with the baby over her shoulder.

"Aunt Polly?"

"Yes, child."

"Aunt Polly—"

I don't know what I would have said to her, but Sid chose that moment to burst into the room.

"Aunt Polly! Mrs Thatcher's come calling!"

"Well, show her in," Aunt Polly said. She looked at me over the rims of her spectacles, but I pretended to be busy with my reticule.

Sid bustled back in, Mrs Thatcher in tow.

"Don't get up, Sarah Mary," that lady said to me. "Nor you, Miss Polly."

The two ladies pecked each other on the cheek, and Mrs Thatcher sat down on the settee next to Aunt Polly and let out a sigh.

"Gracious, it's hot," she said. "What a pretty baby! I was sad, hearing of your loss, my dear."

I could feel Aunt Polly's eagle eyes boring into me. "Thank you, ma'am," I said.

The two ladies clearly wanted to talk, so I excused myself and the baby. Aunt Polly called to Sid.

"Take Miss Sarah up to the front bedroom," she said.

"Yes, Aunt."

"Sarah, if you want to take a little rest, you go ahead."

"Yes'm."

Sally-John and I settled ourselves for a nap. As I fell asleep, I heard the faint rise and fall of the two old ladies' voices from the parlor.

It was going to be hard to keep the truth from Aunt Polly. Briefly, I wondered how she'd take to the news that my baby was the grandchild of a man she'd known as a slave. Then I remembered how Aunt Polly had behaved, all those years before, when she'd helped Tom and Jim and me after all that foofaraw at the Phelpses'.

She'd always been kind, and never other than fair-spoken to Jim or to me. Even in the days when I was Huckleberry Finn and decent folks treated me worse than if I'd been a slave myself, or a stray dog, she'd been kind and decent.

I wished with all my heart that I could tell her the truth.

And, if the two of us had been able to manage some time

alone, I might have done it. But the opportunity never presented itself—and I must confess I didn't press for it.

***

Next morning I met the other member of the household.

"Miss Sarah, pleased to make your acquaintance," she said, with a little curtsy.

Sid introduced us. "This is Nancy. She works for us."

Nancy was a reddish-brown colored woman, about my age. She was, I learned, both housemaid and cook. Since Aunt Polly had become even more shortsighted in her elder years (she must, I figured, be at least in her late sixties), Sid had decided that a servant was a necessity.

Sid was still unmarried, and, I gathered from Aunt Polly, likely to remain so. He showed no interest in courting any of the likely female candidates in Hannibal, but spent all his time studying.

"Studying what?"

"Scripture."

It turned out that Sid had "heard the call," as Aunt Polly put it, to the pulpit, and was busy preparing himself to go to seminary, in Danville, Kentucky.[57]

"The school there had just dreadful, dreadful losses in the War," Aunt Polly said. "Sid says they need students, to build it up again."

He was making ready, I learned, to move to Danville at the end of September. The minister in town, Mr Pritchard, was helping to prepare him, and whenever Sid wasn't upstairs at his books, or downstairs eating one of Nancy's excellent meals, he was likely to be at the Pritchard house or in church.

In fact I saw very little of him during my visit—which was not a hardship, Sid never having been an engaging conversationalist. I told Aunt Polly I hoped he'd be successful as a preacher, though privately I doubted it.

---

[57] Eds. note: Now Louisville Presbyterian Theological Seminary, the school began in Danville. Later, it merged with the Louisville school. The site was taken over by Centre College, a liberal-arts institution founded by Presbyterian leaders in 1819. Following the Civil War, much of the teaching at the seminary in Danville was in fact done by Centre College faculty, due to the tremendous losses in teachers and students that the school had suffered.

Leastways, it meant one less person for me to avoid discussing the topic of my late "husband" with.

On the morning of the day Tom and Becky were expected, Sid went off early (with the wheelbarrow) and I helped Nancy and Aunt Polly with the last of their preparations. Finally, we had done, and Aunt Polly asked Nancy to bring us a dish of tea.

"Tom sent it, last winter," she said. "China tea."

"I sell a good deal of that in my store," I said, then remembered something. "Wait a moment, Aunt Polly—" and I run upstairs.

"Here it is—I brought you some Cologne water," I said. I'd wrapped the flask well in a piece of soft chamois leather, and kept it close by me during the whole journey, fearful lest it break. It had survived, however, and now I handed it over.

"Thank you, dear," she said. "What a nice present."

"Before Tom and Becky get here," I said, "I want to show you what I brought for them," and I brung out a small red-velvet-covered box.

"Open it," I said.

Aunt Polly took the box—it was about twice the size of a deck of playing cards, but with a domed lid—and fiddled with the tiny brass catch. The lid sprung open.

"Oh, my goodness," she said.

Inside was two gold nuggets, both pierced at one end and each one strung on a gold chain. The shorter chain (and smaller nugget) could be worn as a watch fob, whilst the longer one would make a pretty ornament for a lady to wear around her neck.

"Is that real gold?"

"Real's can be. And both of 'em's from Sutter's Mill," I said. "Genuine '49 gold."

"My land," said Aunt Polly.

"I'm doing real well in my business, Aunt Polly," I said.

"I guess you must be, at that," she said, staring at the nuggets. She closed the little box and handed it back to me. "Well, that's good, ain't it? That little one of yours won't find herself in want any time soon, then."

"She won't," I said.

There was a moment, then, when I might have told her, but it didn't last, for we heard steps on the porch and the sound of the front door opening, and Nancy's voice calling "Miss Polly! Miss

Polly! They's here!"

And I put the little box away, and went with Aunt Polly to greet my long-ago companion and his bride.

***

Part of me was eager to see Tom, and part wasn't. We'd been comrades in childhood and co-conspirators in our early youth, but since that time in Connecticut—Tom at Yale, me at Miss Edwards's school—we'd lost the knack of easy companionship. To be blunt, I found the grown-up Tom something of a bore, and Miss Becky had never interested me, she being one of those pink-and-gold ladylike females, all frills and curls, that always set my teeth on edge.

Nevertheless, they was family, too, and I smoothed my hair and plumped out my skirts in preparation for greeting them.

Tom was taller and stouter, though far from fat, and he wore a most amazing set of whiskers, long and ginger-colored. His hair was brushed back from his high forehead and fell down his neck in a profusion of ringlets. I remembered how he'd loathed those curls in his boyhood, and tried with every means—water, macassar oil, bear grease, tallow—to make them lie flat, and here he was with every curl rampant on his head, as if on fire. He shook my hand, then kissed my cheek, and handed me over to Becky.

"My stars, Sarah," said Becky, "How thin you are!"

By comparison with Becky Sawyer, I did look a mite scrawny. She, on the other hand, was plump as a partridge, with round cheeks and dimpled chin, and her figure was round as well, with a lace fichu straining over her bosom, and a protrusion at the rear that was only partly due to the bustle underneath her blue silk skirts. She wore lace mitts, too, and little gold rings in her ears, and I saw when I looked down that her boots were blue silk to match her dress.

Judge Thatcher's little girl must cost Tom Sawyer something at the dressmaker's and mantua-maker's, I thought.

Tom inserted himself between his wife and me and took me by one arm.

"What's this I hear about a baby, now?"

"A baby!" Becky shrieked. "Why, Sarah Mary Williams, I didn't even know you were married!"

"He died," I said. "In the war."

"Oh, how sad for you," trilled Becky. "But at least you have a memento of his love! Where is the little darling?"

The little darling, who was having a bath at Nancy's

competent hands at that precise moment, set up a howl.

"I must see her!" Becky cried. "Take me to her, Sarah, do!"

Becky and I threaded our way past Tom and Aunt Polly and down the passage to the kitchen. There we found my daughter, naked as the day she was born, sitting happily in a dishpan and batting soapsuds about with her chubby hands.

"Ain't she a darlin'? Ain't she just?" cooed Nancy.

"She's the sweetest thing!" Becky said. "Can I hold her, Sarah?"

"I'd wait until Nancy gets a diaper and a nightgown on her," I said. "She's awful squirmy and slippery at the moment."

"I'll bring her out to you soon's she's ready," promised Nancy.

"All right," Becky said, and pulled my arm through hers. "Let's go out on the porch—maybe there's a breeze blowing. I want to hear all about your poor husband."

So we sat on the porch and I made up all kinds of lies about Sally-John's daddy, hoping devoutly that I'd remember them. That was always my downfall—I could lie just fine; it was keeping track of the lies that give me grief.

"I'm so sorry for your loss, Sarah Mary," Becky said at last. "If anything was to happen to Tom, I don't know what I'd do."

"You don't have any children yet," I said.

"No. Leastways," and she blushed, "I don't know but as I might have—expectations—that is, I think—I mean—"

"When?" I asked.

"January," she said. "I think."

"Well, I wish you healthy and happy—expectations," I said.

"Don't tell Tom," she said. "I'm not sure . . . I mean, I hope so, but—"

"I won't say a word," I promised.

"We've been married thirteen years," she said. "I was about to lose hope, I think."

"You'll probably have a whole passel of 'em now," I teased her. "One right after another."

"Sakes," she said. "I hope not! I'd like some time in between, to enjoy myself. Oh, Sarah, Washington is so much fun! I mean, the city itself isn't much—it's not at all like Philadelphia, or Baltimore. Why, the streets are all mud when it rains, and ladies have to go across on stepping-stones, or else wear high wooden shoes like stilts! And there's a lot of shiftless folk about. But the parties—oh, I do love the parties. And Tom lets me buy all the pretties I want."

She prattled on about this dress and that fan and so on, and I listened with half an ear. She had six servants, I learned, including her own coachman and footman, and a maid to dress her hair and take care of her clothes, and their cook was the great-grandson of Thomas Jefferson's own cook, who'd been schooled in France. [58]

Finally, Tom came in and rescued me from a recital of, I believe, every Sawyer social engagement of the preceding decade.

"Honey, go on and chat with Aunt Polly; she's dyin' to hear what you've been up to," he said to his wife. Becky kissed me and kissed her husband and sailed off in a cloud of lace and lilac perfume. Tom sat down across from me and took out his cigar-case.

"May I smoke?"

"It's your own home," I said.

"Aunt Polly don't like smoking," he said, and lit a cheroot.

"I don't mind it," I said.

"Aunt Polly tells me you're a-doing well out there."

"I am."

"I was sorry to hear of your husband's death."

"Thank you," I said.

"The baby's a nice little thing," Tom said. "I suppose Becky told you we're having one?"

"She said she hadn't told you!" I said.

"She hasn't," Tom said. "But I know it just the same. A man knows the woman he lives with." He smiled. "It means a lot to her, to think she's going to surprise me."

"She said—January," I said.

"It does feel strange to me, talking about a child of my own," Tom said, examining the lighted end of his cheroot. "I don't feel hardly more than a boy myself."

I laughed. "You look grown enough to me!"

"It's these whiskers," Tom said, stroking them. "Becky made me grow 'em. She says a Senator has to have whiskers."

---

[58] Eds. note: Jefferson's cook was James Hemings, brother of Sally Hemings, Jefferson's slave and the mother of at least one of Jefferson's children.

"That's what she hopes for you? That you'll be a Senator?"

"She'd like to be the wife of the President," Tom said, grinning. "But that's more'n I can promise."

I laughed. "You might surprise us all."

He smiled and stretched out his hand. "I might. Let's go on inside, now, and see the rest of the folks." He threw his cheroot away and gallantly assisted me to my feet.

"I miss those days," he said softly. "I wisht I hadn't come so far from them, sometimes."

"I know," I said. "I know.

Chapter Seventeen: Sorrow and Secrets

Well, Judge Thatcher's birthday party was indeed "some shindy," and I was glad enough to drink his health, but gladder to be going.

I'd thought of going down to Arkansas, to see Aunt Sally and Uncle Silas, but she'd written to say not to come; Uncle Silas warn't bad off, and she'd likely see me on my next trip East, which she hoped wouldn't be too far in the future.

So I went home.

The train ride back to Tahoe City remains to this day a blur in my mind—I know I rode with half my mind on a gravestone in a cottonwood grove and half in memory of my "boyhood" days.

Getting back into my customary routine was harder than I'd expected. David had done well, and business was good; still, I couldn't settle down, and spent much of my free time riding out along the trails, up into the mountains.

"You should not go so far alone," David scolded.

"I need to be alone," I said, and his stern look softened.

"Be careful, then," was all he said, but I made an effort, after that, to stay closer to home. And then, one day, the mail coach brought a package for me, from St Joseph, Missouri.

There was a letter—a single sheet, the writing blurred in places. Tears had fallen on the paper, and soon my tears also fell. The letter was from Julie:

Dear Sarah Mary,

This come a week ago. I do not know where he is buried, but I have asked my dear son-in-law Mr Drewery to set up a stone for Johnny next to his daddy's. I thought that you had ought to have these things, for the baby.

I am glad that you were able to come to us. Elizabeth is well. She and Mr Drewery send their love along with mine.

Yours in sorrow,

Julie Finn

Inside I found a newspaper cutting, a set of silver spurs with stars engraved along the rowels, a necklace of wolf teeth strung on a length of braided horse-hair, and a telegram, folded small.

I unfolded the flimsy yellow paper, smoothed out the creases, and read:

Dear Madam,

I regret to inform you of the death of your son John Hannibal Finn, of St Joseph, Missouri. Corporal Finn died in an action against Quantrill's Raiders, on May 10, near Taylorsville, Kentucky.

Signed,

Colonel J— S—

For some time, I couldn't catch my breath; I sat there, staring at that paper, trying to take it in. Johnny dead! In an action against Quantrill's Raiders!

He had died a soldier—a Union soldier.

When he'd left me, he'd been headed for a cattle drive to Abilene, in Kansas. I never did find out how, or when, he decided to enlist on the Federal side, nor how he ended up a corporal. But he had.

Perhaps—I thought back to our last few hours together—perhaps he'd decided that freedom was a debt he owed to someone, and determined in this way to pay it.

And in the paying he'd also struck a blow for my future safety, and his daughter's, too.

I scanned the newspaper clipping. Quantrill's Raiders—all of them dead.

*****

It was a long time before I gave over thinking how the cost of my freedom lay rotting in an unmarked grave.

William Quantrill would never trouble me again.

But Johnny would never see his daughter, nor his sister's children-to-be; he'd never stand with his step-mama on the hill where the cottonwoods stood sentinel around his daddy's resting place. His own was in some unmarked corner of bloody Kansas, and none of us—not Julie nor Elizabeth nor I—would ever know where his bones lay.

I wept a long time for Johnny Finn.

I wrote to Julie.

"When Elizabeth's first baby is born," I wrote, "Please write to tell me, for you are all the family left to us now."

And Julie wrote back, many times. I have kept her letters safe all these years.

*****

And so David and the baby and I settled into Tahoe City, easy as a hot knife into butter. There was so much building going on, we had our pick of rentals. For a year we operated out of a storefront I leased from one of the first white men to lay down roots in the region, John Calhoun Johnson[59].

Mr Johnson was rich enough not to mind competition—in fact, he welcomed it, as having a choice of what to buy generally stimulated most folks' desire to do so. He kept a store that was the equal of mine in Virginia City—or the one I'd had in San Francisco, for that matter—but, with folks heading east and west across the mountains, he allowed as what was good for the gander was good for the goose. So we shook hands on a deal that garnered me a store building, a small house with attached shed, and a friend.

That friendship included, on his side, a wife and nine or ten children (he himself frequently lost count), and his Indian friend Fallen Leaf, who'd been a scout with him and with Fremont. On my side I could offer David, whose medical skills put him in great demand (there being few doctors in the region, and generally none of any use). Mr Johnson had no prejudice against Chinese. In fact, he owned Celestials was superior to most white men in many areas. He even spoke, or attempted to speak, some few words of Mandarin, and I often heard him trying them out with David, who listened courteously whilst hiding his smiles.

In our native tongue, or leastways his version of it, which was most colorful, Mr Johnson's stories was thrilling in the extreme, and many's the evening I spent with him and his family, and David of course, who, in addition to helping me with the store and providing medicines and salves for those in need of doctoring, was Sally-John's nanny.

A Chinese cook or houseboy was a usual sight out West in those days, and the fact that David ran my household was no cause for remark. And his care of my daughter was taken for granted—Chinese nannies, too, being common enough.

The two of them made quite a pair, and folks smiled to see

---

[59] Eds. note: Johnson was a companion of John Charles Fremont, the American explorer who claimed to be the first white man to see the lake, in 1844. Johnson, for whom Johnson's Cut-off was named (now US Route 50), ranched, mined gold, and practiced law in the region; his main property holding, called "Six-Mile Ranch," was just east of Placerville (now Camino, California). Travelers crossing the Sierras (in both directions) usually stopped at the ranch, where there was a general store and a boardinghouse.

them together, the curly-headed girl-child and the slim Oriental in his long black sateen gown (for David never would put on Western dress, except on one occasion). She called him "Ah Bok," which he told me meant something like "Elder Uncle."

Indeed, she chattered to him in a mixture of Chinese and English that was something to hear. Later she picked up some Washoe from Fallen Leaf, and Spanish from the Mexicans who worked for the Colonel, and smatterings of German and Danish and I don't know what-all from merchants and horse-traders coming through. She even learned some Hawaiian.

She had a quick ear and a quicker step—there never was such a child for vanishing whenever it was time to do anything she didn't want to do. The only one who could make her behave was David, and if I'd been glad of his company and care before I became a mother, I was trebly glad after. Alone, Sally-John's care would have sent me to an early grave.

Not that she ever sassed me nor disobeyed me with any kind of defiance. She just would not be made to do anything she didn't want to do, and likewise could not be kept from doing whatever it was she did choose. It was like living with the weather—you couldn't do anything with it but let it be what it was. And like the weather she could blow up unexpected, and go stormy or moody, then sunny again. She simply did anything, or not, as she pleased.

Unless it was Ah Bok who forbid it. Then she was meek as they say a lamb is supposed to be (having no experience with sheep, I can't speak to the truth of that).

It was a mystery to me, how David managed to keep Sally-John on the straight and narrow, but I was content to leave her to him, along with the other duties that had somehow fallen to him. He had taken over so much of the running of our daily life, and done it so well and with so little fuss. From employer and employee we had passed into a kind of partnership, which I long since took almost wholly for granted. When something did call his presence to my attention, it was like seeing him for the first time.

He had cut off his queue shortly after we came to Tahoe City, and wore his hair rather like Colonel Johnson's—falling to the collar in back and brushed off the forehead—but David had no whiskers. His golden-skinned face was smooth as a woman's, his hands were well-kept and his breath was sweet, for he took great care of his teeth. Indeed, he was clean and neat, slender and straight, and if one overlooked his Chinese dress, he could be considered a fine-looking man.

I could see that some other women found him appealing. One of Colonel Johnson's older daughters—Clara, a girl about nineteen—clearly did. I often saw her walking with him when she came to town, and observed the pains she took with her dress, and the way she smiled up at him—for she was a tiny thing—but he took care on these excursions to keep Sally-John between them, and though Clara always held her hand out to him on parting he never would take it, but tucked his own hands inside his two sleeves in the way Chinamen do, and bowed her away with a smile that hid nothing, there being nothing to hide.

That David loved Sally-John was obvious to anyone who cared to look. And he had a great affection for his younger brother. Young Chung, I learned to my amusement, had taken his elder's example and now called himself Solomon Chung (for that same king I'd once argued about with my old Jim, so very long ago). Solly Chung had left the Stroethers' employ two years since and now worked for Colonel Johnson as a cook in the hotel that the Johnson family owned and operated for its permanent guests. This establishment catered mostly to mining men and others employed by the Colonel in his various business ventures.

But David was as different from Solly as chalk is from cheese. For one thing, Solly was a family man, having taken a Mexican wife, the daughter of one of Colonel Johnson's drovers, and, in between teaching her to cook Chinese-style, had begun to sire a troop of brown-skinned, almond-eyed children. Whilst David seemed content with the care of only one, and she not of his blood.

Sometimes I looked at David as he bent to tie my daughter's shoes or mended a cut on her small knee with sticking-plaster and dried her tears on a spotless pocket-handkerchief, and wondered what it would be like to have a Chinaman for a husband, but the thought raised no feeling in my body to go along with it.

I could—and did, often— have a fleeting memory of Johnny and feel my breathing quicken and my face begin to flame, but nothing like that happened when I looked at David. Contemplation of my daughter's Ah Bok left me feeling only grateful for his presence, and appreciative of all he did for Sally-John and me.

I did worry, though, that he might someday decide he wanted a family of his own, and leave us.

I asked David if he had ever thought of marrying.

"But I *am* married," he said, "In China."

I must have looked as astonished as I felt, for he began to laugh. "Oh, yes, it is true. I have a wife, Sarah Mary. [He had long since ceased to call me 'Missy Sarah.'] Indeed," he went on, "All Chinamen, or nearly all, have wives at home, waiting for us to return. Did you not know?"

"I never," I confessed. "Is Solly married in China, too?"

"Of course."

"What is she like, this wife of yours?"

He hesitated for a moment, then said, "Wait."

He left the room, and I wandered about for a while, drinking another cup of tea from the porcelain pot that seemed always to stand steaming and ready.

The cups were handleless thick white porcelain, smooth and heavy in the hand, and the tea smelled of flowers. This tea-drinking, Chinese style, had become a habit. I still put sugar in mine, though David shuddered whenever he saw me doing so.

He returned with a flat packet wrapped in red silk and tied with ribbons, which he undid.

"There," he said, laying aside the wrappings.

In a silver case was a photograph. I picked it up.

The picture showed a woman, seated in a tall chair of some dark wood.

I saw a small pointed face, smooth and oval-shaped, in which large, liquid eyes glowed under brows like slender ink-strokes. She was outlandishly dressed, in robes so thick and stiff they looked carved, like the chair she sat in. Her face was white (with rice powder, David explained) and her lips and cheeks had been painted red. Her dress was red also, trimmed in gold; some skillful hand had tinted her face and clothing, but left the background of the picture gray, so that her small figure stood out stark and shining.

Under a headdress like a crown her hair showed black as paint. Her feet rested on a high, carved footstool that matched the tall chair she sat in, and those feet looked scarce as long as my own little finger, in shoes with upcurved toes, shoes of embroidered velvet glimmered over with pearls.

"Her golden-lily feet," said David, "They are the size of Sally-John's little feet, but my wife was sixteen when this picture was taken, at our wedding, and Sally-John is only five."

I looked at him in wonder, and he told me, then, how it was done: how the little girls' feet are bound tight, so that the bones stop growing, and the toes are forced under the arch so that the feet turn eventually into useless stumps, but tiny, tiny, and always covered in white cotton bandages and white silk stockings and the tiniest and most ornamental of shoes.

"It is said to be beautiful," David said. "That is why such feet are known as 'golden lilies,' and the 'lily-footed lady' is she to whom poems are written and love songs are sung."

"Can she walk on—those?" I felt sick with horror and pity.

"With difficulty, and in pain. And she must have two maidservants—slaves—with her, to support and steady her, one on each side."

"How does she live? How can she do anything? Why, she's crippled!"

"Yes. Yes, she is. But Sarah Mary, she need not 'do' anything at all, except bear sons. That is all a woman of her class ever need do. She has servants to attend her every need. She does not think of herself as crippled, but as beautiful."

"How can she bear sons, if you are here?" I hadn't intended the question to come out so flat, but he seemed not to mind.

"We were married a week before I left for Gold Mountain," he said. "All of us young men who were leaving to seek our fortunes in America were wed, in the hope that we would beget sons to take their place among the generations. And that is why I must send money home, that my wife will know that I have not forgotten. At least she has my money if she has not my sons. And so she is welcome to her place at the family's table, and she prays for me to the ancestors, that I may come home and give her sons before it is too late."

"What's her name?" I asked.

"Mei Yin."

"What does it mean?"

I remembered that day, seven years before, when I had asked Cheung Ka Yat what his name meant. And Cheung Ka Yat's wife waited for him six thousand miles from where we stood and looked at her photograph.

"'Mei' means beautiful; Yin means 'Woman,'" he said. "Or, written another way, the same name can mean Wonderful and Desire."

I looked at him. His brows were narrowed as if he felt pain, and he held one hand out and took the picture back from me and stared at it for a time, as if he did not recognize the woman he saw.

"I cannot go back," he said.

"Why not?"

"Because I am no longer Chinese." He saw my expression, and smiled. "Oh, I am still one of the Sons of Han, but I have become an American, as much as you or Colonel Johnson or your Johnny, the father of our small angel. In China I would be an alien to those of every generation, including my own."

"But don't you miss your family—miss your wife?"

"I did, for a long time."

"Don't you ever—want a woman?" I had never talked about such things with any man before, not even Johnny.

"Sometimes," he said. "But it is a longing that can be mastered, and I have mastered it."

"Solly hasn't," I said.

"Solly is even more American than I," David said, and laughed. Suddenly the tension that had been in the room vanished, and I laughed too.

"What does Solly's Chinese wife think about the wife he has here?"

"If she knows," David said, "She would not think it strange. Our people believe that human nature must be allowed to fulfill itself."

"Your wife, would she think it strange if you were to marry someone else?"

"I do not know what she would think," David said slowly. "She is very different from Solly's Chinese wife. My wife, you see, can read and write."

"And Solly's wife can't read?"

"Solly's wife comes from a very old-fashioned family. My wife's family are more—modern. They thought it reasonable that a scholar's wife should be able to read. Perhaps it has been some consolation to her, in my absence. I hope so."

"So she knew she was going to be your wife, even when she was a child?"

"Our parents promised to join the two families when I was still in my nurse's arms, before my wife had even been born. When she was eight years old and I was sixteen, the betrothal contract was signed. And when she was sixteen and I was twenty-four, I returned home from my studies at the Imperial Academy in Peking[60], and we were wed."

"Why are you telling me all this, only now, after all these years?"

"Because we are both lonely people, Sarah Mary, and lonely people must learn to master their loneliness or it will devour them."

I looked into his face then and saw what I had not fully known, that he was in truth lonely. And that he recognized the same feelings in me.

And I believed, then, that he preferred to remain as he was.

As I did.

"I won't speak of these things again," I said to him.

"Nor will I," he said, returning the photograph to its wrappings. I thought of a corpse and a winding sheet, and shivered.

"It is nearly time for Sally-John's bath," he said, and his voice was just as before, tranquil and soft. "Will you come? She likes an audience, to watch her travails and to hear her screams."

"I will come," I said, and he smiled and left me alone once more, with a cup of tea fast growing cold.

I pondered what I'd learned as I carried cup and the teapot back to the kitchen, remembering the eyes of the woman in the photograph.

I knew that she was lonely too, despite her beauty, despite the money that she received, money that arrived once a year, wrapped in a letter marked with characters written in her Chinese-American husband's hand.

***

The next few years continued peaceful. The railroad brought more traffic to the region, and eased the transport of freight (which had, previous, come by wagon road, hauled by mules and oxen). Much of that freight included iron to build the pipelines to carry water through the tunnels that were dug for that purpose. And of course the freight-lines carried the silver that men (and some women) dug from the Comstock Lode.

We saw a number of Chinese, and all sorts of white, Mexican,

---

[60] Eds. note: This may refer to the Guozijian, the highest center of learning in China prior to the establishment of the Republic.

and Negro seekers after the wealth that lay hidden in the Sierras. The governor of California—Bigler—had taken out after Chinese immigration, saying that the Chinese was yellow heathens who would destroy the country if let to come in any numbers. David often said that he and his brother had been among the lucky ones, to have come to America early on. The Chinese folks we saw now had tales to tell of being beaten and robbed—some even killed— and the white folks in charge was busy making more laws to keep the Chinese out.

The Chinese warn't allowed to bring their women, so those who wanted women took wives from amongst the local Mexicans (like Solly had done) or Indians.

Once in a while you'd see a Chinese husband with an Irish wife, for Irish miners had come with their families, along with so many others. Some of the married Chinese soon took to keeping wash-houses and bath-houses and became prosperous, for most of the miners hadn't the time nor the inclination to do their own laundry or haul and heat their own bath-water (when and if they chose to bathe, which was mostly seldom).

And like most folks in business, leastways those with any sense, we made money. Lord, lord, but we made money. We even filled orders by mail, which David took on, helped by Sally-John, who spent a couple of hours every day after school, filling orders and getting the packages ready for the mail train.

Sally-John, by now, had read every book she could get her hands on, even those I'd have thought a child would have little use for—the Johnsons had a library, in fact, Colonel Johnson being a lawyer, and he allowed Sally-John free access to it. She'd carried home various works, such as *Blackstone's Commentaries*, a couple of handbooks of veterinary practice and *Doctor Gray's Anatomy, The Autobiography of Benjamin Franklin*, and something called *Ree's Cyclopedia*, which was about scientific topics—and zipped right on through them all—and I ordered books for her from several companies back east.

But by her tenth birthday, David said, he and I had both reached the limits of what we could provide for her.

"She's too young yet to go away to school," I said. I remembered Miss Edwards's Academy all too well.

"I have made inquiries," said David. "A day-school has been started in Truckee."

Truckee—about fifteen miles away. "What kind of school?"

It appeared, from what David told me, that a maiden lady from Poland had come out to the region with her brother, a metallurgist; he'd gone East to work in laboratory there, but she had taken to the area and decided to remain behind, opening a school by which she earned her living. Her name was Judith Levy.

We—David and I—said nothing to Sally-John, but I made myself ready, early next morning, to go and see Miss Levy. And so I drove over in a light chaise, and arrived, shortly after eleven o'clock on the following afternoon, when school was still in session.

I parked the chaise under a tree and let the check-rein down so the horse could crop at the grass. I didn't knock nor make my presence known, but stood outside on Miss Levy's porch and listened and looked, the windows being open.

The building whose porch I stood upon was a low, wide structure built of logs, with a room that ran the full width of the building in front, faced by that same porch. Windows on three sides let in plentiful light, for I could clearly see the pupils' faces and their teacher's, too.

The children were reciting their spelling lesson, which was written on the blackboard. Miss Levy stood at the front of the room, holding a long pointer, with which she indicated the words to be spelled aloud, each in turn.

The desks was arranged in rows, and each child had its own seat. I could see bookshelves filled with colorful volumes, and geranium plants bloomed cheerfully on top of the shelves. The children appeared very clean—they was mostly white, but I saw one or two that could have been Indian or Mexican.

Their teacher wore a gray dress with white collar and cuffs, and her dark hair was pinned up neatly. "Again, please," she said, in a voice soft but firm.

The children resumed their chanting.

I saw their teacher's eyes flicker toward the window where I stood. She did not stop the lesson, but when it was over, she laid the pointer down.

"It is time for dinner," she said. "As the weather is fine, you may eat your dinners outdoors. Take out your dinner pails."

There was some clattering as pails were brought out from beneath desks.

"You may stand up."

All of them stood.

"You may form two lines," she said.

They ranged themselves obediently into two rows.

"You have one hour," she said, and moved to the door. She opened it, and said, "You may go out. No pushing, please."

I moved quickly to stand well clear of the door as the children filed out. The recess yard was a fenced enclosure, well shaded by cottonwoods, with a few half-log benches and a large area of bare earth where a few boys began almost immediately to scuffle about. Others, including all of the girls, moved off a small distance to the benches and begun quietly to eat their dinners.

"Yes?" Miss Levy's voice reached me. She was standing in the doorway, looking calmly at me with an expression of polite enquiry.

"My name is Sarah Mary Williams," I said.

"Judith Levy," she said. We shook hands, and she waited.

"My daughter is in need of schooling," I said.

"How old is she?"

"She's ten," I said.

"And what sort of education has been provided for up, up to this point?"

"She's had a different kind to what you do, here," I said. "She's been alone, mostly."

"Is she lonely?"

I was startled by the question. I never had considered if Sally-John might be lonely. She had David, she had me; she had all of the people who came to the store; she'd had the Johnsons and their large and active brood; she'd had Solly and his Conchita and their children,

"I don't know," I said.

"Tell me about her," she said.

So I did. I explained how David had been my daughter's nanny, how we had come to Tahoe after her birth, how she'd had no playmates but the Johnsons and Solly's brood, how she could chatter in a mix of six or seven languages, how she could read anything in print and tell you what it meant—and how dear she was to me, how dear and how strange.

"She ain't—isn't—like me at all, that I can see," I confessed.

"And her father?"

"He died."

"What sort of future do you envision for your daughter, Miss Williams?"

That was a stumper. "I hadn't thought about it much."

"Do you want her to take on your business interests?" (I'd explained about my enterprises, so's Miss Levy could see I had the wherewithal to pay.)

"No'm, not really."

"Do you see her making a successful marriage?"

"If she meets somebody she wants to marry, and he ain't a cattle rustler nor a horse-thief, how could I do otherwise but give her my blessing? But I ain't thought about her marrying, no. Seems too far in the future."

"Let me put the question again, another way. What do you want for her?"

"I want her to be happy," I said.

"That is not something education is likely to lead to," Miss Levy said. "Not if it is successful, at any rate."

"I don't understand."

"Many people think of schooling as a preparation for life," Miss Levy said. "And it is, for some. Or can be. For others—and I suspect, from what you tell me, that your daughter may be one—it is not an end but a beginning. But never mind that now," she said. "Bring her to me. Tomorrow is Saturday, and there is no school. Let me see. Shall we say, Sunday, around noon? We will have dinner together, yes? And we will talk about what Sally-John wants. She should be consulted, don't you agree? Good."

We spoke, then, about fees, and about such things as Sally-John would need—"school supplies," Miss Levy called them, and wrote out a list. And then she stood and rang the school-bell to call the children in from their recess. I watched as they marched up to the steps, formed two lines, and entered, each going to his or her desk and stowing a dinner-pail neatly beneath it, then waiting, hands folded, until all were assembled.

"I shall expect you on Sunday," Miss Levy said to me. "With your daughter."

"And David," I said. "He knows her better than I do."

"And David as well," she agreed. "Good day."

As I left, I heard her say, "Please read pages thirty to thirty-three in your history books now, children. Quietly, please, and remember not to move your lips as you read."

I unhitched my horse, climbed into the buggy, twitched the reins and turned for home. For some reason, as I drove, I found myself thinking of Johnny.

Nearly eleven years, it had been, and I could still see him clear as clear: his smooth skin, the color of caramel candy; his full, red lips and the softly curling black mustache he wore above them; his eyes, the color of expensive whiskey.

I could feel, crisp and springing under my fingers, those glossy dark ringlets he'd handed on to his daughter. I could feel, also, his strong-muscled arm beneath my neck, and smell the scent of him, clean male sweat and soap and the musk of sex.

And I could hear his voice, deep and soft.

"You're too loving a woman to live for long without a man," he'd said to me, all those years ago, as we lay together in the sweet darkness, skin to skin.

"You were wrong, Johnny," I said now, aloud.

Love! What did I need of his kind of love? I had all of love I wanted, no less and no more.

And a man—even a man as beautiful as Johnny— was in no way a necessity.

I'd had my man—the only one I'd ever wanted. There could never be another.

I chirped to the horse and he began to trot.

I was anxious to get home. David and Sally-John—my family—would be waiting.

Chapter Eighteen: Departures and Returns

Well, Sally-John did in fact go off to school to Miss Levy. The distance being what it was,[61] we decided she should board with the schoolmistress, coming home on weekends. Miss Levy had three other boarders, she told us; there was room for another, and she welcomed my daughter.

"These are my other boarding pupils," she said, and introduced them all around: Soledad and Ysabel Garcia, sisters aged nine and eleven, daughters of a mining engineer from Mexico whose consumptive wife was trying to cure her sickness in a mountain sanitarium. Their father was working on the Sutro Tunnel, and he had left his girls with Miss Levy and instructions to educate them as modern American young women.

The other girl was Miss Levy's own niece, a dark, slender girl of fourteen. "My cousin Albert's only child," Miss Levy said, stroking the girl's dark curls off her shoulders with a fond though critical look. "Her name is Sophie, Sophie Michaelson.[62] She intends to be an astronomer."

"A what?"

"She intends to study astronomy. The stars and planets," Miss Levy added, taking pity on my blank expression. "We have fitted out a little observatory for her, where she keeps her telescope," and she pointed up the hill. I saw a tiny shack. "The roof is made of glass, on one side."

The stars and planets.

I remembered floating down the river with Jim, nights, and how we'd speculated about the stars—how they had come to be, and what they was made of. And now here this girl, no older than I'd been in those days, fixing on studying them. "Where might a girl go, to study that subject?" I asked.

"At Vassar College, in New York State," Miss Levy said, and Sophie nodded, her dark eyes shining.

---

[61] Eds. note: A fifteen-mile buggy trip lasted three hours or more.

[62] Eds. note: Albert Abraham Michelson (note different spelling of last name), Polish-born physicist known for his work on the measurement of the speed of light, grew up in a mining town near Virginia City. His mother's maiden name was Levy.

"That is a college for women," Sophie explained, carefully, "And they have an observatory there. A real one."

A college for women. I felt a sharp pang as I remembered another young woman's voice saying she intended to go to a college for women. My once-upon-a-time, my long-ago lover, Antoinette. I pushed the memory from me.

"Yes," said Miss Levy. "And Miss Maria Mitchell is the professor in charge."

I had never heard of Maria Mitchell,[63] nor of any of the other female scholars and inventors, doctors and professors whom I was to hear much of in the next several years. But clearly my daughter had.

"Oh, Miss Levy," Sally-John said, "Do you *know* Maria Mitchell?"

"Indeed I do," said Miss Levy. "We have been friends since we were eleven years old. I was a student at her father's school, on Nantucket. She and I were fellow pupils there."

Sally-John was bursting with excitement.

I wanted to ask her, *where did you learn about this Maria Mitchell?* But I kept my mouth shut. No doubt the answer lay in one of the books that David ordered for my daughter, books I peeped into occasionally but found difficult and strange, full of words I had never seen.

"Well, why don't we let these young ladies get acquainted?" Miss Levy asked. "Girls, go on out and take a walk together, or you may spend some time in the schoolroom, if you like. Mr Chung and Miss Williams and I have business to talk about."

"Yes, Aunt Judith," Sophie said, and the other girls chimed in, "Yes, Ma'am." All three of the others curtsied as they left, and I noted that Sally-John observed this phenomenon with open mouth. It was high time that she learned how proper folks did. Not that I wanted her to be proper herself, leastways not too much so, but I thought she ought to see how it was done.

---

63 Author's note: Of course, I looked her up when I got the chance, and found out she was a Quaker and a relation of Benjamin Franklin, and also she won a medal from the King of Denmark for discovering a comet (how, the book did not say). She didn't marry, which did not surprise me; she also worked against slavery and for women's suffrage, which also was what I would have expected.

The upshot of that day's conference was that Sally-John would board with Miss Levy and the other girls from August through November, spend December and January at home, and resume her schooling in February. That term would run until the end of June.

"I intend to put her through a fairly rigorous course of study," Miss Levy said. "Her preparation has been, shall we say, uneven. Depending on her progress, though, she should be ready for university in six years. Sooner, if she makes good on the promise that she shows."

"University?"

Miss Levy smiled. "She may decide that six years of education at my hands is enough. But I think, yes, she will want to go on. And if so, I shall see that she is ready."

And she was.

***

As it turned out, Sally-John did not come home on weekends, preferring to stop at Miss Levy's with the other girls, who stayed with Miss Levy year-round.

I expected to be lonesome for her, and I was, but David fared worse than I.

I hadn't really thought, before, how close the two of them had become. She wrote to him more often than to me—he got six letters to my one—but whilst I read my letters aloud after dinner, sometimes, he seldom shared his. But I knew that he kept them in his red pigskin box, under his bed, the box that held his queue, tied with a black silk cord at both ends, and the picture of his wife, and a tablet with his ancestors' names carved into it.

There were three more things in David's pigskin box: a pair of Sally-John's first baby shoes—embroidered Chinese shoes, in gold thread on red satin; a lock of her curling black hair, wrapped in a piece of red silk; a silver locket he'd hung about her neck when she was tiny, to protect her, he'd said, laughing, from evil spirits. It had been his mother's, he said.

I knew that it contained a paper with prayers written on it, for he'd opened it and showed it to me, years before, when he'd asked me if Sally-John could wear it.

"I ask, because often Christians object to Buddhist prayers," he'd said.

"I ain't a Christian," I had told him. "If you think this thing can protect her, go ahead."

"I don't know if I really believe that," David said, "But my mother did."

"Then go on," I said. "Put it on her."

And so he had. I could remember her as a tiny baby in my arms, the silver chain around her neck. The locket itself showed the marks of her teething. She'd worn it until she was three. Then David had put it away, saying she didn't need it any more. He'd given her a string of jade beads instead.

They were pretty, those beads, each one carved into a tiny animal or bird or flower.

"Does she still have those jade beads?" I asked David after supper one night.

"I believe so," he said, looking up from her latest letter. "When she comes home, shall I ask her?"

"No, that's all right," I said, then, "When *is* she coming home?"

"In two weeks. Just in time for Christmas," he said. "And she wants to bring the other three with her."

"Well, all right," I said. "What does Miss Levy think?"

"Miss Levy is agreeable," he said. "With our permission, she will use the time to go East and visit her cousin."

"Fine," I said. "Now, let's set to work."

"What work?" He looked up again. "We have finished for the day, have we not?"

"Not," I said. "If we're playing host to three more young girls, we'd better get busy. Here, let's make a list—"

An hour later, we were wrangling over a new bedstead.

"There isn't room for another bed in there," David said. "We can put a truckle-bed underneath."

"That's for babies," I objected.

"I'm afraid it's the only solution. Two can sleep in the bedstead, and the other two in the truckle," he said. "We will need more bedding, though."

"If we don't buy another bedstead, we can get an armoire in here," I said.

"That is an excellent idea." David wrote busily. "That chest she has now is far too small already."

I prowled around the room, considering. "Could we fit a dressing table in that-there alcove?" I pointed at a niche that was created by the jog the hallway made at the top of the stairs.

"I believe so," he said. "I will measure to be sure."

And so, when David sat down to write out the order, it included not only two new sets of bedding but a dressing-table, curved, with a mirror atop, and a new armoire big enough to hold the wardrobes of half-a-dozen.

"I still don't feature a truckle-bed," I said. "We ought to have two regular beds. But we'd have to knock out that store-room partition to make this room big enough." I stood in the middle of Sally-John's bedroom, revolving slowly. "There ain't enough space in here."

"Even making this room that much bigger won't solve the problem forever." David said. "If we intend to keep on, we will have to add on *again*, I'm afraid."

When we'd put up the store building, we'd tacked on a largish addition at the back. The ground floor was kitchen, scullery, David's room (off the kitchen), and a large room that we used as a combined office-and-living-room (the privy was in the rear of the property, and a covered passageway led to it from the woodshed; baths we took in the kitchen, using the tub that hung in the woodshed between times). Upstairs we'd partitioned off into two small bedrooms—mine and Sally-John's—and a storage room under the eaves, which at this point held only a few empty crates. Taking out the partition would give us enough room for the new furniture, though the girls would probably have to climb over the beds to reach the dressing-table.

"We don't have time to build on now," I said. "Three weeks and they'll be here. No. Here's what we'll do. I'll move downstairs to the sofa and let two of 'em have my room."

"You can't do that," David said.

"Why not? It'll just be for a few weeks."

"It isn't proper."

"Why not?"

David only looked at me in that way he had—what folks like to call "the inscrutable Oriental" blank-faced stare that meant I warn't seeing something that was as plain as the nose on my face.

"You don't mean it," I said.

But he did.

As long as Sally-John and I slept upstairs, and David kept to his downstairs room, folks had no reason to gossip. A servant—

even a Chinese houseboy—was entitled to sleep on the premises. But not within arm's reach of the mistress of the house.

"That's ridiculous," I said, and meant it.

"You have a position to maintain," he said, serene as always. "I will go and sleep in the barn while the young ladies are here."

"You will not!"

"Yes. It will be perfectly comfortable. I will take the portable stove—[this was a small coal-oil setup we'd bought for extra-cold nights]—and the extra lantern, and the camp kettle."

"You're out of your mind."

He went on, blithe as anything. "And I have plenty of quilts, and there is more than enough straw for bedding."

"You can't sleep out there!"

"Sarah Mary." When David Chung took that tone, it was as well for a body to listen. "I have decided."

"Well, then, go on and suffer, if you want to that much," I said.

"Thank you, Sarah Mary. I assure you that I shall not suffer."

So he got his own way, as usual. (It was like arguing with a river; it just went on its own way, carrying you along with it, and never-you-mind.)

So I give over my room to the Garcia sisters, and Sophie and Sally-John shared Sally-John's room. I slept on the sofa, and David, who woke before the sun, got dressed and waited in the barn until he saw my light, which was the signal that I was up and doing. That meant he could come in and start up the fires and get the water to heating, and whilst I folded my bedding and put it away, the girls come piling down in their wrappers for breakfast.

That was a merry time.

It surprised me, how much I enjoyed the company of four lively girls. I'd never been around children much, and David had cared for my own daughter with such smooth ease I'd scarcely been aware of her presence, except in the evenings, when, clean and sweet, she appeared in David's arms "to spend some time with Mama." And later, as a toddler and then as a small girl, clinging to my hand, we'd taken walks and inspected flowers and stones, fallen logs and mountain streams, until Ah Bok came and bore my daughter away again to bath or supper or bed.

Latterly, she had spent her time off on her own, with the Johnson children and Solly's, or by herself. Coming in from these excursions, it was to David she brought what treasures she'd found—an arrowhead, a curious rock with ferns or fishes in it— though she kissed me good-night with warm affection.

How different she was, in the company of her peers!

For one thing, she was a great deal louder.

Those who believe that girls are quiet, dainty things must not know any, or only those who resemble Tom Sawyer's wife Becky and her ilk. Those ladylike flowers of Southern gentility are nothing like our Western wenches, even those transplanted from elsewhere, like the Garcia girls and Sophie. They, and our Sally-John, shrieked and shouted, romped and galloped, and generally carried on like wild Indians was supposed to (but seldom did).

"What in the world—?" my lady customer started, put her gloved hand to her throat and appeared to totter for a second, before I slid a chair under her bustled rump and pushed her into it. "Set," I said, "It's only my daughter and her school chums."

"Heavens," the lady said, "It sounds like—"

"I know," I said. "A troop of wild Indians."

"Well, I didn't mean—"

"That's all right, Mrs, don't worry about it. Now, was that six yards of the blue four-ounce worsted you wanted?"

"Yes, please, and a bottle of Florida water."

I fetched the goods, wrapped them, took the money, and give the parcel and the receipt to my customer, who turned to go, then stopped as four girls come leaping like antelopes through the front door, their leader snatching up a fistful of licorice ropes as she passed. "Thank you, Mama!" came floating after her, as four sets of feet pounded up the stairs.

"Heavens," my customer said again, and shook her head as she went out. "I don't believe I've ever seen anything the beat of it," her voice floated back to me.

I could have told her: this was all new to me, too.

As the weeks passed, the noise and commotion settled down, or maybe I just got used to it. David, I noticed, spent a good deal of time doing accounts in the kitchen, or reading, whilst the girls played Happy Families or Beggar-My-Neighbour. Soledad and Ysabel had brought their guitars, and entertained us with Mexican songs, which they sang in two kinds of voices, very low and throbbing or high with lots of trills and "Aiii-yiii-yiii's." Sometimes Sally-John read aloud to all of us, and David left his solitude to come and listen at those times. She read very clearly, and somehow managed to give voice to the different characters in a way that made the books come alive.

One that made a deep impression on us was a popular story by Miss Louisa M. Alcott, called *Little Women*, about four sisters and their family and friends, and though it all ended happily, it had some sad parts, such as when the youngest sister, Beth, died, and also when the oldest one, Jo, told Laurie, the boy who loved her, that she would not marry him. They was too much alike, she said, and if they married, each would try to have the mastery of the other. The girls thought she ought to marry him anyway, as he was rich and handsome and loved her dearly, but I thought she was right, and said so.

And in such ways the time passed.

I determined that, come Spring, we'd set about things in a more businesslike way, and build on an addition with space for two big bedrooms and a sitting room, and maybe a bathroom as well. I was growing tired, myself, of taking baths in the old tin tub in front of the cookstove.

So I dreamed—and sketched plans. Christmas arrived, and we had two dinners: one with the Johnsons, Christmas Eve, and next day's with Solly and his family. Solly's made me smile, for he'd put together a real American feast of turkey and ham, oyster stuffing and corn bread, squash pie and apple dumpling, all served alongside rice and pork and cabbage, with Mrs Solly's addition of *frijoles refritos* (which I noticed with interest her children ate mixed into their rice).

The girls gobbled up several helpings of everything, exclaimed in bliss over the Christmas tree—a white pine fully ten feet high that cleared the Johnson ridgepole only by inches—and next day put away enough food for twice their number. I could only shake my head in wonder.

Then all too soon it was time to take them all back to school. We spent several days packing, whilst David baked cookies for them, and a loaf cake for Miss Levy, and I went over my accounts, writing a cheque to Miss Levy for the next term, and counting out spending money for my daughter. There warn't much in Truckee that a girl would part with her money for, to be sure, but I liked Sally-John to have as much as the others did, to spend or to save as she chose.

We made the trip to Truckee in the big wagon, with the girls riding behind on the luggage, wrapped in blankets. The weather was clear though very cold, and we stopped several times for them to run about and get the blood running warm in their hands and feet. I had given each girl a warm hat and mittens, for Christmas: red for Sally-John, yellow and green for the Garcia sisters, and deep blue for Sophie, whose eyes was as blue as Tahoe itself. They chased each other around the wagon, laughing, until David called that it was time to go.

When we got to Miss Levy's, she was waiting with hot coffee, and we gave our girl back into her care, along with the others, and turned the horses' heads for home.

All the way back, David was silent. Finally, I spoke.

"I know how much you're going to miss her," I said. "I will, too."

He didn't say anything. I drove on for a time in silence, then said, "Do you reckon we'll be able to get the addition up and painted and papered in time for June?"

"I suppose so," he said.

"Would you like me to see to it?"

"Sarah Mary, I have something I must tell you."

Now, I have noticed that whenever folks say they have something to tell you in that particular tone of voice, you can bet that whatever it is won't be pleasant.

In fact, it will probably be painful enough that you will decide you'd rather not have heard it in the first place, but what usually happens is, you don't have that choice.

"I am going away," he said. "Very soon."

"Where?"

"Back to China."

"You told me you warn't never going back there!" It burst out before I could stop it.

"I did not think that I ever should," he said. "But the last letter I received brought news that has changed my mind."

"What kind of news?"

"My presence is required in my ancestral village. I have already booked passage from San Francisco."

"Why is your presence required, after all this time?"

"My parents have died, and I am the oldest of the next generation."

I pulled up the horse and stared. "What did they die of?"

"There have been many floods, followed by widespread sickness in the region. Typhoid, most probably," he said.

"Was—were they very old?"

"My father was seventy-five, my mother seventy," he said.

"And you are their oldest child?"

"I am the oldest son. I have a sister, married long ago to a merchant in the nearest city."

"And no brothers?"

"Only Solly."

"Is he going with you?"

"He will not go."

"Why not?"

"He says that his home is here now. China is too far away, too strange, he says, and he is content with his life as it is. He has no wish to change it."

"Will you come back?"

"Most likely I shall not." He sighed. "China is not like America. I am the head of the family now."

"You told me once that we was your family, Sally-John and me."

He looked sad and sorry, both at once. "That is true, but only here. In China—"

"In China, we are a pair of foreign devils. I know."

He sighed again. "I cannot make you understand. Indeed, I hardly understand myself. I can only say that I am sorry, sorry that I must go, sorry to leave you both, sorry that I cannot write to my relations and say, 'find another to take the place of the old ones who have gone.' For in truth there is no one else. If there were, I tell you this: I would *not* go."

It was in my mind that his Chinese wife had written this most recent letter, calling for him to return. But I did not ask him if she had been the one to write. He would not lie, and I did think I wanted to hear the truth.

When we got home, after we'd unhitched the team, rubbed them down, and fed them, I walked ahead of David to the back door. Inside, I took down from a high shelf the bottle of good whiskey that was kept there, for occasions such as this.

I poured a drink for each of us, handed David's to him, and said, "Well, *bon voyage*."

"Sarah Mary, don't," he said. "I cannot say it any other way:

this is a journey I must make; I have no other choice."

"Will we ever see you again?"

He was silent, for a long, long time. Then, "I don't know," he said.

"What will I do, without your help?"

"Hire someone. One of the Johnsons, perhaps."

"It won't be the same."

"No, of course not."

"They'd just be an employee."

"Yes."

"Not like you."

"We have been—what you Americans say," he agreed. "A good team."

"You practically raised my daughter single-handed. She's more your daughter than she is mine," I said.

"She *is* your daughter, though, and not mine."

"She will miss you even more than I will."

"If that is true, then I am relieved," he said.

"What do you mean?" I asked.

"You have been alone for many years," he said. "I would not like to think that I had been in any way the cause."

It came to me that a body could take what he was saying in two different ways.

One, that my having a Chinese man about the place kept off any possible suitors. Which was possible, people having the attitudes they did. Or, two, that he thought maybe *I* had feelings for *him*, feelings that kept me from wishing for any suitors.

A man don't think of your feelings for him unless he has some for you.

This was a poser. But I had to be honest. "You never have been the cause of my being alone," I said. "It's been my wish to stay that way—it's what I'm used to, I guess."

"I am happy to know that," he said. "Sarah Mary, what will you do when the child is grown? Will you still live alone and lonely?"

"Most likely," I said. I drank my whiskey, then poured another. I gestured with the bottle; he shook his head.

"This is enough," he said, and sipped.

"I'm going to miss you," I said.

"And I shall miss you," he said, and finished his drink.

"Good night, Sarah Mary."

"Good night, Cheung Ka Yat."

I did not hear him leave the kitchen and go into the back of the store, where his little cell was, with its narrow couch. I sat at the kitchen table and stared at the wall until my eyes burned and my head began to throb.

The woman in China who was his wife did not have his heart. That did not matter.

Nor did it make any difference that I did not have his heart, either, for I had never wanted it, nor imagined, even, that there was a chance of its being offered.

If matters had been otherwise, would he be leaving now?

In the end, I put my head down and wept a little, for an ending that I thought had come too soon. Perhaps I wept also for the end of my youth. And his.

Next morning we met for breakfast, as usual. In the same tranquil voice with which he always greeted me, he said, "I have written a letter for Sally-John. Will you send it to her, after I have gone?"

I took the letter, which was unsealed.

"You may read it," he said.

"It is not for me," I said.

"Be sure that I have said nothing of which you would not approve."

"I wish I could understand."

"Someday, perhaps, we both shall."

And that was the last we spoke of it. A week later, he was gone.

He went in Western clothing, the first time I'd ever seen him in trousers and coat, with a white shirt and a necktie and polished boots, and an overcoat of thick wool, with a full-brimmed felt hat on his head: David, who for all the years I'd known him went always in black cotton Chinese trousers under a long black sateen gown, with Chinese cloth shoes peeping out from under; David, whose smooth golden features looked more Chinese than ever under his Western hat.

He had only his old grip, and a leather satchel over one shoulder. When I asked about his other luggage, he said, "This is all I wish to take. What remains, I give to you and to our Sally-John. Let her take what she likes, as keepsakes, and do you do the same."

"I want no keepsakes," I said. "I will keep the things safe, against our next meeting."

He said nothing, but his eyes searched mine, and then he smiled.

"Goodbye, Sarah Mary Williams," he said, and took me into his embrace for the first and last time.

"Goodbye," I whispered against his collar.

I did not see him leave the house. I did not see him enter the coach, nor watch it pull away.

I went into my store and shut the door and sat for a long while in the dark.

It was late that night, the moon riding high over the Sierra Nevadas, before I could bring myself to open the armoire that held his belongings. When I found the red pigskin chest, I could not look inside it, for a long, long minute.

Finally, I opened it.

I saw immediately that the picture of his wife was gone, and so was the thick brown envelope of old letters. There remained a pair of Chinese baby shoes in red satin, a few curls of black hair and a silver locket, and a piece of paper folded around a small, rectangular package. The package, which was unsealed, was labelled, in English, in David's beautiful curved writing:

For Sally-John, From Ah Bok.

I unwrapped it and saw a stack of paper money—spirit money, it was called.

David had told me of this Chinese custom, long ago: when someone died, the money was burned at the grave. Some of it was for the ancestors and some for the gods, and some was for the soul of the newly-dead.

I unfolded the note addressed to Sally-John and read,

"Daughter of my spirit, for so I think of you: when you learn that I have departed this life, burn this paper money for me, in place of the daughters and sons I have not begotten. You who are not the child of my loins are yet dearer to me than those never-born could ever have been. And so I sign this last letter to you with all my love, Ah Bok

Cheung Ka Yat 張家逸 *David Chung."*

I folded the paper back around the bundle of spirit money, and replaced it in the chest with the other keepsakes.

When Sally-John was grown, I would give them to her.

In the meanwhile, these few things—and a fan, a teapot, and four small cups without handles—were all that was left to me of someone who, in another time and place, I might have loved.

Someone who could have loved me.

If I had not been blind and deaf.

But I had been, and he had given up trying to make me hear and see, and gone back to the woman whose blood could hear the call of his blood, to the beautiful one whose skin was smooth and golden like his, whose hair was shining black silk like his, whose eyes was almond shaped like his, under brows like slender ink-strokes.

But losing him was not the worst of it.

I knew now, and the knowledge scorched like flame, what had stopped me from loving David. I knew, and I was flooded with shame.

He was Chinese. And I was white.

I had loved Johnny, who counted in those days as a black man. I knew and anyone seeing him would have known that he was more white than black, but still such love was not unnatural, not in the world I came from. After all, black and white had loved one another for generations, as Johnny's color—and that of his sister, and his mother—so clearly proved.

But a Chinese.

I'd not been able to bring myself to see a Chinese man as a man, not with my body at any rate. And that caused me now to feel flayed alive. I had, with every word and action—for ten years!—denied a man his manhood.

He was not a man like other men; he was only David, dear and familiar, more than servant but less than equal.

What if he'd come to me and said, "Sarah Mary, I want you the way a man wants a woman." What then?

Oh, I might have been horrified at first, but I would have felt his wanting, the way a woman does, whether she wants the man in turn, or doesn't.

Did I feel myself to be, still, a woman? Or had I, in the years since Johnny had gone, lost my womanhood, put it from me as surely as I had put David's manhood from him, in my own mind?

I looked at myself in the mirror that hung inside David's armoire, trying to see what he had seen.

The passage of years was clear.

My hair had grey threads in it and was unrulier than ever. My skin was mostly unlined but it had weathered brown—and it had never been smooth as yellow cream.

My eyes had lost some of their brightness. My lips had growed thin and pale, with lines about them—how long had those lines been there?

I was tall, as tall as David himself, with flat breasts instead of soft curves. I was scrawny, that was the plain truth, scrawny as an old turkey hen, with a neck lined and corded, and hands big and rough, with veins ropy across the backs, hands that looked older than my years warranted. I had used them hard, those hands.

And my feet—

I remembered the picture, and David's face when he spoke of Mei Yin's "golden lilies." However much he might despise the practice, and deplore it with his mind, in his body the memory had lingered, and it had stirred him. He too might deny it, but I knew that it was so.

I closed the armoire and left the store.

Later that day I paid a visit to the lumberyard, where I ordered materials and labor. "I want a complete renovation," I said.

By the time Sally-John and her schoolmates came back to Tahoe City, the building had been almost completely redone. Besides the new bedrooms and bathroom, I'd had the kitchen enlarged and the store's premises as well. Instead of the old office, partitioned off from the living room, I had a special corner built and fitted out with desk and files, with the safe concealed behind swinging doors.

And so I bent myself to my new task.

I would make enough money to be able, once Sally-John was sixteen or so, to be able to sell out and go.

Where, I didn't know, but trusted it would come clear in time.

Chapter Nineteen: Aunt Polly

The next years did, in fact, speed by.

I did not replace David with a live-in servant, but hired such help as I needed it by the day. Whenever Sally-John came home, I asked Solly's wife to come and cook and clean for us, and often she brought with her one or more of her Mexican-Chinese children.

Watching those small brown boys and girls running about the place, I was both glad and sorry I'd let David go without either of us acknowledging what could have been. I was too old, I knew, to have another child, and David needed children.

I prayed—to what, I didn't really know, being an unbelieving heathen myself—but I did pray that David's wife, who was still the right side of forty, might still give him a son. And, perhaps, a daughter, too, to take the place of mine for him; a daughter who looked like him and called him whatever the Chinese word was for Pa.

I remembered my own little girl, as she had been, toddling after his black sateen skirts and calling, "Ah Bok! Ah Bok!"

And I remembered his face as he turned and held out his arms for her.

Daughter of my spirit, he called her, in his letter. That, I knew, was as true as any truth could be.

The years after David's departure were hard ones, not only because I'd come so to depend on him in terms of the business, but because Sally-John and I had only each other to turn to. We'd always had Ah-Bok before; now it was only the two of us.

My daughter, she was—and her pa's too. Sixteen years old, now, she looked to my eyes very much like her aunt Elizabeth at that age, tall and slim, long-legged and long-necked, with masses of black curls that she wore braided and piled atop her head. There was more than a hint of Johnny in her length of bone and the way she moved, graceful as a cat. I could even see, in certain lights, a hint of my old Jim in the breadth of her wide forehead and the way her eyes set atop cheekbones that were higher than my own.

I watched, and I planned.

And Sally-John was sixteen, and ready, Miss Levy said, for Vassar College.

"There is nothing more that I can teach her," Miss Levy said.

"And you think that this Vassar College will give her what she needs?"

"I do."

"I don't begrudge the money," I said.

"I know that," she said.

"I only want to be sure that this is what she needs," I said.

"Without this chance, she will die a living death," Miss Levy said. "This child of yours has a formidable intellect . . . would you offer her a stone instead of bread?"

"I don't know what you mean," I said.

"The reference is to the words of Jesus. He said, in one of his teachings, that no one who asks for bread should be given a stone . . . . Miss Williams, will you deny your daughter the bread she needs in order to live?"

"I want her to have everything she needs," I said, "Including what I cannot myself give her."

"Then you must let her go," Miss Levy said. "And take the risk that the bird, once flown, will not return to the nest that gave it birth. Are you able to do this, Sarah Mary?"

"I can't do anything else," I said. "She's not a child any longer."

"She is not," Miss Levy agreed. "So let us both give her our blessings, and help her to make this journey . . . for you know that if we ask it, she will remain?"

"I know it."

"Then—let her go."

And when Sally-John came to me, her eyes open wide with wonder at all the newness she had learnt, and filled with eagerness at all there was still to discover—

I knew nothing must be allowed to keep her from the life that awaited her, however far it might take her from me.

***

We had quite a job to get her ready to travel. Books and clothes and boots and coats, underwear and nightgowns, towels and sheets and blankets ("the young ladies are requested to furnish their own linens")—but finally everything was packed, the trunks corded and labeled, and it was time to go.

I'd already made arrangements for Solly's oldest boy, Seraphim, to take charge of the store in my absence. And so my daughter and I boarded the train and set off. Our final destination was, of course, New York, but I had made arrangements to stop along the way at St Joseph and at Hannibal, Missouri, for who knew when the chance might come again? And it was time for my daughter to make contact once again with her father's kin.

When we got to St Joe, I asked the stationmaster to keep our baggage overnight; I'd telegraphed Mr Drewery, and he met us at the station.

"This is your Aunt Elizabeth's husband, Mr Robert Drewery," I said to Sally-John.

"I'm happy to know you," he said.

I sat between the two of them on the wagon seat.

"How is Elizabeth?" I asked. "And Julie, is she well?"

"Elizabeth is blooming," Robert Drewery said. "And Julie— well, she's just as she's always been." He chuckled. "She's got more get-up-and-go than most women half her age, my wife included. And that's a good thing, for my children lead her quite a dance."

I heard the softness in his voice as he said "my wife" and "my children," and that made me glad.

When we reached the farm, the buggy was surrounded by what seemed at first to be at least a dozen small fry. When the flurry sorted itself out I saw that there was only seven children, six boys and a girl. "Ladies, meet your youngest relations, so far," Robert said, laughing.

"Line up, you all, and let me see you," I ordered.

Of course Julie had written to tell me of each new arrival, and chatted in letters in between of what little Jimmy did, or Henry, or young Robert, Sidney, Louis, or Jake, and she'd written a letter that practically shouted with joy when Naomi was born, but the full impact of the whole tribe could only be felt in person. As it was now.

The children had lined themselves up, as ordered, and stood now, chattering under their breaths, some of them giggling, all of them looking up at me and Sally-John with bright eyes.

Those eyes were all shades of brown: leaf-brown and bark-brown, brown like the water of the Mississippi at full flood, brown like the good earth under the plow, and one or two a goldy-brown like their mother's—or their uncle Johnny's—or their cousin Sally-John's. Likewise in complexion they varied. Young Robert was darkest and Louis the lightest, and all had dark curling hair, but I could see their father's features blended in them too, and in the littlest, Naomi, I saw an expression I'd last seen on her grandpa Jim: she was looking at me with starry eyes, and next minute she flung herself into my arms and give me a hearty kiss.

"Thank you, darlin'—" I held her tight for a minute, then set her down. "That was a fine welcome."

Elizabeth had come out to greet us, and waited whilst the children jumped and shouted. I saw that she was pregnant again, and close to her time, if size was any indication.

Robert jumped out of the buggy and helped me and Sally-John to descend. I laid my cheek against Elizabeth's, and turned to greet Julie, who had bustled out onto the porch.

"There you are, finally!" she said. "Come inside terreckly . . . I've got the coffee-pot to boiling, and they's fresh dough-nuts ready." She flapped a hand in our direction and vanished back inside.

Robert put his arm around his wife's shoulders and grinned at Sally-John and me.

"She's been cooking and baking for two days straight," he said. "Wanting to welcome you, the best way she knows how."

"Well, a cup of coffee and a dough-nut would suit me right down to the ground," I said. "Let's go wash up."

Sally-John and I went inside, followed by Elizabeth and Robert. Julie insisted on a tour of the house. "The coffee ain't ready yet," she said. "Take a look around, and tell me what you think!" Her face wore a proud and satisfied look, and so did Elizabeth's.

Robert had, indeed, made a number of improvements to the house.

The porch we'd entered fronted an ell that had been added onto the original building, and there was a dining room now, and a pantry, and the kitchen shed in back. And three new bedrooms upstairs, Robert mentioned, "for these barbarians of ours"—ruffling the hair of Jake, who was closest, and smiling down at him.

There was also a bathroom, just off the kitchen, complete with an enameled cast-iron tub with huge claw feet, like the one I'd recently had installed, but a size or two larger.

"Next thing," Robert said, "I'm going to put in a water-closet."

"Little house in the back was good enough, once," Julie said, "But Robert, he want things *modern*." She pointed to the kitchen stove, large and gleaming black, with flourishes of bright nickel trim. "Look at that range—would you believe it, two bread ovens *and* a hot-water reservoir." She shook her head.

"I don't feature my family living like the old days," Robert said. "Times have changed."

Everything I saw was as neat and pretty as it could be. "You've done yourself proud," I told Robert, and he beamed.

In the dining room, the big round table was set with a fine embroidered cloth, silver teaspoons, and gleaming china—the set I'd sent the Drewerys for a wedding gift. Julie sailed in from the kitchen with an enormous granite-ware coffee-pot in one hand and a platter of dough-nuts in the other.

"Set," she ordered, and the four of us took our places. The children each took a dough-nut and scampered off outdoors.

"Get those chores done, now!" Robert called after them. Then he took the coffee-pot and went around the table, filling the cups. Julie took her apron off, hung it on the back of her chair, and sat down.

"Say the blessing," she said to her son-in-law.

"We thank you, Lord, for the safe arrival of our sister Sarah Mary and our niece Sally-John," Robert said, standing behind his chair. "And for the bounteous refreshment that our dear mother Julie has prepared. And we ask that all under this roof continue under your loving protection. Amen." He sat down. "Mama Julie, pass me a dough-nut!"

As the cream and sugar went around, I watched as Elizabeth's bright eyes followed the conversation. I motioned to her and spoke as clearly as I could. "When is it due?" I asked.

She held up seven fingers, then quickly flashed four, then held up one. "Four weeks—one more month?" I asked, and she nodded vigorously. She then pantomimed a cradle, rocking, and pointed upwards.

"You have the nursery all ready, cradle and all?" I asked. She nodded again.

"It's the same cradle we've used for all of them," Julie said. "Poplar-wood, smooth as satin, and carved all around the hood with little stars and flowers."

"I didn't know you did wood-carving," I said to Robert.

"Oh, I have done some in my time," he said. "I have built a few chests and a cupboard or two." He pointed at the large china cupboard against the far wall. "I made that, to hold our wedding china that you sent."

"It's beautiful work," I said, and it was.

"Robert is handy at most things," Julie said. "But he says he ain't no great shucks as a midwife, and he ain't a-going to bring this baby, so I guess I will have to do it, same as always."

I knew Julie had presided over the births of the other children.

"You have always done a good job, Mama Julie, but I had thought," Robert said, "Maybe this time, we ought to have the doctor."

"Why?" I asked. "Ain't Elizabeth well?"

Elizabeth caught my eye and nodded. She smiled and patted her belly.

"She's just fine. Like as not the baby will be here before that doctor is," Julie said.

"Like as not," I agreed.

Robert said, "I have spoken to Doctor Nathan, though, and he says he will come."

"Well, another pair of hands can't go amiss around here," said Julie. "Have some more coffee, now, do! Robert, hand me that cream pitcher, and cease your fussing. Elizabeth's going to be all right."

The rest of the day passed pleasantly. I helped Julie with the dishes, whilst Elizabeth took Sally-John on a tour of the barn and farmyard.

"She's happy with him," I said to Julie. "Elizabeth is."

"He's a good man."

"Have they picked a name for the baby?"

"If it's a boy, they're going to call him Frederick," she said. "After Mr Douglass. And a girl will be Angelina."[64]

"Those are fine names," I said.

"I wish Jim could see all his grandchildren," Julie said.

"Amen," was all I managed to say.

***

---

[64] Eds. note: Possibly after Angelina Grimke, the abolitionist and suffragist. Interestingly, Grimke's great-niece was the biracial poet-playwright (and her namesake) Angelina Grimke Weld, born in the same year as this child of Elizabeth and Robert Drewery, 1880.

Next morning, whilst Sally-John helped Elizabeth with the milking and egg-gathering, I took Julie into town to buy some things for the baby. We also stopped at the telegraph office, and I sent a quick wire off to Seraphim to tell him we had arrived safely. Then we set out for the general store, which was a big one, dealing in all sorts of goods, including ironmongery—small items like pot hooks and door latches and so on. I made a mental note to look into including some similar merchandise when I got back home.

Whilst we were in the store, looking at bolts of dry goods (Julie wanted some fine flannel for baby clothes, and some birdseye for diapers), a messenger boy came in.

"Did I see Missus Finn come in here with another lady?" he asked. He was a redheaded white boy, about ten, with freckles all over his face, and he had a telegram in his hand.

"Yes, here we are," Julie said. "Is that for me?" She looked troubled—telegrams usually meant bad news.

"No'm," the boy said. "It's for this lady—that is, if you're Miss Williams?"

"I am," I said.

"Here you are, Miss," he said, and handed me the envelope. "I was all set to ride out to your place, ma'am," he said, turning to Julie. "But the telegraph man said you all was in here."

I give him a dime and thanked him for his trouble, and he lifted his cap and run off.

I slit the envelope with one finger-nail and drew out the yellow paper.

"What does it say? Who is it from?" Julie asked.

"It's from Tom Sawyer," I said, and I read it aloud:

AUNT POLLY VERY ILL STOP DOCTOR SAYS PNEUMONIA STOP COME SOON STOP WILL MEET YOUR TRAIN STOP TELEGRAPH ARRIVAL STOP

"I'll have to leave right away," I said.

"Of course," Julie said. "You go on and get your tickets. I'll go back home and pack your bag and bring Sally-John to the station."

"Thank you," I said, and hugged her. "I'll send you word as soon as I know."

Julie drove off, looking sad and sorry. I headed over to the station, where I booked two berths for Hannibal.

"Train leaves at twelve noon, sharp," the stationmaster said.

It was peaceful on the station platform. I sat down on a bench to wait for Julie to come back with Sally-John.

Aunt Polly, dying.

Would I get there in time?

There was nothing to do now but wait. And I have never been very good at waiting.

***

We got to Hannibal early in the morning of the second day of travel. I'd been able to take advantage of a stop in Meadville to send a wire to Tom Sawyer, letting him know that we'd be on the next morning's train.

He was waiting for us when we pulled in.

"How is she?" I asked. It was a short walk to the house, and the morning was already a warm one. A tiny breeze stirred the leaves of the trees overhead as we stepped along, and I recalled how the air hung hot and sticky along the river in Augusts past.

"She's hanging on," Tom said. "Becky will be glad to see you—and you too, Sally-John," he added. "And Mary."

"Mary's here?"

"She and her husband come in two days ago."

Mary Penniman—Mary Johnston now. She had married a fellow missionary, and the two of them "toiled in the vineyard" as Aunt Polly's letters put it, this particular vineyard being a mission to the Cherokee out in Indian Territory.[65] I had not seen Tom's Cousin Mary since before her marriage, but I'd been kept abreast of her enterprises by Aunt Polly, who was proud of her only child and never lost an opportunity of referring to "my daughter, the missionary to the heathen."

"Is Sid here, too?" I asked.

"He's on his way. He wired, too. He's on the train from Richmond."

Sid taught Bible history at the Presbyterian seminary.

"And Aunt Sally and Uncle Silas?"

"Aunt Sally's here. Uncle Silas stayed behind, on the farm. He's getting on, you know, and it's hard for him to travel far."

---

[65] Eds. note: This may have been Dwight Presbyterian Mission in Sallisaw, Oklahoma (then Indian Territory). The mission was founded near Russellville, Arkansas by the Rev. Cephas Washburn and moved to its present location near Sallisaw in the 1830s.

We had reached the house. I looked up while Tom opened the gate and held it for us. It seemed the same as ever: a two-story frame house, weathered gray, with a front garden full of fragrant, old-fashioned flowers: hollyhocks, carnations, foxgloves, sweet-Williams, calendulas, lavender. The fence was overrun with rambler roses, and purple clematis climbed up one side of the porch and cascaded down the other.

"What a lovely garden," Sally-John said.

"Aunt Polly's pride," Tom said. "We'd best go in now."

After the brightness outside, the house was dim; all of the shades had been drawn down tight, and over the smell of beeswax polish and potpourri was another smell, astringent and medicinal.

"I'll see if she's awake," Tom said. "Go on upstairs. Your room's the farthest back."

We went upstairs, walking soft as we could, to the back bedroom. I remembered that it had been Mary's room long ago—a small narrow chamber, painted blue, with a serviceable washstand and plenty of pegs on the walls. We took off our bonnets and shook out our skirts and had a wash and brush-up. Tom knocked softly.

"Ready?" he said. "If you want to see her, now's a good time."

When we entered the sickroom—what had been Aunt Polly's front parlor so many years ago—I saw the furnishings I'd known so well in the past: the big brass bedstead with its embroidered coverlid, the rocking chair and footstool, both with cushions that Aunt Polly herself had needlepointed in her girlhood, the parlor stove and the square table where Aunt Polly kept her Bible and sewing-basket.

Several other folks stood by the windows (partly open now, to let in what was left of the morning breeze) and two sat by the bedside. One was Sid, who sat with his face buried in his hands, his shoulders heaving silently. The other was Mary, who nodded to me, then took Sid tenderly by the arm and led him from the room.

"Aunt Polly?" I advanced to the bed and looked down at the slender form lying under the coverlid. That coverlid, embroidered all over with flowers, had been on Aunt Polly's bed ever since I could remember. She had made it herself, when she was just a girl, she'd told me, pride bringing a flush to her thin cheeks.

I bent down and kissed her forehead. Her eyes was closed,

and her two plaits of gray hair lay on either side of her face, pale now as the white cap she wore, tied neatly under her chin as always.[66]

"She ain't said more than a few words since we got here," Tom said.

"I'll set with her a while," I said. Tom nodded, pressed my hand briefly, then tiptoed out. I drew up a chair beside the bed and studied the woman who lay there, dying.

Mary Hopewell Penniman. Aunt Polly.

I remembered some of what she'd told me, about her own life. She'd been born in Kentucky, the oldest of three sisters. She had married Mr Penniman when she was twenty-five and come with him to Hannibal. They had one child, Tom's cousin Mary. Tom had come to live with them when his mother died at his birth, his father being unable to care for him. Then the father remarried, and took Tom back; Sid was born, and then both parents got fever and died. Aunt Polly adopted both boys after Mr Penniman died; she sold his lumberyard and some acres of farmland and settled in town for good.

Widowed at thirty-five, she'd raised her daughter and two nephews, Tom and Sid, kept her house and her self-respect, given what she could to charity, gone faithfully to church, cooked and mended and washed, tended her garden and plied her needle, gossiped a little and fretted more than she ought over Tom and Sid and the state of the world. She'd had her few vanities—her spectacles, which she wore for style only, hardly ever using them to look through (as Mr Twain said in his book about Tom[67]), her skills as a housewife, her ability to "handle" a pair of harum-scarum young boys, her devotion to God and His ministers—no traveling preacher ever came to Hannibal but was feted at Aunt Polly's table, and sent on his way with whatever small contribution she could manage, for his "good works."

Now she was dying, this good old woman who'd been as kind

_____

[66] Eds. note: These caps, often frilled or beribboned, were worn indoors by most women well into the late nineteenth century. Outside, a bonnet or hat was worn over the cap. The small netting caps worn today by some Amish and Mennonite women are a reminder of the time when respectable women (and girls once past puberty) did not appear with uncovered heads.

[67] Eds. note: See the first page of the text of *TAOTS*.

to me as to any creature she'd ever had dealings with, man or woman, black or white. I took one of her hands gently in mine and stroked it. "I'm going to miss you, Aunt Polly," I said.

She lay there, breathing softly, her eyes shut.

The door behind me opened, and Aunt Sally peered in. "Don't get up, child," she said, and came into the room. I got up anyway and give her my chair. She sat down with a sigh that seemed to come all the way up from deep inside herself.

"Oh, she does look bad," Aunt Sally said, low-voiced.

There was the sound of feet on the porch, and a rumble of voices. I went to the window and moved the shade a little so I could look out.

"Judge Thatcher and his wife," I said.

"You go on out and tell them to wait," she said. "Let me have a few minutes with her."

"All right," I said, and left her sitting by her sister's deathbed, gazing down at that still face on the pillow.

***

The rest of the day is a blur in my mind of people and faces and voices, coming and going, and the regular opening and shutting of the parlor door as Aunt Polly's neighbors came to pay a final visit. The minister was one of the last to arrive, and he gathered us all together around the bed and led us in a prayer that lasted near as long as the train ride from St Joe to Hannibal, so that I a'most fell asleep on my two feet and only came to myself with a start when everyone else broke out with "Amen!" at the end of it.

Finally it was evening, and the visitors had melted all away. It was just Aunt Sally and Tom and Becky and me around the table. Sally-John was outside in the garden, sitting on a bench by the sundial. Nobody needed to fix supper, for there was bread and cakes and pies a-plenty, and a ham, and fried chicken and other edibles, but nobody was hungry.

"We had ought to take turns setting up with her tonight," Tom said.

"I don't believe I could sleep, even though I'm tired as can be," Aunt Sally said. "I'll set with her. You go on to bed, Tom."

"I ain't tired either."

"Well, go on and lay down, anyway, and take Becky up too. Make her get some rest. She looks peaked."

"So she does," I said. "Go on. Aunt Sally and I will take

turns. We'll call you, if—"

"All right," said Tom. "Good night, then. Come along, darlin'—" and he reached down and helped Becky to her feet.

They went upstairs, arms around each other. Aunt Sally went back into the parlor, and I walked out on the porch and called softly to my daughter, "Sally-John! I'm going to set up with Aunt Polly tonight. You go on and get some rest, now."

"Don't you want me to stay with you, Mama?" she asked, getting up from her bench and coming closer. She looked a little lost, so I said, "No, indeed; I need you to go and sleep, because I am going to need your help tomorrow, whether Aunt Polly passes tonight or not."

She knew what I meant. There are nursing tasks to do, even for someone on her deathbed, and they take a lot out of you, especially if you ain't used to such.

"Good night, then, Mama," she said, and turned to go.

"Sally-John, wait," I said, and put out my hand. She stopped. "I wish we didn't have this sorrow right now. You ought to be having a fine time, getting ready for college, and instead you're stuck here. I am sorry."

"Don't be, Mama," she said, and smiled at me. When Sally-John smiled it was like the sun coming out on a dreary day. "It's no more than right you should be here, and I want to be where you are as long as I can."

She raised up her face toward me, and I bent down for her kiss.

"Good night," I said. "Sleep tight." It was what I'd always said to her, from the time she was a tiny baby. "Sleep tight," her voice floated back to me, as she passed down the hall and started up the stairs.

And so Aunt Sally and I settled down to our watch.

We had the one lamp, turned down as low as it could go, and in the dim reddish glow Aunt Sally's face was barely visible to me on the other side of the bed. Aunt Polly lay still. We'd washed her and put a clean nightgown and cap on her, after Aunt Sally took out her plaits and brushed out her hair and re-braided it, tying the ends with blue ribbons like a girl's. Through it all Aunt Polly lay limp and still, giving out a little moan from time to time, but when we laid her down again on her pillows she resumed that labored, raspy breathing.

I sat and watched and waited. There was no telling, I knew, how long a person might go on in this state. And no knowing, either, if she would wake and know us, or gasp and struggle, as some did when death came nearer.

But she went almost before we could know it, from one breath to the next fading out of life forever . . . so that Aunt Sally was the first to say, "Hist!" and turn up the lamp, and hold it up over the bed, and then to say, "Lord ha' mercy, she's gone." And set the lamp down, gentle, take up Aunt Polly's two white hands and cross them over the dead woman's breast, and then sink down and put her face in her hands and begin, quietly, to weep.

And I wept too, remembering.

And then it was time to call Mary and Sid and Tom, and to stand back while they sank to their knees by the bed and fell to sobbing. Tom cried so hard that Becky reached out and held on to his shoulders and put her head down and wept alongside of him, until at last he raised his head and said, "She was as good to me as any mother could be."

"I never wished for any other," Sid said.

Mary said nothing, but bent her head, and took my hand in hers, and squeezed it.

And so Aunt Polly passed from us.

I have thought many times that her manner of going was a gift to those she left behind. She simply slipped away between one breath and another. I hope it will be given to me to do the same, when my time comes.

***

The funeral was a fine one, as such things go, with wreaths and pots and ribbons of flowers of all sorts, and the church full to the rafters. How the people did sing, when at last the minister had finished his sermon (his text was Proverbs 13, "the value of a worthy woman is far above rubies") and we all stood up as the casket was carried out.

The hearse belonged to the best undertaking concern in town, and the four black horses with their black plumes looked most imposing. Tom and Becky and Sid and Mary and Aunt Sally followed in the undertaker's carriage, but Sally-John and I and most of the others chose to walk to the little graveyard—it warn't far, and the day was fine.

We saw Aunt Polly laid beside Mr Penniman, waited for the

minister to say one final prayer, and wended our way back to Aunt Polly's house. There we discovered that some of the church ladies had been in, cleaned the place spick-and-span, and set up a luncheon. Already folks was walking to and fro with loaded plates. I have seen it before, that a funeral does make people hungry.

Sally-John went out in the garden with Becky and a few of the younger women. I drifted along the hallway until I came to the parlor door. It was shut.

I reached out and turned the knob and went in.

The bed was made up with fresh linens. Aunt Polly's coverlid was gone; probably someone had given it to the washer-woman, along with the other bedclothes. Instead, the bed was spread with a pieced quilt. All of the other furniture was polished and bare. A body would never have been able to tell that a woman had slept here, prayed here, gossiped and laughed here, wept here—as I knew Aunt Polly had done. And some of those tears had been for me.

She warn't any relation of mine by blood, but she'd cared for me. I was glad she'd lived long enough to see Tom wed and know his child would at last be born. For so Becky had informed me, on the day I had arrived in Hannibal.

"It's a miracle," she said.

I thought, watching Tom when she said it, that he didn't look as pleased as she did, and I found later on, when we h ad a private talk, that I was right.

"Becky's old for a first child," he said. "Forty-nine. I'm afraid for her. I could almost wish for her to lose it, like she lost the others. Might be that she ain't meant to have a child."

"It ain't for us to say, is it?" I pressed his hand. "She'll do fine."

I hoped I was right.

Becky had spoke of "expectations" to me when I'd come East all those years before, but that turned out to be a false alarm, and since then only "dashed hopes," Becky had written. Apparently that meant miscarriages, which was a word I doubted Becky knew how to spell, not that she'd use it, of course, even if she could. She was much too proper even to say the word "pregnant," and so at first I did not understand what she was hinting at.

Finally, she come right out and told me, next morning after breakfast. She was expecting—in November, she said.

I counted on my fingers. This was the end of August. "So

you're, what, five months along?" I said.

"Six," she said.

"You don't look it," I said, surveying her. "Just a little plumper than before, that's all."

"I don't lace much," she said. "Just a little, and I wear a fichu or a shawl all the time; that hides a good deal."

"Well, that's good, ain't it?" I said. "You've always wanted a family."

"Yes," she said, "Specially since Mary hasn't any children, and Sid ain't married and don't look to be—"

(I privately thought that anyone who married Sid would be worse than desperate for a husband, but miracles have been known to happen.)

"I just wish Aunt Polly could see the baby," she'd said, and begun to sniffle a little.

"Don't cry, Becky," I said.

"I suppose I ought not to," she said.

"That's right, you oughtn't," said Tom, who'd been leaning against the door frame, listening to us. "It ain't good for you nor for the baby, to get yourself in a state." He put his arm around his wife and give her a quick squeeze. "Ain't she just blooming like— like one of Aunt Polly's roses?"

I allowed as how she was, and the conversation ended there.

Now, as I stood looking down at Aunt Polly's empty bed, I hoped that all would be well with Becky and Tom and the baby that was coming. And I hoped, for everyone's sake, that there was in fact a heaven and that Aunt Polly was there, watching over Tom and his family.

"She ought to be able to put a word in the Almighty's ear," I said aloud.

"Mama, you have to quit talking to yourself that way," my daughter said, popping her head in at the window and giving me a turn.

"Sally-John, don't do that," I said. "You give me such a start!"

"If you hadn't been standing there daydreaming, you'd have noticed me watching you."

"Watching me? Why?"

She came into the room through the window, bundling her skirts around her and stepping through over the sill with ease.

"I like to watch your face when there's nobody else around," she said. "It tells me things I wouldn't otherwise know, for you don't talk of them."

"Such as?" I asked, feeling that maybe I didn't want to know, but unable to help asking.

"I know that you wish Aunt Polly had been your mother," she said. "Or Aunt Sally. Or anybody but the mother you did have."

"What do you know about my mother?" I asked. "I never told you anything about her!"

"No," she said. "But Ah Bok did. And Cassius."

I was dumbstruck. "David? And Cassius? When did—what—"

"They didn't tell me everything, not for a long, long time," she said. "But I was curious. Where was my father? I knew he was killed in the war. What about his folks? You took me to see Grandma Julie and all when I was small, and they wrote to me and I wrote back . . . But what about your pa and ma? Where were they? Who were they?"

"So you asked David." I felt queer. "What did he say?"

"At first he didn't say anything. He told me I was too young to ask questions like that."

Against my will, I was tempted to laugh. David ought to've known that wouldn't wash.

"But I kept asking, and one day he told me," she said.

"I ain't going to ask what he said," I said. "This is not the time nor the place."

"Don't be sad, Mama," she said. Putting both of her slim arms around my waist, she laid her head upon my shoulder. She was most as tall as I, now, but slenderer, so that my own arms went clear around her and held her to me, tight.

"I ain't sad any more," I said. "Not since I had you."

"Not even about Ah Bok?" she said.

So, she knew about David, too.

"No," I said. "Not about him nor any other. At least, not sad enough for it to matter."

And we stood together in Aunt Polly's parlor for a long time, until someone called at the door to say that supper was ready.

Chapter Twenty: Farewells

Most of the important folks in Hannibal come to Aunt Polly's funeral, and not a few others arrived from near and far, including Mr Sam Clemens, or Mark Twain as he was known. He was famous by then, of course, having written not only his book about Tom Sawyer but many others, mostly about life on the Mississippi, and about his travels out West and abroad, and plenty more, some of which I even recall reading with some pleasure (though he lied nearly as much as I did, albeit he did it rather better than I ever managed to do).

He called the day after the burial, wearing one of his famous white linen suits, and asked to speak to me in private.

I showed him into Aunt Polly's parlor, took a chair, and invited him to sit. He took off his hat, ran a hand through his thick mop of graying red hair, and spoke.

"I don't know if you remember me, ma'am," he said. "But it occurs to me that a lady of your name and general appearance run a concern selling general merchandise out in Virginia City, Nevada, some fifteen or so years back."

"That was me," I said. "And I recall you as well, Mr Clemens, when you worked for the *Territorial Enterprise*, and when held Literary Talks in various ladies' parlors. I even attended one, myself."

"I thought you was the same Sarah Mary Williams," he said.

"I am," I said. "And knowing that, you will also remember why I left Virginia City."

Now, Mark Twain in his life as a literary hero always tried to represent himself as a roughneck and uncivilized and one not tied to society's ways, but truth is, he hankered after respectability (and fame, and fortune) and tried as well to be a gentleman, at least his conception of one (though his wife despaired of his ever actually succeeding, as he often confessed). He looked this way and that when I said these words, for he knowed very well I had left Virginia City in an advanced state of pregnancy and without a husband to account for my condition.

He no doubt also remembered that he had snubbed me or at least declined to acknowledge my presence—once the ladies who were his patrons had made it clear that I was, in their eyes, no better than a harlot.

"Well, I left the place right after you did," he said. "You was still running your Emporium at the time—you and that Chinaman."

I recognized this as an attempt to avoid apologizing, and didn't say anything, just waited to see how he'd manage to winkle himself out of the spot I'd landed him in.

He raised his shoulders in a shrug and looked down at the hat in his lap.

"I can see how you might not want to have anything to do with me," he said. "I cannot excuse my conduct of the past. But the past is behind us. The future beckons us both onward, don't it? It might be that I can make up in future for some of my past deficiencies."

"How so?"

"I have something to propose to you," he said, "that might make you look on me more kindly. More to the point, it might serve to improve both of our financial circumstances."

"Go ahead," I said. "Let's hear it."

"Well," he said, "Seeing you at the funeral yesterday, I thought you looked familiar, but I didn't register who you was at first. Finally I asked Mr Sawyer who the tall woman was, with the dark hair and the pretty dark-haired daughter, and he said you used to be Huckleberry Finn."

"He didn't have no call to tell you that," I said. "Those days are gone."

"I am sorry if my conduct has offended you, ma'am," he said. "I'm afraid I presumed too much on my previous connection to Mr Sawyer. He did not want to tell me—it just slipped out."

"I'll bet it did," I said. "Tom Sawyer never could resist making a sensation."

"Well, he did so, in your case," Mr Twain said. "Miss Sarah, I understand that you are a businesswoman."

I acknowledged that that was so.

"And you have a daughter to educate and equip for her place in the modern world," he went on. "And you have only yourself to look to for the wherewithal involved in providing that education and equipment?"

I nodded.

"That being the case," Mr Twain pursued, "You would not be averse to earning a substantial sum of money?"

"That depends on how I would be earning it," I said.

And that was the point when Mr Twain laid his cards on the table, so to speak.

"I have had it in mind for some years now," he said, "To write a story—kind of a companion volume—to the book I wrote about being a boy here in this blessed old town, in a time long past—you recall the work I am mentioning?"

"I am not illiterate," I said. "I have read *The Adventures of Tom Sawyer*, along with most folks in this nation who can read and have the leisure to do so."

"Then," he said, "You recall that I used you—or rather your former self—as a character in that book?"

"Of course," I said. (I didn't mention then that I found his description of Huckleberry Finn something lacking in several areas, as I have noted earlier.)

"And so," he went on, "I have had it in mind, as I said, to write another book, but this time I want to use your story, ma'am, as the basis for the work I have in mind."

"Which story?" I asked. "The village pariah who run off with a runaway slave down the river—that story?"

"That is the one I had in mind," he said.

"The whole story?" I said.

"I don't know the whole story," he said. "You will have to tell me what happened. I will decide what to tell and how to tell it. That is what writing fiction is all about."

I had to hand it to him, he come right to the point. So I did, too.

"How much?" I said.

"Pardon?"

"How much do you intend paying me for the right to tell my story?"

He didn't hesitate. "Five thousand dollars."

"That is a lot of money," I said.

"Will you do it?" he said.

"I will," I said.

And we shook hands.

"I will come back tomorrow, with your permission, and take some notes," he said.

"That will be agreeable," I said.

"There is one more thing," he said. "The Huckleberry Finn of my book must remain a boy. I couldn't possibly tell the tale I have in mind if the character were female."

"Huck Finn's a boy in the first book," I said, and shrugged. "Might's well stay that way. He ain't me, in any case. Leastways, I ain't him. And never truly was," I added.

Mr Twain smiled. "That's between you and him, ain't it?" he said, and bowed, and left me sitting there.

I sat like that for a long time, remembering, before I got up and rejoined the rest of the household. The remainder of the day passed without my paying much attention to it, but that was all right, because I hadn't much to do beyond helping to receive those mourners who continued to call all through that day and the next. My thoughts was all on what Mr Twain and I would talk about next day—and on that five thousand dollars, for I could foresee many ways in which a sum like that would come in mighty handy.

∗∗∗

Sally-John was taking advantage of these days to walk about the town, mostly in company with Aunt Sally, sometimes with Becky, who couldn't walk very far but enjoyed a brief stroll in the morning or late evening, when there was sometimes a breath of air. It was hot and sticky and muggy as can be, and my clothes stuck to me so that I wished I could rid myself of at least my topmost petticoat, but I didn't dare. I was here to honor the memory of Aunt Polly, who always looked respectable no matter what the weather, and so I supposed it was the least I could do to try to be the same. It made me think, though, of how it had been thirty years back, when Huckleberry Finn wore a suit of rags so well-ventilated that the slightest cooling breeze found its way inside.

I said as much to Mr Twain when he came by next morning. He had brought his notebook with him, and extracted it and a pencil from his coat pocket.

"Tell me exactly what happened, in your own words," he said.

I had forgot that he'd been a reporter, and used to drawing folks out and getting them to tell him what he wanted to know. The words come slow at first, then quicker and quicker, and his pencil flew over the paper.

"Tell me about your pap," he'd say, or "What did the Widow do then?" or "What was Tom Sawyer's Gang like?" He laughed til the tears come when I told him about ambuscading the A-rabs, and he made me tell about Jim and the hairball oracle over and over again til he was satisfied he got it right. And when I got to the part about how I'd faked my own murder, he bent over his notebook and his pencil fairly whizzed along.

Well, I talked and talked til my mouth was parched, and Mr Twain stopped me along about luncheon-time and we halted to eat a bite, and then we went back at it for the rest of the afternoon. I was most tuckered out when he left, and didn't eat no supper, just crawled off to bed.

Sally-John had met Mr Twain by this time and was flattered at the courtly way he behaved to her, but she told me before we went to sleep that she wasn't sure she trusted him completely.

"That just shows that you have good sense," I said, and blew out the candle. "Well, we'll see what happens if he ever does get this book written out complete."

For I had told her what his plan was. It warn't possible to keep such things from her, and I didn't try. She knew the greater part of my childhood history as it was—I'd left out a few things, here and there, but mostly I'd told the truth—and she only said, "Well, Mama, you go on and do what you think is best."

And so I did.

Well, it got to the last week in August. Pretty soon Sally-John and I would have to depart, for her term at Vassar would begin shortly, and I wanted to see her settled before I headed back out West.

The Sawyer family finally said farewell to the last of the mourners, and Aunt Sally went back to the farm in Arkansas, taking with her my love to give to Uncle Silas. Mary had gone back to her heathen Cherokee and the mission where she taught little Indians how to be Christians, and Tom and Becky was making their final arrangements to head home to Washington.

"I have gotten tickets for all of us on the same train East," Tom said. "If you and Sally-John care to stop off in Washington, we'd be pleased to have you for a few days."

I thanked him and said we'd have to push on. "Maybe next year, when I come to fetch her back home in the spring," I suggested, and Becky agreed that that would be better.

"Washington is still bearable then," she said. "But summertime—that's just awful."

"Can't be much hotter than here," I said, fanning myself.

"Oh, but it is," she said. "You have no idea."

"There's plenty trains north from Washington," Tom said.

"You won't have any trouble getting Sally-John up to New York from there."

"Well, I have sent her up to finish packing," I said. "We'll be ready first thing in the morning."

That left the rest of the day for my final sessions with Mr Twain.

By now, the whole household knew that Mark Twain was going to use my story for his next book, and he had some trouble getting everyone to promise not to say a word about anything to do with the name Huckleberry Finn until the book was published.

"For," he said, "if everybody knows the story already, no one will want to buy the book," and so everybody promised, and he signed autographs and scattered them like confetti, and shook hands with anyone who stuck a paw in his direction, and let himself be photographed with Tom, and Becky, and even with Sid, who was trying hard to balance his feelings of pleasure at the honor of entertaining America's greatest living writer under his own humble roof with his feelings of horror at what the Presbyterian authorities of his seminary might have to say about the matter, Mr Twain's works not being found sufficiently Christian and reverent by many of the churchly profession.

(Mary, for example, had asked Mr Twain to sign three new copies of *Tom Sawyer* to take back to the mission school, but she also pressed a parcel of tracts on him and implored him to take time to think on his latter end, which both he and she told me about later. *She* said he was mighty humbled by her concern for his soul, and thanked her with tears in his eyes; *he* said he had some trouble to keep from telling her that he found such things as tracts useful only for lighting his cigars.)

So we come to the end of our interviews, him and me, and when I had reached the last of the story—the part where Jim told me that Pap warn't going to bother me no more, for he was dead, Mr Twain said, "I guess you're mighty glad that pretty daughter of yours won't have old Finn to make her life a hell, like he done yours," and I said that was truer than he could know.

"Well," Mr Twain said, as he rose to take his leave, "I thank you, Miss Sarah Mary, for all of the help you've given me, and when the book is finished, I'll be honored if you will allow me to dedicate it to you."

"No, thanks," I said. "That's closer than I care to having

anybody remember who I used to be, outside of those within these here four walls, that is."

So he laughed, and promised he wouldn't do it[68], and left me to gather up what was left of my composure. It does take it out of a body, to do that much remembering at one clip.

I warn't much good at the conversation at supper that last night, for I kept on seeing shadows in the corners of the room, and my mind kept on a-wandering back to a time when a room like this looked like a palace, and the empty hogshead that I slept in was the only shelter I had from any storm sent by God or humankind.

***

Next morning the station dray rolled up just as we was sitting down to breakfast—Sid had hired it to carry our luggage to the train. We finished eating and Becky and I washed up, whilst Tom and Sid and the drayman took care of the various bags and trunks.

Then it was time to go. There was quite a flurry of farewells there on the porch; I even hugged Sid and told him to come out West for a visit sometime—"Tahoe City could use some preaching," I said—and then Becky hugged Sid, and Tom shook his hand and clapped him across the shoulders, and Sally-John took Sid's hand in hers, and he told her to study hard in college, and she said she would, and everyone came out again with words to the effect of how sad times like these are full of sorrow on account of the one that's gone and departed, but how good it had been to see each other nonetheless and to enjoy the company of them that's left to carry on, and all that sort of blether that people do say on such occasions, and we were ready.

The dray's driver looked familiar. As he swung himself up onto the wagon-seat I realized who he was.

"Why, it's little Tommy Barnes, ain't it?" I said, and shook his hand. Tommy had been the youngest member of Tom Sawyer's Gang. [69] Tom Sawyer leaned over and pumped Tommy's hand, too.

---

[68] Mark Twain did not, as it turned out, dedicate Adventures of Huckleberry Finn to anyone, though the famous "NOTICE" regarding motive is given as "Per G. G., Chief of Ordnance," generally interpreted as a reference to General Grant, but which subsequent research suggests was intended to refer to the Clemens' butler, a freed slave named George Griffin (see Robert Hirsch, editor, *The Mark Twain Project; Bancroftiana*, Vol. 117, 2000).

[69] Eds. note: See Ch. 2 of *AOHF*, "Our Gang's Dark Oath."

"So you work for the railroad, do you?"

"I own a delivery service that contracts with the railroad," Tommy said. "I run this-here dray and I deliver the mail to the post-office, too, and handle cargo, and I also hire out carriages for passengers, and drivers too. I offered to have a nice surrey drove over for you-all, but Sid here said you was a-going to walk."

(As the station was less than a quarter-mile from the Sawyer house, a carriage ride had seemed less of a necessity than a last chance for some days of getting a little exercise, and, as the day was fine, Sid had let himself be persuaded.)

Tommy drove off, and we followed. When we reached the station, Tommy had already piled the luggage on the platform. He touched his cap to us and turned his team, then headed off towards his next errand.

Sally-John and Becky stood a few feet away, chatting about something or other. I watched Tom Sawyer's face as he stood looking down the street.

"It's more than just Aunt Polly passing," he said, without turning his head toward me. "Do you feel it too, Huck?"

I slipped a hand into his. There was no need to say anything. We both knew what he meant.

A train whistle sounded—not too far off. Tom squeezed my hand, then let it go. "Best get ready to board," he said. He moved toward Becky, who took his arm; Sally-John picked up her holdall and came and stood next to me.

"Are you all right, Mama?"

"I'm all right."

"Do you think you'll ever come back here, Mama?"

I took a last look around, and let out my breath in a long sigh. "No," I said, finally. "I don't believe I ever will. There's nothing I need to come back here to find."

We stood there watching as the train came in. Sally-John put her arm around my waist and leaned her head against my shoulder.

"Uncle Tom called you 'Huck' just then," she said.

"So he did," I said.

"Mr Twain's book—he's going to write about Huckleberry Finn, but not about you," she said. "His book will be about someone else entirely—someone he can only imagine."

"He's got imagination enough to do it, I reckon," I said.

"Why did you change your name, Mama?"

"Well," I said, slowly, "I guess it didn't fit who-all I thought I was supposed to be."

She was silent for a moment. Then, "You told me once it was your mother who named you," she said.

"She did," I said.

"But you never talk about her," Sally-John said.

"No."

"Why not?"

"There's some things I'd rather not remember," I said.

"Oh." She didn't say anything more after that, but waited by my side until the train came roaring in, with great whooshes of steam and a screeching of metal on metal. Our bags went on, and then we boarded, and the conductor showed us to our seats.

I had the seat nearest the window, and I turned and watched as we pulled out of the station. Sally-John's question echoed in my ears—and my answer.

I was looking on Hannibal, Missouri for the last time.

***

The rest of our journey passed without incident. Tom had engaged sleeping-berths for all of us, so the usual discomfort of train travel was somewhat lessened. I was glad to find that I fell asleep easily—the rocking motion of the car seemed to help. The miles flew by under us whilst we slumbered, and soon we pulled into Washington, where Tom and Becky left us and we changed to another train for the trip North.

Our leave-taking of the Sawyers was brief. Becky was tired and pale from traveling, and Tom said he would write as soon as he could.

When Tom and Becky had gone off, followed by a porter trundling their baggage along on a hand-cart, I arranged for our trunks to be transferred. The porter who took charge of them was a tall, dark-brown man with a wide smile. He took the two bits I offered him and thanked me. He reminded me of someone, but I couldn't think who. Finally it come to me: he was the dead spit of Uncle Silas's hand, Cuffy, who had drove us to the steamboat landing after Jim was finally free. This man, though, was twenty years and more younger than Cuffy would be, were he still living.

It warn't often that I felt old, but I did now, and didn't much like the feeling. Part of it was, of course, due to the past few weeks' events, including the time spent with Mr Twain, remembering a past that seemed more and more like it had happened to somebody else. And part of it, I guessed, was that Sally-John was so much younger than I had been at her age.

And part of it was that she was about to leave me.

I shook off these thoughts as best I could. There warn't nothing I could do to change the way things had been or the way they was going to be.

"Let's have some pie and coffee," I said to Sally-John.

The coffee at the station café was hot and strong, and there was cherry pie—Sally-John's favorite. I stirred sugar and cream into my coffee and watched her as she took in the sights all around her.

She had thrown off her solemn mood and looked about her now with pleasure, calling my attention to this or that, or exclaiming when she caught sight of a woman in fashionable dress.

"Look at those feathers, Mama," she said, as a hat laden with billowing white plumes sailed by atop a plump woman in a maroon and white striped jacket with pagoda sleeves worn over a maroon skirt.

"Egret," I said.

"She oughtn't to wear that color," my daughter said, craning her neck to watch the woman's passage.

"You're right; it don't suit her at all," I said.

"*You* always look nice, Mama," she said.

I brushed at the front of my jacket. It was a gray checked worsted with braid-trimmed lapels, worn over a black silk shirtwaist (most practical for rail travel), and my gray skirt was fashionably puffed in back. "I don't want the folks at Vassar College to form a poor opinion," I said. "It matters how people dress, here in the East."

"I'd forgot, you went to school here, too," she said.

"Connecticut," I said.

"Did you like your school? You never talk about it," she said.

"It was good enough," I said. "I learned what I came there for."

Toinette, her dark hair falling about her face, her lips full and rosy in the candlelight . . . I shook myself free of the unwanted memory, with a jerk. "Let's go and see if we can get aboard now. I'd like to make sure of our seats," I said.

"All right, Mama."

As we left the café, I noticed the woman in maroon again.

She was seated across from a girl about Sally-John's age. The two of them was talking with great animation. The girl was a small, slender little thing in violet, with yellow hair caught up in a matching velvet snood. She looked up as Sally-John passed, and smiled.

"Sally-John," I said, as we came up to our train, and I saw the conductor coming up, ready to help us board.

"What is it, Mama?"

"I hope you make some good friends at Vassar College," I said.

"I expect to," she said.

"But don't forget your old friends, when you do," I said.

"Why, of course I won't," she said.

We took our seats and made ourselves comfortable, putting our holdalls at our feet and taking off our hats and jackets. The car was hot.

"It'll cool off once we start moving," the conductor said, taking our tickets.

I leaned my head back against the scratchy blue plush seat. "I think I'll close my eyes for a while," I said.

"I'll read my book," Sally-John said, reaching into her reticule. She was reading a book by Jules Verne, the Frenchman, called *Around the World in Eighty Days*. She had read some parts of it to me during our travels, translating from the French (which she'd learned from Miss Levy, who said every educated person ought to know it), and soon she was deeply absorbed, so that I relaxed and let myself drift.

Eighty days to go around the world…it had taken upwards of fourteen days for us to get from Nevada to Washington, D. C…. but close on a week of that was taken up with Aunt Polly's passing, and her funeral…

I must have dozed off, because some time later I opened my eyes to see that Sally-John had fallen asleep over her book. It lay on the floor, open, so I bent to retrieve it.

I picked it up and turned it over. It was not the Verne book after all.

My daughter was reading words I knew almost as well as if I myself had written them. Hadn't I read this same book, over and over? The page before me was as familiar as my own face in the mirror—and as alien:

Huckleberry came and went, at his own free will. He slept on doorsteps in fine weather and in empty hogsheads in wet; he did not have to go to school or to church, or call any being master or obey anybody; he could go fishing or swimming when and where he chose, and stay as long as it suited him; nobody forbade him to fight; he could sit up as late as he pleased; he was always the first boy that went barefoot in the spring and the last to resume leather in the fall; he never had to wash, nor put on clean clothes; he could swear wonderfully. In a word, everything that goes to make life precious, that boy had. So thought every harassed, hampered, respectable boy in St Petersburg.[70]

I closed the book and put it down, gently.

Huckleberry Finn was dead—dead and buried as Aunt Polly, as Jim, as everything from those long-ago days. But I knew with a sinking heart that he wouldn't stay dead. I myself had unlocked the tomb and put the key into Mr Mark Twain's hand. And I had a suspicion that the resurrection would prove as much a trouble to me as Lazarus's had been to him.

When the Widow Douglas first read the story of Lazarus to me, I'd been troubled. I tried to talk to her about it, but either I didn't know how to ask the questions so's she could hear them properly, or else the bare fact of questioning Holy Writ put her in to a tizzy.

"Land sakes, Huckleberry," she'd said. "Jesus raised him from the dead. It was a miracle, child; you don't question miracles."

"I ain't questioning that he done it," I had said, "Just—I was wondering how Lazarus felt about it, that's all."

"What on earth do you mean?" She'd been awful put out with me, so I left off asking what I wanted to know, and to this day I hadn't found anyone else to ask.

But I still wondered.

If there was a Heaven—as everyone seemed to think, even David, who warn't even a Christian—then Lazarus must have been in it, being dead, for, having been a friend to Jesus—his best friend, the Widow had said—he must have been a good man.

So, Jesus calling him back from the dead meant He was calling him back from Heaven.

That was what I wondered: did being called back from Heaven—even when Jesus was the one who did the calling—did it feel like going home again, or was it more like Hell?

And how could Jesus do such a thing, to a man who was

---

[70] Eds. note: *TAOTS*, p. 71.

supposed to be his friend?

And then, once Lazarus had come back, what about everyone else who knew him?

What do you say to someone who's been dead and buried and come back from the grave?

And what will the dead person tell you, that you can bear to hear?

If, that is, you choose to believe that he or she is telling the truth, and not a collection of wishes and hopes and other lies.

I picked up the book again and opened it to the Preface:

Most of the adventures recorded in this book really occurred; one or two were experiences of my own, the rest those of boys who were schoolmates of mine. Huck Finn is drawn from life . . .

I closed the book. Something that is drawn from life is not the living thing itself; it is created by the one who does the drawing, who sees only what he or she wishes to see.

Mark Twain had taken my story down with his nimble, flashing pen, but what would emerge would not be me, but someone else, and I wondered if anywhere in the portrait I would recognize the image I held in my own mind of the boy I had once appeared to be.

***

We got into New York late on a Sunday afternoon. There was a delay whilst I arranged for Sally-John's trunks to go on by rail up to Poughkeepsie. The porter got us a cab and loaded our hand-luggage whilst I conferred with the driver. Then off we went, moving smartly through the still-crowded streets, and I settled back next to Sally-John, who was staring out at the passing scene, her eyes shining. My own eyes kept on darting left and right as well. After all, I hadn't seen New York in nearly thirty years, myself, and there was a lot to look at, including several buildings taller than I could have imagined a building could be.

I had forgot how fast everyone and everything moves in the Eastern part of the nation, as if time itself was in short supply. In what seemed a very few moments, we drew up outside the Grand Central Hotel on Broadway. As we both was tired, we ate a light supper in our room and turned in early.

Next morning, we set off on the last stage of our journey.

***

Getting Sally-John settled into her room at the college and

paying her first year's fees took up most of the day. We had a tour of the campus given us by a member of the Dean's staff, a bony woman of indeterminate years, dressed severely in black serge and wearing pince-nez, who introduced us to several girls—my daughter's classmates-to-be. All too soon, Sally-John was deep in conversation with them, and I turned to my guide, a Miss Brawley.

"Could someone call a carriage for me? I'd like to catch the evening train back to the city," I said.

"Certainly," and she rang for a porter, who touched his cap and went out.

"I take it you've been with the college for some time?" I asked.

"I came here in 1870," she said.

With very little prompting from me, she spent the next half-hour expounding on the many virtues of the College, and was in the middle of a recitation of the various honors that had been awarded to the valedictorians of the last eight or ten graduating classes, when the porter returned and announced that my carriage was waiting.

I took my leave of Miss Brawley, and, asking the porter to tell the carriage I would be along directly, went in search of Sally-John.

I found her in a common room, in the midst of a lively discussion of President Hayes's foreign policy—I caught the words "Argentina" and "Triple Alliance"—and I waited in the doorway, not wanting to interrupt.

"I believe you are wanted, Sally," the blonde girl sitting next to her said, and Sally-John turned and saw me.

"Oh, Mama, are you going already?" She jumped up. "This is Miss Hapwood, and Miss Lorimer, and Miss Sutematsu," the last being a young lady of Oriental features (I later learned that she was Japanese).

"I'm pleased to meet you all," I said. "Sally-John, you stay and finish your conversation, honey. I'll write you as soon as I get home."

And I give her a little push back towards her new comrades. "Go on," I said. "I'll be just fine."

She hugged me, then, quick and fierce, and I hugged her back, then turned and walked as steady as I could away from her. In just a moment I had passed into the corridor and turned to make my way to the big front door, where the porter stood, waiting to see me out.

"Good day, ma'am," he said, holding the door for me.

"Good day to you," I said, and in another moment I was in the carriage.

The day had turned to rain, and through the slanting grey lines I watched until the buildings of Vassar College disappeared.

Chapter Twenty-One: A New Acquaintance

I returned to the hotel in New York and spent the night more or less sleepless, and so the next morning I was somewhat the worse for wear as I boarded the train for Chicago. [71]

It too some time, therefore, for me to become aware of the man sitting across from me.

"My name is Theophilus VanDerWalk Osterhouse," this personage said, raising his hat the prescribed inch and leaning forward with a smile. "Whom do I have the honor of addressing?"

"My name is Sarah Mary Williams," I said, and shook the hand that he held towards me.

"Are you traveling alone, Madam?"

"I am."

"Please call on me for any assistance that you might require," Mr Osterhouse said, and he set his hat carefully down next to him. Then, leaning back in his seat, and crossing his arms over an expanse of embroidered waistcoat, he fell asleep.

I shrugged, wrapped my shawl tightly around my shoulders, and, relieved of the need to make conversation, examined my seatmate attentively.

He was around my age, fifty or thereabouts, as far as I could judge; his hair (what I could see of it under his high silk hat) was black, streaked only a little with gray, like his profusion of side-whiskers. He was a tall, somewhat bulky man, broad in the shoulders, and his clothing was well-tailored and of good quality though clearly not new. His hands was clean and the nails cut short, and he wore a gold ring on his left hand, with a red stone in it. As he breathed in and out regularly, I discerned a slight scent of wintergreen.

All in all, I reflected, I could have been landed with much worse; railroads being a highly democratic form of travel, my seatmate could have been anyone from a fat Bohemian farmer

---

[71] Author's Note: with trains running clear across the nation by 1880, the year in which these events transpired, travel to the West could take only seven days from New York to California, given good connections and a sturdy constitution. When I think of the months it took to go overland in the 1850s, I was able to undertake the discomfort associated with trains in a much better spirit—though I still disliked railways and always would.

smelling of beer and pipe tobacco to a deaconess with a basket of tracts and a proselytizing disposition. Or, what was far worse, to my mind, a harried mother with a brood of quarrelsome, noisy children and at least one infant at the breast whose mission was to wail unceasingly when not at suck. I'd shared many a train compartment with such examples of familial devotion, and blessed Providence for sparing me the same on this particular journey.

I must have drowsed off, for I found myself being shaken by the shoulder, and opened my eyes to find myself staring directly into those of my companion.

"I am heartily sorry to wake you, madam, but the conductor says that dinner is being served, and I thought perhaps you might care to take a little nourishment. May I escort you to the dining car?"

I sat up straight, smoothed my hair, and managed to thank him.

"Shall we go?" he motioned to me to precede him down the corridor, and I did so, both of us managing the car's sway by holding on to various seat-backs as we went. The dining-car was only two cars behind, so in a very short while we was seated across from one another again, this time at a table covered with a linen cloth and set with china and silver as fine as any hotel's.

The waiter was a small, lean, saddle-colored man with gray hair combed back; he reminded me a little of Ned, Captain Sellers's servant, and the memory brought a lump to my throat. Mr Osterhouse leaned toward me.

"Why, what's the matter?" he asked.

"I just—remembered someone," I said.

"A sad memory," Mr Osterhouse said.

"Yes, it is."

"All memories should be cherished, even the sad ones," he said. "Perhaps especially the sad ones."

"Why is that?" I asked. "Don't most folks try to forget the sadness that they've left behind them?"

"They do," he said. "And that, I believe, is a mistake. For what you try to leave behind will surely follow after you . . . to embrace that which makes us sad is, therefore, the better course." He cleared his throat. "Let me explain."

And explain he did, through three courses and two cups of coffee.

Mr Osterhouse was convincing. He pointed out that everyone has memories that make them sad or angry, but that we can't go back and change the events that give rise to those memories. "Therefore," he said, "It is our responsibility as intelligent creatures to say to those memories that cause us grief or ire: it is the past that has led to the present, and the present is what it is precisely because of the past; therefore, since nothing can be altered of what *is*, let us accept what *was* and go on with our lives. We are as we have been, and we will be as we are; that is fact. Fact cannot be argued; it can only be accepted. Q.E.D."

"Q.E.D.?" I asked.

"Quod erat demonstrandum," he said. "Thus it has been demonstrated."

"Oh," I said. "Are you some kind of a preacher, Mr Osterhouse?"

"My dear lady," he said. "Nothing could be farther from my choice of career. I deal not with metaphysics—except as an avocation, you understand—but with the physical, to wit: the human body."

"You're a physician."

"Ah. Of a sort."

"What sort?"

He went on to explain that, while he had studied anatomy and physiology "since my early youth," he had not chosen to pursue formal studies in medicine due to circumstances—here he hesitated for a long moment before confessing what those circumstances had been.

"I grew up," he said, "On a farm, dear lady, but for my part was never drawn to the practice of agriculture, despite the efforts by my noble father, a man of some education, to inculcate in me a love of the soil by reading to me from that splendid work by Cato the Elder, *De Agri Cultura*; and certain of the odes of Horace, in which the poet celebrates his beloved Sabine farm. Indeed, I say, despite the weighty evidence provided by such approved and approving authors, before I had well commenced my second decade of life, I was persuaded that a life tied to the soil was not for me."

"I take it your folks was farmers," I said. "How did they respond to the news of your, ah, persuasion?"

"I was never in a position to communicate my feelings to them. My father had by that time departed this life," he said, "My

311

mother had passed away some years before. I had only a stepmother, who cared little for me. Therefore, I elected to seek my fortune in a different sphere entirely."

"In other words, you run off."

"I did."

"Where'd you run?" I was curious, now—especially as I'd done much the same thing.

"By a happy chance," he said, "I found congenial employment, and did so speedily. My new profession required me to travel extensively, and in the next few years I had occasion to visit over thirty of these great United States, several provinces of Canada, and not a few of the districts of Old Mexico adjacent to our own fair nation."

"And what was this new profession?"

"It was, madam, a traveling circus."

I found myself recalling the many circuses I'd enjoyed in my own youth, and laughed for sheer pleasure at the memory.

"That news pleases you," he said.

"It does," I said. "Tell me more."

He went on to relate that, for over twenty years, he'd sojourned with this particular traveling show. He'd begun, like most youngsters in the same situation—for, he said, the circus was a time-honored refuge for such boys as he had been, in a hurry to get away from home and to leave few traces behind them—he'd begun by doing menial chores: feeding the animals and cleaning up after them; carrying wood and water; making fires and helping with the cooking; assisting the performers in their various needs.

"It was all very splendid at first," he said. "And then of course, when the new wore off, it became sheer drudgery—but I persevered, dear lady; I persevered, and in the end I too became one of those happy few whose calling it is to entertain as well as to edify."

And he proceeded to tell how he'd spent several years as the general factotum to the circus's medicine man, a snake oil salesman[72]

---

[72] Eds. note: This was not originally a pejorative phrase. Chinese immigrants brought many ancient remedies with them to Gold Mountain, including snake oil (the rendered fat of various water snakes), which was rubbed on the skin to relieve joint pain. Modern science confirms that such oils do contain useful compounds, notably EFAs. The term "snake

of the first rank, he said, and one whose name deserved to be written in letters of fire—to match the tonic that he sold, at one dollar per quart, to sufferers from Atlanta to Albuquerque.

"Was it—the tonic—like Dr Rush's Thunderbolts?" I asked.

"Worse," he said. "Oh, far worse. It was a point of pride with Professor Marvel—that was his *nom de guerre*— that his 'prescription,' as he termed it, stripped the lining of the esophagus on the way down and burned its way through the stomach and the intestines as well, on the way out, if you will excuse the indelicacy of my saying so. But folks seemed to relish it, all the same."

I thought of Aunt Polly and her devotion to Painkiller, and nodded. Mr Osterhouse went on, "My employer and mentor—for so he became, and I learned much from him over the next few years—eventually unloaded enough of the stuff to retire to a little village in Mexico where he'd stashed a pretty senorita, and he sold the concern and all his supplies and equipment to yours truly."

"And so you've taken on the burden of relieving suffering humanity, yourself."

He bowed. "Indeed. And thus began a series of happy and productive years. I traveled, and I prospered, and along the way I studied what I could of the art of medicinal preparations. I learned from old black herb-women who'd doctored entire plantations over the better part of a century; I learned from Indian shamans and witch-doctors, whose knowledge dates to a time before the Great Pyramid was raised; I even consulted a *brujo* or two—"

"What's that?"

"A Mexican conjuror. They know a great deal, madam, about various species of beneficent plant life, including a particular cactus they call *peyotl*—it produces visions, they say, like to those related by the Apostle in the Book of Revelation, though I myself cannot attest to the truth of this, having declined to indulge, though I was, to be truthful, mightily tempted . . . Oh, I spent a long time, and filled many notebooks with my findings, and eventually, I concocted a new tonic, one far more pleasing to the taste as well as being supremely efficacious in the treatment of a host of the ills to which the flesh is heir."

---

oil" as used to refer to patent medicines without any real value came about partly due to the peddling of fake "snake oil" and other "cure-alls" by unscrupulous salesmen.

"Sounds as though you was headed for that Easy Street they tell of," I said. "What happened?"

"War." He was silent. "I was thirty years of age when the South seceded, and though you may find it difficult to believe, I felt the call to take up arms on behalf of the Union."

"So, you're a Northerner by birth," I said.

"Ah, yes. Ohio is my home state," he said. "And a notable free state . . . and, although my parents and I had not seen eye to eye about my life's intended purpose, they had in fact imbued me from earliest childhood with a love of freedom and a hatred of slavery."

"So you enlisted."

"I did. I found myself," he said, "Serving in the Union Army, and although I longed to acquit myself with honor on the field of battle, before I ever fired a single shot in an engagement, I had the misfortune to fall into the hands of a Rebel scouting party, and was carried off a prisoner."

"When was that?" I asked.

"The precise date," he said, "I cannot now recall, but it was in the spring of 1863 that I found myself in Andersonville prison, and I was not freed until the War came to its end in 1865."

I said, "And since then?"

"Since then," he said, "I have devoted considerable energy to continuing my studies. And I believe that that effort has borne fruit. The results of my labors will, I believe, benefit mankind to an extent never before seen, at least since the days of Aesclepius, the god of health, and his daughters Hygieia, Panacea, and Aglaea—to be brief: I have found the secret of eternal youth and health, madam, and it has become my mission to carry this secret to the farthest reaches of this, our great Nation."

"Tell me more about this secret," I said, and after we finished our meal, he escorted me back to our coach. When we were seated comfortably, and I had declined his offer of a wintergreen lozenge (from a packet he produced from a pocket of his waistcoat), he continued his exposition:

"My dear lady, the man you see before you is the product of an amazing set of circumstances, which I will relate in the hope that you will then better comprehend the gift that I wish to bestow upon our human species. As I mentioned earlier, I was a prisoner for over two years in one of the most horrific settings of degradation, squalor, and brutality the world has ever known: Andersonville Prison."

Like everyone else, I had heard of Andersonville. I nodded.

"When I was liberated from that Confederate circle of hell," he went on, "I weighed less than 120 pounds, on a frame some six feet and two inches tall. I was nearly bald, madam, for my hair had fallen out from a vile skin disease with which many of us were afflicted; my entire body was covered with boils and eruptions; my teeth were so loose in my gums that I could have, if I wished, plucked them out one at a time with my own finger and thumb. I was, in short, in a condition of such physical weakness that I could scarcely hold my own self upright. I was a ruin of what had been, if you will forgive my boast, a fine figure of a man."

"Please go on," I said, fascinated.

"I was thirty-five years old when I was freed," he said, "And I looked, and felt, nearer eighty. Why, when I returned at last to the circus, madam, even those persons with whom I had spent the bulk of my years before the war intervened failed to recognize me, until they heard me speak!"

(At this I had to turn and hide a smile, for Mr Osterhouse's voice was certainly unique: deep and resonant, it throbbed with emotion, and when deeply moved it took on what I can only call a syrupy quality, like honey or molasses. No one who had ever heard that voice could mistake it for anyone else's, I was sure.)

"So, you may ask, madam, how did I recover this physique, that of a well-nourished and well-preserved mature male, and also regenerate these profuse and lively locks which flourish upon the head which you now behold? How did my teeth resume their whiteness and solidity, fixed anew, as before, within this oral cavity? How did my skin resume its previous customary rosy glow of health? How did I regain the strength which allows me, today, even at my age of half a century, to lift and carry fifty pounds with ease, and to walk for miles at a pace that would tire a man half my age?"

"How?" I asked, as he paused and gazed at me.

"Why, with this simple preparation," he said, and dived into the carpetbag that reposed near his feet, producing a tall, cobalt-blue glass bottle with a porcelain cap. I took it from him and read the label:

DOCTOR Th. VanDerW. OSTERHOUSE'S

ELIXIR OF LIFE

}A Proprietary Mixture{
The Secret Formulae of Ancient Egypt, Arabia Felix, Mycenean Greece, and Cathay
Containing Aromatic Oils, Tinctures of Rare Herbs, and Spices of the Orient
Conveyed to the Ancient Aztecs, Incas, and Mayans in Times of Yore
Rediscovered and Prepared In Healthful Modern Form
In a Pleasant-tasting and Efficacious Preparation

Take TWO Tablespoons BY MOUTH
THREE TIMES DAILY

Recommended for Men, Women, and Children
CURES AND PREVENTS:
dysphoria, dyspepsia, neuralgia, nephritis, neurasthenia,
calcification of the joints, bowel and bladder complaints,
female ills, consumption, infant colic, summer complaint, cancer, boils,
sore gums, tooth decay, pimples, brittle nails. STIMULATES: male
potency, luxuriant growth of the hair of the head, pleasant breath, and
suppleness of the skin. *CONTENTS: thirty-two ounces (one quart)*.

PRICE: <u>ONE DOLLAR US</u> $1.00

I handed the bottle back to him and said, "Sounds cheap at twice the price, if it does all that."

"Oh, it is, dear lady, most economical, and I make no claims that cannot be substantiated by testimonial," he said, tenderly receiving the bottle and putting it carefully back into his carpetbag. "Not least my own. For, as I say, this preparation enabled me in short order to regain my previous health and vigor after my unfortunate sojourn in captivity."

"What's in it?"

"Ah . . . they are *secret* ingredients, madam."

"I'll take a gross," I said. "What's your wholesale price?"

"Pardon me?" He looked astounded.

"You've told me all about what you do, but I guess you don't know what *I* do for a living," I said. "I'm a businesswoman. I own a store—general merchandise—called Williams' Emporium. In Tahoe City, California. I'm on my way home now, and I'd like you to deliver a gross of your Elixir to me, on consignment. I'll see if I can sell it to the unhealthy, weak, balding, toothless, nervous and afflicted population of the region. If, that is, you care to branch out into that area of the country."

"My dear madam! I am touched at the trust that you reposit in me—I have dreamt of just such an opportunity, ever since I had occasion to briefly visit the area in question, some years ago, when to my sorrow I happened to note the pervasive debility of the inhabitants."

"It *is* pretty pervasive," I said. "The climate accounts for it."

"No doubt, no doubt," he said. "And a life of arduous toil."

"So, do we have a deal?" I asked.

He hesitated. "Sixty percent?"

"Fifty. On a gross of bottles—delivered. If they sell fast, I'll want more, on a regular basis."

"It's a deal," he said.

And we shook on it.

***

I was sorry to bid farewell to my new acquaintance when the train pulled into Salt Lake City.

"Don't you go and let these Mormons convert you, now," I teased, as he made ready to depart.

"My dear Miss Williams," he said, taking my hand in his, "I have no desire to compete with the American Moses,[73] though some have alleged in my hearing that I resemble him to some degree."

(This was true; he did look something like Brigham Young, though Mr Osterhouse wore no beard and had a kindlier, less carved-from-Vermont-granite expression, and a deal more humor about him—if the stories I'd heard of the Prophet were true, *he* hadn't much of the latter quality about him, though by all reports he didn't seem to require it. Perhaps having thirty or so wives took the need for humor from a man, though I'd'a thought it might could be a help.)

"I'm glad to hear it," I said. "I'll look for you in a month or thereabouts, then, with my order."

"I shall be there, I shall be there, with wings upon my feet, like to Hermes himself," he said, and pressed my hand warmly, then placed his tall silk hat firmly upon his head, smiled, and bustled off.

I found myself staring after him, suddenly lonely. He was a rascal, that was plain, and probably had never uttered an honest statement in his life (I doubted his story of his military service and his imprisonment, for example), but he was warm and solicitous; he had tried his best to cheer me up, and had in fact done so.

---

[73] Eds. note: This sobriquet was in fact applied by contemporaries to Brigham Young, who led the Mormons to Salt Lake following the death of John Smith.

It had been a long time since I'd laughed so much, or so long.

I sat down and took up the book I'd been attempting to read, but had put by whilst Mr Osterhouse entertained me. It was one that Sally-John had long been pestering me to read, having decided that my education (spotty as it had been) could use some spiffing up, and soon I was deeply involved in reading the life of *Nana*, by Mr. Emile Zola.

I was reading it in English, of course, not ever having learnt French, but Sally-John said that the book warn't harmed at all by being translated. Further, she'd told me that it was destined to be a classic, being highly representative of the literary movement called "naturalism," and it wouldn't hurt me to read good literature once in a while. Also, she'd thought the story that might interest me, the character's earliest years having some similarity to my own history.

Well, Nana's father was, like mine, an ignorant sot with a heavy hand, but the fifteen-year-old Nana was beautiful (as I had never been) and quickly ended up the toast of Paris as a stage actress, a profession that had never tempted me in the slightest. However, Zola's descriptions of the theatrical world made me think once again of Mr Osterhouse and his claim to be an entertainer—which he surely was, given the act he'd put on for an audience of one!

For the remainder of the journey, I slept, off and on, when not immersed in the increasingly depressing life of Nana—she died a loathsome death of the smallpox, as it turned out, and deservedly so in my view, having driven one suitor to plunge a pair of scissors into himself, and sent others to the brink of financial ruin and beyond. Mr Zola spared none of the gruesome details, and despite Nana's being a completely irredeemable character, as far as I could judge, the tale of her rise and fall was absorbing. By the time I finished the novel, I was gladder than ever that I had never had the need to visit France, and I resolved then and there to avoid the place if at all possible.

I woke just as we pulled into Reno from a dream in which Mr Osterhouse appeared in front of Williams' Emporium in broad daylight, dressed like pictures I'd seen of ancient Greek gods in a tunic that revealed his powerful chest and shoulders, and driving a red-and-yellow circus wagon full of bright-blue glass bottles labeled "Snake Oil."

***

In actual fact, when Mr Osterhouse did show up in Tahoe City, his arrival warn't that far short of the apparition he'd presented in my dream (though he was clad not in a tunic but in a long canvas coat over what appeared to be the same black suit he'd worn on the train).

It was no circus wagon that he drove up in, but it was likewise designed to attract attention: a large wooden conveyance, painted bright blue, with white-and-gilt side-boards advertising not only The Elixir but a variety of medicaments from cures for warts to ointments that promised instant relief from eczema, skin rashes, insect bites, shingles, and the like, as well as cough lozenges, soothing syrups, plasters, tonics, and pills for everything from lack of stamina (these was labeled "FOR MEN ONLY") to leaky kidneys.

I didn't see his arrival, for I was in my office, busily trying to track down a bank error (in my favor) of twenty dollars and fifty-seven cents, when Solly's and Conchita's boy Seraphim, who was clerking for me, come running into my office. "Missy Sarah, there's a man come, says you contracted with him for a big sale. He's outside in his wagon, ma'am."

I knew who it must be, and when I went out onto the board sidewalk in front of the store, I couldn't help but smile.

"My dear lady! I am here, as promised," he announced, jumping down from the wagon seat, "With the first of what I hope will be many future orders, to our eventual mutual enrichment and to the increased health of the residents of this splendid region." He opened the back of the wagon to show a dozen large wooden cases. "If you will permit me—" and he carefully pried up the lid of a case, to reveal twelve straw-filled compartments, in each of which nestled a large blue bottle. "The rest are exactly the same—constructed to my own design, as you see."

"Thank you, Mr Osterhouse," I said. "Seraphim, round up a couple of boys and unload these-here, please. It's bottles, medicine bottles, so be extra careful. Put them in the front of the store—we'll set up a display later this afternoon."

"Yes'm," said Seraphim, and disappeared.

"Would you care to take a dish of tea, or perhaps you prefer coffee?" I said.

"Coffee," he said, "If you please. Ah, coffee, that aromatic gift to the world of the sons of Araby!" And he went on, discussing the merits of this particular bean and that particular method of roasting, whilst Seraphim and two of his brothers unloaded the cases.

Mr Osterhouse hadn't lost his gifts of oratory. He kept right on talking whilst I led him into the store and through to the back, where my office was. He settled himself onto the large rocking-chair that I kept next to the parlor stove, where the coffee-pot reposed. He accepted a cup of coffee, to which he added three spoonsful of sugar and a large splash of cream. I poured a cup for myself and waited.

"My, my, but that's good coffee," he said.

"Arbuckle's,[74]" I said. "I am the local agent for the company. Glad you like it."

"Ah, yes, Arbuckle's Arioso—the coffee with the candy in each package," he said. "It is famous, deservedly so."

We sipped in silence for a time. Then Seraphim appeared in the doorway.

"We've unloaded the crates," he said.

"Thank you, young man," said Mr Osterhouse, setting down his cup. "Let me give you a token of my appreciation," and he took a coin from his pocket and handed it over.

"Thank you, sir," Seraphim said. "Do you want me to take your rig over to the livery stable, sir?"

"No, no; I'll just take care of that myself, in a moment." He turned to me. "I have reservations at the hotel for tonight, dear Miss Williams. May I have the pleasure of your company for dinner?"

"All right," I said, conscious that Seraphim had not departed, but was watching and listening, with an expression of great interest.

"Then I will take my leave," Mr Osterhouse said, getting to his feet, "And return to escort you to the hotel at, shall we say, six o'clock?"

"That will be just fine," I said.

"And may I borrow the services of your young assistant for a short time?"

---

[74] The Arbuckle company, after the Civil War, developed a process for selling roasted coffee beans in airtight packaging, and marketed their product with coupons printed on the package, redeemable for various items (each bag also contained a peppermint stick).

"Of course," I said. "Seraphim, you help Mr Osterhouse."

"Yes'm."

"Now, young man. Will you do me the kindness to accompany me to the livery stable so that I may make suitable arrangements?" Mr Osterhouse said, turning to Seraphim and putting one large hand on the boy's shoulder.

"Sure thing," said Seraphim. "Missy Sarah, I'll be right back."

"Don't hurry," I said. "Mr Osterhouse's arrangements may take some time."

Mr Osterhouse raised his hat to me and walked off with my clerk, who was staring up at him with a mesmerized expression. I sighed and pulled the ledger I'd been working on toward me again and picked up my pencil. Where was that dratted twenty dollars and fifty-seven cents?

It warn't til I found the error, finally (someone, probably Seraphim, who had no head for figures, had forgotten to deduct $20.57 in freight charges from last month), that it dawned on me: I'd agreed to go to dinner. At the hotel. With a supplier.

I put my pencil down. I had never before mixed business with social doings.

Why had I accepted Mr Osterhouse's invitation? And why did the prospect of dinner with a middle-aged, portly windbag of dubious ethical propensities cause me to feel an unaccustomed warmth and pleasure?

I shook my head and closed the ledger. "You're going batty, Sarah Mary Williams," I said, aloud. "Just plain batty."

And I went upstairs to see what in the world I could possibly wear that didn't make me look quite so much like the middle-aged, scrawny female storekeeper I was.

Chapter Twenty-Two: A New Arrangement

It is funny what a person will remember, even after years and years have gone by. I elected to wear conventional clothes, choosing a new dress, a deep-blue challis, for that first dinner with Mr Osterhouse, and it was only whilst I was buttoning the high collar that I realized the same blue was the color of his wagon as well as the color of the bottles that contained his Elixir.

And not until I was seated across from him in the hotel dining room did I notice that blue was the color of his eyes as well—not a dark blue like my own, but paler, like the sky on a late summer afternoon, shaded by thick curly black eyebrows threaded with gray.

"I've taken the liberty of ordering a bottle of wine," he was saying, as he poured a golden liquid into two goblets, "So that we can drink to our mutual success in the noble grape."

"Thank you," I said, taking the stemmed glass from him.

"To success," he said, and sipped appreciatively at the wine. "Splendid, splendid—I hadn't thought to find a Moselle quite as good here in the hinterlands, but your hotel's cellar appears to be of excellent quality, Miss Williams."

"I don't drink wine much," I said, "But this is right tasty."

We sipped in thoughtful silence for a while, and then the waiter came and took our orders. The fare on this night was, as I recall, roasted saddle of venison with ground-cherry sauce and mashed turnips, and Mr Osterhouse did justice to his well-filled plate. I watched him eat, noting that his hands were deft in their use of the tableware, and that he kept his lips firmly closed whilst he chewed (and that silently), used his napkin liberally, and paused often to ask me if I required another helping of sauce, or bread? I shook my head at these questions, and applied myself to my own plate. The food was delicious, but I seemed to have lost my appetite.

"I perceive that you appear not to be relishing this fine meal," Mr Osterhouse said. "Is something the matter?"

"It appears that I ain't—am not—very hungry," I said. "I'll take some more wine, though."

He poured another glass for the both of us. Then, "I hope that the company you are keeping has not put you off your victuals," he said.

"No, no," I said.

"Perhaps some dessert?"

I didn't usually care that much for sweets, but I knew that men usually did, so I nodded. He conferred with the waiter, who brought us each a thick slab of pie—apple—and coffee.

Mr Osterhouse forked up the point of his slice, chewed, swallowed, then contemplated his pie with reverent attention. "I don't believe that I have ever had such a fine piece of pie before," he proclaimed.

It was good pie, but not much out of the ordinary, to my taste. "Mr Osterhouse, I believe that you are exaggerating," I said.

He smiled. "Do you think so?"

"In fact," I said, "I believe that exaggeration is your ordinary form of expression."

"Ah. That propensity has been laid to my door, ere now," he said, cutting another piece of pie and lifting it to his mouth. He chewed, swallowed, dabbed at his lips with his napkin, and said, "It is, I fear, the result of too many years spent in appealing to a largely indifferent public. In order to capture anyone's attention, hyperbole must be the order of the day. Mere adherence to plain facts, while less subject to challenge, also brings, regrettably, less custom."

"That's so." I pondered. "It seems like cheating in a way, though, don't it? If a person needs a thing, he will pay for it, regardless."

"Ah, but does he *know* that he needs it? That is where salesmanship comes in. And where a skill in what you term 'exaggeration' may spell the difference between making the sale and losing it."

I shook my head. "I guess I have fallen behind the times."

He finished his pie, plied his napkin, and sat back from the table. The waiter come and cleared the dishes away. "Another coffee?" he asked.

My dinner partner quirked an eyebrow at me; I nodded. "Yes, coffee for two," Mr Osterhouse said to him, then turned back to me.

"Now, I've recounted to you, dear lady, how I came to be in the business of dispensing health and vigor to suffering humanity."

I smiled, remembering. "You surely did!"

"Well, then: turn about is fair play: how did you come to take up the profession of storekeeper?"

"Why, I don't rightly know," I said.

"Come, come," he said. "A person don't usually take up a life's work without some sort of inspiration . . . it needs inspiration, don't you find, to maintain one's strength of purpose through the vicissitudes of commercial enterprise?"

The coffee arrived, and I drank some of mine. "I guess."

"For instance," Mr Osterhouse said, adding cream to his cup, "I took up my own profession out of a desire to promote health and vigor amongst the populace, as well as to gratify my own creative impulses, which, in the crafting of my Elixir, have been so supremely satisfied."

I had to smile. "I'm sure your 'creative impulses' are much grander than mine."

"I am just as sure that you wrong yourself by saying so," he said. "I observed, earlier today—and this is but a single example— that your Emporium is arranged in such a way that the customer's eye cannot but be captured . . . before such plentitude his pocketbook must perforce open itself, and all its contents spill into your clever hands."

"Why, setting out the merchandise so's to show it off to best advantage, that's just good business," I said.[75]

"Perhaps," he said. "It is also art." He ate some more pie. "I am curious by nature, and so I ask you again—and you may tell me it's none of my business—why storekeeping? Why not school-marming, or cattle-ranching, or—" he put up one hand, "—you needn't tell me, but—why not marriage to some fine and deserving man, and children, and a home of your own?"

I looked across the table at him. His eyes shone with kindness, and the expression in them encouraged me to say more than what my response might otherwise have been.

"Storekeeping . . . well, it just seemed like a good thing . . . folks always need this and that, you know, and I've got an eye for what people want and will pay to get," I said.

"And how is it that you know what folks need?"

"Because," I said, "It's generally what I myself would have wanted, or what I would have wanted for them as I cared about to have."

---

[75] L. Frank Baum, author of the *Oz* books, was for a time a store proprietor in the Dakotas and may have been one of the first to recognize and put into practice the art of window-dressing.

He nodded. "And for yourself?"

I thought about those years when I'd slept in empty hogsheads and waked before dawn, bone-chilled and hungry, and scrounged for scraps of food in the alleys outside of taverns; when I'd crept to the backs of houses and caught glimpses of such comforts as I never imagined could be for such as I. Those parlors and kitchens came before my eyes in patterns of light and color, peopled by well-fed women and men and children whose clothes were whole and clean, who sat at table and ate hot meals off patterned china-ware, who slept at night under soft, warm blankets.

On more than a few occasions I'd dared to enter some of those houses, when their inhabitants was away from home, and stolen food or an article of clothing—once I'd stolen a pair of socks, the first I'd ever worn: I could still feel the wonder of their warmth and softness inside the broken boots I'd taken from a rubbish heap and mended with my own clumsy fingers, a rusty nail for an awl, and a bit of waxed thread—that last item stolen, too, from the town cobbler.

I remembered how I'd wandered past Hannibal's shops and peered inside as folks came and went, seeing splendors spread on counters and stacked on shelves, and how I'd wished I'd been anyone but Huckleberry Finn, who'd never dare to set one toe inside such places. Why other reason would Huck Finn have, but to steal? Those owners who'd spied me outside in those days was only too prone to step up and tell me—and in so many words, and often with curses, too—to make myself scarce if I didn't want to have the law on me. That was usually enough to make me vanish back to my hogshead, to wrap my skinny arms around myself and try to sleep, for when I slept I could forget that I was cold and hungry . . .

"I'm sorry," I said abruptly. "I was remembering . . . "

"And not pleasant memories," he said.

"No."

"I'm sorry, too," he said. "I have no desire to be the cause of any discomfort on your part."

"I'm aware of that," I said.

"I envy you, in a way," he said. "I envy your stability, at any rate."

"Because I stay in one place, you mean?"

"Yes. Unlike my way of life, which requires more or less constant movement."

"I worked out of a wagon myself, when I first came West," I said.

"Did you?"

I described my original, mobile Emporium, and related how, for the first months of my sojourn in San Francisco, I'd slept inside it with my guns ready to hand, and Cassius sleeping beneath, armed as well.

"I kept that wagon," I said. "It ain't as pretty as yours, but it's still roadworthy."

"Perhaps you have thoughts of taking to the road once more?"

"No. I aim to stay on here," I said.

"Whilst I," he said, "I was born under a wandering star, I fancy."

We were both silent for a spell. The waiter came, presented the bill with a bow, and left, bearing a pile of notes. "You may keep the change," Mr Osterhouse said to him, grandly.

"You ain't going to get rich that way," I said.

He laughed. "Perhaps not. But I find that I enjoy being the giver of largesse, once in a while. It allows me to feel rich, in other words, even though I have not yet achieved such a state."

"Well, I ain't rich, either," I said. "But I'm comfortable enough."

"I take it that you have found storekeeping a prosperous undertaking, in the main?"

"In the main, yes," I said. "It ain't been easy, though. Since the railroad come, shipping's been more dependable, but I don't figure on dying a millionaire, if that's what you're angling to know."

"Ah," he said. "There, we differ. For I do."

"You do what?"

"Aim to die a millionaire."

"What, on one-dollar bottles of snake oil?" the words were out of my mouth scarcely before I'd thought them. "I mean—that is—"

"Do not, I beg, distress yourself," Mr Osterhouse said, pouring more wine into our glasses. "I am quite aware of the common view attached to purveyors of, ahem, patent remedies—"

"I'm sure your Elixir has excellent qualities—"

"It does, dear lady. For example, you used the term 'snake oil' just now—"

"I do beg your pardon!"

"Not necessary. You see, 'snake oil'—the real thing, derived in China from certain species of water snakes—is in fact a medicinal substance of great antiquity."

"I had a Chinese assistant some years back," I said, "And he talked a great deal about Chinese medicines, so I believe that what you say might even be true."

"I am glad to hear it . . . then you accept that my Elixir may in fact have some value?"

"What's in it?" I leaned across the table. "I've undertook to sell a gross of bottles, ain't I? I'm an associate. So tell me: what's in it?"

"Miss Williams," Mr Osterhouse said, putting his empty wine glass aside and signaling to the waiter for more coffee, "My dear Miss Williams: I will tell you. But not in this public venue."

"Let's go back to my place, then," I said.

"My dear madam—your reputation—"

"Let me worry about my reputation," I said. "Come on."

I stood up before my companion could rise and pull out my chair. I picked up my reticule. "Well?"

Mr Osterhouse handed several bills to the waiter. "Madam, I am at your disposal!"

As we left the dining room, I nodded to several folks I knew.

"You've made a life for yourself here," Mr Osterhouse said, taking my arm.

"I have," I said.

"It must be hard for a woman alone," he said.

"No harder than for a man," I said.

"A different kind of hard," he said.

"Yes," I said. "That I'll allow."

My apartments above the store was dark as the tomb; it took a moment to find a lamp, and several tries to light it, for the dratted thing's wick seemed to wave about, back and forth, moving just out of the reach of the match.

When at last I had the lamp going, I turned to see Mr Osterhouse, arms folded across his ample front, surveying me with something close to a frown.

"My dear lady," he said. "It occurs to me that you are not yourself."

It occurred to *me* that I'd had several glasses of wine, and that he was probably right.

"Maybe not," I said.

"I shall withdraw immediately," he said.

"Oh, hell," I said. "You might's well stay put. I'll be right back."

In my small kitchen, I lit the stove and put the teakettle on. The routine of scalding out the teapot and measuring out the leaves steadied me, and when I come back into the sitting room with the tea tray, I felt more like myself. Mr Osterhouse took the tray from me and set it down.

I lit a second lamp, and then a third. In their warm glow my sitting-room looked snug and cosy, with the two armchairs drawn up next to the small round table with its red embroidered cover. I took my seat.

"Have some tea," I said, passing Mr Osterhouse a cup. "Do you take sugar?"

"No, thank you," he said.

I added sugar to my own cup, remembering briefly how David had deplored the habit, and settled back in my armchair. "Well?"

"My dear Miss Williams," Mr Osterhouse said. "Do I have your word of honor that none of what I tell you will go beyond these four walls?"

"Word of honor," I said.

"Well, then," and he began.

I won't at this point go into detail about what was in it—it had a grain alcohol base, which I'd pretty much surmised beforehand, that being the major ingredient of most such patent remedies. This Elixir of Mr Osterhouse's, though, did contain some substances that, as I later discovered, was indeed truly beneficial: ginseng and chamomile and comfrey and mint; mullein; blackberry leaves; ginger; blackstrap molasses; alder bark; sagebrush; purple bee plant; sumac leaves and berries; rose hips; fenugreek; black cohosh; water snake oil (the real McCoy); honey; horehound; cayenne pepper; asafetida; Peruvian bark and willow bark extracts; senna; and, last but not least, a decoction of hemp that Mr Osterhouse swore was in all respects save country of origin the same as what in India was known as *bhang*, a remedy as ancient, he said, as the Upanishads—whatever they was.

"One moment," Mr Osterhouse said. He got up, took a lamp, and went clumping downstairs. He returned with a bottle from the display that Seraphim had painstakingly created, and dexterously opened the porcelain cap. "You should really taste it for yourself."

He poured a small amount into my empty teacup. "Go on," he said. "Try it."

I smelt it, first. There was a strong whiff of alcohol that dissipated instantly, leaving something herby in its wake, a scent that was almost familiar, but when I tried to identify it, it vanished. I tasted the liquid. Pepper, I thought, sensing heat, and spiciness, like nutmeg and cloves; a tanginess, paired with the sweetness and smoothness of honey, and over all that same elusive flavor, green and pungent, almost leafy. There was a sensation on the back of my tongue, faintly bitter but far from unpleasant. I set down the cup.

"It don't taste like medicine," I said. Most such, in my experience, were nauseous when not actively purgative.

"My Elixir," Mr Osterhouse said, lifting his chin, "is not medicine. It is *health*."

"I ain't a-going to argue with you," I said. "This stuff tastes pretty good."

"Miss Williams," he said, "I took care to make my Elixir palatable, but its benefits are, I assure you, what renders it worthwhile."

I was getting sleepy. "I believe you," I said, with a yawn.

"The hour is late. I must take my leave of you, dear lady," he said, and stood up.

I stood also, though I felt somewhat wavery about my feet. "Good night, Mr Osterhouse," I said.

"Good night, madam," he said. "Sleep well."

I lit his way down the stairs and saw him out. His feet went clacking down the board sidewalk towards the hotel. I locked the door and went back upstairs.

I blew out two lamps, then stood, holding the third. In its gleam I saw the bottle of Elixir standing on the table where he'd left it. I stoppered it, firmly, then carried the bottle into my bedroom and set it, with the lamp, down atop my dresser. The blue glass shone softly in the lamplight.

I undressed and got into my nightgown. I brushed out my hair and gazed at the bottle. There was two of them, just as there was two of *me*: the one on the dresser and the one in the mirror.

"He's a rogue," I said to my reflection in the mirror.

My reflection stuck its tongue out at me. I blew out the lamp and crawled into bed.

"He's a rogue, but I like him just the same," I said, and fell sound asleep.

***

Next morning I awoke, expecting a headache from the wine I'd drunk, but I felt fine, in fact I felt so energetic that I spent most of the morning reorganizing the window display to show off the Elixir. I stepped outside to gauge the effect, and failed to notice that Mr Osterhouse had come up behind me until he cleared his throat. I turned at the sound.

"Good morning. I trust you had a restful night?" he asked.

"I did," I said. "And yourself?"

"The hotel accommodations are comfortable enough," he said. "I must be off, however, before the day wears on further apace."

I held out my hand. "When will I see you again?"

"I shall return in a month," he said.

"I hope to have sold all of those blue bottles by then," I said.

"Until next we meet!" he cried, and, tipping his hat, he turned and strode off in the direction of the livery stable.

I watched him go, feeling that the day had lost some of its fine brightness. Then, sighing, I went back inside. Seraphim was waiting on two ranchers' wives in the dry-goods section. The doorbell pinged and a burly miner came toward me.

"I'd like a bottle of that stuff there, that Elixir you got in the window," he said.

"Yes, sir," I said. "You're familiar with it, then?"

"I surely am. Bought some a couple of months or thereabouts, down Sacramento way. That doctor feller that makes it, he was selling it out of a wagon," he said.

"A blue wagon," I said.

"Yes. That there is good medicine, missus. Do you aim to be carrying it from now on?"

"I hope to," I said.

"I'll tell the fellers," the miner said, taking his bottle, which I'd wrapped in two thicknesses of brown paper. "See you around, ma'am."

"I'll look forward to it," I said, ringing up his dollar.

"This way, ladies," I heard Seraphim say, as he shepherded his two customers in my direction. "Miss Sarah, these ladies have bought ten yards of muslin each."

The two customers stood by, chatting, whilst I took their money and wrapped up their purchases.

"Why, Miss Williams," one of them said, pointing to the window. "I see you're carrying Doctor Osterhouse's Elixir."

"Yes, ma'am," I said. "I just undertook a consignment, yesterday."

"I'll take two bottles," she said. "It's just the best tonic!"

"Is it?" asked the other lady. "I guess I'll try it, too, if you recommend it, Madeleine."

"Oh, I do," her companion said. "My husband bought a case of it when we were in Santa Fe, and I've been looking for it ever since we run out. It's wonderful stuff."

I wrapped up the bottles (the second woman ended up taking one) and thanked them, and they bustled out. I leaned on the counter, thinking.

I'd never heard of this stuff before, but apparently plenty of other folks had.

Perhaps—just perhaps—the arrangement I'd made with Theophilus Osterhouse would prove more profitable than I'd anticipated.

And—if this rate of sales kept up—I'd need a new supply sooner than I'd anticipated.

I could reach Mr Osterhouse, he'd said, via general delivery, San Francisco.

I called Seraphim over. "Mind the store for me a few minutes," I said. "I've got an errand over to the telegraph office."

***

Well, as it turned out, I sent the telegram, but Mr Osterhouse didn't get the message for another week, he being out on the road, selling, so it was ten days more til I got his reply: GRATIFIED REGARDING SALES STOP WILL BRING NEW SUPPLY NOVEMBER 30 STOP ONE GROSS QUERY STOP IF MORE DESIRED PLEASE ADVISE STOP T.VDW.OSTERHOUSE

I thanked the telegraph boy who brought the message and told him to send this reply:

BETTER BRING TWO GROSS STOP SELLING LIKE HOTCAKES STOP S.M.
WILLIAMS

That was the literal truth—most folks who came in for Elixir
bought a couple or three bottles at a time, and whilst I wasn't about
to run out right away, I could see the supply dwindling steadily.

The weather had turned colder than usual, and with a howling
wind, more like January than November. I was writing a letter to
Sally-John, trying my best to describe Mr Osterhouse and his wares.
"Now I know," I wrote, "That you don't approve of patent
medicines, but his Elixir is pretty powerful stuff. When you
come home for Christmas I intend to send you back to college
with a few bottles, for it really is wonderfully strengthening,
and I know how hard you are working at your studies."

I posted the letter and stopped off at the milliner's, Mrs
Rakaczy's. She was a Hungarian lady, a widow, who'd set up shop
about a year since. Her hats was always well-made and fashionable
without being ridiculous in size or amount of trimming, and, looking
forward to Sally-John's graduation, I'd ordered one for myself, in
deep red—the color that suited me best—the whole ornamented by
a cockade of red-and-bronze feathers.

"Your hat is ready, Madame," Mrs Rakaczy said, turning to
take it out of the case where she kept her "originals," as she called
them.

"It's beautiful," I said, trying it on. The feather cockade was
jaunty, and the hat's color lightened my skin to cream.

"You should have your portrait taken in it," Mrs R. said,
decisively. "Then you can put the picture in a frame, yes, and give it
to your daughter."

I thought that sounded like excellent advice. Sally-John did
have one picture of me, but it was an old one—taken at Tom
Sawyer's wedding, in fact—and I thought, myself, that I had
improved in appearance since then. Having put on a few pounds,
my face had filled out some, and I looked less gaunt than formerly.

"I believe I just might do that," I said to Mrs Rakoczy.

She settled my new hat into a nest of tissue paper in a round
box printed all over with her initials, and tied a string round to carry
it by.

I walked back down the street, swinging my hatbox slowly.

The photographer, a tall, spare, dark party named Fortin, had his studio upstairs over a tiny shop where his wife, also an artist, sold hand-painted china articles and suchlike. She also illustrated the cartes de visite[76] that he produced, with delicate hand-tinted wreaths of flowers and leaves. I'd not had occasion to visit their establishment since they'd opened it a year since, but now I pushed open the street door and stepped in.

A long counter heaped with paper goods stretched nearly the length of the shop—a good ten feet—and behind it a folding screen half-hid Mrs Fortin. She was seated at an easel, paintbrush in hand, but she jumped up when she saw me and came around the screen.

"Miss Williams, how do you do?" she said. "May I help you?"

"I'd like to have my portrait taken," I said.

"Will you wait? I shall have to ask him when he is free," she said.

"Of course."

At the end of the shop a door stood half-open; I heard her mount a flight of stairs. Then she came tapping back down.

"He will see you now."

She escorted me to the rear of the shop and pointed upward. I gathered my skirts and mounted the stairs. At the top, a door stood hospitably open, and I heard a cheerful male voice call, "Come in, come in!"

The voice belonged to Mr Fortin, of course, a tall, lean man; as mentioned before, completely bald, but with a neatly-trimmed Vandyke beard.

The room was small but well-lit by three large, uncurtained windows. I was interested in the camera, which consisted of a big, polished wooden cube, commodious enough for a packing box, on three legs, with a protrusion of brass and enamel knobs and dials on it, and in front a huge glass lens on a sort of bellows-like structure. There was a black cloth like a cape thrown over the top of the

---

[76] Eds. note: These small portrait photographs on visiting cards (later, larger versions were known as cabinet cards) were popular in the period. They served as advertisements for the photographer as well as calling cards; often the fronts were decorated with the sitter's name in fancy script and with designs such as vines, flowers, birds, and the like.

camera. Mr Fortin seated me in a comfortable armchair and begged to know what-all I had in mind. I took off the top of the hatbox and showed him what lay inside.

"I thought I'd have my portrait done wearing this hat," I said. I knew that the portrait would not be in color, but the hat was stylish; I would look fashionable, at least, and not like some frowsty frontierswoman.

"A splendid idea," he said. "How many copies?"

I hadn't thought that far, but now I imagined sending a picture to Tom and Becky and one to Julie and Elizabeth and another to Dr Thannheimer—along with the one for Sally-John.

"Five," I said.

"Five," he repeated, and wrote the information in a tiny account book that he took out of his coat pocket. "Framed?"

"Yes."

"We have frames in brass, silver-plate, and sterling. My wife will show you a selection when you go back downstairs," he said. "Now, if you'll seat yourself over there—" he pointed to a tall stool, which stood in front of a wall painted a pale silvery gray.

"All right," I said, taking my seat on the stool. "Now what do I do?"

"Just sit quietly," he said, and took his place behind the camera. "Try to hold as still as you can."

I warn't ready, and he had to stop and adjust the thing, and take more pictures, but finally he seemed satisfied, and shook my hand, and told me to tell his wife to put me down for five copies and to show me the frames they had in stock.

When I left he was tenderly polishing the lens of his contraption.

Downstairs, Mrs Fortin helped me select several styles of frame—I wanted something different for each recipient—and then remarked, "If you order six prints, you get twenty free cartes de visite."

I'd never required such things before, but I thought it might be good business to leave with special clients. "All right," I said. I didn't know who I'd give the sixth print to, but it seemed too good a deal to pass up.

We shook hands and Mrs Fortin promised to send a messenger as soon as the prints was ready for me to approve. I put my hat back into its box, nodded, and walked home, where I put my hat in the wardrobe and sat until it was nearly too dark to see, there by my parlor stove.

When Sally-John come home, I decided, I'd take her to have her portrait done, too. It would be pleasant to look up and see her smiling at me. I wondered that I'd never thought of it before. Surely photography was becoming commonplace in these modern times!

That night I went to bed early.

Sometime in the night I woke, or dreamed I did, and saw a framed picture atop my dressing-table. I tried to focus on the face in the photograph, but I could not make it out.

I got out of bed and crept up close, but still I couldn't make out whose portrait it was. The frame itself give off a glow, kind of greenish, like marsh gas, and where a picture ought to be was a dark gray empty oblong full of mist that moved and swirled. Finally, though I felt a shiver of dread, I put out my hand and picked up the thing.

The mistiness cleared. I was holding a picture of Pap, just as he'd looked when I last saw him alive, in all his rags and dirt. He was glowering out at me with that same expression he'd worn when he was still this side of sober, a kind of narrow-eye'd scowl, as if he was a-saying the meanest and dreadfulest things he could think of, and enjoying it, too.

And I felt a chill of fear run through me whilst I looked into that face that I'd feared and hated so long ago. And my hand shook so that the image blurred into mist again, and shifted and changed—

I was looking at Jim. Not as he'd been when I first knew him, but as he was the last time I'd seen him: his hair all silver, and his broad brown face all wreathed in smiles. He turned toward me and held out his arms—

And then he was gone, and I found my hands gripping a frame that bore a picture of Johnny.

I stared down into that face I had loved with the last love of my youth. I marked the clear lines of brow and chin, the full lips and bright eyes. So like his daughter—our daughter. And with something of Jim as well—something in the way those full lips curved into a smile as warm as sunshine after a cold winter.

And then, just as before, this image too melted away and another took its place:

Gazing at me out of the frame was a high-cheekboned

smooth Chinese face, grave and patient, out of which two almond-shaped black eyes gazed at me with sorrow and regret. The man in the picture held up a hand as if in farewell—or in warning—and then he too had disappeared into the mist, and another man's face swam into view.

He was round and rosy and jovial, with waving black-and-grey whiskers, a nose like a potato, and blue eyes, small but intensely kind.

"Mr Osterhouse," I murmured, "Mr Osterhouse, is that you?"

"The very same, dear lady, the very same!"

"Come in! I have been waiting for you," I called, and woke at that same instant, my arms reaching out—

I was alone in my room.

There was, of course, no picture on my nightstand. None at all.

No one was there. It was only a dream.

I hadn't wept in many years, but I did so now; and when I finally fell, exhausted, asleep, the pillow under my cheek was sodden with tears.

Chapter Twenty-Three: I Am Surprised

Well, as you might expect, I felt a touch bit shy when Mr Osterhouse did come a-rattling up to my store a week or so later. But as soon as he'd bounded out of the wagon and held out his hand to me, booming, "Dear lady!", I shook off my notions and chatted with him just as natural as ever.

"You look well," he said, as we sat down and I poured out coffee for both of us.

"Thank you," I said. "You, also."

He did in fact look uncommonly sleek. His clothes was all new, and I marked that he'd seen a barber within the last day or so, for his whiskers was brushed to a curl, and there warn't no stubble on his solid pink chin.

"I have had a successful half-year," he said. "So much so that I have had to lease more property in order to extend my manufacture."

That was how I heard about how the Elixir was in fact produced.

"I began to make and sell the Elixir in Ohio, following the War," he explained, "In partnership with a friend of mine, a druggist. We made up the mixture in small batches and bottled it ourselves. What was for my friend a sideline, and but mildly profitable, seemed to me to promise the potential for considerably more, given time and dedication."

"And what did you propose to your friend?" I asked.

"Namely: that he should provide the necessary capital to purchase a manufactory and employ workers in order to produce the Elixir in quantity."

"I take it that he was disinclined to do so."

"Dear lady, you are correct."

"And so?" I prompted.

"And so I determined to make a fresh start, alone. I bought out his share of the enterprise, and took legal possession of the formula—he was most insistent that his name not be connected with the Elixir in any way, if it were not to be made under his direct supervision— and made my way to that most beautiful and wicked city, San Francisco, where opportunities continue to abound for those who seek them. There I leased a warehouse and employed such workers as were obtainable—the bulk of them being Chinese, of whom San Francisco boasts a great many—"

"I know," I said.

"—a great many," he continued, "most of whom were happy to enlist with me, for I gave full value for their labor. And, with production thus assured, I set out in pursuit of wealth and fame, selling my Elixir to eager customers in mining camps and cattle ranches, in small towns and remote settlements, across the high plains and up into the mountains and down to the sea once more, to re-equip and re-supply. Over the past five years, madam, I venture to say that the miles I have traveled might have put three girdles 'round the planet!"

"You don't say."

"I do say. When I first met you, dear lady, on that happy occasion when you and I found ourselves in joint occupation of those railway seats, back East, I was just returning from a profitable venture with an Eastern glass manufacturer, for those handsome blue bottles which you currently display in the front window of your own fine establishment."

"And your manufactory in San Francisco?"

"Has been twice enlarged, madam, and currently employs a hundred Celestials."

"That's quite a payroll."

"It is. I have had to hire an assistant, in fact, both to supervise the work force and its output and to handle the details of manufacture, including supplies, bottling, labeling and so on."

"Must be someone you can trust," I said. "To leave all alone whilst you go a-traveling, drumming up sales."

"He is a most trustworthy person."

"Chinese?"

"Indeed. I was of course cautioned by some business associates against employing a Chinaman in such a position, but I have found, dear lady, that trust repays trust, more often than not."

"That's true enough," I said. "And Chinese folks are not more dishonest—nor less so—than anyone else who works for a wage."

"The wages I pay are neither stingy nor stinted," he said.

He went on to describe his manufactory: the laboratory where the Elixir was compounded; the bottling plant; the warehouse, well-placed on the waterfront, with its own pier to which the ships that brought the blue glass bottles could draw up and unlade; the workers who toiled for him and whom he rewarded not only with pay comparable to that paid to white men (a rare thing indeed in those days) but with feasts on their festival days, such as Ching Ming, when he provided a seven-course dinner for all of this workers and their families, capped off with a show of fireworks.

"Sounds as if you've succeeded in your aims," I said.

"So much so," he said, "that this will be my last selling excursion. I have decided to hire a team of salesmen to take over for me, and intend to devote my time to cultivating such interests and individuals as will guarantee continued success."

"You're giving up the road," I said.

"I am."

"I shall miss our visits," I said. "I'm sure whoever you hire will be able to take my order for more bottles of Elixir, but I'm just as certain the process won't be nearly as entertaining without you."

He reached over and patted my hand. "Dear lady, you compliment me."

I poured some more coffee. "I used to live in San Francisco, myself."

"Did you?"

"A long time since. It ain't—isn't—a place with friendly associations for me, up to now, that is," I said.

"I am sorry to hear it. If you can overcome your misgivings, I shall be honored to show you over the premises, should you decide to visit," he said.

"I have friends in Oakland," I said. "Maybe next time I go to see them, I'll keep on and look you up."

"Do," he said. "Please do." And he took out his pocketbook and fished out a visiting card, on the back of which he wrote down the address of his factory.

"Good day, then, my dear Miss Williams."

We both stood up, then. He smiled down at me. I am a tall woman, but Mr Osterhouse was at least half a head taller. He took my right hand in both of his and raised it to his lips.

"Until next we meet," he said, and bowed himself out.

***

It was a few weeks later that I received a letter from Ernst Thannheimer.

It read: "My friend: The Doctor has had a stroke. He is in no immediate danger, but it would be well if you could come soon.

339

Your loving friends, Ernst and Gerda and the children."

I wired Ernst to expect me in a day or so, and bought a ticket for San Francisco on the next train.

"Make sure and keep detailed records for me, now," I said to Seraphim, who would be managing the store in my absence. Seraphim had grown up to be a steady young man. He hadn't much imagination, but he was cheerful and energetic.

"I will, Miss Sarah," he said.

"And don't drink all of the Elixir—it's two weeks until the next shipment," I said. Seraphim was devoted to the Elixir and accounted for at least two bottles a week all by himself. He often told customers how effective it was on such varied ailments as ringing in the ears, headache, nervous stomach, and spots before the eyes, all of which he suffered from something dreadful, after a Saturday night on the town.

"I'll take care, Miss Sarah."

"All right." I gathered up my gloves, valise, and reticule and found my seat on the train. This time I'd decided to spend the extra money and travel first-class. My compartment was comfortable, with purple plush seats and mahogany fittings, and as usual the spectacle of the lake and the Sierras held me spellbound despite the rattling, swaying motion of the train as it hurtled around curves and across trestles.

When we pulled into Oakland station, I was most dead with fatigue, for every attempt I'd made to sleep on the train had been frustrated; I just couldn't seem to settle. Also, I was hungry. The food had been a disappointment: stringy beef served cold, with dumplings the consistency of paste (and about as flavorsome), and no green vegetables. The bread was stale, the butter rancid. I drank coffee that was burnt rather than roasted, and nibbled on some chocolate that I'd thought to bring along, but I was perishing for a real meal when I hailed a cab and give Doctor Thannheimer's address.

It's just turned six, I thought, th*ey might still be eating dinner when I get there.* "Can you go a little faster, please?" I called up to the driver, who spat brown tobacco juice off to one side and said, "This hoss ain't no racer, lady."

"Right," I said, subsiding. The animal in question was built long and rangy, with ears almost mule-sized; he seemed unable to travel at any gait faster than a walk. I unwrapped another piece of chocolate and sat back, resigned. Might be we'd arrive by morning, and I could have breakfast.

Finally we were there. The driver carried my bags up to the front door, rang the bell for me, and accepted his fare—and the tip I included—with a grimace that I realized was meant to be a smile.

"Good day," I said.

"Ma'am," he said, touching his cap, and he and his long, languid horse clopped away.

I hardly rang the bell when the door burst open and Albert, Ernst's oldest boy, nearly up-ended me.

"Aunt Sarah! Aunt Sarah!" he shouted. "Come in—we've been waiting for hours!"

I let him pull me inside, then bent and planted a kiss on his cheek. "How are you, Albert? Tell me about school."

"School's all right. I wish I could leave school and come work for you, though," the boy said. "Papa says I can come out and work this summer, if you want me."

"Of course I want you," I said, and ruffled his hair, giving his ear a playful tug.

"Ouch," he said, and we both laughed.

Ernst had married a local girl of German extraction and settled down to run his uncle's practice. I knew that he had hopes that Albert would succeed him, but that did not seem likely. Albert insisted that he wanted nothing to do with medicine; he wanted, he said, to keep a store like his Aunt Sarah and make lots of money, and, he added, "never have to go out at night, as Papa does." His Papa had ruefully agreed that this aspect of medical practice was difficult to avoid.

"What did you bring me?" Albert asked, taking my elbow and guiding me down the passage toward the dining room. I could hear voices, and the clink and clatter of china and utensils.

"A switch and a lump of coal," I said. Albert hooted.

"That's what Santa Claus brings bad children," he said. "I'm not bad, and it's not Christmas!"

"Then why are you expecting a present?"

"Because you always bring me something."

"Well, I guess I do, at that," I admitted.

I sent Albert to fetch my holdall and rummaged for a moment. "Here you go."

Some years earlier, as more families with young children

settled around Tahoe, I had begun to sell a selection of toys, and this had proved a successful innovation indeed. They were mostly small wares—dolls and marbles and such. The item I now produced was rather bigger. "Here you are. This is for all of you to play with, so no fighting."

It was a Noah's Ark. The Ark itself was in two pieces, a top deck that lifted off and a lower deck where the animals was stowed, two by two: giraffes and elephants, lions and ostriches, crocodiles and anteaters, foxes and antelopes and hippopotami every sort of animal you could imagine, right down to ordinary ones like cows and horses and pigs and sheep and goats, even grasshoppers and ladybugs. And, of course, Noah and Mrs Noah and the three sons and their wives.

"Thanks, Aunt Sarah," Albert said. "Papa, Mama, Opa— Aunt Sarah is here!"

There followed the usual commotion of hugs and kisses and exclamations.

I found myself in the midst of a noisy throng of children— Albert and his two little sisters and the baby, who was just beginning to toddle—when I heard Ernst clear his throat.

"Sarah Mary," he said. "There is someone I would like you to meet."

He was holding the hand of a tiny Chinese girl. She was dressed all in pink—a padded rose-colored silk jacket over deeper cerise trousers—and her straight black hair was cut even with her chin, except for the bang across her forehead.

"Sarah Mary, this is Chung Hsaio-yen," he said. "David's daughter."

David's daughter?

In a daze, I shook the little girl's hand and said, "How do you do?" She nodded sedately and let Ernst lead her away, while Albert capered at her side.

Still bemused, I allowed Gerda to take my hand and lead me into the dining room.

I found myself seated next to Dr Thannheimer—known as "Opa" to Albert and the other children, though of course he was their great-uncle, not their grandfather. I sat there, feeling curiously numb, with a napkin in my lap, and Gerda—Ernst's wife—busily mounded a plate with roast chicken and carrots and boiled potatoes. Ernst passed the plate over to me, along with the gravy boat.

The little Chinese girl sat next to Albert, who watched over her solicitously. I tried not to stare at the child, but concentrated on my plate. I accepted second helpings, as did Ernst, Albert, and the two little girls, Clara and Katie. Hsaio-yen, I noticed, ate only a wing of the chicken and a little fruit. Gerda was kept busy feeding the baby minced chicken and mashed potatoes and applesauce—she was, she said, watching her figure, which tended toward plumpness—and helping Dr Thannheimer with his meal, which was pretty much the same as the baby's, he being unable to manage a knife and fork any longer. I noticed with a pang that his hand shook as he lifted each spoonful to his mouth. The conversation was merry enough, however, Albert and his sisters vying with each other to tell me what Santa Claus had brought.

"It was indeed a fine Christmas," Gerda said, wiping the baby's chin. He wiggled as he sat on her lap, chuckling fatly as babies do. "And we had also a surprise," she added, nodding at Chung Lin. "Ernst, tell Sarah what happened Christmas Eve."

"It was just after we came back from church," Ernst said, laying down his fork and turning to me. "Gerda was putting the baby to bed, and Albert and the girls were getting into their nightclothes, when there came a tremendous banging at the kitchen door. I was still dressed, so I hurried downstairs, and opened the door, and who do you think was there?"

"Who?"

"An old friend of yours. David Chung. And this little one, his daughter Hsaio-yen."

The little Chinese girl stirred in her seat, but said nothing.

"Albert," Ernst said, "Take Hsaio-yen and your sisters upstairs, ja?"

"Yes, Papa," Albert said.

We grownups waited until the children had departed.

"How can David be here?" I asked. "He is in China."

"No more," Ernst said. "He is in San Francisco."

"He came here to bring the child to you?"

Ernst hesitated. "That, and other business."

"What business?"

"David will be here tomorrow. He will tell you himself," Ernst said.

Gerda rose to clear the table.

"Let me help you," I said, but she shook her head. "It's better

I do it," she said. "I know where everything goes. But if you like, you and Ernst could take Uncle Josef into the parlor and sit with him, ja?"

"Ja," I said. Doctor Thannheimer had fallen asleep in his wheeled chair, his hands loosely curled in his lap atop the blanket that covered his legs. Since an earlier stroke had taken away the use of those legs a year ago, he spent his days in this chair—it was a regular kitchen chair, fitted with wheels—in which he could be pushed from one room to another; luckily, his bedroom was downstairs, off the kitchen—the room that had been Margaret's, I realized now with a pang. Margaret had died nine years before, just after Ernst had married Gerda.

Ernst pushed the Doctor in his chair into the parlor. The motion woke him a little and he stirred and smiled in his sleep. I sat down on the divan. The room was warm and the lamps all lit made it cosy. Ernst sat next to me.

"How is he?" I asked, nodding at the Doctor.

"He sleeps most of the time," Ernst said. "In the mornings sometimes he is a little more animated. It is hardest on Albert, I think. Before this stroke he spent many happy hours with his Opa." He sighed.

"He ain't—isn't— so very old," I said.

"Seventy." Ernst said. "What does the Bible tell us? Threescore years and ten, that is man's allotted span."

I thought how tall and handsome the Doctor had been, thirty years before, as we headed West in our wagon train. I remembered his curling dark hair and beard. Both were now snow white. His eyes were closed, his head sunk upon his breast.

"Gerda is wonderful with him," Ernst said. "She takes good care of him."

"You mustn't wait, if anything should happen," I said. "Wire me right away, and I'll come."

"I will."

"Good night," I said, and went up to bed, then, in a most thoughtful frame of mind.

***

When I come down to breakfast next morning, David was already there.

He was the same David, and yet he wasn't. He looked much older—a trifle heavier about the body, and there were lines about his mouth and eyes that had not been there before. His hair, brushed straight back in the old way, was heavily threaded with grey.

"Sarah Mary, I am here illegally," he said. "And I need your help."

We sat at the kitchen table, across from one another. Gerda brought in a pot of tea, smiling, and left us. Ernst too had vanished. Dimly, I heard the sound of the children as they played upstairs in their nursery: Albert and his sisters and their baby brother, and the Chinese girl Hsaio-yen, David's child.

"How do you mean, illegally?" I asked.

"I am not a U.S. citizen," David said. "The laws have changed. [77]It is difficult for Chinese to enter this country, and so I have been smuggled in. I cannot stay long."

"When do you leave?"

"Very soon. I must hasten home," David said. "There is a great famine in my home province—there have been many such in the last few years—and part of my errand has been to secure a shipment of food."

"Part of your errand?"

"Yes. The other part concerns you, Sarah Mary. That is, if you consent."

"Consent to what?"

He hesitated. "I had a letter from Sally-John not too long ago."

"She told me long ago that you and she write each other. I'm glad."

"You have seen my daughter, Hsaio-yen," he said. "What do you think of her?"

My mind flew, for no reason that I could name, to the picture I'd seen, all those years ago, of the beautiful Chinese woman who was David's wife. "She seems like a nice little thing."

"She is also very bright."

"I would expect that," I said, smiling. "What does her name mean?"

He smiled. "Little Swallow—is she not like a small bird, my Hsaio-yen? Ah, Sarah Mary, you are the only Westerner I have ever

---

[77] Eds. note: Legislation forbidding the entry of Chinese nationals continued to pass during and after the 1880s, culminating in the Chinese Exclusion Act.

known who cares for the meaning of Chinese names. Do you remember, when we first met—?"

"I remember," I said softly. "Tell me about your daughter."

"My wife does not love the child. That may seem strange to you, I know—"

"Not so strange," I said, remembering Hagar, with a little shiver.

David went on. "The child is unhappy at home. And I have, since Hsaio-yen's birth, hoped for a different sort of life for her. A life where her sex need not be a hindrance. A life where she can be free to grow, to live, to be."

"So you have brought her to America."

"I have brought her to *you*," he said.

"To me? Why not to Solly and his wife? They're her kin," I said.

"They are," David said. "But I do not wish my Little Swallow to grow up as the poor relation, the tag end—so to speak—of a crowd of children, all pushing and shoving for what each can get—you see I know my brother's family well, even though I am so far away—"

"That's true," I said. "They're a nice enough bunch, but rough in their ways."

"Sarah Mary, I do not know how to say this," David turned to me and there was real pain in his eyes, "But here it is: I am afraid for my daughter, if she stays in China."

"What do you mean?"

What he went on to tell me might have made another woman's blood run cold, but I had had my own taste of what a mother's feelings toward her child might be. Remembering, I listened with horror but without surprise. Most of what I felt, in truth, was pity.

"My wife was most unwell after Hsaio-yen was born," David said. "She did not recover for several years; in fact, it has been only a twelvemonth since she regained sufficient health and strength to resume her wifely duties." He avoided my eyes. "We have met with good fortune. Three months ago, she gave birth to a son."

"Congratulations."

He continued as if I had not spoken. "The birth of a son is a most significant event in a Chinese family. My wife had almost given up hope, but now she has her place in the generations, as my

346

son's mother."

"She was a mother already."

"A girl does not count."

"What do you mean?"

"Girls, when they grow up, marry and become part of their husbands' families. Only a son can carry on the family name and do honor to the ancestors."

"And so, now you have your son."

David's voice was bitter. "And my daughter must be sent away."

"Why?"

"My wife says that she cannot bear to see Hsaio-yen. She detests her."

I brushed aside the feeling of sickness that came with his words.

"Can't you keep her out of your wife's way, somehow?"

David said, "Our house is large, but not that large. My wife says that I must send Hsaio-yen away, or she will do so, herself. And I cannot bear for my daughter to go where her mother would send her."

"Where is that?"

"She intends to give Hsaio-yen to a monastery, where she will live forever apart from her family, shut away behind walls, never to see any of us again. She will become a nun, a Buddhist nun. In that way my wife will gain merit, by making the gift, and Hsaio-yen's prayers will also provide spiritual benefit for our house."

"Can't you stop her?"

"If I gainsay my wife, she says that she will hang herself."

I thought (but didn't say) that maybe that was the best solution all around.

David went on, "She has the ability to do this thing. My wife is a woman of very strong will."

"I believe it," I said. I could easily envision that small, pointed face with its eyes narrowed in fury, the beautiful mouth twisted in anger and vengefulness.

"There is more."

I waited.

"She says that she will hang herself, but before she does, she will give poison to our son, so that his soul will accompany hers to the Yellow Springs—the Underworld."

"No," I said. "She couldn't. No mother could—" and then I was silent.

He went on, "And so I have agreed," David said, "I have come here—smuggled myself and Hsaio-yen into this country—and I shall smuggle myself out again, but my daughter will remain. And my wife—"

"How can you live with someone like that!" I burst out.

"I hope," David said, "That my son continues to thrive. And I hope that my wife takes sufficient joy and pride in being his mother, such that she will not mind if he is an only son."

"You mean—"

"Yes. I have finished with her," he said. "I cannot divorce her. I have no cause. She has done nothing wrong, under our law and customs."

(His tone was dust-dry when he said "our law and customs.")

He went on, "And her family is powerful, and a divorce would cause trouble. But—there will be no more sons. She will be the mother of my only son, and nothing more. Never anything more."

"Oh, David," I said softly.

"My wife says that Hsaio-yen would make a fine nun," he said. "But I do not want my Little Swallow to be a nun. I do not want her to have to shave her head and wear coarse homespun cloth and live only on a handful of rice a day and maybe some cabbage— nuns eat no flesh food. I do not want her to live without music or laughter. I do not want her to sleep on cold stone, to spend the years that are given to her in hunger and empty toil, praying to gods who perhaps do not exist and in any case do not care." He bowed his head in grief. "But I cannot prevent it without further sorrow. And so I have done the only possible thing. I have taken her away."

Above us, the murmur of childish voices continued.

"How old is she?"

"Six."

"And I'm fifty. What's a woman my age going to do with a six-year-old child?" I asked. "And a Chinese one at that. How much English does she know?"

"A little. She learns quickly. You will send her to school. Does Miss Levy still have her establishment?"

"She does," I said, sighing. "Well, after all, if Aunt Polly could take in Tom and Sid at fifty, and survive, I ought to manage with one little girl."

David said. "She should not write to me directly. Later I will find a way for her to contact me, if she wishes. I should like to have news of her, though. Perhaps when Sally-John writes to me, she can tell me how Hsaio-yen does."

"And how'm I supposed to tell Sally-John that she's got herself a Chinese little sister?" I asked.

"I think you will find that she knows already," David said. "It was her suggestion, in fact, that I bring the child to you."

"Was it, now," I said. "Was it, indeed." Somehow the news did not surprise me.

"I must go," David said. "The ship sails two days from tomorrow."

"So soon."

"Yes. So, here are these documents," and he reached into a pocket and pulled out a packet wrapped in dark-blue cloth, "I have written out my daughter's lineage in Chinese and in English. Someday she will want to know it. Also there is money here—American money—and I will send more, of course, as time passes."

"You don't need to send money," I said. "I've got plenty."

"Save it for her education, then, or for her dowry," David said.

"All right."

"I do not know if we shall see each other again. I have missed you, Sarah Mary."

"I've missed you," I said.

"You have been lonely for too long. You should marry," he said.

"Who'd marry me?" I said.

"Any man with sense," he said.

"Well, that lets most of 'em out," I said.

"You're right." He leaned forward and kissed me on the cheek, which I believe surprised him nearly as much as it did me. "Thank you. I do not need to say, 'be good to her,' for I know that you will love her as your own."

"Take care of yourself," I said.

"I shall."

He smiled at me one last time, and then he was gone.

I went in search of my new daughter, and found her at the window, waving.

"Yes, he has gone," I said. "Do you understand?"

She nodded.

"All right, Miss Chung," I said. "We'll be going home soon. But I have one more errand in this benighted city."

***

I took a horsecar to the waterfront, and soon found myself standing in front of Mr Osterhouse's premises.

A Chinese in blue smock and trousers, his pigtail hanging over his shoulder, answered my knock. "Yes, Mr Osterhouse is here," he said in good English. "I will fetch him."

When Mr Osterhouse came out, he looked startled, but his expression cleared immediately and he beamed with pleasure. "My dear lady, what a surprise! Come in, come in."

I stepped inside the warehouse, which was stacked with wooden crates. The Chinese hovered in the background.

"Wu Wen, please wait for me in the office," Mr Osterhouse said. The Chinese bowed and disappeared through a wooden door with a window in it. Mr Osterhouse took both my hands in his and bent toward me. "I am honored, dear lady, at your visit. Dare I hope that you might enjoy a tour of our little concern?"

"Not so little, I'd say. Yes, I would enjoy a tour," I said.

"Excellent, excellent." He rubbed his hands together, looking pleased. "Wu Wen!"

The Chinese man's head and shoulders appeared in the window of the office door.

"Wu Wen, I am giving this lady a tour of our operation," Mr Osterhouse boomed. "Man the fort."

"Yes, Mr Osterhouse," the man's voice came faintly through the partition.

Mr Osterhouse took my arm and proceeded to show me over the supply depot, where the ingredients for the Elixir were sorted and stored for use; the "kitchen," as he termed it, where the Elixir was compounded in large brass kettles watched over by Chinese workers in clean blue smocks, and then filtered through a series of pipes to the bottling room, where more workers oversaw the filling and capping of the blue glass bottles, to the labeling room, where more workers pasted labels on the bottles, and to the warehouse, where the filled bottles were packed in crates well padded with straw and stacked for dispersal, and thence to the shipping room, where more workers filled orders for what Mr Osterhouse described as "our burgeoning mail-order trade."

"I engage in some mail-order business," I said. "It don't pay, though, what with shipping costs."

"Ah, but it is the wave of the future, madam," he said. "Many of my best customers live far from retail outlets, and they gladly pay those same shipping costs themselves."

That was something that hadn't occurred to me. "You mean, make the customer pay to ship the merchandise? That's brilliant," I said.

"Yes, isn't it?" he said. "I do not claim to have originated the concept. But it pays, madam, it pays." We strolled back along the side of the shipping depot to the front of the building and went back inside. There was a light on in the office; I could see an amber glow through the window in the door.

"I guess it does," I said. "You have quite an outfit here, Mr Osterhouse, quite an outfit."

"Thank you."

"No doubt my little store looks like pretty small potatoes to you," I said.

"On the contrary. Without retail establishments like your own, fully half of my own business would disappear."

"That's so."

"And for a woman alone to have made a success of her own business, that speaks highly to your intelligence and perseverance. In fact, Miss Williams, you really are a most unusual woman altogether."

"I suppose so," I said.

"I confess that I would be deeply honored to hear the chronicle of your success from your own lips," he said. "Will you, perhaps, dine with me this evening?"

"I would like to," I said, "But I have another engagement."

"Well," he said, "I am sure that my interests will occasion my traveling to your 'neck of the woods,' as they say, before too many weeks have passed."

"Well, fine," I said. "Let me know, and I'll take you up on that invitation."

"Good, good. Wu Wen!"

"Yes, sir?" The Chinese popped up in his window again, his silhouette dark now against the light behind him.

"Call a cab for this lady!"

"Sir!" Wu Wen vanished.

"Thank you for an interesting experience," I said.

Mr Osterhouse took both my hands in his. "It has been deeply gratifying to me, madam."

The cab drove up, and Mr Osterhouse helped me in.

"Well, goodbye," I said.

"Until next we meet," he said, and bowed. "Drive on!" he shouted to the cabbie.

As the cab pulled away, I looked back. He was standing in a spill of light from the open door, a solid, reassuring blocky figure. As I watched, he raised his hat, and I heard him shout, "Bon voyage!"

***

When I got back to the Thannheimers' it was nearly dusk.

"Sarah Mary, we have been wondering where you were," Ernst said.

"I had business."

"Ah. Gerda has packed Hsaio-yen's things. Are you leaving tomorrow?"

"I expect so."

"Are you sure you wish to take her, Sarah Mary? You can leave her here with us, if you'd rather," Ernst said. "One more won't make any difference."

"No, indeed," I said. "Her pa give her to me. She's mine."

And so, next morning, we went home, Hsaio-yen and I.

Chapter Twenty-Four: Sisters

I wrote to Sally-John right away, of course.
Her letter came quicker than I'd expected.

> *Dear Mama,*
>
> *I was glad to learn that you and Hsaio-yen made it safely to Tahoe City, and that Hsaio-yen has begun the new term at Miss Levy's school. What does Miss Levy think of her? Is she (I mean Hsaio-yen) learning English quickly? David has written to me that he believes she will pick it up fairly readily. He hopes she has inherited his facility with languages. He also writes that she is good at numbers. It occurs to me that she might be some help to you in the store, after school—that is, if Seraphim is agreeable. Is he as pompous as ever? Tell him hello for me.*
>
> *I will be leaving here in mid-December, as usual, and expect to be home as soon as may be.*
>
> *Please give my 'little sister' a hug and a kiss from her 'big sister.'*
> *Until Christmas,*
> > *Love,*
> > *Sally-John*

Some five months later, I was re-reading this missive and thinking how accurate David's prediction had been. Hsaio-yen now chattered fluently in English to everyone she met. She had learned to read it just as quickly, and now a small sum every month went to books that I ordered for her from a bookseller in the East, at Sally-John's recommendation.

"Seraphim!" I called. "Seraphim!"

"Yes, Missy Sarah?" His voice floated up the stairs.

"Has Hsaio-yen come home from school?"

"Yes, Missy."

The local roads and general traffic had improved so much since Sally-John's time at Miss Levy's that Hsaio-yen, along with two local girls, the daughters of an engineer and his wife who lived just outside of Tahoe, could ride to school on the milk wagon in the morning and travel back with the mail in the evenings.

"Mama Sarah, I have got the mail!" Hsaio-yen's voice floated up the stairs.

"I'll be right down," I said. I'd been upstairs in my room, going through chests and boxes, looking for Sally-John's old winter coat. I knew I hadn't given it to Solly for any of his girls, having a sentimental fondness for this particular garment, a gift to my daughter from Cassius and his Rogue River wife. It was Indian-made, of sealskin, with a hood and mittens to match. And somewhere there was a pair of child-sized kamiks, too. The cold weather would be coming soon, and Hsaio-yen was used to a softer climate than ours.

When I got downstairs, Hsaio-yen had already taken off her macintosh and leggings and was seated at my tall stool.

"I am minding the store," she announced. "Seraphim has gone to the barber's."

"Has he?" I stooped and kissed the top of her shining black head. She leaned against me for a moment. "Did you miss me, Mama Sarah?"

"I always miss you," I said. "But you like school, don't you?"

"Oh, yes, I like school very much," she said. "Miss Levy is ex-treme-ly sat-is-fied with me, she says."

The big words sounded quaint, coming from such a small body. The slight accent she still had made them sound even more so. "Does she?" I said, smiling, thinking how her English had improved. Except for a little difficulty with 'r's she sounded like she'd spoken it all her life.

Hsaio-yen nodded. "I have a lot of homework to do tonight," she said.

"What are you studying this week?"

"Miss Levy wants us to learn a poem by heart," she said.

"Any poem?"

"No. She gave us each a different one. And when we have learned them, we will have a recital," she said. "Everyone will be invited. We will have re-fresh-ments," she said. "What are re-fresh-ments, Mama Sarah?"

"Cookies," I said. "And candy, and punch."

"Punch?"

"A drink made with fruit juice," I said.

"I like re-fresh-ments," she said. "Will you hear me say my poem?"

"Yes, later," I said. "Look, here is Seraphim."

"How was the barber, Seraphim?" Hsaio-yen asked.

"He has taken off too much hair again," Seraphim said, looking gloomy. "Always happens. I say, 'just a trim,' and he takes off too much."

"You do look sort of scalped, come to mention," I said, surveying him. "What's the occasion, anyway? I wouldn't have said you was due to be barbered for another month."

"I wanted a haircut and a shave," Seraphim said, "Because I am going out to a party tonight."

"A party! Who is having a party?" Hsaio-yen asked.

"It is a church party," Seraphim said. "To dedicate the new window."

Seraphim's church—the Episcopals— in Placerville had recently put in the first stained-glass window the region had ever seen. It was a pretty thing, too, all blues and reds and greens.

"That sounds fine," I said. "Who are you taking?" I was teasing, because I knew that Seraphim was sweet on Alice Calumet, whose daddy owned the tavern.

Seraphim refused to say, though, and skulked on out of the store looking mightily aggrieved. I called after him, "Hope she likes you scalped as much as she does hairy!" but he pretended not to hear me.

"You should not tease him," Hsaio-yen said in her precise little voice. "He is very sen-si-tive."

"I have been teasing Seraphim since he was smaller than you," I said. "He expects it."

"He is in love with Alice Cal-u-met," Hsaio-yen said. "He bought her a hand-ker-chief all covered with roses, and a bottle of scent, and a comb for her hair, with diamonds."

"Rhinestones," I said absently. "Seraphim couldn't afford diamonds, even if we sold 'em, which we don't."

"Do you think they will get married?"

"Landsakes, child, how should I know? Probably," I said. "Why?"

"Because Seraphim said that if I help him to woo Alice, he will let me be a bridesmaid. I would like to be a bridesmaid," Hsaio-yen said.

"What does a bridesmaid do?"

Hsaio-yen was vague. "Oh, wear a pretty dress and carry flowers in the wedding pro-ces-sion," she said. "I love pro-ces-sions, don't you?"

"I don't know as I've even seen one," I said.

"Oh, Mama Sarah, how sad!" Hsaio-yen said in a sorrowful voice. "I used to see many, many pro-ces-sions back in China."

"You remember that?"

"Of course," she said. "I was six when I came here to America to live with you. I was not a baby."

"No, you were a big little girl," I said, laughing.

"That does not make sense," she said severely. "'Big' and 'little' do not go together."

"You're right," I said. "Tell me about the processions, back in China."

"Well," she said, "P-pa took me many many times—hundreds of times—"

"Hundreds?" I objected.

"Yes, hundreds," she said. "We saw all dif-fer-ent sorts of pro-ces-sions. Monks in orange and red, carrying shining brass pots of incense, and with banners flying, and brides in red robes and red and gold veils, in sedan chairs, with servants, and ox-carts carrying the bride's furniture and trunks, all dec-o-rated with flags and pen-nants, and children running alongside shouting, and drums playing, and sometimes flutes. And soldiers on big horses, with tall lances and guns, all shining bright, and some of them carrying banners too, with the names of their war chiefs painted in red and black. Every day or so a pro-ces-sion went past our house, and I watched from the gate with my amah, and sometimes she bought candy for us from a street vendor, if P-pa gave her the money. And u-su-ally he would."

It was almost as interesting to watch her as to listen to what she said, for her pretty little face lit up with remembering, and her eyes were bright when she said "P-pa."

"It must seem pretty tame around here," I said. "We don't have anything to compare."

"No," she said. "But I like it better here. And I like Ser-a-phim better than my amah. She used to pinch my arm when I was naughty, and she told me ghost stories that made me afraid in the night."

"I'm glad you like it here," I said. "Your pa thought you would."

For a moment her little face looked somber. "Will he come to see me some-time, do you think?"

I sighed. David's infrequent letters mentioned nothing about visits, being mostly tales of the unrest and continued famine in his province. He expressed hope that Hsaio-yen was growing well and directed her to obey me, to be dutiful, and learn her lessons, and that was all.

"I don't know, sweetheart," I said. "I hope so."

"If he comes for Ser-a-phim's wed-ding, he will see me in my bridesmaid's dress."

"Yes," I said. She was only seven. In a year she would be eight. Soon enough she'd be a big girl, big enough to dream of being a bride and not a bridesmaid. Perhaps in a few years the pain of separation would ease. I didn't really think it would, but I could hope.

"Smells to me like Seraphim's started dinner cooking," I said. "You can tell me your poem whilst we're waiting."

"Yes, Mama Sarah," she said, and got down off the stool. She rummaged in her school bag and pulled out a book. "It's a very in-ter-est-ing poem. It's by Robert Brown-ing. It's called 'The Pied Piper of Ham-e-lin.' Have you ever heard it before?"

"Can't say's I have," I said. "Let 'er rip."

The poem she read was something long—it went on for pages and pages, all about a pied piper who told some city leaders in Hamelin (wherever that was) that he would get rid of the rats that had been plaguing them for a long time.

Well, the piper played his pipe and the rats danced along and followed him, you see, and he made them all dance right into the river and drown. Then, after he'd gotten rid of the rats, the mayor and the council refused to pay him what they'd promised, so he played his pipe again and this time all the children come dancing away with him and disappeared forever.

I thought it was a sad poem, and said as much, though it had some funny rhymes in it.

"Why is it sad?" Hsaio-yen asked, putting down her book. "The children went away to a beau-ti-ful place. The poem says so."

"Ah, that's what the lame lad said, the one who couldn't keep up with the others," I said. "He might have been wrong."

(The piper didn't seem like a very pleasant character to me, and though I sympathized with his feeling ill-used when the Council refused to pay what they'd agreed on, it didn't seem fair in return for him to take all, or nearly all, of the children.)

357

"I believe the little lame boy. After all, it is a magic poem," Hsaio-yen said firmly. "Like the stories my amah used to tell me, about the girl who rode the dragon and saved the hand-some prince from his wicked uncle, the warlord."

"Is that a Chinese story?"

She nodded.

"Well," I said. "I haven't your acquaintance with magic. You'd have to ask Tom Sawyer about magical things—he knows about such."

"He was your friend when you were a boy," Hsaio-yen said.

"Who told you *that?*"

Coming out of the blue, so to speak, I was that startled, my question came out in a sort of squawk, like a scalded cat.

"Sally-John."

"For heaven's sake. Well, I was never really a boy," I said.

"I know," Hsaio-yen said. "It was magic."

"I suppose it was, in a way," I said. "All right, then. Say your poem again, if you really mean to get it by heart."

"All right," she said, and began:

> Hamelin town's in Brunswick
> By famous Hanover city;
> The River Weser, deep and wide
> Washes its walls on the southern side;
> A pleasanter spot you never spied;
> But, when begins my ditty,
> Almost five hundred years ago
> To see the townsfolk suffer so
> From vermin was a pity—
>
> > Rats!

She read on. I listened with half an ear, for the other half was remembering ...

Two youngsters lay under a tree by a wide, wide river that flowed lazily by, brown ripples gleaming under the midday glare of a summer sun. One was reading aloud while the other seemed to doze.

The words rolled out with Tom's best oratorical flourishes:

In Xanadu did Kublai Khan
A sacred pleasure dome decree
Where Alph, the sacred river, ran
Through caverns measureless to man
Down to a sunless sea ...

Tom Sawyer interrupted himself. "Huckleberry, wake up and listen. You ain't never going to amount to much if you don't learn to appreciate good literature."

Huckleberry yawned and tipped her hat down further over her eyes. "It's too blamed hot for poetry, Tom. Read about the Count of Monte Cristo instead. That's a rattling good story."

"I want to read poetry," Tom said. "Listen: don't this just give you the shivers? 'Through caverns measureless to man/ Down to a sunless sea.' Wonder what a sunless sea is?"

"Well, go on ahead and read, then," Huck said. "Just don't pester me no more about listening to it. I'm goin' back to sleep."

"The trouble with you, Hucky," Tom said, "Is just that you ain't got no imagination to speak of."

"An' you got too much. Spaniards an' A-rabs," Huck said. "Elephants an' camels an' sumpter mules loaded with di'monds."[78]

"You c'n sneer all you want," Tom said. "This here Samuel Taylor Coleridge, now: he knows what imagination is. Listen, Huck: 'For he on honey-dew hath fed/ And drunk the milk of Paradise.' "

Huck yawned again. "Milk of Paradise'—huh. Sounds more like he drunk too much of Pap's forty-rod."

"Huck, if you ain't the ignorantest—"

I sat up with a jerk. Hsaio-yen's voice had stopped, and she was closing her book. "I'll say it for you again, tomorrow," she said.

"All right," I said. "Let's go in and have dinner now."

She helped me lock up the store and pull down the shades. We put out the lights and went back to the kitchen to wash up.

***

Well, one day slid into another, and soon it was time for Hsaio-yen's recital. Miss Levy had timed it for the first week in October, so that the roads would still be clear of snow.

We'd had Miss Furbush, the local dressmaker, make us both new outfits for the occasion. Hsaio-yen had on a pale-blue muslin

---

[78] Eds. note: See *AOHF*, Chapter III.

dress with a sash of deeper-blue silk, and a silk bow the same color in her hair, with new white stockings and black strap shoes, also new. I wore a blue velvet ensemble trimmed in black-dyed Mongolian lamb, and a hat to match; Hsaio-yen said I looked "most imposing," and didn't I want to borrow her silver locket? This was the same locket that her father David had given to Sally-John when she was tiny. I'd gotten it out of its silk wrappings when I'd first brought Hsaio-yen home, and Sally-John had been wholehearted when I asked her if I could give it to her new little sister.

She'd written, "Of course you must—it was David's own mother's, and I'm sure some virtue must still cling to it. And it is something of his, which I'm certain will be as meaningful to her as it was to me."

Not for the first time, I reflected on the relationship between my elder daughter and her former nanny.

"No," I said. "You just wear your locket yourself, and think how proud your Papa would be if he was here."

"I believe he would be," she said. "Shall we go now?"

The recital was held in the school building, of course, and all of the children's parents and most of their relations seemed to be there, despite the cold weather and the several feet of snow that had fallen in the past weeks. Miss Levy had had some extra chairs brought in for those who couldn't fit into the children's desks (or who come in late) and we all sat and fidgeted for some minutes before Miss Levy come in and introduced herself and thanked us all for coming.

The children was all out in the porch waiting to be let in. I held my breath when Miss Levy opened the door and introduced them one by one. The youngest ones went first, they having too many fidgets to wait for their elders. So the boy who headed the primer class, a minute specimen of about five years, stood up, put his hands behind his back, and recited "The Boy Stood on the Burning Deck," to much clapping and cheering. Then the second grade representative stepped out, a little girl this time, with red curls and about a hundred freckles. She spoke her piece pretty well, though she bogged down a mite in the middle. I recall that it was a saddish selection, called "The Wreck of the Hesperus," by Mr Longfellow. She got a tremendous hand, and sat down looking well pleased with herself.

Then it was time for Hsaio-yen. Miss Levy introduced her:

"And, representing the third-grade class, Chung Hsaio-yen, whose adopted mother is your friend and neighbor, Sarah Mary Williams."

There was a little murmur of voices, and then Hsaio-yen started in.

Well, she sailed right on through to the end without a blink or a stutter, and when she was through I expected to hear the same kind of clapping and cheering as the little red-haired girl had gotten, but there warn't no applause at all.

I was startled, and swiveled around in my seat to see what the matter was.

Most of the folks present being parents and family of Hsaio-yen's classmates, I knew the greater part of them by sight if not by name. They looked back at me with stony eyes, and Hsaio-yen turned to Miss Levy and hid her face in her teacher's skirt.

I begun to clap again, all by myself, very loud.

Nobody joined me. And then, very soft but very clear, I heard the whisper: "Chink."

"Who said that?" I said, very fierce.

Silence. Then it came again: "Chink."

Miss Levy put Hsaio-yen to one side and said, "Thank you, dear, that was very good. Now, if you'll all give your attention, the fourth-grade reciter is—"

She went on to introduce the next child, and the next, right up to the big girls and boys of thirteen and fourteen, and I sat rigid in my seat and clapped when everyone else did—and never heard a single word.

All I could see was my Hsaio-yen, sitting in her blue dress with her book pressed against her chest and her black eyes shut tight to keep out the staring white faces. Her own face was palest ivory; there was no sign of tears, but I knew as if she had become part of my own body—as if she was in truth my own child—that she felt the hurt like a stab right to her vitals.

"Don't let them see it, Hsaio-yen," I whispered, and she must have heard, for she never let out a sound or gave them a look. And when the recital was over, I rose and passed among the crowd as if it did not exist, and took my daughter's hand and led her out of the schoolhouse. We rode home in the moonlight, both of us silent, and it warn't til I was helping her to get ready for bed that she finally spoke.

361

"I think my P-pa would be proud of me, don't you think so, Mama Sarah?"

"I know he would," I said. "Now, scoot on under the covers. That's right."

She lay in her little bed, looking up at me.

"Mama Sarah, what does 'Chink' mean?"

"It means that some folks have got big mouths and very small brains," I said. "I'm sorry you heard that. It's an ignorant way of saying 'Chinese person.'"

"Is it wrong to be Chinese?"

"No, sweetheart. It ain't wrong. Just different."

"Patty O'Malley has red hair," referring to the little girl who'd recited the Longfellow poem. "Nobody else in the class has red hair, so she's different, isn't she? Why don't folks call her names?"

"Some folks would," I said. "Some folks call red-haired Irish people 'Micks.'"

"Nobody called Patty a Mick, but they called me a Chink," she said.

"I know," I said. "It ain't fair."

"Miss Levy said I did very well. She's a good teacher, isn't she?"

"Yes, she is."

"Good night, Mama Sarah."

"Good night. Sleep tight."

When I closed the door to her room, I stood outside in the hallway for a long time, listening. But I didn't hear anything, just Hsaio-yen's soft breathing, and after a while I went downstairs.

In the office I opened the drawer to the file cabinet where I kept David's letters, and taking out the most recent one I read,

And if she comes in contact with the ignorant and fearful, she will hear herself called ugly names; this is something experienced by any Chinese who travels outside the Middle Kingdom. It is best that she hear it and learn to armor herself against it, for no one who is undefended can survive for long in this world. Sarah Mary, teach my daughter to be Chinese AND American, to love freedom and to honor her heritage, for those who would call her names are the enemies of liberty, and, in addition, they know nothing of the glorious history that lives on in my child's very bones and blood.

362

Of course, David, you are right, I thought. But what do ignorant folks like these know or care about your glorious history? Why, it's just the same as me, forty-odd years ago, trying to imagine Tom Sawyer's Spaniards and A-rabs and sumpter mules. *It's like having blinders on*, I thought. Worse. With blinders, a horse can only see what's dead in front of him, but people ain't horses. People ought to be able to see more; that's what Tom meant about imagination, only he took it for a game. It ain't a game; it's real. If you can't even begin to imagine that someone who looks different is really just like you, feels what you feel and thinks like you do, then it's easy to say "Chink," or "Mick," or "nigger." But giving folks names like that is just like putting blinders on a horse. *Oh, David*, I thought, *if only I had knowed these things all those years ago.* For me, for us, the blinders had come off too late.

I folded the letter and put it back into its file, closed the door, turned the key, and took myself off to bed.

***

There warn't no more public recitals the rest of that school year. When I went with Hsaio-yen on the last day of term, before Christmas, Miss Levy apologized for what she called 'an unfortunate incident.'

"It warn't your fault," I said to her, as Hsaio-yen cleaned out her desk.

"No. I had hoped for more tolerance from this community," she said. "After all, there are Mexican children in the school, and Indians, and—"

"And Irish," I said.

She smiled faintly. "And Irish. And then there is myself, as well—"

"What do you mean?" I asked, startled.

"Well, I am Jewish," she said. "Some people take exception to Jews, as you know."

"I have heard it," I said. "And I must confess it don't make sense to me at all. I ain't got—haven't—any religion of my own, to speak of, but most of these folks follow Jesus, don't they? And he was a Jew, or so I'm told."

"That is so," she agreed.

"It don't seem reasonable."

"No."

"Well, then," I said. "As far as the Chinese, I know that some

363

people say there's a problem with Chinese labor, but Hsaio-yen ain't about to take any jobs from anyone else, at least not for a few years yet—"

"I think the problem is racialist[79] rather than economic," Miss Levy said.

Racialist. I carried the strange word away with me. I had not known that there was a word for these feelings. That knowledge did not make me feel any better. In fact, I felt worse.

***

Soon it would be Christmastime, and Sally-John was coming home.

"Will she bring me a present?" Hsaio-yen asked.

"I expect so," I said. "Do you have a present ready for her?"

"I do," Hsaio-yen said. "I gave Seraphim the money, and he sold it to me. It is a secret."

"Even from me?" I pretended to be upset. Hsaio-yen saw through my pretense, though, and begun to giggle.

"Of course from you," she said. "It is only for sisters."

"Oh," I said. "Well, I never had a sister, so I suppose that's all right."

That made me think of Mary Jane Wilks, who was the closest thing to a sister I had ever had. I'd written to Mary Jane to tell her about Hsaio-yen, but hadn't heard back yet. Most likely a letter would come at Christmas; that was when folks mostly wrote to catch up with the home folks and those who were far away. I had ordered a present for Hsaio-yen and Sally-John both, but I warn't at all sure it would get to Tahoe City in time. I went out back of the store and crossed my fingers and spat three times for luck, and felt more hopeful. Maybe . . .

And then she was home. I was upstairs putting the last touches to her bedroom—hot-house roses in a vase on her night-stand, and a new lace dresser-scarf—when I heard the bell jingle as the store door opened.

"Mama! Mama! Where are you?" I heard her calling.

"Hold up, hold up," I shouted, "I'll be there terreckly."

---

[79] This term, no longer used, preceded "racist" by some decades.

When she come in, Hsaio-yen was sitting on a stool near the dry-goods counter, writing out a list of numbers on a pad of yellow paper.

"Hello, little sister," Sally-John said, plopping herself down on the counter. "Goodness, it's cold out." She peeled off her coat and scarves and mittens and held out a hand.

Hsaio-yen shook it gravely. "How do you do? I am pleased to meet you," she said.

"I am pleased to meet you, too," Sally-John said. She and Hsaio-yen both burst into giggles.

I waited for them to subside. "Hsaio-yen, will you mind the store for a few minutes? I want to speak privately to Sally-John," I said.

"Of course, Mama Sarah," Hsaio-yen said, putting down her pad and pencil and coming to stand next to the cash register.

Sally-John followed me to the kitchen. Seraphim was rolling out pie crust.

"Welcome home, Missy Sally," he said, his eyes shining with pleasure.

"Oh, Seraphim—pie! What kind?"

"Mince," he said.

"My favorite! Be sure and put lots of rum in it," she said.

"I open a new bottle last night," he said.

"You sure did," I said. "And drunk up half of it."

"Just tasting it," Seraphim said. "Got to see if it's all right."

In spite of myself, I had to grin. "I suppose that's so," I said. 'But you oughtn't to make a habit of it. That rum costs plenty—it comes clear around the Cape, you know, and it's mighty fragile cargo. Sally-John, come over here a minute." I pulled her to the far end of the kitchen and spoke low. "This is Hsaio-yen's first Christmas. I want it to be extra nice."

"Of course you do, Mama."

I said, "She's smart as a whip, and she knows more than she lets on. She suspicions that I have something up my sleeve, so to speak, but she ain't said nothing."

"Do you?" Sally-John said, smiling. "Have something up your sleeve?"

"I ain't about to tell you," I said. "Just make sure she stays upstairs until Seraphim calls us for breakfast, and you stay up there too, all right?"

"All right."

I could tell that she was puzzled, because in past years I'd always hung her stocking on the mantel in the back parlor, and she had leave to take it down and rummage as soon as she woke. Often she come running in before daylight, even, jumping up on my bed to wake me, showing off this present or that.

"See what Santa left!" she'd say, and I'd admire the doll or book or trinket.

"What about the stockings?" she asked now.

"I'll put them on your beds tonight. You can let her show you hers if you like." I smiled. "Maybe I'll get some sleep that way."

"Oh, no," Sally-John said. "I'll come in and show you my presents, just as I always have."

"Well, come ahead, the both of you," I said. "Just keep her upstairs until Seraphim calls."

"All right," she said.

We turned back to Seraphim, who had finished rolling out the piecrust and was busily fitting it to an enormous pastry dish.

"That looks like enough pie for a regiment," I said.

"Maybe we have visitors," Seraphim said. I shot him a warning look, and he bent back to his task. "Welcome home, Missy."

***

Our traditional celebration of Christmas always begun after supper on Christmas Eve, when the tree (a small pine chosen in summer and marked with a red ribbon) was brought in by Seraphim, placed in a bucket at one end of the parlor (the bucket being carefully covered with a red tablecloth arranged artistically by Sally-John), and decorated with paper chains, popcorn strings, gilded walnuts and such homemade baubles. In the past few years I'd added new ornaments from the stock I ordered from New York: strings of glass beads and "silver" tinsel (made from lead foil, actually) that reflected light in tiny sparkles.

We always had the same supper: bean soup and corn bread, to

save room for Seraphim's roast turkey and mince pie on the day itself. After supper, I read aloud from Sally-John's favorite Christmas books: "Twas the Night Before Christmas" and Mr Dickens's story about miserly old Mr Scrooge, *A Christmas Carol.*

I looked around me at the familiar scene. Familiar, and yet not so: Hsaio-yen sat cuddled up against her "big sister," and my daughter's cheek looked very brown next to Hsaio-yen's ivory one. Sally-John's hair was pinned up, but her curls still sprang out in every direction, while Hsaio-yen's hair fell stick-straight in a frame around her small face. Both girls were in their long ruffled nightgowns and both held mugs of cocoa.

I'd lit only the lamp by my chair, and the room was dim except for the pool of yellow light that fell on the book in my lap. Supper was over long since, and Seraphim had taken himself off to bed in his room behind the kitchen.

I pulled the lamp closer, settled myself, and began to read.

> Twas the night before Christmas,
> And all through the house,
> Not a creature was stirring,
> Not even a mouse . . .

As I read, I heard Sally-John softly whispering the words along with me. Hsaio-yen listened, and when the poem was over, she clapped her hands.

"That was beautiful, Mama Sarah," she said. "Is Saint Nick the same as Santa Claus?"

"The same," Sally-John said. "Mama, read *A Christmas Carol* now, please."

And so I began:

"Marley was dead, to begin with . . . "

The girls sipped their cocoa and nestled closer together. The tree in its corner gave off its fragrant smell. I read straight through to the end, then closed the book with a sigh. Mr Scrooge's transformation had always moved me, but the part of the book that spoke most to my heart was the visit he made to his childhood with the Ghost of Christmas Past.

It seemed to me as I grew older—especially now that Hsaio-yen had come to share my life—that the griefs of childhood never quite go away. We keep them within us in some secret place, and think ourselves grown beyond them, but they are still there, their power to hurt as sharp and strong as it ever was. Perhaps that is why so many grown people try to pretend that childhood is a time of innocence and sweetness. Anyone who was honest would have to disagree. And yet—

Even someone like me, who scarcely had a childhood: even I could remember a time when a day of sunshine and soft breezes felt like heaven, and a body wanted nothing more but to laze by the river under a green canopy of leaves. You could, if you sat very still, *feel* the river, the deep currents like a heartbeat, and the little ripples like music that you could almost but not quite hear, that came and went upon the shore.

The river had another face, when storms drove the ripples into waves that ate away at the shoreline and made the riverbanks give way. I had seen them soften and collapse as they turned from solid ground to yellow mud. People and animals and even whole houses might topple into the swirling water, and the child who saw it would run away from the river, to huddle in her empty hogshead and pull her scanty rags over her head and wait, cold and hungry, for the storm to end.

A child has no way to keep the horror out except by denying it.

Scrooge could keep himself alive only by becoming a stranger to his own life. In a way, he was as dead as Marley, when the story started. Only he didn't know it, until the Spirits came and showed him. Then he was able to come alive again, and that was what Christmas was for him—it was a rebirth. He was able to become, not like a child again, exactly, but to understand Christmas in the way a child might.

I never had any religion to speak of, so Christmas as the birthday of Jesus didn't mean much to me, and I suspected that the same was as true of Scrooge as of his creator, Mr Dickens. What seemed to matter to Dickens was the way that Christmas called to folks to come out of the lives they led—lives that were really like tombs, like Scrooge's cold and empty house was a tomb that held his body and the spirit inside it—to come out of those lonely lives and touch one another's hearts with tenderness and laughter and compassion—to eat and drink and play games and just love each other for who they were, without wanting anything more from them than that—

A child's voice broke into my reverie.

"What does that mean when the book says 'he kept Christmas'?" Hsaio-yen asked.

"It means he had Christmas just the way we do," Sally-John said. "With a tree, and good things to eat, and presents."

"Oh, presents," Hsaio-yen said softly. "I'd for-got-ten."

"Presents tomorrow," I said.

"From Santa," Sally-John said.

"Good night, girls," I said.

"Good night," they chorused.

I was the last to leave the room. I stood for a few minutes, taking deep breaths of the resinous scent of the Christmas tree. I put the books away, stirred the coals in the stove and laid on more wood for the night, and took myself off to bed, holding my lamp up high and watching the woman-shaped shadow that, as always, followed me as I climbed the stair.

***

Next morning, of course, both girls rushed in and flung themselves on my bed, their hands full of the contents of the stockings that I had stuffed whilst they slept.

"Look, Mama Sarah," Hsaio-yen said, holding up a paint-box. "Now I can make pictures for you!"

Sally-John cradled a jeweler's box. "It's beautiful, Mama." She lifted the box so that we both could see and admire the brooch inside. I had ordered it from Tiffany & Co. in New York, nearly a year before: a crescent moon in silver against a dark-blue enamel sky, with three tiny diamond stars. "Thank you," she said.

I leaned over and kissed her cheek. "Wear it with my love, dear."

For Hsaio-yen there was a French doll with real hair, black like hers, and brown eyes that opened and shut, and a trunk full of doll's clothes. Also several books, including Mr Tennyson's "Idylls of the King," which Miss Levy had recommended, and a new copy of *Alice's Adventures in Wonderland*, since Sally-John's copy had gone off to college with her, a beloved treasure in spite of its tattered condition.

"Let's read *Alice* tonight," proposed Hsaio-yen. "I'll read a chapter, then you."

"All right," Sally-John said. "Mama, open your presents now!"

Hsaio-yen, I knew, had chosen her gift for me with Miss

Levy's help, and had hidden it somewhere in the kitchen with Seraphim's connivance. Now she handed me a parcel wrapped in brown paper, about the size of my hand.

I undid the wrappings and gasped with pleasure.

"Oh, Mama," Sally-John said. "Hsaio-yen, did you do that all yourself?"

"Miss Levy showed me," Hsaio-yen said in a satisfied voice. "You like them, don't you, Mama Sarah?"

"I like them very much," I said, finding my voice. "They're just lovely, Hsaio-yen. Thank you, dear."

"They" were six linen handkerchiefs embroidered with my initials in blue, red, purple, black, green, and grey:

$$s\mathcal{W}_M$$

"That's very nice stitching," Sally-John said, examining them. "How long did it take you to do each one?"

"Oh, days and days and *days*," Hsaio-yen said. "I had to do them when Mama Sarah was busy, so she wouldn't see me."

I shook out the handkerchief with the red initials and tucked it into my belt so that the embroidery showed. "I'll use this one today."

Hsaio-yen clapped, and then Seraphim come in to thank me for his present (a bottle of rum and six pairs of wool socks), and to give the girls his gifts. For Sally-John he had made a box of fudge—three kinds: chocolate, penuche, and chocolate-walnut—for her to take back to college, and for Hsaio-yen he had made a platter of Christmas cookies in shapes of wreaths and fir trees and stars, all decorated with colored sugar and silver dragées. For me, Seraphim said, he had something very special, and he went back into the kitchen to fetch it.

"I wonder what it is?" Sally-John said.

"Maybe a cake," Hsaio-yen said. "Choc-o-late, with cherries!"

"Here it is," cried Seraphim, coming through the door. And there, following close on his heels, come another man, muffled to the ears in a thick woolen coat, and calling out to all of us in a familiar voice, a voice that we all loved: "Merry Christmas! Merry Christmas!"

It was David, of course. Both girls jumped up and ran to him.

And that was not all. Behind him we heard stampings and thumpings, and yet another visitor came leaping into the room on a blast of wintry air, this time a vast bulk in a cape the size of a carpet, with a hat tied down with a red scarf, and another scarf, a blue one, wrapped around his neck, the whole enterprise jammed down tight over greying side-whiskers.

"Mr Osterhouse!" I said.

"The very same, the very same," he said, taking off scarves and hat and gloves and heaping them on a chair, then bestowing the cape over all.

"Merry Christmas!"

***

Well, that was a wonderful reunion. Hsaio-yen flew to her Papa's arms. (She spent most of the day on his lap, holding her doll and smiling a blissful smile.) Sally-John ran to hug her Ah-Bok and found, to both her and his surprise, that she was fully as tall as he.

"You have grown into a young woman," David said, and he smiled at me over Hsaio-yen's shining head. "It's a good thing I still have my Little Bird here. Christmas is for children, after all."

"There I must disagree," Mr Osterhouse said. He had settled himself in the big chair by the stove, and was holding out his hands to its warmth. "I like Christmas pretty well myself, and I'm no spring chicken."

"What is that, 'spring chicken'?" asked Hsaio-yen, peeping out from her father's coat skirts at this giant.

"It means, my dear young lady, that I am no longer young," Mr Osterhouse said.

"Are you as old as Mama Sarah?"

"Older."

"Then you must be very very old indeed," Hsaio-yen said.

This brought gales of laughter at my expense. "I ain't so very old," I said. "And I agree with Mr Osterhouse. Christmas, seems to me, is for everyone, of any age. And I certainly do like my present," I finished.

"Thank you," David said. "I had quite the time getting here, though. If it hadn't been for your friend Mr Osterhouse, I'd still be in San Francisco."

"Mr Osterhouse is a business associate," I said.

"And friend," Mr Osterhouse put in.

"When I got to San Francisco I was afraid at first that I would not be allowed to land," David said. "The immigration authorities do their best to keep Chinese out, you know—"

371

"I know," Mr Osterhouse said grimly. "I employ quite a few of your countrymen. Sometimes I have the dickens of a time getting them out of the hands of the harbor police."

"Yes," David said. "Since the Exclusion Act was passed earlier this year, only Chinese who can prove they were born on American soil can pass freely in and out of any port. And in San Francisco, Dennis Kearney and his thugs make walking on the streets a hazardous endeavor for any Chinese. And Chinatown itself is not safe."

"How did you manage?" I asked.

"Why, Mr Osterhouse met me at the ship and told the authorities that he would vouch for me," David said. "And so we travelled up here together, he and I." He grinned at me. "It gave us a good opportunity to become acquainted."

"I've told your Ah Bok that he can come to work for me any time he wants to change China for the States," Mr Osterhouse said to Sally-John.

"So you know about my Chinese nanny," I said.

"Oh, he filled me in all right," Mr Osterhouse said. "And about your new little daughter here."

"How did you come to meet David's ship, Mr Osterhouse?" I asked. "That seems like quite a coincidence."

"It was nothing of the sort," Sally-John broke in. "I wrote to Mr Osterhouse and asked him to do it."

"You did!" I could only stare at her, amazed.

"Yes, I did. I knew that he'd have trouble, and also that Mr Osterhouse is well known to employ Chinese and to vouch for them."

"Ah." I looked at my pretty dark-haired daughter. "And how did you learn about Mr Osterhouse and his Chinese workers?"

"Why, Mama, you told me, yourself," Sally-John said.

"I did?"

"You wrote to me about Mr Osterhouse ages ago," she fished in the pocket of her skirt. "Here it is." She waved the letter.

I recalled writing it only too well.

"I would like to tell you about a man I have met," I had written. "He is a large and bulky person with long side-whiskers and an orotund, pompous voice. He's a snake-oil salesman and a rogue, but I like him nonetheless," the letter went. "He sells those blue bottles of Elixir that are so popular; I am sure you have seen them even in New York State. I imagine that he is getting rich from selling the stuff. One of the most interesting things about him is that he employs only Chinese workers. I suppose that he can pay them less than Americans—he seems a shrewd enough businessman to take advantage of such a thing."

I cringed a bit, recalling other passages just as uncomplimentary. "Put the letter away, if you please," I said hastily. "Mr Osterhouse, I do thank you for your having helped David to come to us. It is a great surprise and a joyful one. Will you stay to Christmas dinner, sir?"

"I was hoping to be asked," he said. "That turkey smells mighty good."

Chapter Twenty-five: Frisco

I expected that Mr Osterhouse had not come a-visiting just to be social. And in fact it was not long before he put his new proposition to me, which was that I would advance the money to finance the expansion of the Elixir business to the eastern part of the country. Mr Osterhouse had an option on a factory in Philadelphia. We spent several days going over the details, and in the end I agreed to provide $25,000 in capital in return for one-third share in the company.

Where was the money to come from? There was no difficulty there. You may recall that I'd received $5000 from Mr Twain a few years earlier. I'd added that sum to what I had invested over the years. Allowing for what I needed to keep in reserves, I still had over $100,000 that I could draw from, in cash and property. I had to give Mr Osterhouse full marks for finding out just how considerable my assets was, as well as for making a successful pitch to part me from some of them.

"My dear lady," he said, "We can't lose."

And of course he was right.

That Philadelphia factory was soon churning out thousands of blue bottles every month of the year, and shipping them to retailers from Florida to Maine. Mr Osterhouse and I went into partnership in 1881; by 1882 we was seeing a return of over twenty percent, and by 1884 our profits grew so sufficient as to sustain us through one of the worst depressions the country had ever seen. We weathered those hard times in fine shape. In fact, we managed not only to hang on but to expand. Mr Osterhouse was fond of saying that you could find a bottle of Elixir in every medicine cabinet in America, and he was probably right. At any event, we got richer and richer— and we also become better and better friends.

He was a rogue—true enough. But a jolly sort of a one, and—this is a quality that is unusual in a businessman—he was completely without malice.

In plain fact, he was kind, one of the kindest men I'd ever met. And he didn't show off his kindness, neither. I found out about it mostly by accident, like when I'd review a stack of business statements and find listed a receipt for a sum of money he'd been paying to a worker who'd been sick for months.

"What's this?" I'd ask. "You've been paying this man wages

for no work."

"Oh, yes. Huang Erh. Well, he's got a wife and five children to feed. He'll come back to work once he's well. I'm holding a foreman's slot for him. He'll make good; you'll see."

And then I found out he was paying school fees for some of his workers' children. He'd even sent two boys to Yale College—the same Yale College that Tom Sawyer'd gone to.

"Their fathers have worked hard for me, and their sons are very bright young men," he said. "They deserve a chance in this country—a better chance than their fathers will ever have, for all their labor. It will prove a reliable investment in the end," he went on. "The Chinese community is behind me—behind us—a hundred percent. You can't buy support like that."

"You seem to be able to," I said drily.

"It's just simple good business," he said, but I was not fooled.

When he come to visit, I saw that he paid close attention to those whose lives were tied to mine. For Seraphim he usually brought some exotic cooking utensil or a packet of spices or fancy chocolate. He had a soft spot for Hsaio-yen, always bringing her a present whenever he come to visit—a book, usually, or some bit of lacquerware or porcelain from China. "Here you are," he'd say, "A bit of your ancestral homeland, to console you in your exile here in Silver Mountain." His pronunciation of the Chinese for this—Yin Shan—always made her laugh.

And he made me laugh as well. Not the kind of laughing that goes along with joking or making game of someone. Although he could tell a funny story, it was never the kind that showed people up or made them look foolish. He had what wears better on a body than good looks or good manners or even high intelligence: he had the most and good humoredness that I have ever met in any human being—kind of a largeness of heart that went along with his big body and big voice. (In that, if in nothing else, he reminded me of Jim.)

How can a person mark when feelings begin to change, and you see someone you thought you knew with new eyes?

I won't deny that I begun to feel an unaccustomed pleasure at the news, whenever I received word to expect a visit. Nor will I deny that I begun to take a lively interest in what Seraphim planned for dinner on such occasions, and to suggest that Mr Osterhouse was fond of beef and dumplings, or that perhaps we could have peach pie, which was Mr Osterhouse's favorite. And I began to take more pains with my own appearance than I'd done formerly, and to wear red whenever he was expected, because he'd said that it became me.

And so it went, until his visit on one bright October day.

"Miss Williams," he said, "I hope and trust that you are aware that I hold you in the highest possible esteem." He was sitting across from me in the parlor. We had just returned from luncheon at the hotel. Mr Osterhouse, I recall, was wearing a plum-colored coat, black trousers, and a waistcoat of cream satin embroidered with tiny purple flowers. His cravat was plum-colored as well. Above it his ruddy face beamed at me.

"I am glad to hear it," I said, sitting there in garnet velvet, with my hair done up becomingly (so the hairdresser had assured me) in puffs and twists. "Likewise."

"Do you mean that?" he said. "For if you feel the same as I, then let me be brave and ask you this: have you ever entertained the thought of changing your estate?"

"I think it's time to put my cards on the table, before I answer," I said. "And I'll ask you to show me yours as well."

"All right," he said.

"I ain't never been married," I said. "If that's what you mean."

"It is. Neither have I," he said.

"I have a daughter who was born out of wedlock," I said.

"Ah. I suppose," he said, "that that might matter to some men."

"It don't matter to you."

"Not a whit."

"Well, then," I said. "Her pa was a colored man. Or let's say he warn't white."

"Is that the case? That would explain the warm hue of your daughter's complexion, and also the profusion and luxuriance of her ebony curls," he said. "Her pa, as you call him, must have been a handsome fellow."

"So that don't matter to you neither."

"My dear lady, why should it? These events are past and gone. You did not marry him at the time. Why not?"

"We never talked about marrying."

"And he left you?"

"Yes. But he never knowed about Sally-John. And then he died. He has a sister, though, and a step-mother. They know. We ain't close, but we visit now and again. His sister has a girl about Hsaio-yen's age, in fact."

He brushed all this aside. "Would they object to your marrying, after these many years? Would your daughter?"

"I reckon not."

"Are you concerned about Hsaio-yen? Would she object?"

"No. She likes you." That was true.

"She will be going away to school soon in any case. You will be lonely without her."

"I don't mind being alone."

He looked down at his clasped hands. "Until recently, I could have said the same. You know, I have never wanted to marry any woman before."

"Then why me? Why now?"

"My dear Miss Williams, let us be frank," he said. "I am a man facing the final years of life. I have no ties, no relations, nothing in this world but a business—true, it is a successful one—and many memories." He cleared his throat. "I find that memories are a poor substitute for the prospect of the kind of lively affection that is ideally shared by a husband and wife."

"That sounds fine," I said. "But how can I be sure that all this ain't just a sly way of getting control of my property?"

"I don't suppose," he said, and those genial blue eyes turned steely for a moment, "That I could persuade you otherwise, if you really believed that to be the case."

"You're right," I said. "I apologize."

"Accepted. And so I take it," and his eyes were warm and merry again, "That you do not in fact suspect me of any such evil scheme?"

"No," I said, "But also I don't pretend to understand why you want to change the arrangement we've got. It seems to work all right."

"Ah. That puzzles me as well," he said. "For I swore long ago that I'd never allow sentiment to dictate how I'd comport myself in business. And I swore also that love was not an emotion I'd allow to get in the way of attaining the success I dreamed of."

"And now?"

"Now none of that success seems to matter, my very dear

377

Miss Williams, if you are not a part of it."

"We're in business together."

"That's not enough any longer," he said. "For, you see, I am no longer content with a mere business arrangement. I want you to be my wife."

"Are you saying that you love me, Mr Osterhouse?"

"It would seem so, my dear lady; it would seem so." He leaned toward me and put one hand on his chest, being careful not to crush his cravat. "This heart no longer possesses any defense against Cupid's darts." He settled back in his chair and clasped his hands on the table. "I have declared myself. Will you be mine?"

I looked across the table at him, at his curly black-and-grey whiskers (of which I knew he was extremely vain), at the absurd way his eyebrows flared into owl-like tufts at the ends, at his potato nose and double chin, at the small blue eyes that shone with such benevolence out of that large, bland, ruddy face. It was not a handsome face, but it had become very dear to me.

His eyes beamed at me, and I felt a kindling warmth begin to stir in my heart, a warmth I had not felt for any man since Johnny rode away forever.

I reached across the table for his hand and I said, "The answer's yes."

We sat there, hands clasped, for some minutes, and then he said, "My dear Miss Williams, you see before you a completely happy man."

"Good," I said. "Now perhaps you'll oblige me by telling me your real name."

***

Love is well known to cause the victim (if that is the right word) to go what Tom Sawyer used to call "soft in the head." However, though my feelings for Mr Osterhouse were strong enough for me to call them "love," I didn't see, then or later, why I should allow those feelings to take over whatever good sense I still possessed.

"My real name," Mr Osterhouse repeated. "Well, my dear 'Miss Williams,' I could ask you the same question."

"And I'll answer," I said. "But—you first. If you please."

"Have I ever been other than honest and aboveboard in our dealings?"

"Probably," I said. "But I'm willing to overlook the past."

"Well, then," he said, and his small blue eyes danced, "As long as we're going to be completely open with one another—"

"You first," I repeated.

"Of course."

Here, in my best recollection of his own words, is what he told me:

You are correct, dear lady, in your assumption that my original appellation was not in fact the euphonious collection of syllables that constitutes my current public identity. I was born plain Theodore Oster in a small Ohio village called Paradise Falls. My father was of German ancestry; he grubbed a small but adequate living from the soil. My mother died when I was five, and my father remarried a woman who conceived such a dislike for me that nothing would serve but that I should be made to leave home and be sent to school. I was then seven years old.

My stepmother chose the institution, which was run by the Religious Society of Friends—the Quakers. I suppose that she chose it because it was cheap, rather than from any personal conviction, for she was not a member of that Society. And so I was sent. I received the rudiments of an education in that place, but two years later I fell ill and was returned to my home for a prolonged convalescence.

The malady which seized me began with a fever and progressed to a profound lethargy and weakness. Eventually I was confined to my bedchamber, and I did not leave the compass of those four walls for some months.

During that time, reading was my only solace. My father undertook to join a subscription library, and books arrived weekly by mail, offering me a refuge within their pages from my stepmother's strident harangues. She believed that I was malingering, and if my father had not prevented her, would many times have forced me from my bed . . . on one such occasion she belabored me with her tongue to such an extent that my father, who was the mildest of men, shouted and stormed at her to cease, raising himself to such a pitch of excitement that he was struck with an apoplexy. He died two days later.

After the funeral, my stepmother, citing my many delinquencies and deficiencies, bound me over to a pharmacist. She paid the apprenticeship fees with a share of my father's estate and kept the rest for herself. In a year, she sold the house that had been ours and moved away. I never saw her again.

The pharmacist, Dr Ettinge, was a learned man who had aimed for a medical degree but discovered in himself such fastidiousness, indeed such delicacy, that confrontation with illness or injury was impossible for him to manage. Consequently, he took up the preparation and dispensation of medicaments and was moderately successful. He treated me well, and I might have gone on to

379

succeed him, for he was a bachelor without relations of any kind.

However, he made some unfortunate investments and was ruined, and his property was seized and sold to pay his debts. He himself took to drink and died a pauper; I, being still a minor, for I was had just passed my thirteenth birthday, was conveyed by law to yet another master, this time a coal merchant who was ready to overlook my lack of brawn in return for my ability to write and figure.

I decided to run away, and as luck would have it, a traveling circus had come to town and was about to continue on its way. I waited until my new master had gone asleep, stole out of his house, and took up a new and more congenial way of life. This continued for five years, during which, as I have related, I made the acquaintance and became the assistant of the late, great Professor Marvel—born Jacob Grossmeyer in New York. He taught me all that he himself knew, and upon his retirement, sold me his wagon, his horses, and all of his equipment, for which I gladly paid the sum he requested, which amounted to a mere bagatelle—that is to say, my entire savings.

And so I became—

"A snake-oil salesman," I interjected.

"Just so."

"Please continue."

I took my erstwhile mentor's example and rechristened myself: Theophilus Osterhouse sounded more impressive than Theodore Oster! I chose a middle name that seemed to me to bespeak a certain solidity, nay, even nobility, of heritage, and as Professor Theophilus VanDerWalk Osterhouse I pursued a most remunerative career as a traveling purveyor of various nostrums and remedies.

I pride myself that the "snake oil" I sold was not valueless; I had always taken care to learn of those who knew something of healing—I have spoken to you before of my sojourns in various locales. I also endeavored to learn what I could from whatever published sources were available, and amassed a small but valuable library; I retained some of what I had learned from my first master, the pharmacist, and I was able in time to present myself and my products—my preparations—as at least the equivalent if not the superior to what the ordinary druggist could, for a fee, provide.

And then the war came.

I had never been one to argue politics, such argument being generally bad for business and prone to cause contention, but I confess that my travels had borne in on me the sorry fate of the Negro slaves who toiled so that their masters need not. Although I had spent the better part of two decades far from my Ohio home, I recalled my father's confident pronouncement that the evil of slavery would someday end, and his equally fervent but fearful contention that abolition would come only at the cost of many lives and through no peaceful means.

When the President called for volunteers, I was ready; I presented myself to the recruiters, who dismissed my desire to serve at arms—"we don't need no more old farts," they said, although I argued that I was only just turned thirty, but they readily hired me for transport duty. And, in the event, I was able to serve, for the war went on so long and our regiment sustained such losses that men even older and less able than I were equipped for combat and directed to join our comrades on the front lines.

I was no soldier, and perhaps my capture by Rebel forces was inevitable. The Johnny Rebs were contemptuous of my age and bulk, but I had the last laugh, for my captors had all themselves died of wounds or disease when I staggered out of Andersonville Prison a free man once more.

I joined a band of similar refugees who struggled through the swamps and ruined fields of Georgia up along the Carolina coast and thence to Virginia, and finally I reached Washington, where I worked for a time as an orderly at the Army hospital there, for I was not yet mustered out. When the surgeons there discovered that I had had training as a dispenser, I was given the duty of helping to compound medicines, salves, ointments and lotions for the sick and wounded.

This allowed me to begin the process that led to my own return to health, for I now had access to a full complement of materials with which to concoct various remedies, including many herbs, the uses of which had been revealed to me in my earlier travels. Having completed my military service at last, I purchased an ancient cart and an equally venerable nag, equipped myself with a few basic supplies, and returned to the profession which availed me the greatest likelihood of survival if not prosperity. I was once more Professor Osterhouse, and I was well on the way to perfecting what would become Osterhouse's Elixir. And in a few years I had prospered to the extent you yourself have witnessed.

"Your turn," he said.

I took a deep breath.

"Have you ever read the book *The Adventures of Tom Sawyer?*" I began.

Well, he had, thanks to goodness, and so I didn't have to do very much explaining, once I got it through his head that I started out in life as someone very different from the Sarah Mary Williams sitting across from him, that it was I who had been "the pariah of the village," the ragamuffin with whom Tom had witnessed a murder, stalked a killer, and discovered a chest full of gold.

"You mean to say," he finally got out, "That Mark Twain's book relates true and actual events?"

"Well, some of it he made up," I said. "For instance, that whole part about goin' to our own funerals—we never done—did—that, and Tom warn't so very sweet on Becky Thatcher back then as the book makes it seem, though he did fall in love with her later."

"But the people and events—?"

"Mostly true and real," I said. "There was a murder, and Injun Joe did die in the cave, and we did find the gold. I invested my share with Judge Thatcher, and even taking out what I did to move out West and start the Emporium and raise Sally-John and all, I still have somewhere in the neighborhood of a hundred thousand, I'd say, in gold and securities."

He sat there and looked at me with the most indescribable expression I have ever seen on another human being's face.

"And in between finding the gold and making your way out West, what happened then?"

So I went on and told him about having to decide to be a girl, and how I managed it.

He laughed when I told about Mary Jane helping me turn myself into a girl, especially when I got to the part about all the different pieces of underclothes.

"And yet you've turned into quite a fashionable woman," he said, still chuckling. "I don't believe I've ever seen you in male attire."

"I seldom do wear it, these days," I said. "Only for riding astride, and then I wear a split skirt over my riding trousers, so as not to cause a commotion."

"I can't picture you riding sidesaddle," he said.

"I did learn how, once," I said, and told him about Miss Edwards's school.

"You were unhappy there," he said.

"I was. Until I met—someone." I hesitated. I'd never mentioned Antoinette to anyone, ever. Not even Johnny.

"Did you ever love someone," I asked him, "Who you oughtn't to have loved?"

"You mean, someone too high for my reach?"

"Not exactly . . . more like someone folks wouldn't understand your loving the way that you did."

He shook his head, then stopped. "I suppose—"

And he told me this story:

Her name was Penny. She was only a mongrel, small, about the size of a fox terrier, but with curling copper-colored fur—hence the name. I'd had her from babyhood; she and I were the same age exactly. She slept in my bed, at least until my stepmother came. Then dogs on beds were forbidden, and I had to smuggle her upstairs after everyone else had gone to sleep. (It was easy enough to sneak her downstairs in the morning, in all the commotion of breakfast and fire-making and washing up and getting ready for school and chores). Even after my stepmother came, Penny was my companion in all my boyish deeds—she fished with me, swam with me, walked with me, sat by my chair at meals, waited for me every day after school, listened to my daydreams and childish hopes. I almost believed that she could speak, if she wished—her eyes were that eloquent.

My stepmother did not like dogs—they were dirty, they shed hair, they had fleas, they were noisy—and she said once too often that Penny was a pest and should be got rid of, but my father at least on that one occasion stood his ground. "It's the boy's dog, his pet," he said to her in my hearing. "It was a gift from his own mother. Leave the beast alone, and the boy too." She hated me even more after that, both because I had witnessed his forbidding her to do what she wanted, and because in her eyes I had led him to mention the woman who had preceded her. My stepmother had banished all mementoes of my mother from the house—her pictures, her curtains, the little rug she wove that always lay before my father's chair. Nothing remained of my father's dead first wife but Penny—and I.

She died the first year after I was sent away to school. Of a distemper, I found out later—much later.

She died, but they lied to me; they said that they had given her away— my dog. The only thing I had to love, the only being who loved me, since my mother's death. They said that they had given her to a farmer in the next town, who'd wanted a dog for his children to play with. "You were away at school. You had no need of a dog, and the beast was pining," my father said to me, and I remember that I shouted at him, for the first time in my life, "If she was pining, it was for me! You had no right to give her to someone else."

Eventually the truth came out. My father tried to smooth things over. "We didn't want to upset you, telling you that she was dead," he said, and I flashed back at him, "Didn't you realize that it would be far more upsetting, as you term it, to learn that she belonged to someone else?"

To that he had no answer. It was, I think, the only time I ever saw my father's eyes wear an expression of shame.

"What did your stepmother say?" I asked.

"Ah. She only said that it was more childish foolishness, although that was all she had come to expect from me, and if I couldn't take the loss of a dog with more manly fortitude, I would find that the world would deal harshly with me when I became in truth a man."

"And what did you say then?"

"I said that she was an evil woman and I hoped that she would die. And for that my father beat me—the only time in my life he ever laid a hand on me in anger—and shortly after I was sent back to school, a week before term, because, my father said, I had hurt my stepmother's feelings so badly that she could not bear to have me in the house."

He stopped speaking and sat for a long moment with his hands on his knees and his eyes closed.

"The loss of my dear companion was grievous," he said. "But I think even worse was that they had lied to me, my stepmother and my father—and such a lie. A really diabolical lie. I don't think," he went on, "I don't think that I ever trusted him again, after that. The woman, I had never trusted, and now I was but confirmed in my belief that she was Satan in human form." He turned to me. "But you asked me, had I ever loved where I ought not."

"Yes, I did," I said. "Because I loved someone, long ago, and was betrayed."

"A common enough event, in human life," he said. "The entire corpus of literature deals with love and betrayal when it does not deal with hate and war."

"That's true enough," I said.

"You told me that you searched for your mother, after you left your school," he said. "I take it that that ended with a betrayal of some sort, as well?"

It took all my courage to tell it, but I managed. The better part of the afternoon had gone by when I had done. These was things I'd never told another human being and never had expected I would.

As for what had happened with Antoinette—I'd never spoke her name before, not to any human soul, and did not now. But I did relate the story of my search for my mother, and its dreadful end—when I described what had happened to me at the hands of my blood relations, and how I'd lived in terror that William might someday find me—he said not a word, but only took my hand gently in his and sighed.

"And so I come up here to the Sierras, only I started out in Virginia City, at first," I said. "And that is where I met Sally-John's pa. And here is a wonderful thing—" and I told him about how Johnny was Jim's son, and a little about who Jim was.

"He sounds as though he was a far better father to you than your own 'Pap,' as you called him," Mr Osterhouse said. "I wish I might have known him."

"I would be a very different person if it hadn't been for Jim," I agreed.

"I take it that your enterprise in Virginia City was as successful as the concern that you have built here?"

"It was. Do you know, Mr Mark Twain was there as well?"

"Really? Did you meet?"

I told him about the town and the people, then, and about how bad I felt when folks I thought were friends had taken against me.

"I've thought since," I said, "That perhaps I ought not to have left Virginia City. I should have stayed and brazened it out."

"Maybe you could have done so," he said. "Or maybe you and your daughter would both have starved."

"That's so," I said. "I guess I made the right choice."

"Whether or no," he said, "It was a lucky choice for me, to find you here on the shores of this heavenly lake, on that fateful day—when was it? Ah. It was in October—"

"It was August," I said. "And you stomped off in a temper when I told you I was all out of those fancy cheroots you like."

"I did?"

"Said I ought to carry a better stock of goods."

"Hmm. And you allowed me to return and darken your door again?"

"You had something you wanted to sell, and I wanted to buy."

"So it was purely business?"

"At that point it was."

"When did it change?"

"When you first made me laugh."

"It is my fate, to be only a clown, a figure of mirth—"

"I do not depise mirth," I said. "Having had little enough of it."

"Perhaps, if we spend time together, you will amass more."

"I hope that's so," I said. "It comes strange to be talking about—love, for instance."

"But you have loved," he said.

"I have," I said.

"You have a lot more courage than I," Mr Osterhouse said finally. "As I said a while since, I have never loved anyone besides myself, until now."

"I don't know if you can call it *courage*," I said. "Mostly, I have done what seemed to need doing, is all."

"Ah," Mr Osterhouse said. "Would you be surprised to learn, my dear Miss Williams, that I envy you the loves that you have experienced—even those that caused you pain and grief?"

"I would be very surprised to hear that," I said. "Grief and pain don't seem to me to be anything to envy."

"Nothing in life comes free," he said.

"That's a fact," I said.

He was silent for a moment. Then he said, "Did Mr Twain ever write that book about Huck?"

"No, not so far's I know," I said. "He did say once that he'd begun it, but didn't come to finish it."

"If he does," Mr Osterhouse said, "I wonder how much of the truth he'll tell."

"Only as much as will sell," I said. "That is one way that you remind me of Mr Sam Clemens. The both of you have a clear eye for what sells and what don't. Only," I added, "You seem to have better success at business than he has had."

"Business is business," Mr Osterhouse said. "Perhaps Mr Twain should, so to speak, stick to his last."

"Pardon?"

"He has had success as a writer. Perhaps he ought not to try for worldly gain in any other field."

"He's always coming up with some scheme or invention that will make him 'rich beyond the dreams of avarice,' as he once said to me."

"That's quite an ambition. Do you know why he desires such wealth?"

"Well, his wife comes from well-to-do folks," I said. "I suspect that quite a good part of Mr Twain's ambition is aimed in that direction."

"A wife can indeed inspire a man."

"I suppose so," I said.

"I am not, myself, looking for inspiration," Mr Osterhouse

said. "Never having thought that I, myself, would ever take a wife."

"Let alone a wife who started out as a boy," I said.

"Indeed."

"It warn't the easiest way to start out," I said.

"No. I must confess, however, that I do hope Mr Twain will finish the book," Mr Osterhouse said.

I said I'd just as lief he didn't, but in any case it had nothing, really, to do with me. Not any more. It was all too long ago, and nobody would believe it anyway.

***

Well, of course I was wrong on all counts.

Mr Twain did finish. The book was published in 1884, the same year that Mr Osterhouse and I tied the knot. And although it come in for a great deal of harsh criticism ("trashy" and "vulgar" was only two of the epithets aimed at it), it did sell. Nobody in Tahoe City knew that I had once been Huckleberry Finn, of course, but some folks in other places did know, and some of them wrote to me. I have kept a few of the letters.

Tom of course sent a telegram straight off:

DEAR HUCK STOP THOUGHT I'D CALL YOU THAT ONE MORE TIME IN HONOR OF THE BOOK STOP DIDN'T MR TWAIN DO A BULLY JOB STOP WELL WE ARE BOTH FAMOUS NOW STOP LOVE, TOM

Tom had asked for the message to be delivered to Miss Williams, of course, but all messages get read out by the operator when they come in, and Mr Whipperson at Western Union did give me some awful funny looks for a while, after Tom's little joke.

Most of the letters was from Missouri folks. Mary Jane Wilks wrote a beautiful one, signed with a whole row of kisses.

She could not come to the wedding, for her husband was very ill with heart trouble and she did not want to leave him (he died soon after). Mr Twain did not come, either, although I did send him an invitation. But Tom Sawyer and Becky made the trip—Tom was in fact a Senator by this time, and very grand; he'd put on a great deal of weight and was even more portly than the bridegroom. Cassius and his wife Snow-on-the-Mountains come, and Ernst and Gerda Thannheimer come along with young Albert Thannheimer and his beautiful wife Melinda and their baby son Josef. Elizabeth and her husband Mr Drewery made the trip from Missouri, with Elizabeth's stepmother Julie and their little girl Julia. My Sally-John stood up with me, and David was Mr Osterhouse's best man. Yes, David made the journey, and Hsaio-yen was a bridesmaid, just as she'd wanted to be. Miss Levy was there, and she and Sally-John had a regular love feast. Solly and his family come all the way from Lamy, New Mexico, and Seraphim made a cake that was too big for any table in the house; we had to put boards across two trestles to hold it.

That was a fine wedding. Nobody put on any airs, and Seraphim's cooking was as good as could be; the weather was fine, and we all enjoyed ourselves.

I hadn't wanted to wear a wedding dress, but David had brought a length of lace from Macao—it was Portuguese lace, made by nuns in a convent—and I wore that for a veil, and my garnet velvet dress, and Mr Osterhouse had on a new black coat and striped trousers and a hat as tall as a smokestack.

The minister of Seraphim's church spoke the words over us from the Prayer Book and when he was done, I was Mrs Theophilus VanDerWalk Osterhouse.

***

Well, everyone stayed for another week, visiting, but finally we set off for our honeymoon, which Mr Osterhouse had persuaded me we should spend at the Palace Hotel in San Francisco. Sally-John stayed on with Hsaio-yen, and Seraphim had the store well in hand, so I was easy in my mind and ready to enjoy myself.

The Palace Hotel was the grandest establishment I'd ever stayed in, and that was saying something, but it warn't the decorations nor the furnishings nor the food that moved me to tears of joy.

That honeymoon was a revelation to both of us, Mr Osterhouse and me.

For one thing, he told me that no one else had ever called him "Theo."

"I don't recall that my father ever called me by name," he said. "He addressed me as 'boy,' and sometimes as 'son.' My mother called me 'Sonny.'"

"And your stepmother?"

"She called me 'you' to my face. In front of others, she referred to me as 'Philip's boy.'"

"Philip being your father's name."

"Yes."

"What was your mother's?"

"Dorcas."

"I have thought of you as 'Theo' for some time," I said.

"And I have longed to call you 'Sarah,'" he said.

"Sarah Mary Osterhouse," I said, trying out the name. "It don't sound like me."

"Perhaps," Theo said, drawing me to him, "You only need to get used to it."

***

The physical side of our relationship did not cause us any difficulty or concern. That we had any such congress might surprise some folks, especially those who think that people in their middle years are beyond such things. I knew that I had been at one time capable of taking pleasure in the act of love, and Theo's gentleness soon reassured me that that pleasure was still to be had.

As for my husband, he told me, after our first night together, that he had not imagined such contentment could ever be his.

I suppose some might find the idea of two elderly persons wrestling about under the bedclothes a topic for mirth. And in fact Theo in his striped nightgown and tasseled nightcap was far from the conventional depiction of a Romeo, whilst I, even with my hair down, and clad in a long nightdress trimmed in lace and ribbons, did not even faintly resemble Juliet.

But in each other's arms we forgot how we might seem to others, and existed only for ourselves. There was pleasure in our embrace, true, but also comfort and tenderness, which to my mind are as great a good if not greater. And to wake and see Theo's nightcapped head on the pillow next to mine and to feel the reassuring bulk of him, warm and solid—why, that was pleasure too, of a kind that made me feel, not young again, but ageless, as if time had decided to lay only gentle hands on me from now on.

And indeed I did not feel that I was growing old. Only when I looked at Theo, sometimes, did I see that time in fact was racing by.

Theo's health begun to decline in the latter part of 1899, just after the war with Spain ended. He was approaching seventy, and even I had to admit that he looked his age. His hair had gone white, what there was of it, and so had those curling whiskers of which he was so vain, and even his eyebrows were silvered. He still had his teeth, and his color was still ruddy, but he tired easily and was often out of breath.

"You ought to take it easy," I said one day, when he had climbed the stairs to our room too quickly. "You're wheezing like a grampus."

"Maybe I will," he said. "If you agree to take that trip around the world with me."

This was an idea he'd been proposing for some time. We could visit China and see David. We could go to Japan. We could travel to India and see the Taj Mahal by moonlight. Egypt and the Pyramids. Constantinople—the Golden Horn and Saint Sophia. Greece, and the Parthenon. Italy. Florence, Venice, Rome . . . He tossed place names into our conversation like a man peppering his breakfast eggs, and the more I resisted, the more he argued.

"We have plenty of money," he said.

That was true. The Elixir was as popular as ever.

"It's not the expense," I said.

"Then why not?"

"I don't know," I said. And that was true. For one who'd covered as much ground as I had done, I had, it appeared, lost my desire to travel. But Theo continued to plan for my change of mind, leaving steamship pamphlets and Cook's Tour brochures on my night-stand, and subscribing to that new magazine from the National Geographic Society. Whenever somebody come to town to give a lecture on some Place of Interest, Theo insisted that we go, and so I sat through many hours of lantern slides and Professor So-and-So droning on about the Hottentots or the Hindus, bored and sulking, whilst by my side Theo beamed and clapped.

I have wished many times since then that I'd gone on that World Tour with him.

How many times do we fail those we love, only to regret those failures over and over, once time has made certain that we can never remedy them?

Theo died in 1901, just as the old century passed and the new one started up.

***

The years since Theo died have been good ones, on the whole. I miss him, of course, but at my age a body expects to miss most of those who were near and dear, when above ground. I am seventy-six or thereabouts, near as I can figure, and healthy except for a tendency to stiffness in the morning, which I attribute mostly to the damp climate of this city.

Yes, San Francisco is still my home.

I never loved it as Theo did, but when he prevailed upon me to sell the store to Seraphim and move here, I agreed. And I found that I grew fond of the place, especially of Chinatown, where I often go; there is a tea shop where I like to sit and watch the people pass.

There are more Chinese in San Francisco than there ever were in the old days, despite the laws passed to keep them out. Of course, many were born here, and more are being born every day. And there's Mexicans and Indians—a few—still around, and I still sometimes see Hawaiian sailors when I visit the wharfs—enormous copper-brown men in canvas drawers and rope-soled shoes. There were Hawaiian miners in Nevada, back in the silver days; I had learned a greeting from them, and sometimes I use it now, just to see a brown face split into a gleaming white grin and hear a powerful bass voice roar it back to me: "ALOHA!" And there are black men of every shade and coloration, and white men, Americans and Europeans and even Russians in baggy breeches and embroidered tunics and tall boots, and once in a while the occasional Eskimo come down from the north, all swaddled about in furs.

And of course there are the women.

The Chinese women walk along swift and silent in their black cloth shoes; they wear black smocks and trousers and their hair tied up in white kerchiefs. Often they carry baskets and bundles, and just as often I see one with a child tied on her back. They sell vegetables and fruit and dried fish and shrimps. The Mexican girls walk in pairs or groups, with mantillas over their hair, and skirts in bright colors, with white blouses trimmed in ribbon. They chatter in Spanish and the sound is like a tree full of birds.

The white women I see on the streets are mostly poor—cooks and maids and washerwomen, those being largely Irish and Swedish or Danish, I think. Then once in a while I see a woman in a carriage or a motorcar, wearing furs and a hat with feathers. The women who walk alone without bundles or baskets are prostitutes, of course.

These are mostly white girls, though not all. I give them money from time to time, not a great deal at any one time, because I don't wish to be robbed; I know that the girls' macquereaux are as vicious today as they were forty years ago, and a girl who goes home with less than she's supposed to have earned will suffer for it.

The word has gotten around that Mrs Osterhouse will help a girl who's in a bind, and one or two I've even spoken for to employers and helped to get out of that life once and for all. Some of them have babies they never see, put out to nurse God knows where. I'd like to spend some money on a foundling home for children like these—since the places that already exist are full, mostly, and not much better than the workhouse in Mr Dickens's book *Oliver Twist*. There was a man who knowed what it is like to be poor.

San Francisco has changed so much since the old days.

There have been a number of very large and destructive fires. The street where the brothel used to stand and where I nearly lost my own life has been gone for a long time. There's been new building everywhere, stores and houses and hotels. The cable cars go up and down the hills, and there are motorcars everywhere, too, and fewer and fewer carriages. There's even talk of a bridge across the bay someday.

Everything is different, in fact, except for the hills themselves and the bay that sparkles below. Angel Island is still there, of course, and Alcatraz, though the Miwok Indians who used to live there are long gone, too; a military prison occupies Alcatraz, and Angel Island is an outpost now, called Camp McDowell; there is an Army garrison where Cassius and I and an old Chinese boatman once camped.

I miss Tahoe City sometimes, especially the clear air and the scent of Ponderosa pine. Seraphim bought the store from me and continues to run it with his children—he married Alice Calumet and they have a large and noisy family, all boys. Last time I visited there was steamships on Lake Tahoe!—a thing I could never have believed.

Sally-John finished her studies at Vassar and then went on to the University of Chicago, where she studied Oriental languages. (Did her being raised by a Chinese have anything to do with that? I imagine that her Ah Bok would be proud.) Sally-John is now a full professor. She never married, but lives with a dear friend from college, a writer and editor from Boston named Louella Radclyffe. I have never asked if their "friendship" is more than that, but I suspect so. If that is the case, I am glad. Louella is very lovable, and Sally-John is the kind of woman who needs someone else to care for (and be cared for in return).

Their home in the Hyde Park district is a comfortable warren of books, musical instruments—they both play, Sally-John the cello and Louella the viola—friends, students, dogs (they have two King Charles spaniels), and about a hundred potted plants. Louella has what folks call "a green thumb." Last time they visited here, she brought me a fern which has grown nearly to the ceiling of the morning room.

Hsaio-yen went to Vassar as well, where she made a name for herself as a scholar and artist. She lives in Paris, where she paints. She married a fellow painter, a Frenchman named Louis D'Ormonde. They have two children, a boy and a girl, named David and Sarah. Just a few weeks ago, Hsaio-yen wrote to say that they are expecting another child in the spring. If it is a boy, she promises to name him Theo.

Mr Twain has become the most famous writer in America. From time to time I send off a letter or card; I did so when he lost his beloved daughter Suzy a few years back, in 1896. He wrote back, thanking me, but we haven't seen each other in twenty years at least. The book *Adventures of Huckleberry Finn* continues to sell, as does *Tom Sawyer*. Tom and his wife Becky traveled West for Theo's funeral. Their son Thomas is a minister back in Hannibal, a fact that probably would cause Mr Twain a great deal of mirth if he knew it. I must remember to ask Tom in my next letter if he has communicated the fact to Mr Twain.

David is still alive. He writes twice a year to me, more often to Hsaio-yen and to Sally-John. Both of them give me news of him in their letters, which come frequently. I have asked both girls to visit me this spring. They want me to come to them, of course, but I don't feel any more inclination to travel than I did when Theo was still alive. In fact, I leave this house less and less.

The only friend I see with any regularity is Cassius.

He's very old now, is Cassius—ninety-four. He's shrunk some but is still spry as a cricket, though his head is egg-bald and he has to wear a knitted cap to keep it warm. He grew a pair of long mustaches when he first came out here and they are all white now. His wife Snow-on-the-Mountains is still living, too, and the two of them come here several times a week to take supper with me. Her hair still falls to her knees and is still coal black, though she is in her eighties. Their sons and grandsons manage their property. They tell me that one boy, named Lincoln, has opened a fine restaurant up in

393

San Bruno and called it "Lincoln's Log Cabin."[80] When spring comes, perhaps I can persuade Cassius and Snow to take me there. I'll ask them tomorrow. They are coming here for supper. I wrote the date on my desk calendar: April 18, 1906.

It's late and I am tired.

Before I take these old bones of mine off to bed, I must remember to put this manuscript back safe in its envelope. I keep it in the second drawer of my nightstand (the top drawer is where I keep my handkerchiefs and scarves). I don't suppose anyone in my family will care much (one way or t'other) about what I've written, after I'm gone that is, but Mr Mark Twain might be a mite sensitive about having "his" story about Huck Finn turn out to be somebody else's, so I keep these pages private and I intend them to stay that way. I've marked the envelope "not to be opened for a hundred and one years after my death"; that ought to keep Mr Twain's literary reputation safe enough.

As for my own reputation, I don't suppose anybody will ever read this, but if you do, think kindly on the writer. I done my best. The record of these pages is all I have to leave in defense of

Huckleberry Finn

P.S. Mr Twain might'a' done it better, but at least my version is true.

---

80 Eds. note: There was a restaurant in San Bruno called "Uncle Tom's Cabin."

394

Gina Logan lives in Vermont and teaches in the College of Liberal Arts at a private university.

Made in the USA
Charleston, SC
21 December 2013